Enchanted Enemies

Even though he was a Confederate, something about Wesley was compelling Serena to be more daring than ever before in her life. True, Wesley was a soldier, but he was also wounded. Perhaps this was why she felt unthreatened by him. Or was it because she desired his kisses? His dark, beguiling eyes were drawing her to him, it seemed. She shook her hair to hang down her back, then leaned closer to him. "Do you want to kiss me?" she asked quietly.

Wesley's heart was beating so wildly, he wasn't sure he could endure the sweetness of Serena's lips against his. But, yes, he had to. He needed her, as strange as it seemed.

And without further words, Serena placed her lips against his and felt a rush of desire consume her in massive waves of forbidden pleasures. "Wesley," she murmured, pulling away. Then, his free hand reached up to engage her again in a kiss. And as Serena brought her lips down, once again, to Wesley's, tears surfaced in both their eyes. These were the tears of a new found love—between enchanted enemies. . . .

HISTORICAL ROMANCE IN THE MAKING!

FORBIDDEN EMBRACE

BY CASSIE EDWARDS

ZEBRA BOOKS
KENSINGTON PUBLISHING CORP.

ZEBRA BOOKS

are published by

KENSINGTON PUBLISHING CORP.
475 Park Avenue South
New York, N.Y. 10016

Printed in the United States of America

Lovingly to Delores, Barb, Mary, Geneva, Dale, Dave, Linda, and Norma, and their families, and to my father-in-law Avon.

Acknowledgments

The author is grateful to the following for helping
to supply historical data for her novel:

Mattoon Association of Commerce
Mattoon, Illinois

Kiawah Island Company
Charleston, South Carolina

Betty Shirley, History Teacher
Northwest High School
House Springs, Missouri

Charles Edwards, Husband and Teacher
Northwest High School
House Springs, Missouri

St. Louis County Public Library,
    Tesson Ferry Branch
St. Louis, Missouri

High Ridge Community Library
High Ridge, Missouri

For oh! so wildly do I love him
That paradise itself were dim
And joyless, if not shared with him.

                    —*Moore*

So lost in love
is she
who forsakes all
for the man
she loves,
only to then
discover that
to find love
in an enemy
is to find danger
in every
heart's beat.

Chapter One

The sunset was coloring the gracefully blowing prairie grass in brazen oranges, and the only sound was the faint, remorseful cry of a loon, hidden away in a low marsh, intermingling with the whisperings of the ever-swaying grasses.

The lone grave lay silent. It had sunk a bit into the ground after the long Illinois winter.

"The winter of 1864," Serena Kassia Calvert murmured to herself, staring at the grave. "It's a winter I shall never forget."

It was now the fifth day of March, when an occasional warmer breeze might blow, but this evening Serena still felt the need to pull her brown velveteen cape more snugly around her shoulders. A chill always seemed to accompany her to her mother's graveside.

Julita Kate had been a casualty of this harsh winter, even though her husband Hiram Milton Calvert was a much sought after physician in Mattoon.

Hiram Milton hadn't been able to cure his wife of pneumonia; being so frail and overtaxed from assisting Hiram in his hospital duties, Julita's lungs had just given out on her.

"And all because of this darn war, Mother," Serena whispered harshly, doubling her fists at her side. "If Father hadn't insisted that we use our house for a hospital to fill with wounded soldiers, you wouldn't have been overworked. You would probably still be alive today."

Serena couldn't help but think back to that steaming hot day in July, 1861, when her father had said, "Now that the United States Sanitary Commission has been created to guarantee that all our soldiers are taken care of in the best way possible, then I'll see to it that my house will be Mattoon's hospital. What better place to bring our wounded heroes?"

He then had addressed his wife in his loud, authoritative voice. "Julita Kate, it will only be for the duration of the war. We can move our valuables to the third floor of our house. Surely you are loyal enough to the Union to sacrifice a little something."

Serena stooped to place a bouquet of yellow jonquils on the grave, and spoke softly, "But, Mother, you sacrificed much more, didn't you? You are the true heroine of this war."

Serena then rose, her dark eyes flashing. Oh, how she hated the war. To her it was such a useless thing. She admired President Lincoln tremendously, but still couldn't understand him, and why he so feared the spread of slavery into the new lands in the west.

She couldn't understand why Lincoln felt the need to dictate how one might live . . . with or without slavery. Serena felt it was the individual's choice, as well as the state's, and if one chose to use slaves, they should be allowed the freedom of such a decision.

To Serena's way of thinking, any other way was to be

making even the white people slaves, slaves dictated to by laws.

Even though Serena was from the North, she could understand and sympathize with the feeling of the southerners that any law passed against slavery was a danger to their way of life, since most of the wealth of the South was in land and slaves. But Serena had to remember her loyalties, and not speak these feelings aloud . . . to anyone.

A shrill whistle echoed across the ocean of grass that spread out on all sides of Serena. Her heartbeat quickened when she turned and caught sight of a train in the distance. As the train traveled along the horizon, its long trail of black smoke wound upward behind it, then caught in the wind and became many small gray clouds against the sky.

The train was a reminder of two things to Serena. The captured Rebels were being brought to Mattoon, to the town's new, stronger jail; the seriously wounded, among them would go to Serena's father's hospital quarters, to lay only heartbeats away from wounded soldiers from the North.

It hadn't been in Hiram's plans to doctor the enemy. But when word had reached Mattoon of the overcrowding of the other makeshift hospitals of both the North and the South, Hiram had quickly let President Lincoln know that he wasn't a physician only to an elite group of wounded, but to any man whom might be placed on one of his hospital beds.

The townspeople had at first frowned upon this decision, saying that Rebels in their jail were enough threat to the community. But Hiram had said that no wounded would escape from *his* hospital quarters. He had then ordered shackles for each bed that would be occupied by the enemy.

Serena continued to watch the train, thinking further. . . .

The train's engineer was Edward James Carlson, Serena's suitor, hand-picked by her father. Edward was twenty-eight years her senior.

Being only eighteen, Serena was not yet prepared to say yes to any man's proposal. She was too restless to settle down, to be tied to one man, with daily wifely duties, even though her father's choice was known to be one of Mattoon's most respected citizens and most admired by all who knew him.

It hadn't taken many years after Serena's birth for the Calverts to realize that their first-born daughter was too high-spirited for her name.

As now, her brown eyes gleaming with flecks of gold and her hair the color of ripe picked strawberries, so wild and free, with its long, natural curls lifting and blowing in the breeze, she looked the part of the seductress.

Her daring personality and her perfect features—wide, sensuous lips and a slightly tilted nose with its dusting of freckles—had been the cause of many a young man's hands to attempt to creep where they shouldn't. Suspecting this, Hiram Milton had decided that he would sleep better nights if his daughter was safely wed.

A stirring in the grass close to her brought Serena quickly around. For so long now, she had anticipated a jail break. Whenever she heard strange noises in the night, a shimmer of excitement would ripple through her; she hoped that some Confederate soldier would find a way out of the dreaded jail that seemed to have sprung up overnight after that first gunfire had echoed around

12

Fort Sumter, where the war had begun.

Serena hated jails as much as she hated war. Jails meant snuffing out one's free spirit. Oh, if she were ever to be restrained, she would just rather die!

The shadows of early evening were playing around her now, making it almost impossible to see who was coming through the small grove of trees that lay between the Calvert house and the family's private, white-picket-fenced cemetery.

"Serena?"

When Serena heard the familiar voice, disappointment made her lips curve downward a bit. It was only Priscilla, her sixteen-year-old sister, a sister who so tested Serena's patience at times. How Priscilla lacked in personality! It was as colorless as the drab hair that hung in limp strands around her face.

"Yes, I'm here, Priscilla," Serena finally answered. "By Mother's grave."

Priscilla moved through the opened gate and to Serena's side, panting for breath. Her eyes wavered a bit when she glanced toward the grave, then back to Serena. "It's father," she whispered, as though she feared disturbing her mother's peaceful rest. "He's been asking for you, wondering where you've disappeared to."

"I've worked by his side in that dreaded hospital all day," Serena said glumly. "I even fear I smell of the wounded. Doesn't he realize that I have to have some time to myself?"

"Serena, if you don't return with me, father will most assuredly make me work with him," Priscilla whined. "Please, Serena? I hate working around all that blood and stench." She screwed her face up, closing her eyes. "It sickens me so," she added weakly.

13

"Yes, I know," Serena sighed. "And what would you do instead? Settle down in a velveteen chair and read? That's all you'd ever do, if allowed. Just read romantic novels."

Serena's gaze raked over Priscilla. Priscilla's face was a perfect square, with brown eyes set wide apart. Serena knew that what lay beneath the fullness of her sister's cape was a cotton dress that had been chosen too hastily with its gathers and folds, hiding a body that would draw any man's attention, possibly even away from Serena. But Priscilla hadn't thought much about her better qualities yet. She had chosen to live in a fantasyland.

"Just look at you, Priscilla," Serena blurted. "Don't you care about yourself and what your laziness is doing to you? It would do you good to help father. At least you would see that a true world does exist outside the covers of your books."

Tears shone at the corners of Priscilla's eyes. "Serena, must you always annoy me about my reading?" she said.

"I'm sorry, Priscilla," she murmured. "But you could look beautiful, if you tried."

Priscilla felt as though her show of tears had been a success. Her dark eyes brightened as she said, "You *will* go help father, won't you, Serena?"

"No. I will not," Serena said firmly. "I've things to do tonight."

"Things? Do you mean to say, with a man? With that handsome Edward James Carlson?"

Serena couldn't have heard right. Was her sister actually showing an interest in Edward? But surely not. Priscilla hadn't yet shown an interest in *any* man. She dismissed the thought from her mind, tossing her windblown hair from around her face. "Yes," she groaned. "With him, though I detest every moment of it."

Priscilla's face broke into a wide grin. "Maybe father has picked the wrong daughter to wed up with Edward," she giggled.

Serena's eyes widened. "Priscilla," she said. "Have I been wrong in my assessment of you? Could it be that your mind has learned to focus elsewhere?"

"Possibly," Priscilla said, blushing a bit. Then she quickly added, "Are you going to see Edward tonight?"

"Yes. Tell Father that Edward has asked me to meet him at his house," Serena said, moving from her mother's grave. With Priscilla close beside her, Serena hurried through the grove of trees, then to the clearing that stretched in four directions around the Calvert house. "Tell Father that he should be pleased. Maybe Edward will even seduce me tonight. How else to be assured of my hand in marriage?" Serena added, watching her sister's reaction.

Priscilla paled. "Serena," she gasped. "You can come out with the most . . . the most . . . *brazen* of statements. I shall not tell Father such a thing."

"Then tell him what you like," Serena laughed, not having meant to shock her sister so severely. She untied the sleek black mare's reins from a hitching post and said further, "But one thing for sure, I will *not* work in the hospital quarters tonight, and you'd better not tell Father where I'm going. It is not the proper thing to do, you know, to go to an unmarried man's house without an escort."

She climbed aboard her carriage and clucked to the horse, then looked back across her shoulder, at Priscilla, still standing with her mouth agape. "Looks as though

15

you'll have to muss your hands a bit tonight, Priscilla," she said, smiling triumphantly.

"Oh, *you*," Priscilla shouted, stomping a foot.

Serena ignored her sister as the buggy took her past the house that she had been a part of for the last five years, ever since the Calvert family had moved to the state of Illinois, after having grown tired of living where their aristocratic descendant, Cecelius Calvert, had founded the colony of Maryland in 1632.

Hiram Calvert had heard of the Illinois settlers dying of cholera, even malaria, and had decided that's where he could best serve. And after having chosen Mattoon, a town that had been built around the spot where the Illinois Central and the Terre Haute and Alton Railroads intersected, a huge house had been erected close to where an enormous elm stood with its majestic wide-spreading limbs.

This at one time solitary elm, that stood back away from the grove of smaller trees, had already made its mark in history. While the other trees had been only sprouts, this tree had become a sentinel for those who traveled the prairie, a trail marker for both Indians and pioneer white men. Those moving westward had often paused in its shade to rest.

Now, in the shade of its limbs, the Calvert house stood, a house that most people would envy, with its three stories, wide porches, stained-glass windows and mansard roof. A decorative iron fence enclosed its grounds, emphasizing its grandeur.

But Serena wished never to enter that house again, especially now that the sweet aromas of logs burning on the hearth and apple pies baking in the oven had been replaced by the stench of the hospital. Serena just knew that the Calvert home would never be the same again.

As her carriage now moved on along the deeply rutted dirt street, Serena's thoughts turned to the house she was urging her horse toward. She set her jaw firmly. She didn't wish to be a part of that house either. Oh, what was she to do . . . ?

How many times did she have to tell Edward that she didn't love him, that it was only her father encouraging this so-called courtship.

"But I now know what loneliness is, Serena," her father had said. "Now that sweet Julita Kate is gone, I understand the empty evening hours that Edward must have since having become widowed not only once, but twice."

"Darn it, Father," Serena had stormed, her face crimson. "Is that what you are truly wishing on me? An early grave like Edward's first two wives? Surely you must see that's what the future would hold for me. . . ."

"Nonsense," he had argued, caressing his thick, gray mustache. "Utter nonsense. Edward lost those wives when this land was only a wilderness. Do you see any wilderness now?"

"My heart has become one," Serena had murmured.

"Nonsense. Utter nonsense," he had further grumbled. Then with fire in his dark, usually brooding eyes, he had added, "And you watch your temper. I wish that you would behave like a lady, not a trollop who feels free to rant and rave to all she chooses. I would wish for quiet, gentle words to come from such delicate lips as yours."

"Darn it," she now mumbled, snapping the reins a bit too harshly, causing the horse to whinny. "I shall raise my voice whenever I choose to do so. Until I have a wedding band on my finger, I am still my own person.

And even then, I shall remain my own person. No man has the right to dictate to a woman. Not even a husband!"

Serena slowed the pace of her horse when she found herself on Corral Road. Along this road, on each side of her, she could see row after row of horse corrals. She now watched as many blue-uniformed men guided their horses in and out of the corrals, which had been built especially for the war horses so that they could get proper care and rest before being used again in battle.

Snapping the reins again, Serena moved on until she found herself mingling with other horses and carriages, and many lone horsemen who were busying themselves along Broadway, the main thoroughfare of town.

The wood-plank sidewalks were free of women passersby, even though the two- and three-storied brick buildings displayed, by way of lights from many kerosene lanterns, all sorts of enticing merchandise that had been carefully arranged on shelves behind wide expanses of glass windowpanes.

The war had brought a change to Mattoon. Even though the town was known to outsiders principally for its fine hotels and its connection with the many stories of Abraham Lincoln, what seemed to be the topic of conversation now around the supper table was the number of blue-uniformed soldiers one might see roaming the streets on any afternoon or evening.

Moving onward, the darkness of the hour and the lack of lights along the street urged Serena to call out to her horse and once again flick it with the reins. She had only a small distance to go now, then she would be at Edward's. For what reason, she didn't know. He had almost begged her to meet him there, having said privacy was now hard to find, "With the town so buzzing with war activities and all."

Serena had at first hesitated because of the impropriety of going unescorted to see Edward, but then her sense of adventure and reckless nature had prompted her to agree.

She truly didn't wish to be with Edward ever. But with the town so filled with uniformed men, she had found it an impossible task to do much without him. All other men that she had known had gone to war. Edward had been too old for fighting, but he didn't think himself too old to take on a younger wife.

"But this won't happen," she murmured to herself. "I will never become his wife." She was hoping that she could convince him of this this night. She was tired of playing games with him, even if he were the only man available that wasn't dressed in blue.

Guiding her horse and carriage on past the town's two most famous hotels, Serena was reminded of the Lincoln/Douglas Debates. Stephen A. Douglas, Abraham Lincoln's opponent for the United States Senate in 1858, had stayed at the Essex House, and Abraham Lincoln at the Pennsylvania House. The very next day Lincoln had traveled by buggy with three Mattoon men, and Douglas and his wife had gone by train to Charleston, a town a few miles east of Mattoon, where one of their many famous debates had been held.

It was during these debates, where the speeches centered on the extension of slavery into free territory, that the rising young Abraham Lincoln, scarcely known outside of the state of Illinois at that time, had added greatly to the luster of his growing reputation.

Douglas had stood for the idea that the people of new states should decide for themselves whether or not they wanted slavery, as Serena herself had always believed.

Lincoln did not want any more slave states. He did not believe that the United States could remain "half slave and half free."

"Sooner or later," Lincoln had said, "the country would become all one thing, or all the other." Lincoln was against the idea that the people of each new state should decide for themselves whether or not to have slavery. "If slavery is wrong," Lincoln had said, "then people do not have a right to choose it." Lincoln did not believe that any people have a right to choose to do wrong.

Lincoln's speeches against slavery had received loud cheers. People in the North began to think of Lincoln as a leader. Politicians began to think of him as a winner. In 1860, the Republican party chose Lincoln to run for President.

In January 1861, Abraham Lincoln had returned once again to the outskirts of Charleston to pay his final visit to his stepmother Sarah Bush Lincoln before he left for Washington to become President.

Serena could remember it so vividly. Lincoln had come from Springfield via the Central Illinois Railroad to Mattoon. A little later, he had taken a freight train to Charleston, where Serena and her family had stood among the swelling crowd, watching this tall, lanky fellow with the sober face and stovepipe chimney of a hat, waving to the crowd.

Serena had been impressed by this man and how he so cordially greeted everyone, as though he were simply "Friend Lincoln" and not, indeed, among the most noted personages in the civilized world, even though some Southern states had already said they would secede if

Lincoln won, knowing of his strong feelings against slavery.

But that had been the last of the excitement for Serena for a while, until that following May, when Ulysses S. Grant had come to Mattoon after the news of the Civil War outbreak had spread to all parts of the North. Governor Yates had appointed the shabby, former West Pointer from Galena, Illinois, to muster in ten National Guard units, all to rendezvous at convenient railroad centers.

Mattoon had been one of them. All eyes, Serena had stood by in the shadows of a general store, as Grant had mustered into service the Seventh Congressional District Regiment. Only a few men had been willing to join up, but Grant had finally succeeded in getting his quota. He then headed them toward Springfield, where Serena later heard that Grant had taken over command of the unit, when the regiment had refused to serve under their elected leader, Colonal C. C. Goode.

Since then, Ulysses S. Grant had made history, and when he had made another brief stopover at Mattoon this past year, Serena had marveled at the change in the man. He was now the commander of all the Union Armies; his black boots had shone like mirrors, and his blue suit had been pressed to perfection, his gold buttons gleaming. Serena would never forget his sword and how it hung so threateningly at his side.

Turning onto a street of white frame houses, Serena slowed the horse's pace. Faint glimmerings of light from kerosene lamps reflected from front windows, and the aroma of evening meals cooking traveled along with Serena as she watched for Edward's familiar fenced-in yard and the chestnut mare tied to a front hitching post.

21

When she did sort his house out from all the others, a feeling of apprehension swept through her. Edward's horse wasn't there and his house stood in utter darkness. Now what was she to do?

She looked from side to side, wondering if she was being watched. To her, the many windows of all the houses along this street were eyes. If she didn't make a move quickly, not only would the blue-uniformed soldiers be gossiped about at this evening's supper table, but she would be, too.

She urged her horse to a stop in front of Edward's house. "I've come this far, I shall not turn back," she said to herself. To turn back would also mean having to return to the hospital duties. She would do anything to get away from those hospital quarters for a while—even if it meant entering Edward's house in the darkness of night.

She climbed from the carriage and secured her horse, then moved quickly to Edward's front porch, hoping to find the door unlocked. She slowly turned the doorknob, barely breathing, when the door squeaked slowly open.

Once inside, she peered through the darkness, trying to make out what was on each side of her. The apprehension inside her built, as she realized that she had just become an intruder. She could just hear the housewives' whisperings: "Scandalous. Tsk, tsk. Just scandalous."

But Serena blamed her father for any connection with Edward. She, herself, had thought it scandalous that her father would even suggest that she marry a man so much older, even though, in truth, he was kind and pleasant enough to be around.

"But, love, Father?" Serena had argued. "Mustn't

22

there be love in a marriage?"

"Bah," he had said. "Love comes after marriage. You see, love means different things to different people."

"What do you mean by that, Father?" she had asked.

His face had colored a bit and he had averted his eyes from Serena, while toying nervously with his mustache. Always when not busying his fingers while doctoring, they would be at his mustache, twisting, smoothing, bristling. "What do I mean?" he had said, coughing absently. "Well, uh, to some love means what one shares in bed, to others, it has a fancier meaning . . ."

"And for you and mother?" Serena had interrupted. "How had it been for you?"

Her father had clamped his lips onto the stem of a pipe, and looked reproachfully toward Serena. . . .

Feeling more and more uncomfortable in the darkness of Edward's house, Serena began to feel around as she inched her way along the hardwood floor. She thought about her mother's and father's relationship. She knew how it had been between them. She had heard the sounds from their bedroom those many, many nights. Yes, she knew the kind of love they had shared. . . .

Serena wanted more. When she loved, she wanted it all. She wanted it to be so special that to be separated from the man she loved would be the same as plucking her heart from inside her. With Edward, she didn't even get the slightest twinge of a racing pulsebeat. He was just another man. Nothing more. Nothing less.

At last she found a kerosene lamp. She moved her fingers downward and scooted them along the table's surface until she found a small tray filled with matches. After striking one, she lifted the chimney from the lamp, screwed the wick up higher, then moved the match to it, filling the room with gold, dancing shadows.

Serena turned and gazed slowly around her. The room was small, plain, and in much need of a woman's touch. She grabbed a handful of matches and went about lighting two more lamps in an effort to cheer the place up a bit. She stood with hands on hips, gazing around her.

The walls were wallpapered in a pale beige, leaf-design, and yellowed priscilla curtains crisscrossed limply at the two windows. A huge rocker, with padded seat and arms, sat beside a potbelly stove at the far end, and a settee and odds and ends of tables and chairs filled the rest of the room.

A few, sepia-toned family portraits, framed by tarnished gold graced the walls, and some books and newspapers lay spread out atop the tables, along with ashtrays deeply heaped with discarded cigars and ashes.

"And now, what else?" she said aloud, swirling around, wondering exactly where the door at the other far end of the room led. She picked up a lamp and moved onward until she found herself in the kitchen. She lifted the lamp higher, to cast light further around her, and gasped at her findings. Not only the kitchen table but the stove and sink also were filled with soiled dishes. The sight appalled her.

"How could he live in such a way?" she murmured. "How could he ever expect me—"

The front door slammed with a loud bang and Serena jumped with alarm.

"Hullo. Who's there?" a voice boomed loudly.

Serena tensed even more, recognizing the deep voice, always so authoritative like her father's; this voice alone was enough reason for Serena to hate the thought of becoming Edward's wife. Eighteen years of her father's

24

lectures and orders had been enough.

"It's me, Edward," she finally answered. "Serena. I'm here in the kitchen." She stared awkwardly around her, suddenly feeling quite out of place . . . especially in this man's kitchen. She placed the kerosene lamp on the table and smiled a bit sheepishly when Edward entered the room, having to stoop a bit to fit his massive six-foot-four height through the door. His thick, brown walrus mustache which matched the thickness of his hair bounced as his toothy smile broke through.

"What have we here, little darlin'?" he drawled in his booming voice. "A touch of domesticity for the betrothed?"

Serena's lips narrowed into a straight line, as she saw the lust in the depths of his pale gray eyes. She could tell that he wasn't angry at all over her illegal entry into his house; he was amused. She didn't want to let herself think of the reasons for his amusement.

"I only—" she began, but stopped when two strides from his long legs brought him to her side.

"How damned sweet of you to come tonight," he said, taking her hand in his. "And I'm glad you've made yourself at home. Makes me mighty proud."

Serena became annoyed at his joy in seeing her and jerked her hand free. "You are so late, Edward," she stated flatly. "I didn't want to sit alone in my carriage waiting. You know, gossip . . ."

He laughed raucously as his gaze traveled around the room. "So you decided to play wife before the big day, eh?" he said. "I like it. It's nice comin' home to. Is that why you were in my kitchen? Were you ready to prepare a bite to eat?"

"In this mess?" she gasped, visibly shuddering. "It's

ungodly, Edward. And the answer to your question is no. I did *not* plan to prepare your supper." *Now or ever,* she thought further.

"Yep. I know it's a mess," he said, lifting a suspender from one shoulder, then placing his thumbs beneath the other, ready to also slip it downward. "And sorry you're not preparin' my meal. It would've been cozy."

Serena paled and her fingers went to her throat while she watched as he removed the suspenders from his shoulders; she half-expected to see his breeches drop to the floor at any moment. "What are you doing, Edward?" she gasped.

"Wash off a mite," he said, wide-eyed. "I always do, first thing upon arrivin' back home evenings."

"But . . . here? Now? In my presence . . . ?"

"Don't I look like needin' it?" he chuckled, holding his arms out, gesturing with his head.

Serena's gaze moved slowly over him. Compared to her own crisply clean, blue-flowered cotton dress, his shirt and breeches, soiled black from the engine's coal dust and the black coal-dust lines around his eyes and mouth did reveal to her that he was in need of some sprucing up.

"Yes, I . . . guess . . . you do," she murmured, moving toward the living room.

"Then while I splash some water over my face and arms, just make yourself at home," he laughed, going ahead to flip the other suspender from his shoulder, which left his breeches resting only barely on his hips. When his fingers began to work with the buttons of his shirt, Serena gasped loudly and moved on into the living room. Not even her father had been so bold in front of her. *Ever.* She was shocked by Edward. Absolutely shocked.

She eased down onto a chair, listening as he hand pumped water into a basin, then further to the distinct noise of his splashing water onto himself. She wasn't sure where . . . and didn't truly wish to know.

"Sorry to be so late, little darlin'," he yelled, still splashing.

Her eyes moved upward in despair. She hated to be called little darlin'. She wasn't anyone's little darlin. "Why were you?" she said, forcing conversation. She now hated herself for having come.

"A good damned amount of prisoners rounded up this trip," he shouted. "Poor critters. Pushed into the train's cars like cattle. Exceptin' the wounded. And there were plenty of them this time around also."

"War," she said sadly. "Such a disgrace."

Edward moved into the living room, toweling his face. "As far as I can tell, the war's the same as over for Lee's weary troops," he chuckled further.

As Serena turned toward him, she found him stooping down over her, causing her to face his unclothed, hairy, massive chest. She swallowed hard and turned her eyes quickly away, stopping only when Edward's hands gripped her wrists and pulled her up to him.

"What do you think you're doing, Edward James Carlson?" she said hotly, squirming to free herself, but only succeeding at making her wrists burn from his strong grip.

"We've never been alone like this before," he said thickly, eyeing her with raw hunger.

"And we never shall be again if you don't release me," she shouted, still struggling.

Edward's eyes lowered as he released his hold. His fingers went to his mustache and swirled it as he moved away from her. "As I was saying," he said, acting as though nothing had happened, "war's near over." He walked out of the room and then back again with a clean shirt pulled on.

Serena settled back onto the chair, breathing hard, watching him closely for any further sudden movements. "Why is that, Edward?" she asked, placing her hands on her lap, clasping them tightly together.

Edward sat down opposite her and lighted a cigar. "Grant took care of Lee's troops at Petersburg. Don't you know how the Southern armies are wastin' away in Grant's bulldog grip?"

"No. Can't say that I do," Serena said, forcing conversation, occasionally eyeing the door, feeling the need to escape. Being alone with Edward in his house was even more unbearable than being with him in the company of others. Oh, how unwise for her to have come. But boredom caused one to do many things. And she was going to tell him—this night—that she could not marry him, that she *would* not marry him. He hadn't believed her before. Would he this night . . . ? Oh, he had to.

"Sherman's left a wide track of destruction as he marched through Georgia and the Carolinas," he said. He drew deeply from his cigar, then added, "Yep. For the first time ever, I think Lincoln can think he's succeedin' at reuniting the nation."

"That's what you truly think is happening?" Serena asked, eyes snapping.

"What . . . ?" Edward asked, eyeing her questioningly.

Serena's gaze shot upward as she realized what she had just said. She had almost revealed her lack of loyalty. . . .

"Nothing," she stammered. "But, Edward?" she quickly added. "Why did you want me to . . . come to your house tonight . . . ?" She had to change the subject. Speaking of other things than the war had to be managed. She always seemed to be speaking too carelessly of her feelings.

"Where else?" he grumbled. "All the restaurants are filled with uniforms."

"So there wasn't any special reason?"

"Does there have to be, to be with a man's chosen?"

"Edward!" Serena said, annoyance showing once again. But wasn't this the opportunity to tell him once again of her true feelings? She began to speak, but couldn't find the words. They had all been spoken before.

He leaned back into his chair, puffing on his cigar. "I've just had the need for your company, Serena," he said thickly. He rose from the chair and went to a window, putting his back to her. "A man has needs. All sorts," he said. He swung around, eyeing her with the raw hunger she had seen earlier.

Knowing this, Serena rose and moved toward the door, definitely ready to take her leave. She could tell of *her* feelings later. She was angry at herself for not having been smart enough to know that nothing proper could have been behind this invitation. Suddenly she didn't feel safe with this man of her father's choosing. He was so much larger than she. He could force his way on her, if he so desired. She had only been jesting when she had spoken the word "seduce" to Priscilla. Surely Edward wouldn't . . . Surely he had more respect for her and *her* wishes.

"I don't wish to hear of your needs, Edward," she said softly, reaching for the doorknob. When she heard his footsteps and felt his arms circling her waist, the breath caught in her throat and her eyes grew wide.

"You must have the same needs," he said thickly. "Or else why would you be here? A woman does not come to a man's house alone unless she has more than conversation on her mind."

Serena jerked free from him, glowering. "Do you want to know why I truly came?" she said between clenched teeth. "Because I was bored. *Bored*. And because I wanted to tell you that I despise you and will *not* marry you. Do you hear? How many times do I have to tell you? I did not come to your house because I had a need to be with you. I hate you. I hate the sight of you."

He laughed and reached for her once again, grabbing her roughly into his arms. He held her there as though in a vise and crushed his lips against hers, emitting a deep, throaty moan as he moved a hand beneath her cape to feel the curve of a breast.

"All I've thought about today is you, Serena," he whispered into her ear, panting as his fingers fumbled with the buttons of her dress.

Serena continued to squirm, dread filling her veins. "Edward, you must stop," she stormed as his fingers made contact with the softness of a breast. "Release me. *Now*. I demand—"

With one quick movement he swooped her up into his arms and carried her into the dark recesses of a bedroom and placed her on the bed. When she struggled to move from it, he held her in place with one hand and lifted her cape off. Then he reached beneath her skirts to pull her underthings off with the other. Then, when she heard him unbuttoning his breeches, she swung her free hand upward, slapping him noisily across the face.

"Let me go!" she screamed. "I'll tell Father! I will!"

"He's a man. He will see what you've done this evening as an open invitation for me to do just what I'm doing."

"You're wrong. I'm his daughter. Why, he'll shoot you!"

He laughed. "I think not," he said. "I think not. Do you even dare tell him you so brazenly came to my house? And after dark?"

"Why . . . you . . . planned this . . ." she gasped.

"How else . . . ?" He loomed over her now, holding her down. Suddenly he leaned against her and plunged into her. Serena let out a cry of pain. And when he began to move deeply inside her and kept thrusting in and out, over and over again, Serena lay in shock, feeling nothing but humiliation and pain, now wondering why any woman could ever . . . love . . . a . . . man. . . .

Oh, God, would he never end this? It seemed to go on, forever and ever, as he continued to pound his body into hers. She wanted to scream at him to stop, but couldn't, for his lips were once again crushing down upon hers, sealing her mouth, as his body continued to attack her, pushing her more into the bed, hurting her even more. . . .

Then it seemed suddenly to be over after his body had shook with tremors, jerking, as he gasped for breath between loud guttural groans of pleasure.

Tears of humiliation wetting her cheeks, Serena turned her face from his. She had not been seduced but raped. She had wanted it to be right that first time. She had wanted to love . . . to truly love. . . .

She tensed when Edward's lips sought out a breast that he had forced free from the front of the dress.

"I love you, little darlin'," he whispered, now reaching

31

up inside her dress to run his hands over her stomach, and down between her thighs, parting her there, caressing her.

Serena's breath caught in her throat, afraid that he would attack her again. She clamped her legs together, wishing to be set free, oh, so badly wanting to leave Edward's house.

"I'm sorry, Serena," Edward said, rising from the bed. "I shouldn't have done that. I should've had more control. Please, I beg of you, please don't hate me."

Serena's fingers quickly secured the buttons of her dress, then fumbled in the darkness and succeeded at finding her underthings. She pulled them quickly on, unable to quell her trembling.

"It won't happen again, Edward," she hissed. "You'll never have another such opportunity. For, you see, I'll refuse to ever even speak with you again. *Ever.*"

"Oh, little darlin'," he whimpered, moving to pull her from the bed. "Please . . ."

She jerked free from his grip. "Don't touch me," she hissed. "I told you that I hated you. Why didn't you listen? Now my hate is tenfold. . . ."

She scooped her cape up into her arms and ran from the bedroom and into the living room. She threw her cape across her shoulders, then rushed on outside to release the horse's reins, not stopping to look back when Edward came yelling after her.

Too angry even to cry now, she shouted at her horse and snapped the reins. She was glad to be leaving the scene of the last hideous moments behind her.

Oh, how could I have ever let this happen? she thought angrily to herself. *How?*

Chapter Two

Shimmers of golden came across her bed, a warning to Serena that the time had arrived to rise to another day.

But this day, something else had been added. She rose to a strange soreness between her thighs, an ugly reminder of what had happened the night before. She groaned as she lifted first one leg then the other from the bed, wondering if having sex with a man would always leave her with such terrible aftereffects. If so, she couldn't see why any woman would choose to wed.

A voice broke the silence in the room, making Serena turn with a start.

"Serena?" Priscilla persisted with impatience.

Serena eyed the closed bedroom door with caution, then hurriedly pulled a robe around her shoulders. She felt as though anyone could see the telltale signs of having been with a man if she didn't cover herself completely. And she most certainly didn't want her sister to know. Priscilla just was not a sister to confide in.

"Coming, Priscilla," she finally answered, running her fingers through her hair in an effort to loosen its tight curls. She hated her natural curls. They seemed to be forever springing in directions that weren't of her choosing. She shook her head, causing the hair to rise and fall around her shoulders, then went to the door and swung it aside, letting Priscilla enter.

Serena eyed her sister in amazement. "You're already dressed, Priscilla?" she said, shutting the door behind her. Priscilla's dress was a crisp, blue silken material with a pleated bodice and gathered puff sleeves, and it tapered to the waist to an extreme, accentuating the swell of her bosom and the smallness of her waist. "Why are you? Is there some special occasion?" Serena questioned further. "You are always ready to seize the opportunity to sleep late. It is I who always have to awaken *you*."

Priscilla moved to Serena's dressing table and lifted a brush, pulling it in long, smooth strokes through her straight, brown strings of hair. "I've listened more closely to your recent words, Serena," she sighed, pursing her narrow lips as she then ran a finger over them while looking into a mirror. "I'm going to change. I'm going to make myself just as beautiful as you. I will then have any man that I want. Maybe even then Edward will want me instead of you." She swung around to face Serena. "You truly don't want him, do you, Serena?"

Serena could feel her face coloring. She quickly averted her eyes for fear Priscilla could read the guilt in their depths. "I would never want that man," she hissed. "He is despicable." She smiled wickedly as she gazed toward Priscilla once again. "And you do want him? How interesting." She now knew how to rid herself forever of this man. The previous evening, she hadn't taken Priscilla seriously when her sister had spoken of Edward.

But now Serena would take full advantage of this knowledge. Knowing of Edward's weaknesses, Serena knew that the proper thing to do was to warn Priscilla of

Edward's ways. But yet she couldn't believe that Edward would seduce a second daughter of Hiram Milton Calvert. To do so could mean Edward's possible demise. So, yes, that would now be her plan . . . to help direct Edward's interests to Priscilla!

She moved to her wardrobe and chose a black serge skirt and white shirtwaist to wear in the hospital quarters, where endless chores always awaited her. How long had it been since she had been able to wear a beautiful, lace-trimmed evening gown? Balls and parties had ceased when the war had begun. But Serena was remembering Edward's words about the war. Maybe Grant *was* going to succeed at defeating Lee. Though her loyalties traveled from one to the other, the end of the war wouldn't be soon enough to please her. Only then could her life change back to what she could consider normal.

"I've also come to tell you that Cora has breakfast ready in the sitting room," Priscilla said, swirling around, lifting her silk dress up, pretending to be dancing.

Serena eyed her quizzically, then said, "Please go tell Cora that I'll be up in a few minutes. I need to get dressed and brush my hair. And also tell Father that I won't be long."

"Okay," Priscilla said, fluttering her lashes in a teasing fashion.

"Priscilla," Serena snapped, "you are acting like an idiot today."

"Rather I'd be this way than reading novels, huh, older sister?" Priscilla laughed, then rushed from the room.

Serena's eyebrows raised, then she moved around the

room, almost throwing her clothes on, only stopping long enough to brush her hair to long, curly masses of red around her shoulders. She was thinking about where the Calvert family now ate their breakfast each morning; a third-floor sitting room had been established in one of the rooms that wasn't filled with dust-sheeted furniture. As always, Cora, the Negro maid, served them. Their "maid," not their "slave."

To Serena's way of thinking, however, they both were the same. A maid was a slave. But her father would never let the word "slave" escape his lips when he spoke of Cora, nor any of their other servants they had once employed that had kept busy from dawn to dusk before the Calvert's house had been converted into a hospital. Now servants weren't needed. Even their quarters were being occupied by the wounded.

"Oh, well," Serena sighed, pinching her cheeks in an effort to cause some color to rise. She knew that she was much too pale this day and she didn't want her father questioning her about her pallor. She didn't want to have to confess, "Father, oh, Father, it is because I was seduced by a man last night . . . a man that you trusted. . . ."

She smiled almost wickedly, wondering just what he might say or do if she did make such a bold confession to him. "But, I can't," she whispered. "Never. It is something I have to push from my mind. And when Edward comes to call, I shall urge Priscilla toward him. He will see that there is more womanly flesh in this house than he can shake a stick at."

Giggling, she moved from the room, swinging her skirt around as she began to climb the staircase to the third floor. She cringed when she was once again reminded of

none' and 'charity for all.'" Hiram cleared his throat, then continued. "It also says that Lincoln is imploring the people to bind up the nation's wounds, to care for him who shall have borne the battle and for his widow and his orphan, and to do all which may achieve and cherish a just and lasting peace."

Hiram folded the newspaper and placed it beside him on the edge of the table. The wrinkles around his eyes and mouth deepened and his dark eyes saddened. "The photograph of Lincoln in this morning's paper shows the effects of four years of this hellish war," he grumbled. "Lincoln's face has become gaunt and deeply lined. Even his eyes are ringed with black."

Serena shook her hair around her shoulders. "Four years of war has done many things to many people, Father," she said, then sipped quietly on her coffee, eyeing her father as his gaze moved to her and stopped. His graying hair matched that of his thick mustache, and his wide nose had begun to be streaked in shallow purples, a sign of the intensity of his life, with his blood pressure causing many small veins to burst, not only on his nose, but also his cheeks. In her way, Serena loved him, but had feared him so as a small child. She had always hated his loud, authoritative voice. That was the reason she had come to be as stubborn and strong-willed herself. She had had to learn to stand up to him and his overbearing ways. He had led her to become so high-spirited, even reckless at times, with her ways, as well as her words.

"Where were you last night, Serena?" Hiram suddenly blurted, lifting a pipe from an ashtray. He placed it between his lips and began puffing, letting it settle into the corner of his mouth. He leaned the bulkiness of his full weight back in his chair. He was dressed all in black now, but when he entered the hospital quarters, this would always be covered by a long, flowing garment of white. "We had quite a rush of wounded in here last night after the train's arrival," he continued. "We sure could've used another pair of hands."

"I went to mother's grave, Father," Serena said, lowering her eyes. She took another quick sip of coffee, feeling tension mounting inside her. Her stomach was even tightening, for fear of his next question.

He laughed hoarsely. "By carriage? By damn, I think that a bit strange, since our cemetery is only a few footsteps away."

"Well, Father . . ." she said, stammering over her words. She wasn't used to becoming speechless around her father. Since having grown into her late teens, she usually would spout right back at him. But this morning, it was all suddenly changed. And all because of Edward. No man had taken advantage of her before. How could she explain *that* away?

"Well, what?" he boomed, tapping his pipe empty into the ashtray. He pushed himself up from the chair and went to a window. He pulled the sheer curtain aside, peering downward. "Meet with Edward? Eh?" He turned on a heel, eyeing her with a lifted eyebrow. "See Edward last night? Speak up."

Serena pushed her chair back and rose from it, knowing that she was blushing. This was also something new for her. She rarely blushed, especially in the presence of her father. "Yes," she finally confessed. "We met." She began to move toward the door with quick, eager steps.

"A date been set for the weddin'?" Hiram spoke loudly

40

from behind her. "Eh? When's the big day?"

Serena glanced toward Priscilla whom had been sipping quietly on coffee, listening, watching, then back toward her father. She moved her hands into two tight fists. She swirled around, glowering, as she moved a bit toward her father. "Father, will you just forget this thing about Edward and me marrying?" she said between clenched teeth. "I will never, no, never, never marry that . . . man!"

She rushed from the room, steaming. With quick steps, she rushed down the two flights of stairs to the first floor. Anything to get away from the proddings of her father. Anything to get away from the continuing reminder of that brute, Edward James Carlson.

Hesitating at the foot of the stairs, Serena's gaze moved around her. The large living room, the dining room, and other rooms of this lower floor were filled with beds, donated by the local townspeople after Hiram Milton Calvert had volunteered his house for the war's services.

From this vantage point, Serena could see through two large archways, one that led into the living room on one side of her, and the other, into the dining room. Then down a long length of hallway, the other rooms opened up on each side.

She set her jaws firmly, knowing her duties awaited, then went to a wardrobe and pulled out a long, white apron and lifted the neck loop over her head. She wrapped the apron's ties around her waist and tied it securely.

With quick movements, she reached into an apron pocket for a yellow satin ribbon that she had left there the previous day. She used it to tie her hair back from her face, to hang as one long mass down her back. "Wearing your hair in such a fashion resembles a pony's tail," Priscilla had teased.

A low, throaty moan and an accompanying cough caught her attention. It was coming from one of the smaller rooms along the hall, which were used for the enemy casualties. She always hated having to enter those rooms, because the men were shackled to the beds, if not to the headboard, then at the foot of the bed. It was always according to where the soldier had been wounded. If nearer his upper extremities, he would be shackled by the lower, or if nearer the lower, he would be shackled by the upper. Either way, Serena thought it to be quite barbaric. A wounded man should be treated with more respect. She would always believe this. When wounded, surely the last thing a man would have on his mind would be to escape. To escape without proper care would most surely mean a slow, cruel death.

But she also knew that the men doubted they would get "proper care," even in one of the cleanest hospitals in the North. With no ways to combat infection or fever, amputation had become the chief method of treating major wounds. Serena had assisted with more amputations than she would even care to think about. It had become as common in her life as eating.

She knew this was the reason Priscilla shirked her hospital duties. Serena had found that Priscilla couldn't stand to be around a man once a limb had been removed, saying that any imperfection sickened, even repelled her, although in most things Priscilla was kindhearted and compassionate. Serena had wondered if this would also apply to other imperfections that sometimes would afflict a human, even upon birth? Serena had discovered a side of her sister that indeed was most unpleasant.

Priscilla had even been found to have a weaker stomach than Serena, even though Serena had been known to faint when a man's gangrened leg had been uncovered before her eyes. The stench alone had been the cause of many of these faintings. Oh, how she had hated herself afterwards. She had always prided herself as being as strong as her father. That had been her only way to win with him.

Serena entered the first room, where she had counted twelve men only the day before. Now that she was counting heads from behind separate pulled curtains that hung at each bedside, she found that one more had been added, to be squeezed into a corner, next to the outside wall.

Wondering about the seriousness of this latest enemy's wounds, Serena made her way in front of the other beds. She knew to always expect to feel eyes following her, but today that feeling bothered her. Was it because her trust in men had diminished? Even in a man who lay ill, and unable to move from the bed without the assistance of a key . . . ?

Serena thrust her hands inside her front apron pocket as she moved to the new patient's bedside. Seeing one leg fettered to the leg of the iron bed by way of a chain with a lock securing each end made her insides tremble. So often she had thought of sneaking into the sitting room and stealing the keys from her father's desk to release all these men. But she knew that to do so would be the same as aiding and abetting the enemy. So far, the only aid that had come from her was the gentle word or gentle touch to those who needed it the most. It was her father who always did the more extreme of the treatments.

Lifting the window shade next to where the new patient lay sleeping, Serena was able to get a better look at him. His face, framed by black, wavy hair, was ashen, where it could be seen beneath his mustache and thickening black whiskers.

His closed eyes showed dark eyelashes, as thick as one would expect to find on a woman. His nose was straight, and he had a hard, clean set to his jawline. But the thing that caught Serena's full attention was the deep cleft in his chin. It made him different and, oh, so handsome. Something urged her forefinger upward, to touch the cleft, then she gasped and drew back from him when his eyes flew widely open, revealing to Serena the darkest, the most beguiling eyes that she had yet to see on a man. Something stirred inside her as a small smile lifted his lips upward.

"Am I going to make it, beautiful?" he said teasingly. "Or am I going to hang it up right here and now?"

Serena's words caught in her throat. She hadn't even taken the time yet to see how he had been wounded. She had been so captivated by his handsomeness, she had completely forgotten why he was lying on that bed, in her father's hospital quarters, where she was supposed to be caring for patients, instead of studying the better qualities of one of the wounded enemy.

"I don't know, sir," she finally murmured, clearing her throat nervously.

He tried to move a bit, then groaned, closing his eyes as he gritted his teeth. Then he spoke in a tight whisper. "Hurts like hell," he said, reaching up to touch his left shoulder.

Serena's gaze moved there, now seeing blood oozing from his bandaged shoulder.

"Here. Let me help you," she said, bending, pulling the sheet down from where his hand had stopped to rest. She examined the bandage, seeing that it needed changing, and when she heard heavy footsteps coming up behind her, she turned and found her father already attired in his long garb of white moving toward her.

"Needin' changed, Serena?" he said, one eyebrow lifted higher than the other. He was carrying fresh bandages and a pair of scissors. In a front pocket, Serena spied a bottle of whiskey resting precariously inside it.

"Yes, Father, I believe so," she said, moving aside so her father could take over.

"Go get a basin of fresh water, Serena," he ordered loudly. "I'll remove the bandage while waitin'."

"Yes, Father," she said, scooting on away from him. Feeling clumsy, knowing that this new patient was watching her, she moved to the table that held large pitchers of water and several basins to work from all through the day. With trembling fingers, she poured water into one of these basins, then moved back to where her father was slowly and carefully cutting the soiled bandage away.

"Damn wound you got there, lad," he grumbled. "But my whiskey treatment will get it fine in no time."

"The bullet's already removed?" the man said, flinching when the bandage was pulled from the skin.

"Yep. I took care of that late last night," Hiram said, laughing a bit beneath his breath. "I *thought* you were out of it. That makes it much simpler for me, you know."

"It was a long, tiring trip," the man said, sighing, then glancing toward Serena, lifting his lips into another smile.

"You'd better get a good grip on the bed, son," Hiram

45

said, taking the bottle of whiskey from his pocket.

"What are you planning to do with that?" the man asked, licking his lips. "I'd like a drink if you could even spare it."

"Ain't what this whiskey's for, lad," Hiram said darkly. "Serena, go get a clean cloth," he ordered, unscrewing the lid from the whiskey. "Nope. This whiskey ain't for drinkin'. It's for cleanin' the wound."

"Do you mean . . . you're . . . going to pour that on this . . . fresh wound . . . ?" the man said, inching his way from Hiram.

"Yep. Guess so," Hiram chuckled, as Serena returned with the cloth. He poured the whiskey onto it, saturating it, then without hesitation applied it to the bloody, raw mass of flesh. He couldn't help but tense when the young man cringed and bit his lower lip to keep from crying out. "Sorry about that, lad," he grumbled, then handed the whiskey bottle and rag to Serena and then began to wrap the wound with the clean bandage.

Serena felt a rippling in her stomach when she saw the man's pain. She wanted to reach out, touch him, but decided that her father would probably shout at her. She always did these things when he wasn't around. This was a soft side to her nature that she didn't ever let him see.

"This here your nurse?" the man said, panting, eyeing Serena with a keen interest. He'd never seen such a beautiful woman. None of the South Carolina women could ever compete with her, even with her hair tied back away from her face and dressed in such a garb. Ah, if he could see her in a low-cut gown with a full hoop beneath, accompanying him to a ball. Ah, this would be something he could dream about while recuperating.

"Just my daughter, Serena," Hiram said, tying off the

ends of the bandage, rising.

"Serena?" the man said thickly. "Such a beautiful name. Does it mean that she is of a serene nature?"

Hiram hooted with laughter, eyeing Serena with amusement. "Serena? Serene? Think you figured *her* wrong, lad."

"Oh?" the man said, smiling. He had dreaded this hospital stay, keeping him from gathering together another regiment. But with such a beautiful woman to stare at, the hardship could be made a bit pleasurable.

Hiram continued to hand out further orders to Serena as he moved from the new patient's bedside. "Some laudanum for this lad, Serena," he said, then moved on from the room.

"Some character, that father of yours," the man said, sighing.

"Yes. Likes handing out orders," Serena said, starting to move away with the soiled water and bandages. "I'll be back with some laudanum, in just a minute, sir."

"You can call me Wesley," the man called after her. "Colonel Wesley Alston Wyndham. If I wasn't shackled, I would rise from this bed and bow deeply to your beauty."

Serena's eyes widened. She turned and smiled warmly toward him, feeling something foreign stirring inside her that no other man had been able to stir. It was a delicious feeling, a warmth that traveled from her head to her toes. The ache between her thighs had suddenly become of a different kind, a pleasurable thing that mystified Serena. "Glad to meet you, Colonel Wesley," she said over her shoulder, then moved on away. She had to remember that this was the enemy, enchanting though he was. . . .

Feeling slightly giddy from this man's attention, Serena hurried to the cupboard where the laudanum was kept. She poured some into a small glass, added water, then hurried back to Wesley's bedside. "Here," she said, smiling softly. "This should make you feel better, for a little while, that is."

"How can anyone feel better with chains wrapped around his ankle?" he grumbled, then accepted the glass anyway. He tipped it to his lips, eyeing her once again.

"It's the rules set down," she said, turning to look around her, to see if anyone else needed her attention. To her relief, most were drifting off to sleep again, though fitfully. "If Father hadn't agreed to shackle the prisoners, they would have been taken immediately to the jail, wounds and all."

Wesley swallowed the last drop of the liquid, then handed the glass back to Serena. "The damnedest, cruelest thing I've ever encountered," he said, frowning darkly.

"And you, sir, wouldn't you leave, if you weren't so imprisoned?" Serena asked, placing the glass on a table, wiping her hands on her apron.

"Me?" he said, laughing suddenly. "Naw. I'd never think of doing such a thing as escaping."

"I bet," Serena laughed, tilting her head a bit sideways, feeling uncomfortable under his steady gaze. She could tell that it was an appraising one, but she wasn't quite used to the effect it was having on her. Usually such a look would annoy her. But not with this man. She wanted even more of it. There was something about him that was drawing her to him. She just had to get hold of herself. She had to remember the impossibility of the situation. She turned to leave, but was stopped by the pleading in his words.

"Do you have to go? Just yet?" he asked, trying to lean up on his free elbow, but groaning, dropping back down to lie flat on his back.

"I have duties, Colonel Wesley," she said, feeling a strange tingling riding up and down her spine with the mere mention of his name.

"I am one of the wounded," he said. "Surely you can spend just a bit more time with me. I hate the thought of just lying here, staring off into space."

"But you must remember that you *are* wounded," she said. "You have to be quiet. Only by doing so will you be healed."

"And then what? Where will I be sent?"

Serena's face darkened. "I don't think you want to know the answer to that, Colonel Wesley," she said softly, turning to leave once again.

"Serena," he said.

She stopped abruptly. There seemed to be a certain magic in the way he spoke her name. She couldn't help but turn on a heel and smile warmly toward him. "Colonel Wesley, I must—"

He patted the bed beside him. "You must sit right down here and keep me company," he ordered firmly. "For a while. At least until the laudanum begins to take effect. Be my medicine for a while. Please?"

Serena threw her head back in forced exasperation. "Oh, all right," she sighed, then settled down beside him, taking another fast look around the room. She didn't want to be guilty of neglecting the others for just this one man whom had taken her fancy. She didn't care to be chided by her father. Oh, hopefully those days would soon be over.

"And now that I'm here, what do you have to say,

Colonel Wesley?" she added, smoothing her apron around her and crossing her legs.

"What do I have to say?" he said, reaching to trace her arm with a forefinger. "I say that I'd like for you to drop the colonel before my name and that you have to be the most beautiful Union wench I've ever become acquainted with."

"Oh?" she said, eyes wide.

"Yes," he said, laughing hoarsely. "And even more beautiful than any Confederate wenches I've come across also."

Her eyebrows tilted even more. "Oh?" she said even more loudly.

"But you know how beautiful you are," he said, laughing, reaching to touch her lips, causing Serena's heart to begin to beat wildly inside her.

"I've never thought much about it," she said, pushing his finger away. It was unnerving her. She didn't want this stranger to see this. She had to remember that he was the enemy . . . the captured enemy. . . .

"And what else do you do for fun?" he said, moving his free arm to rest beneath his head.

"Fun? You are comparing this to fun?" she gasped, covering her mouth with a hand.

"Well, you know what I mean," he said. "I don't know of anything else you do. What can I even ask about?"

"Well, maybe you can tell me a little about yourself," Serena said, glad to have been led into such a question. She *was* curious. She wanted to know his age, where he lived before he began fighting, if he was married.

"And what would you like to know?"

"The usual things . . ."

"Well," he said, rolling his eyes to the back of his head, as though in thought. "I have ten children, two grandchildren—"

Serena pushed herself from the bed. "You . . . what . . . ?" she said in a rush, paling.

He laughed. "Now do you think I'm truly old enough to have experienced all that?" he said, reaching for her, encouraging her to sit back down beside him.

"What are you? A big tease, as well as a soldier?"

"I've been known to tease a mite," he laughed further.

She arranged her skirt and apron around her once again as she repositioned herself on the bed. "I truly would like to know something about you, Wesley," she said, flirting with her large, seductive brown eyes.

"I'm from Folly Island—"

"Folly?" she said, thinking him teasing once more. She rose again, setting her jaw firmly. "If you can't be serious, I will take my leave," she said angrily. She brushed her skirt in place and took a step away from him.

"It's true," he said. "There is such an island. My father owns a large plantation there. It's just a few miles from Charleston, South Carolina."

"Truly?" she said, settling down beside him again. "There is? And you have lived on a plantation? It sounds so exciting."

"Yes. It was, until the war began," he grumbled, furrowing his brow.

"Yes. I can imagine . . ."

"But, anyway," he continued. "I'm twenty-five. And you?"

"Eighteen."

His eyes raked over her, stopping on the swell of her

bosom. Even beneath the bulkiness of her attire, it was alluring. "A quite ripe eighteen," he said, smiling wickedly.

Serena felt another blush rising. What was happening to her? Did having a sexual relationship with a man, undesirable and unfulfilling as it was, make changes inside a woman to such an extent? Rarely, oh, so rarely had she ever blushed. Now she seemed to be doing it all the time.

She couldn't make words rise from inside her throat. Instead, she let him continue speaking.

"Before the damned firing on Fort Sumter, I was quite content with my way of life on Folly Island," he said, wiping at his eyes, suddenly feeling a bit lightheaded from the laudanum. But he wanted to stay awake. Continue talking with Serena. If not, she might not return. While he held *her* captive, he had to take advantage of it.

"What was your life like there?" she asked.

"I helped my father with the plantation," he said. "I helped to watch over the slaves. We had over one hundred at last count. Now that Lincoln has created this war, I'm sure there will be no slaves left when I return."

Serena looked nervously around her. "Wesley, please let's not talk of slaves while in this Northern hospital," she said. "I don't think it a bit wise."

Wesley laughed. "I thought you would even get fighting mad," he said. "I thought it would bring out the sparks in your eyes. Now what have I got me here, a Confederacy lover on the Union side?"

Serena paled as she rose. When his hand reached for hers and held onto it, she returned beside him. "Please," she whispered. "Please speak of something else."

He held onto her hand, making her grow weak in the knees. "I guess I can tell you how I happened to be here, can't I?" he asked, squeezing her hand. "I've needed someone to talk with. Get it . . . off . . . my chest," he added.

A feeling of contentment overpowered Serena. For the first time ever, a man was calming her. She wondered if she would stay as calm if he were to try to kiss her? Her heartbeat fluttered like a butterfly's wings just thinking about such a kiss from lips as thick and moist as his. "Please tell me what you wish," she said softly. "But speak quietly and please say nothing else about slavery," she hurriedly added. "That is a word best left alone, if you know what I mean."

"I'm sure I do," he said, clearing his throat nervously, remembering the loud voice and the bulkiness of Serena's father. Wesley didn't want to create trouble. Not yet anyway. He had to wait until he was a bit stronger. Then he would make his move. "Well, when I saw that the war was being fought, truly fought, I enlisted as a private with the South Carolina Mounted Rifles. You see, I'm a bit restless at times. Even reckless, so my father has told me. If war was what the North wanted, then I was one of the first southerners to call their bluff."

As he spoke of his true nature, of being restless and reckless, Serena was reminded of herself. It gave her a strange sensation inside, having found a man with the same attributes as she. "So? How did you get captured?" she asked, her eyes dancing with excitement. She hadn't yet allowed herself the pleasure of talking at length with a prisoner. Up to this point, there hadn't been any man who had stirred her interests. None had been as exciting or as handsome as Wesley.

"After I was a private for a short while, I was given a colonel's commission by General Lee. He authorized me to raise and command a regiment of cavalry. It wasn't as all others. Mine was mainly to carry out raids behind enemy lines." He laughed hoarsely. "I've even heard that General Sherman called my raiders the most dangerous set of men which the war had turned loose on the world."

"Truly?" Serena gasped, enthralled even more now by Wesley's exciting words. She would hate to leave his bedside. She now knew that she could stay forever to listen to him. She loved his voice. It was as honey, all spun and sweet.

"Yeah. He said that each and every one of us were splendid shots and utterly reckless."

"And were you?"

"Yeah. Guess so. I've had at least twenty-nine horses shot from under me, and on many occasions I escaped from encircling enemy forces."

"But this one time, you weren't so . . . lucky?"

"No," he said darkly, turning his head from her. "It was at Ft. Donelson, on the Kentucky/Tennessee border. The Union regiment captured it at the first of the war. I had decided it was worth recapturing. But it was one time I got a bit careless, I guess. The Yanks had us circled before I could bat an eye."

"Then, how did you get shot? They surely didn't shoot you while you just stood there."

"No. I dared them, I guess you'd say. I lunged my horse right through the bastard Bluebellies," he said, now laughing softly. "I wasn't going to be captured without a fight."

Serena glanced quickly toward the door, glad her

father wasn't hearing all this talk about the Bluebellies as Wesley and all other Rebs called the northern troops. She then glanced back at Wesley. "And you got shot while doing such a reckless thing?" she asked quietly.

"Yeah. Guess I was lucky it was only a shoulder wound."

"And the rest of your men?"

"I'm not sure. Some killed, I suppose. Not sure about the wounded," he said glumly. "Maybe even in your jail."

"You truly don't know how many were wounded?"

Wesley's eyes traveled around the room. "I don't see any of my men," he said sadly. "I guess I'll never know the true count of the dead or wounded."

"Wesley, don't you think you need your rest now?" Serena asked, hating to have to draw this tête-à-tête to a close. But she could see the heaviness of his eyelids.

"Will you come back, Serena?" he asked, holding her hand tightly.

"Yes."

"When?"

She placed her forefinger to his lips. "Tonight," she whispered. "I shall return . . . tonight . . ."

His heart pounded rapidly as he saw something in her eyes. Was she as attracted to him, as he to her? If only he wasn't wounded. He would show her his skills as a lover. "I'll count on it," he said thickly, releasing his hold on her hand, to reach upward and touch the softness of a cheek.

"I shall return," she whispered. "Don't fear." And she would. No one had ever stirred her heart so. No one . . .

She rose and moved away from him, feeling a wondrous lightheadedness accompanying her each and every step. . . .

Chapter Three

Serena paced nervously back and forth before the roaring fire, glancing occasionally toward the hands of the clock on the mantel. She wanted to see the hands move more quickly around to the hour of eleven, when the lamps' wicks would be lowered in the hospital quarters. Only then would it be safe to go to Wesley, be free to speak with him once again.

"You're as nervous as a cat, Serena," Hiram said, settling down onto a chair, lighting a pipe. "What's got your dander up? Is it Edward? Because he hasn't yet arrived this evening?"

Serena turned quickly, her eyes flashing in golden browns. "Father, once and for all," she blurted. "I refuse to marry him. Is that understood? Will you please know that I mean every word? I don't love Edward. I shall not have a wedding band placed on my finger by a man that I have grown to loathe."

"Loathe? That's a mighty strong word," Hiram said, tilting a thick, gray eyebrow. "Since when have your feelings grown so harsh toward Edward? Has something happened between the two of you that you haven't discussed with me?"

Feeling her face reddening, Serena turned with a start, facing the fire. She was remembering Edward's massive hands traveling over the private parts of her body. Even now it sent a keen sense of revulsion through her. When she then let herself remember how Wesley's touch had sent sparks through her, kindling something beautiful, she knew even more strongly that Edward wouldn't have the opportunity to get near her again.

"Well, Serena? What's the problem?" Hiram insisted, moving to her side, tapping his pipe's ashes into the fire.

"It's as it always has been, Father," she said quietly. "I never wanted to marry him. You know that."

"Well, for now, I won't get into this thing with you," he stormed. "I have to go back to the hospital quarters. Are you coming?"

"No. I don't think so, Father," she said, but knowing that she would be entering the hospital quarters later, when everyone else was hopefully asleep. She had to see Wesley. She had to listen to the magic of his voice. She had never felt this way about a man before. If only he weren't the enemy!

"Priscilla is feigning illness, I believe," Hiram said, moving toward the door. "She'd do anything to keep from her duties. Her loyalties are only to herself. Are yours also, Serena?" He turned on a heel, staring accusingly in her direction.

"Father—" Serena began, but was stopped when heavy footsteps drew close. Serena's heart began to thump wildly, recognizing these particular footsteps. It was Edward. Oh, what did he want with her now? Hadn't he done her enough harm? Serena moved quickly, wishing to escape, but just as she was about to rush from the room, Edward appeared at the door.

Hiram and Edward met with a heavy handshake, while Edward's eyes sought out Serena's, then held.

"Good to see you, Edward ol' boy," Hiram chuckled, glancing toward Serena, then back to Edward.

"Good to see you, too, Hiram," Edward said quietly, still watching Serena and how she stood with her hands so tightly drawn into knots at her side.

"Well, must run, ol' boy," Hiram said, clearing his throat nervously, feeling the tension between Serena and Edward. "I see you two have to get a few things settled between you. I sure can understand lovers' spats." He laughed a bit nervously, moving on past Edward, glancing at Serena, saying more loudly, "Yep. Sure can understand lovers' spats. Had a few in my day. See you, Edward." He stopped with his brow furrowed deeply. "And, Serena, if Priscilla wanders in here by chance, send her downstairs, will you? Edward here has a way of fillin' our beds up with the Johnny Rebs, don't cha ol' boy?" He laughed huskily as he moved from the room.

Serena went to a window at the far end of the room and pulled a sheer curtain aside, glancing upward at the sky. Though it was supposed to be darkening, there was something else about it this night. The clouds of gray seemed heavier, as though they had a burden inside them, needing to be released. *Snow*, Serena thought. *Though it is March, there seems to be a snow threatening*. But nothing was threatening her any worse than Edward who had moved to her side.

"Serena, I'm damn sorry for last night," he said thickly, working his hat in his hands. Serena had noticed how nice he had looked with his black waistcoat and tight-fitted breeches of the same coloring. The harsh color of black had seemed to emphasize even more the bulkiness of this man. To some women, he would even be attractive. But to Serena, he was just another man, one whom she would pass on the street without even a second glance.

Now, Wesley . . . She would have noticed him, would have singled him out from a crowd. No one could be as handsome. She had to wonder how he would look clean-shaven and fully clothed. In a hospital bed, he had managed to capture her heart. Surely clean-shaven and fully clothed, he would capture her soul!

"Serena," Edward said, grabbing her by the arm, forcing her around to face him. "I'm apologizing. Don't you give a damn?"

Serena's eyes began to flash warnings toward this man who was once again forcing himself upon her. "You get your hands off me, Edward James Carlson," she hissed. "If you don't, I shall scream. And when I scream, my father will know, without me having to tell him, that you seduced me last night. He's a very smart man. He already sees something in me that is different." She lowered her eyes, mumbling, "As I also do."

"I love you, damn it," Edward said, releasing his hold. "I love you more than I could ever love anybody else."

"I hate you," Serena said, flipping the skirt of her dress around as she moved back to stand before the fire. She was chilly, and she knew why. This man would always be a reminder of her first sexual encounter, which had left her cold inside.

Edward lumbered next to her with head bowed. "I'll never approach you in that way again," he said. "I truly won't, Serena."

She swung around and faced him, her jaw set firmly. "I know that even more than you do," she said. "I won't

59

ever give you the chance. You shall never be alone with me again except for while you are in this house, and I hope that will never be again after this night. Do you hear?''

More footsteps entering the room made Serena's gaze move to the door. A small smile erupted on her lips when she found Priscilla standing there, looking coyly toward Edward. Serena moved toward Priscilla, now keenly aware of what her next move had to be. "Priscilla, honey," she said, taking her sister's hand, guiding her on into the room. "Father wants me to help him in the hospital quarters. Will you entertain Edward? Maybe offer him a glass . . . of . . . uh . . . fine wine?'' She smoothed one of Priscilla's straight brown locks from her face. "Will you please do that for me, darling?" she said sweetly, glancing toward Edward, seeing fire in his eyes.

"Serena—" he began.

"I'll be glad to pour you a glass of port, Edward," Priscilla said, lifting the skirt of her thickly gathered dress up into her arms, moving toward the liquor cabinet.

"Serena," Edward grumbled, moving to her side. "Your father distinctly said to send Priscilla downstairs to assist him. Not yourself. What is this little game you are playing?"

Serena said with a tilt of the head, "Figure it out for yourself.'' She then whirled the skirt of her dress around and hurried from the room, stopping to breathe a sigh of relief when she was clear from Edward's look of bewilderment. She leaned against the wall, breathing hard, clasping her hands to her throat. She had succeeded at putting Edward in his place. Finally! Now the rest was up to Priscilla. . . .

She touched the softness of the part of her breasts that were exposed, wondering if she should go on to the hospital quarters, pretend to be eager to assist her father, all the while being able to catch glimpses of Wesley, enabling him to also watch her, stir his interest in her just a bit more before the later hour arrived.

She glanced downward, smiling wickedly. She had chosen a dress that had yet to be worn in the hospital quarters. She hadn't planned to enter until later, so that only one set of eyes would see the lowcut dress of rose-colored satin, where she was trying to display her deep cleavage to the man she was falling in love with.

Should she hurry to the hospital quarters now? Yes! She would! The only other alternative would be to return to the room where Edward and Priscilla stood, or to the silence of her own bedroom, where there was nothing to amuse her.

She wondered to herself about the word she had chosen to use. *Amuse?* Until Wesley, she had found no charm or amusement in the hospital quarters. But he had made the change. She would forever be eager to have a chance to be around him. She didn't know why she hadn't thought about it earlier. Why should she wait until the later hours of the night, when she could possibly see him for the entire evening.

Moving down the stairs, she could feel her heart racing, knowing that one look into that room would allow her to see him again. Would he be awake? She hoped he was in less pain than earlier in the day. She wanted him to be totally awake when she moved to his bedside later in the night. She didn't want him to be drugged by that dreaded laudanum.

Taking the final step that took her to the landing next to the door where Wesley lay shackled, Serena's hands began to tremble. She leaned against the door frame, then peered into the room, barely breathing. In each bed was a man of different wounds and miseries. As usual, there were those who moaned steadily, even while asleep, and then there were those who lay with a silent hate in their eyes, obviously plotting a way to escape.

But no man had yet succeeded at that. The locks were too secure. Only a key could set any of these men free. Keys that Serena knew were kept in her father's desk in the sitting room on the third floor. How often she had watched him place them in the lower drawer. It had never occurred to her how easy it would be to remove them. But to do so would mean probably more than harsh words from her father. He would probably even take the razor strap to her back. He had done so when she had been a mischievous child. She could even still feel the blows to her bare skin and how she had refused to cry out each time the strap had snapped at her flesh.

"Cry, damn you," her father had shouted, hitting her even harder. "You're so stubborn. I have to get it out of you before you're grown. No man will have you. Do you hear? No man . . ."

But she had just stood there, gritting her teeth, hating him, defying him, until he had finally given up and had left her be, with welts that had always taken a full month to heal.

"And he's a physician, to now heal the sick?" she scoffed as her gaze settled on the end bed of the room.

"What's that you're mumbling?" Hiram said, moving suddenly to her side. "Somethin' about my healings?"

Serena turned with a start, having not seen him so close by. She cleared her throat nervously, moving away from him. "Nothing, Father," she murmured, going to busy her fingers with stacking fresh bandages in a neat pile. She glanced back at her father and how his white attire was already spotted with blood. He was a good man now. Yes, he did mean well. Maybe in the past he did also, but hadn't known how.

Hiram glanced up the staircase, twisting his mustache between his fingers. "And where is Edward? Why aren't you with him?" he grumbled.

"Edward is still upstairs," she said with a forced ease.

"Then why aren't you?"

"He's with Priscilla . . ."

"Priscilla?" Hiram gasped, jerking Serena around to face him. "Why Priscilla? Why not you?"

Serena smiled slightly, feeling pleasure at being able to get one over on her father. "Father, it seems you've pushed Edward toward the wrong daughter," she said, watching his expression of disbelief cause his eyes to widen in darker browns.

"Priscilla you say?" he said, kneading his brow. "Priscilla?" He laughed suddenly. "Edward isn't interested in Priscilla. He doesn't want a wife who would lay around reading all day . . . and . . ."

"And what, Father?" Serena stormed, hands on hips. "What else?"

"He wants a beautiful wife, like yourself, honey," Hiram said, smoothing a finger across Serena's cheek.

"And why would he? He would only want me to do his cleaning and cooking. Why should I be chosen to do these things instead of Priscilla? Do you think I want to

63

be the one who slaves? Why not Priscilla?"

"Your tongue has always gotten you into trouble, Serena," Hiram said, his face reddening with anger.

Serena saw this and suddenly felt like biting her tongue. Her father looked stricken, but she was always so driven by his rage. She knew that she always went too far both with Priscilla and their father. But she did have much to anger her. She only wished for escape. She wasn't shackled like the prisoners, but her kind of prison seemed to even be worse at times.

"I'm sorry, Father," she said soothingly. "Truly I am. Please don't anger yourself so over what comes from my spiteful mouth."

Hiram reached inside a pocket and removed a handkerchief and wiped at his brow, breathing hard. "If any man is ever able to tame your tongue, he will be highly rewarded by me," he grumbled.

"It won't be Edward," Serena murmured. "Father, it won't be Edward. Please realize that. Then we will all be much happier."

"But, Priscilla? Is she truly interested in the man?"

"Yes. Very."

"Do you think it possible that he—?"

"I'm going to see to it," Serena said firmly.

"How, Serena?"

"You will see," she said, smiling wickedly. "There is a way. I assure you."

"And they are together? Right now?"

"Sharing wine, I hope," Serena said, laughing softly. She leaned toward the door, trying once again to catch a glimpse of Wesley.

Hiram grumbled noisily. "I don't understand you or

your sister," he said, moving toward a table. He lifted a stack of fresh bandages into his arms and turned his gaze back to Serena. "And you have chosen to assist me tonight, have you?"

"Yes, Father."

Hiram's gaze traveled over her. "Then cover yourself, Serena," he said flatly.

"What?"

"You get that apron over the front of you," he ordered in his usual booming voice of authority. "We don't need the wounded having more miseries to cope with."

"What do you mean, Father?" she gasped.

"Seein' your rounded globes hangin' from that dress is enough to set a young man's heart to racin' too fast for his own good, especially one who is lyin' near death."

Serena was shocked at the boldness of his words. "Yes. I guess you're right," she murmured. She reached for her apron and slipped into it, then followed her father into the room where Wesley lay waiting.

Eagerness to get to Wesley's bedside made her frown when her father seemed to be moving too slowly from bed to bed, changing bandages, cleaning wounds, checking for temperatures. "And now for this Wyndham character," he said, finally moving to stand over Wesley. "How's it farin' for you this evenin', lad?" Hiram boomed, hands on hips, having refused from that first day of doctoring the wounded to address the enemy by their proper Confederate rank. Hiram would not address this man as colonal. He didn't look the role of a colonel. A plantation lad maybe, but not a colonel.

"Seems I'm better," Wesley said, moving a bit to

position himself so he could get a full view of Serena. Though he wasn't feeling as well as he pretended, he could feel the ache in his loins and the heat rising. He smiled at her, glad to see the knowing in her eyes, eager now for the later hour to arrive, so they could be together, if only to talk.

This time, he thought to himself. *This time we will just talk. But later, we will do more than that.* His gaze moved over her. She didn't have her hair secured by a ribbon this night. It hung in red masses of curls around her face and across her shoulders. Her lips seemed to be trembling a bit. Ah, so full, ah, so sensuous. He groaned a bit as he scooted back down onto the bed.

"Need some laudanum, lad?" Hiram asked, leaning to push at the bandage around the wound.

Serena's heart skipped a beat, hoping Wesley would say no. Without realizing what she was doing, she was slowly shaking her head no to him, and when he looked upward and saw her, he blurted out a quick, "No. Don't think I do," he said. "Seems I'll be all right without it tonight." He smiled a wide smile back at Serena, seeing her shoulders loosening in a sigh of relief. He knew what was in her mind—the same as was in his own. . . .

"Then I'll take my leave," Hiram said, turning to Serena. "Come on, Serena," he said a bit impatiently. "We've many more bedsides to visit before callin' it a night."

"Yes, Father," she said, then kept looking over her shoulder at Wesley as they moved toward the door. She mouthed a wide "later" to him, then hurried on beside her father to the next room of waiting Confederates, then on to the wounded Union soldiers for another fast see-to since they had been first on the list of priority and always checked first by Doc Calvert.

The Union soldiers were kept in a larger, much nicer room, with fresh coffee always ready for them to drink at their pleasure. Even an occasional glass of wine would be poured for those who requested it. Serena knew just what she would take to Wesley's bedside later this night. It would be more than herself. . . .

Chapter Four

Waiting for the last shuffling of her father's feet as he was preparing for bed, Serena stood in silence beside her bedroom window watching the snow falling in its white softness. It seemed that the Illinois weather had changed its mood once again. Serena had grown used to this. She had found that one day she could be basking in the warmth of an early spring sunshine, then the next day, a blizzard could be raging.

As now, the whole area surrounding the Calvert house had become a layer of white, so serene, it was hard to imagine that a war was being fought anywhere. But there was. And there was even talk of the Confederate regiments fighting in their bare feet and in clothes that fell apart after the first wearing. It made goosebumps ride Serena's spine thinking about this disgrace to humanity. Blood had been spilled in so many southern states and bodies had been left to freeze stiff in the colder temperatures of both December and January, bodies of those who had been no more than boys.

Trying not to envision the way blood might seep into the whiteness of this fresh snowfall, Serena bit a lower lip and shut her eyes tightly. Oh, if the war could only end this night. What a miracle it would be. But it wasn't going to end just yet, and she had her own war raging inside her—a war of a thumping heart against her chest as the moments drew closer to when she would be with Wesley. She only hoped that he had managed to stay awake. She only hoped that his wound wouldn't make it impossible for them to have a few moments together.

Serena crept to her bedroom door and opened it slowly, listening. She had to make sure that her father was settled in for the night. In no way could she take a chance that he would catch her sneaking in the middle of the night to comfort an enemy Confederate soldier he so often called "Damn Johnny Rebs" to their backs, but, so puzzling to Serena, that to their faces, he would treat most like his own long, lost sons.

No matter, though, because to Serena, Wesley was not a true enemy. He was just a casualty of war, a war that even he hadn't wanted. As Serena, he had had no choice but to do his part, as was expected of him by his neighbors whom had also been forced into battle, sometimes even fighting brother against brother when families had been split by marriage, or the earlier pursuit to better themselves by moving to another state, away from family.

"I shall not feel guilty about what I am about to do," she whispered, straightening her back and tilting her chin upward. "It is only natural to go to the man you are attracted to, no matter which side he has fought for. Wesley, oh, Wesley, you are so different from any other man I have ever known, oh, so different . . ." she murmured to herself.

Not able to delay her plans any longer, for need to see him, Serena moved to a table and lifted a kerosene lamp.

She turned the wick to its lowest point, then moved on out into the hall. She looked quickly around her, seeing only her shadow against the side walls of the hall, then crept up the steps to the third floor, where she planned to steal one of her father's better bottles of wine.

With light footsteps, she inched her way upward, barely breathing, looking back occasionally, to see that she was still unnoticed, and safe to carry this plan out to the fullest.

When she reached the third-floor landing, she lifted the lamp, casting shadows on the door as she opened it. She inched her way on into the sitting room, seeing orange flickerings from the ashes on the hearth, then moved the lamp on around so that it cast even more shadows on the glass-encased liquor cabinet.

Smiling almost wickedly, Serena tiptoed across the room, tensing when the floor creaked beneath her. She stopped and listened, knowing whose bedroom was beneath the exact spot that she was standing on. "I only hope father is busy snoring," she whispered to herself. "His snores can outdo even the loudest clap of thunder on a spring evening."

Then after assurances that she hadn't been detected, she moved onward. She turned the latch on the liquor cabinet, then opened it slowly, eyeing immediately a bottle of champagne that she would take with her. Serena could remember her father speaking of this particular type of wine as he had sat leisurely sipping it in front of a cozy fire before the war had started, when one could relax and truly enjoy such simple pleasures. He had liked its pale amber color and the way it pleasured his tongue when the effervescence would tickle it and his nose, and the way it would even leave droplets on his mustache tips, so that his tongue could still enjoy its last drops when the tall-stemmed wine glass would become empty.

Serena hadn't seen her father enjoy any champagne for years now and knew that he probably wouldn't even miss this one bottle, unless he was saving it to drink in celebration to the war's end. *But when shall that be?* she thought, tucking it beneath her arm. *By then, who even knows where I shall be?. Hopefully, not within range of his hollerings when he discovers this bottle missing from his prized collection of wines.*

With deft fingers, Serena rearranged the remaining bottles of wine inside the cabinet in an effort to fill the gap the stolen bottle had left. Then when she felt that all signs of theft had been taken away, she closed the door and tried tiptoing on a different part of the floor, hoping not to find the extension of that board that had squeaked only a few moments earlier. So far, she had succeeded in her flight to be with Wesley. Only a while longer, and she would be at his side. And with that thought, she eagerly moved to the door and opened it slowly, peeked out, then moved out and down the stairs until she found herself safely standing on the landing of the first floor.

Looking around her, she saw the traces of lamps flickering in soft goldens, and at the far end of the room, she saw the lone night attendant slumped over his desk, asleep. No uniformed nightguards were required. The locked shackles were cause enough for everyone to relax most nights. So Serena crept on into the room where Wesley lay. She tried to shield the rays of her lamp with her body, knowing that if she awakened some of the wounded her moments with Wesley might be ruined. One outcry could cause the night attendant to come searching. But Serena knew that these outcries were

71

usually ignored, unless they surfaced from the Union wounded, where they were seen to immediately.

A slight noise behind her made Serena jump with a start, but she sighed with relief when she saw that it had been only a man moving from his back to his side on the bed next to where she stood.

Swallowing hard, she moved onward, now able to make out Wesley's features as the lamp's glow settled across him. Something made her heart flutter. Then when his eyes flew open and saw her approach, she felt consumed by warmth. She hurried on and then fell to her knees, to position herself beside his bed, placing the bottle of champagne and lamp on the floor on the far side of her, where the lamp lit only the small spaces around her.

"Wesley," she murmured, lifting a finger to his hand. "I've come. Did you truly want me to?"

He turned his hand, letting hers rest in his, then moved his fingers around hers, squeezing gently. "I've been counting the moments, Serena," he whispered. "But I didn't think it was you who were serious. What if your father should—"

She lifted her other hand to seal his lips. "Shh," she murmured. "Don't worry about anything. I know what I'm doing."

To Serena's surprise, his lips opened and kissed her fingers with a warm wetness, so sweet she felt as though she might melt onto the floor in one trembling mass of flesh.

"But I wouldn't want you to get in trouble with your father," he said, smiling as his gaze moved quickly over her, stopping to rest on her heaving bosom.

She rose and quietly pulled the curtain around Wesley's bed to assure privacy, then fell to her knees

72

beside him again, now truly feeling alone with him. "I've made sure to be very careful, Wesley," she said, seeing his look of appraisal as his gaze continued to hold. She lifted the bottle of champagne before her, then watched as his eyes began to sparkle, like the champagne itself. "I've even brought you some special nourishment," she said, laughing softly.

"Well, I'll be damned," he said, leaning up a bit, but groaning as he fell back to the bed.

Serena's face drained of color. "Oh, Wesley," she murmured, setting the bottle back on the floor, freeing her hands so she could reach for him, comfort him by caressing his brow. "Maybe I shouldn't have come and disturbed you. You're in pain. I shouldn't have discouraged you from taking the laudanum. Surely you would have been more comfortable if you had."

Even though full of pain, his dark eyes showed a contentment. "You, my beautiful thing, are my medicine, don't you know that?"

Serena lowered her eyes, feeling suddenly shy, a first for her. "Truly? You mean that?"

"I've never been more serious," he said gruffly, reaching to trace her facial features with a forefinger.

Serena closed her eyes as she leaned into his touch. Her insides were trembling. His finger was like velvet, creating a sensation of soft delight with each added touch.

"Oh, if only I wasn't in such a condition as this," he said, suddenly pulling his hand away from her. "You've set me afire inside, Serena. And, damn it, there's nothing I can do about it. Why, if I should even try to kiss you, you'd probably slap my face."

Serena felt as though hypnotized by the purr of his

73

voice. Something was compelling her to be more daring than ever before in her life. Was it because he was shackled? Was it because that was making her feel safe with this man? Or was it because she wanted these touches, and even a stolen kiss from a man who had been a stranger only the day before. She now felt as though she had always known him. His dark, beguiling eyes were drawing her from herself, it seemed. She shook her hair to hang down her back, then leaned closer to him. "Do you really want to kiss me?" she asked quietly.

The heat increased in Wesley's loins and his heart was acting so wildly, he wasn't sure he would be able to stand the sweetness of her lips against his. But, yes, he had to. He needed her, as strange as it seemed, since she was the enemy, oh, so enchanting an enemy. "Would *you* want me to kiss *you?*" he asked quickly, lifting his head from the pillow, no matter if the pain in his shoulder was sending knife-like jabs to his brain.

Without further words, Serena pushed herself upward and placed her lips against his and felt a rush of desire consume her in massive waves of forbidden pleasures. "Wesley," she whispered, pulling away a bit, then when his free hand reached up and tangled his fingers through the thickness of her hair to crush her lips downward against his again, Serena felt tears surfacing, not from sadness, but from the pain of new-found love.

She spread her lips apart and let his tongue move inside her mouth, searching, probing, making her feel almost wet between the thighs where a strange throbbing had taken over, down where she had been so crudely attacked by Edward.

With her fingers, she framed his face, then continued to tingle all over as his lips moved from her lips, to her

74

nose, to her closed eyes, then to the hollow of her throat. "You are so beautiful," he said thickly. "What am I to do?"

"Just kiss me again, Wesley," she purred. "I do enjoy it so. I've never had anything stir such exquisite feelings inside me. Please pleasure me some more. Please."

With a tenderness this time, his lips sought hers out, making her head begin to spin in different colors of the rainbow. She smiled to herself, now realizing what this all had to mean. She had found the man of her dreams. Hadn't she known that such wonderful feelings existed when with the man she loved? When his lips pulled free once again, she whispered, "I love you. I know that I love you. . . ."

"Well, I'll be damned," Wesley said. "I'll be damned." Daringly, he let his free hand travel from her throat, down to her breasts, making a deep moan surface from somewhere deep inside Serena as she leaned into his touch once again. His touch was ecstasy, sweet, sweet ecstasy. And when one breast was completely from the dress, and his fingers worked with the nipple until it was erect, Serena felt as though aflame inside.

She knew that she should be feeling guilt for letting a man touch her in such a way, but she didn't. She had been waiting for this for too long now. She had known there could be such enchantment in life—and she had found it . . . in this room . . . beside this bed . . . with this man . . . her enemy. . . .

"You are ravishing," he purred further. "I only wish my lips could take the place of my fingers. . . ."

Serena's eyes flew open. Should she? She was stunned by such a suggestion, but she was excited by just the thought of what he would do. Ah, she was wicked, so utterly wicked.

"What do you want me to do?" she asked thickly, feeling full of fever and soaring above herself, as though she was another person, witnessing, not a part of it herself, because it was so unreal that she should be here . . . doing these things . . . with a man . . . a man so handsome, her heart had been fully captivated by him.

"I can't lean forward because of my shoulder," he grumbled. "Just you lean forward a mite. Just let my lips experience one taste of that ravishing piece of flesh."

Serena glanced quickly around her, but then remembered the drawn curtain and with a keen excitement of the unknown, she leaned forward and even took it upon herself to guide the nipple between his lips, sucking in her breath rapturously as his lips began to circle and wet the nipple. "Oh, Wesley," she purred, closing her eyes, wetting her lips. "What you are doing to me. This just can't be real. It just . . . can't . . . be. . . ."

His free hand moved lower, touching her through her clothes where her thighs met, making her quickly draw away from him to secure her breast back inside her dress. She suddenly felt like a wanton whore letting a man have such freedom with her body. She suddenly remembered Edward and his touches and how repelled she had been afterwards. She smiled weakly and moved to the floor, lifting the bottle of champagne. "I don't have any glasses," she said. "I couldn't carry the bottle, lamp, and also glasses. I surely would have dropped one or the other and would have awakened the whole household if I had done so."

"We can share the bottle," he said, settling his head back against the pillow.

Serena glanced toward him, seeing the flush of his

face. It seemed to match her own. She felt as though on fire, both inside and out. She quickly looked away from him, feeling the giddiness beginning inside her once again under his steady, warm gaze.

"Don't feel bad about tonight," he said, as though he had read her mind. "I do feel we have something special between us. I know you wouldn't have let anyone else do such a thing. When I am free, I will show you my sincerity of my caring for you."

"How?" she asked, eyes wide.

"Maybe you could travel to South Carolina with me," he said. "See what my Folly Island is truly like. It is quite breathtaking, you know. It's a paradise. It is made for someone just like yourself."

Serena took a quick intake of breath. "You'd really—?"

"Would you go with me?"

"We've just met. You know absolutely nothing about me. . . ."

"I know enough," he said, reaching for her hand. "I know that you stir my insides like no other woman has ever done before. I know that no matter if you are from the North and I'm from the South, we were destined to be together."

"It's all unbelievable. . . ."

"Give me a drink of that champagne, and let me taste the reality of that," he laughed.

"Can you? You can hardly move to a sitting position. . . ."

"I will manage, my dear," he chuckled, moving a bit upward, resting on his elbow. "A little bit of help from you is all that is required."

She placed her hand behind his head to support it, then

helped to lift the bottle to his lips to drink from it. "Delicious," he said. "Just like the taste of you, only you are much sweeter, darling."

Ripples of sensuous pleasure surged through Serena. "Then shall I take a sip?" she asked, giggling softly.

"Dare you?" he asked, laughing throatily. "You sound as though you have already sipped from the bubbly liquid."

"Only because I am with you, Wesley," she said softly.

He laughed a bit hoarsely, then grew serious. "I am finding this all a bit hard to believe," he said.

She took a sip from the bottle, feeling its warmth enter her stomach, then leaned closer to him, smiling coyly. "And what do you mean?" she whispered.

"I would never have thought I would enjoy being in a Bluebelly's prison hospital," he said, reaching for her hand.

She giggled, taking another small swallow, then helped him to another drink. "I've hated these hospital quarters from the very beginning," she said. "My father has a way of forcing his ideas on others. I always seem to be there, the one the closest at hand to reciprocate. When the wounded were brought here, it was my duty as the daughter of the town's physician to assist." She lowered her eyes. "Oh, how I have hated it."

"Thank God you did help him," Wesley said, squeezing her hand gently.

Her eyes flew upward. "I know," she purred. "If I hadn't, I wouldn't have ever met you."

"Am I the first . . . ?"

Serena's heartbeat faltered. Did he think she did this with most men? Surely not. . . . "You don't truly believe that I make this a habit," she said flatly. "Wesley, tell me you don't."

"How is it that I'm the lucky one?" he asked, smiling weakly.

"My dear, you are the one who has made my heart leave me," Serena said, moving to kiss him softly on the lips. She withdrew when she felt him shudder a bit. "Wesley, why did you just tremble? Are you cold?"

His body convulsed once again. "I guess I am," he said thickly. "I seem to have the chills. And so suddenly."

Serena set the bottle down, then pulled a blanket up, tucking it around his body. "There. It's probably the wind making its way through the window," she said. "It seems we have a small blizzard outside."

"Snow? The men who are still fighting on the fields . . ." he groaned, convulsing once again. "There's nothing as cold as an open field in the middle of the night. And then to have to fight snow as well as the damn Yankees? It's hell. Pure hell."

Serena lifted a hand to his brow, tensing. Before, he had felt feverish, but she had thought it to be because of his reaction to their kisses and touches. But his fever was more than that. He was ill. He was possibly chilling because of infection. "Wesley, maybe I'd best get Father," she said beginning to rise. "I do believe you have a temperature."

He stopped her by a strong hold on the wrist. "No. I'm all right," he murmured. "Please don't leave me. Let's talk a bit more. I hate having to lay here all alone. If I do have a temperature, it will be gone by morning. I've never been known to be one down for long. We Wyndhams are a hardy lot. Temperatures are usually a passing thing with me. Stay. Please stay a while longer."

"Are you sure?"

"Yes. Positive," he said. He placed his right arm over his brow, breathing hard. "Now. Tell me a little about yourself. What are your ambitions in life? Things like that."

Serena's face reddened. Her main ambition in life was to be set free from the bonds of her father. But she couldn't tell Wesley that, for she hadn't figured out how yet. When Wesley had mentioned her traveling to South Carolina with him, that had been the first time that she had actually felt hope rising inside her. Had he been serious? If so, she would most assuredly go.

But it would be a dream . . . one that surely would never come true. She knew that she was probably fated to marry such a man as Edward, as tasteless as that was to even think about. "My ambitions?" she finally said. "To be happy." She saw his eyebrows tilt upward. Had he expected more?

"Happy? What would make you happy, Serena?"

"Many things," she murmured. "But now? I would say that you would be first on that list."

"Then I can say the same, that you would make me the happiest of anything else I can think of at this moment," he said thickly, taking her hand once again.

"My mother—I don't think she was ever truly happy with my father," she said sullenly.

"And where is your mother now?"

"Dead," she murmured. "At the age of forty-two. Only a few months ago."

"I'm sorry," he said. "How? How did she die? Your father being a physician . . ."

"He couldn't help her," she answered. "You see, my mother was frail, very small-boned. She took sick quite often. This one time she came down with pneumonia and she didn't make it."

"That's terrible."

"It's all because of this darn war," Serena hissed, doubling her one free hand into a tight fist.

"Why would you say that?"

"She worked in the hospital each day and night until she would almost drop."

"Oh, I see," he said.

"Tell me about your family," Serena said, needing to change the subject. She still missed her mother. Terribly. She missed her soft voice, her soothing words that would always come after Serena would have been yelled at by her father. Yes, she would always miss her mother. But she would never be like her. She would be strong, hold up against all odds.

"My family? Well, right now, I'm not sure about any of their fates," he said quietly.

"Why?"

"The war also. You see, Folly Island is only a short distance from Fort Sumter. As far as I know, my father *and* his house might be gone. I had hoped for better, but one never knows."

"When you were last there, had regiments from the North actually arrived at your island?"

"No. But we were so close to the actual fighting, we could watch the bombardment of Fort Sumter from our bedroom windows. I'm sure by the time I even reached Charleston to enlist the damn Yankees had taken over our island."

"Didn't you hate to leave your family?"

"My father had always taken care of everything. He was a strong man."

"How many are there in your family?"

"My father, Carvell Chatwin Wyndham, my mother Lona Gale, my sister Dorlisa May and my younger brother Truman Firman."

"You speak so affectionately of each. I'm sure you had a pleasant relationship with them."

Wesley laughed. "No. I wouldn't say that," he said. "My brother and I? Well, we never hit it off. I've always thought him to be a sissy. Why, he wouldn't even fight for the South. He hung onto my mother's apron, like a slobbering baby."

"How old is he?"

"He's now twenty. Old enough to fight, that's for sure."

"You speak of your sister Dorlisa May. Is she pretty?"

Wesley's face darkened with shadows. "My sister? Well, how can I put it. My sister, well, she isn't . . . well, she's different," he finally managed to say.

"What do you mean, Wesley?"

"Stays to her room, day and night. Everyone talks about her being a bit odd. I guess one could call it that. But mother takes care, uh, well, she takes care of Dorlisa May, so that no one has a chance to poke fun at her."

Wesley trembled violently. He closed his eyes as his teeth chattered. His fever appeared to have worsened.

Serena rose, desperation seizing her. But when his hand urged her downward once again, she settled next to him, listening to his low ramblings that had just begun. "Ah, my island," he said, as though in a drunken stupor. "It's a paradise. My ancestors first planted indigo there, then cotton. Ah, such a paradise. It takes your breath away."

He continued to mumble beneath his breath while his

eyes stayed closed, then Serena remembered the cure her father used for raging temperatures. He would always laugh and call his cure the 'whiskey treatment.' Not only did he use the harsh liquid on open wounds, but also on bodies, to help lower temperatures.

"It's the alcohol," he had chuckled. "Has a way of reducin' fevers in a body."

Serena eyed the bottle of partially emptied champagne. If whiskey could, then why not champagne? She lifted her dress and tore part of her petticoat off, then saturated it with the champagne and began smoothing it across Wesley's brow, dying a slow death inside as he began talking out of his head, making no sense whatsoever.

How can it come on a person so fast? she thought to herself. *Only moments ago, we were embracing, and now? Oh, Wesley. Was I the cause? Did I get you too excited? Or is the wound not healing properly?*

Feeling the trembling of his skin beneath her touch, Serena knew that more than his brow needed bathing by the alcoholic beverage. Dare she? It had been easy to do to men she felt nothing about, but to touch Wesley elsewhere on his body? She just wasn't sure. But when his teeth began to chatter more wildly, she knew the answer.

Hurriedly, she pulled the blanket down, revealing his bare chest to her. Her fingers began to tremble as she smoothed the champagne through his thick chest hairs, then around each of his nipples. She so wanted to kiss each of them as he had done to her breast, but she had to remember what was important. She had to continue caressing him only with the champagne-soaked cloth. Nothing more.

Then when her gaze lowered, she wondered if she

should remove the blanket and even caress his legs and torso with the liquid, but just couldn't. It would surely be invading his privacy. So she just continued to smooth the liquid across his upper body until she saw that he was in a deep, easy sleep.

She reached her hand upward and touched his brow. "You *are* cooler, Wesley," she said in a low whisper. "I have succeeded. I have." She placed the bottle of champagne on the floor, then lifted the blanket up to rest snugly beneath his chin, then kissed him lightly on the lips.

She pushed herself up from the floor and studied him with deep affection for a moment longer, then reached for the half-emptied bottle and kerosene lamp and began to inch away from him. She stopped as she sucked in her breath wildly, remembering the cloth she had left lying suspiciously beside his bed. She rushed back to the bed, stooped, lifted it, then hurried across the room, stopping to check on each side of her before moving out into the foyer, where she hoped the night attendant would still be asleep. When her gaze moved to the desk and she saw that the chair was empty behind it, her heart faltered. Where was he?

She gasped noisily when a hand reached out and grabbed her by the wrist. She turned and saw the gleaming eyes of Terence, the elderly night attendant, whose eyes were raking over her, resembling dark coals as they rested on her heaving bosom.

"Quite a show you were puttin' on in there, Miss Calvert," he drawled. The wrinkles of his face met in wavy lines from one side of his face to the other, his nose was long and sharp, his lips thin and wet.

Serena tried to struggle free, but her arms were too full

84

to give her the freedom she needed to succeed. "Let me go, Terence," she hissed. "What do you think you're doing anyway? You've never acted so crazily before. Let me go."

He sneered knowingly. "I seen with mine own eyes," he laughed hoarsely.

"You . . . saw . . . what . . . ?" she gasped, knowing there was much to see if one had crept to the edge of the curtain that circled Wesley's bed and had peeked around a corner. *Oh, no. Not this man. Please, God.*

His grip tightened. "I seen you kissin' that enemy fellow," he said, laughing still. "I even seen his hands wander to places my eyes have only been allowed to. Miss Calvert, shame be upon you. Shame be upon you."

"Listen here, Terence," she snapped. "If you don't let me go, I am going to scream. Do you hear me?"

His laugh deepened. "Scream then. Then wouldn't you have a fun time explainin' what you're a doin' here with this bottle of champagne in the middle of the night dressed so's a man can get a hold of such beauties as is hangin' out the front. Yeah. Go ahead and scream."

Serena's eyes narrowed into slits. She eyed the champagne bottle, then Terence. "This is the best bottle of champagne my father has ever owned," she purred enticingly. "Want to share the rest of it with me, Terence? It could set your heart to racing."

Terence licked his lips hungrily, looking from the bottle to Serena's heaving bosom. "You'd share it with me? Huh?" he asked, tilting a brow quizzically.

"Yes. Only if you agree to not tell my father about any of this," she said softly, blinking her lashes nervously.

"Sounds rightful good to me," Terence snickered, releasing his hold on her.

"Shall we move to . . . uh . . . a quiet corner where we can be alone?" Serena said, teasing with her eyes.

"Follow me," Terence said, laughing throatily.

Serena was now smiling wickedly, knowing what her next move was to be. She followed along behind him, and when Terence had guided her into a linen closet and had closed the door behind them, she set the kerosene lamp on a shelf, then slowly pulled the cork from the champagne bottle, watching him as he licked his lips hungrily. She cringed when he reached and touched the softness of a breast. Then after releasing the cork from the bottle, she raised the bottle above Terence's head and quickly poured the remaining champagne over him, laughing softly as his expression turned to shock. "You wanted the champagne? Well you got it," she said, even making sure the last drop fell on him, wanting to be sure that his clothes were completely saturated.

"Miss Calvert, why—?"

"Now that you stink of my father's finest champagne, he will accuse you of stealing it," she said firmly, lifting her lamp again, moving toward the door.

"I'll tell him it was you who done this," he shouted.

She swung around, stiff-backed. "And I shall call you a liar," she hissed.

"Not only will *I* stench of champagne come mornin'," he laughed. "What 'bout that Johnny Reb in there? I saw how you wuz bathin' him in this liquid."

"You don't know much about alcohol, do you?" she snapped. "By morning, it will be evaporated from his skin. But you? Your clothes will stink of it. No way can it evaporate from them. Good night, Terence."

She left the linen closet, laughing beneath her breath. She only hoped that she was right. That all telltale signs of her being with Wesley would be vanished into the air by morning. If not, how could she explain it away to her father? And Terence? Would he be fool enough to tell her father about all that he had witnessed? Knowing her father, he would kill the man for even breathing such insanities about his beloved daughter. . . .

Chapter Five

"Serena?"

Serena awakened with a start. She turned on her side and looked toward her bedroom door, seeing Priscilla standing with it partially open, clinging to it. "Priscilla?" she murmured, wiping her eyes, still feeling so drowsy from her night of excitement. Then she bolted upright, suddenly remembering Wesley, how ill he was, and also, Terence, and how she had left him.

"May I come in for a minute, Serena?" Priscilla asked, still clinging.

"What do you want so early in the morning?" Serena asked, rising from the bed, searching around her for a robe. When her gaze settled on her green velveteen wrap, she pulled it around her shoulders, then slipped her feet into some soft slippers.

"May I? May I come in?"

Sighing absently, Serena answered. "Yes. Yes. Come on in."

Priscilla lumbered on into the room, closing the door quietly behind her. She was already dressed in an attractive cotton dress with puffed sleeves, with a faint trace of lace at her throat. Her face shone as though it had been scrubbed and scrubbed, looking now as though porcelain. "I must speak with you of Edward," Priscilla said, eyes heavy while wringing her hands before her.

"Edward?" Serena said, raising an eyebrow. Then she remembered. "Ah, yes, Edward." She went to her dressing table and lifted a brush to her hair. She gritted her teeth and closed her eyes, again hating her natural curls. Each night they twisted and tangled, becoming many "witch's knots" as her mother had called them. "What about Edward?" she asked cautiously, curious as to how the evening had developed once Serena had left her sister and Edward alone.

"Serena, he stomped from the room last night, without even one sip of wine," Priscilla said glumly. "He never even said one word to me after you left the room. Oh, I am so embarrassed. Why would this man do such an unthinkable thing?"

Serena felt a trace of fear creeping up her spine. If Edward didn't become attracted to Priscilla, then he would persist at pursuing Priscilla's sister. Serena couldn't let this happen. She had had enough of Edward. Wesley was the only one she would ever desire. She went to Priscilla and wrapped her arms around her, thinking to become the mother this morning that Priscilla no longer had. "Honey, I've told you over and over again what men like," she said softly. "Now will you believe me? If Edward had such a reaction, surely you can see what you must do."

"Am I so unpleasant to look at and be around? Honestly?"

"I've told you. You could be beautiful if you even half tried."

"Will you help me?"

This had been in Serena's plan. She was glad that Priscilla was making it easy for her by taking the initiative. "Do you truly want me to?" she asked, eyeing Priscilla closely, wondering where to start. The dress was perfect. Now . . . the . . . hair? Yes. That would be a good beginning.

"Yes. Please, Serena. I know you can. You always look so pretty."

"Okay," Serena said flatly. "First your hair. We must lift its ends into curls. We mustn't let it lay in flat strings of brown any longer. First, you go and get our curling iron hot over the fire, then we shall proceed."

Priscilla swung around, all smiles. "I'm so glad, Serena," she sighed. "I'll only be a minute."

Priscilla opened the door and hurried away; Serena tensed when she could hear loud shouts from her father. Afraid, but curious, she went to the door and peered outward as he raced up the steps toward her. *Oh, no*, she thought. *He has found out. He knows. . . .*

"That damned Terence," Hiram shouted.

"What about Terence?" she asked shakily.

"He stole my best bottle of champagne, drank what he didn't spill in the linen closet, then fled into the darkness of the night."

"Terence?"

"Damn man," Hiram grumbled, toying with his mustache. "Can't depend on help these days. And how'd he get the nerve to go steal from my liquor cabinet?"

Serena's insides eased, knowing that she had done the right thing by pouring the champagne on Terence. It had become the perfect cover for her own crime. "Terence actually stole from you, Father?" she said smoothly. "Tsk. Tsk. How terrible. And your best bottle of

90

champagne? I'm sure you'd like to hang the man for such a terrible deed."

"Just might do that," he grumbled further. "The men could've died for sure being left unattended like that."

Serena started toward the staircase, wishing she could flee to Wesley, to see if he was indeed all right. She did feel a bit guilty when thinking of all the wounded being left unattended. But it was not her fault. How could she have known that Terence would run scared? Then her eyes searched her father's face as she said, "You have checked on the wounded then, Father?" she asked softly. "They . . . are all right? All of them?"

"I made my usual early mornin' check, and yes, appears all is in good enough shape," he remarked, moving toward the stairs that would lead him to a cup of coffee and breakfast. "As well as can be, under the circumstances of the type of wounds we're strugglin' with."

Serena sighed with relief. If Wesley had worsened through the night, her father would have noticed and would have mentioned it. For some reason, her father had shown more of a liking for this particular prisoner than any others in his years of doctoring. But Serena could understand. Hadn't she even singled Wesley out? Wouldn't anyone?

"Comin' up for breakfast, Serena?" Hiram tossed over his shoulder.

"In a little while, Father," she said, moving toward her door. "I've got to dress and . . . Priscilla and I, well, we've something to attend to also."

"Don't dally too long," he said further. "We've much to attend to downstairs. You know I depend on you. Be ready for the usual."

91

Serena's shoulders sagged. "Yes, Father. I know," she said. She was anxious to see Wesley, attend to him, but no one else. She hated the thought of another long day ahead of her that included only drudgeries. The thoughts of the last night, before Wesley had grown so ill, made her insides go soft. The same tingling that she had felt when he had touched her seemed to ripple along her flesh when she could remember his lips against hers, and the way his hands had created such euphoria. . . .

"I've got the curling iron hot, Serena," Priscilla said, rushing down the steps toward Serena, disturbing her pleasant train of thoughts. "Let's hurry before it cools too much," Priscilla added, hurrying into the bedroom.

"Go and sit in front of the mirror, Priscilla," Serena said, following along behind her sister, closing the bedroom door behind them to assure privacy.

Lifting Priscilla's hair upward, she began wrapping one lock, then another and another around the curling iron tongs until Priscilla's hair hung in long, deep coils. "Oh, Serena," Priscilla sighed. "It's just like when mother fooled with my hair all those years ago." She shook her head, watching the coils of curls bounce back and forth.

"I'm not finished, Priscilla," Serena said, lifting the brush. "You don't want long curls like a young girl. You want your hair to hang in waves across your shoulders. It will make you look more a woman than a child." She brushed through the curls, loosening them, working with her other hand pushing, arranging, until Priscilla's hair now settled in soft browns around her face and shoulders, making her look almost lovely.

"Now pinch your cheeks and bite your lips for color," Serena said, standing back, watching.

"Why, you have worked a bit of magic on me,"

Priscilla laughed, standing, swirling as she held the skirt of her dress up.

"Yes. The metamorphosis is a success," Serena said proudly, going to her wardrobe to choose a cotton frock with a low-cut bodice, even though she would be working with the wounded. The apron would keep her covered, except for the moments spent with Wesley. She liked to see his eyes light up when near him. But she wondered if she should play more the role of a lady. Hadn't he spoken of his plantation? She had to be sure he didn't forget. She had to be sure that she looked the part of someone whom would be taken to a plantation to be presented to family.

If the family even still exists after this dreadful war, she thought to herself, pulling the dress over her head.

"I'll go and tell Cora and Father you will be up soon," Priscilla said, almost dancing toward the door.

"Yes. Please do," Serena said, now brushing her hair.

"And, Serena?" Priscilla said, stopping, lowering her eyes.

Serena turned, wide-eyed. "Yes?" she murmured.

"Thanks a lot."

Serena's smile was her response, yet feeling something grabbing at her heart, realizing that she was only taking such pains with Priscilla's appearance because of her own selfish reasons. But Priscilla wasn't aware of this. It was nice for Serena to feel the change that was arising between herself and Priscilla, even though it was for all the wrong reasons. She watched Priscilla move from the room, all smiles.

"Mother would have loved seeing us plotting together," Serena whispered. "Mother would have loved seeing us share moments of laughter. . . ."

She brushed thoughts of her sister aside and leaned

into the mirror, checking her face, seeing something similar to a glow this morning, and knowing why. . . .

If she could only rush to Wesley now, tell him how much she loved him, but she didn't wish to raise any eyebrows. Not today. She had taken such a chance the previous evening. "And almost got caught," she said aloud, sighing heavily.

But she had to laugh when she thought of Terence and what he had had on his mind when he had discovered her game with Wesley. "Too bad, Terence, ol' boy," she said, moving toward the door. She knew that if Terence hadn't left as he had, he would more than likely have tried the same with her once again. She didn't need any added attention drawn to herself now. She needed privacy in order to be able to be with Wesley again. "And over and over again," she purred, stepping out into the hallway. Looking down the stairs, she saw more activity than usual at the front door. She hesitated before moving up the stairs, thinking to rush down and see what was going on, but she shrugged and went on up to the sitting room where she found the usual: Cora had already fled from the room to handle all the other chores; Serena's father was reading the morning paper at the breakfast table; and Priscilla was already positioned at the table, sipping her coffee.

Serena sat down at the table. She poured herself a cup of coffee, then tensed when a loud knock on the sitting-room door drew not only Serena's attention, but also her father's and Priscilla's.

"Come on in," Hiram boomed, lowering his newspaper. He stared a bit harshly when no one entered. "Damn it," he quickly added. "Come in."

A man in full blue uniform stepped into the room,

straightbacked and gloomy faced. "Mr. Calvert, sir," he said, breathless. "There's been an accident. I think you'd best come downstairs."

"What sort of an accident, lad?" Hiram said, pushing himself up from the chair, hurrying across the room.

"A train wreck, sir," the man said, stepping aside so Hiram could move on out into the hallway.

Priscilla and Serena exchanged quick glances, then both rose and rushed toward the door and followed along behind Hiram and the uniformed man, listening.

"Where was this train wreck?" Hiram boomed, grunting as he took the steps more quickly than usual.

"Just a few miles out of Mattoon. Seems some southern sympathizers sabotaged the Illinois Central," the man said, keeping step with Hiram.

"Damn it, you say," Hiram boomed.

Serena grabbed Priscilla by the hand. "Priscilla, that's the train . . . that . . ." she began.

Priscilla's free hand went to her mouth as her color turned gray. "Edward," she blurted. "Oh, Serena, Edward is that train's engineer . . ."

"I know . . ." Serena said, then rushed on down the stairs, looking anxiously around her, then stopped short when she caught sight of Edward stretched out atop a bed just inside what once was the Calvert living room. "Edward," she gasped quietly. His eyes were closed and he had a blood-soaked bandage wrapped around his head.

Priscilla moved to Serena's side, clinging to her arm. "Oh, no," she moaned. "It *is* Edward." She went to him and fell to her knees, touching him so gently on the cheek. "Edward, say something. Please . . . say . . . something."

"Here. Here," Hiram boomed, pulling Priscilla away

95

from Edward. "We can't have that. I've got to have room. Priscilla, now's a hell of a time to make your presence known in this hospital. Get the hell out of the way."

Priscilla began sobbing as she inched her way toward the wall, where she stood, her hands covering her mouth as she watched Hiram work with the wound.

"What must I do?" Serena said flatly, moving to her father's side.

"See to it that a bed is readied upstairs," Hiram answered, looking up at her with deeper worry wrinkles circling his eyes and mouth.

"Upstairs?" Serena gasped, putting her hands to her throat. Though Edward was injured, possibly seriously, Serena didn't wish to treat him differently. To her, he was no better than the enemy. In a sense, he was her enemy, more than Wesley ever could be.

"He'll need to be watched around the clock," Hiram said, working with the bandage once again, then checking the wound. "He must have complete privacy. This man has a terrible head wound. Seems someone hit him with the butt of a gun."

"Oh," Priscilla shrieked even more loudly.

"Damn it," Hiram boomed. "Get your sister out of here, Serena," he ordered. "Better yet. Let her be the one to go upstairs and see that a bed is readied. Give Edward the spare bedroom at the far end of the hall. The one your mother used . . . for sewing. Then we shall see to it that our old friend here gets the best treatment that this hospital has to offer."

Serena's heart pumped wildly. "Mother's room?" she gasped. "You'd use her room . . . ?"

"No arguments, Serena. Just do as you're told," Hiram

said in a low rumble.

Serena didn't approve but knew to argue would be to anger her father to no avail. His mind was made up. He was like a mule that wouldn't budge when his darn stubborn side showed. So Serena went to Priscilla and framed her sister's face with her hands. "Did you hear what Father said, Priscilla?" she asked softly. "Can you do these things?" Then she quickly added, "You will be doing this for Edward."

Priscilla sobbed once again, then wiped her eyes. "I'll hurry," she said. "I'll make sure the bed in that room is readied in the bat of an eye."

"Then get on with it," Hiram ordered loudly. "No time to waste here. I want to get him settled, and at once."

"Yes, Father," Priscilla said, rushing off, leaving a trail of sobs behind her.

"And, Serena, do you think you can find someone to sit with Edward?" Hiram said, rising, wringing his hands nervously.

"What?" she said weakly. Her father hadn't ordered any vigils at any bedside thus far during this whole span of war. But now? Oh, if only she could tell her father about this man. Then Edward wouldn't get any special treatment.

"Serena, you seem to have become suddenly deaf," Hiram said, pacing nervously. "Now do you or don't you have anyone in mind for sitting at Edward's bedside?"

Serena sighed and said, "Priscilla? Can she?"

He laughed raucously. "That girl? Didn't you see how shaken she was? She couldn't hold up next to a sick bed. And you know how she hates blood . . . and everything associated with it."

Serena leaned into Hiram's face and spoke softly.

97

"But don't you see, Father?" she said. "To Priscilla, this patient is different than all the others. This is Edward. Priscilla has a fancy for him."

"Why not you, Serena?" he said gruffly. "Why can't you be the one to help if you know of no one else?"

Serena's insides tightened. "But, Father," she said innocently enough. "You need me here. To help with the *many* wounded. I can serve better here. Don't you believe so?"

Hiram twirled his mustache between his fingers. "Hmmm," he said, tilting an eyebrow. "Yes. I'm sure you're right. Okay. Priscilla can do it. We'll give her a try. If she whines just once about it, though, you'll have to take her place."

"Yes, sir," Serena said, breathing more easily now. She had faith in Priscilla. Priscilla's deep feelings for Edward were sincere. She didn't doubt that. Not for one minute.

Her eyes moved toward the door that led where Wesley lay. She had to wonder if his fever had dissipated. She ached to go to him. But she couldn't. Not just yet.

Her gaze settled back on Edward. He looked so lifeless. His breath was coming in shallow rasps. His face was as pale as the fresh-fallen snow and his arms lay limply at his side. She couldn't help but wonder about his well-being, even though he had seduced her . . . taken her virginity from her. . . .

Hiram quickly wrapped a new bandage around Edward's head, then stood with hands behind his back. "There. That should hold him for a while. Then once we get him moved, we can change his clothes to something looser and we shall start our whiskey treatments. Do you understand, Serena?"

"Yes, Father."

"But for now, maybe we'd best move on through the rooms to get a fast check on the men. Breakfast will have to be forgotten this mornin', it seems."

Serena followed along beside Hiram as he went from room to room, bed to bed. Then when he entered the room where Wesley lay, Serena glanced quickly back at him, smiling when she saw that he had managed to sit a bit upright. His face was still a bit flushed, but his eyes weren't glazed as most when feverish. He *was* better. And when he smiled back at her, she felt her heart melting.

"Harumph," Hiram said, moving on to Wesley's bed. "You look a bit more spiffy this mornin', lad," he added, touching Wesley's brow. "Hmm. A touch feverish though." He punched around the wounded area, then faced Serena. "This one also needs a whiskey rub," he said, moving away. He stopped to sniff, lifting an eyebrow. "Seems that champagne odor even drifted into this room." He turned to walk away, grumbling about Terence and what he had done.

Serena looked sheepishly toward Wesley. "Looks like I have to take care of you again this morning," she said. "Another treatment. Can you stand it?"

"Another?" he said, moving up a bit more, resting on his free elbow.

Serena moved to her knees beside him, leaning closer to him, glancing at her father who had just taken his last step from the room. "Last night? Don't you remember . . . ?" she murmured.

Wesley held a twinkle in his eyes, but he said, "No. Don't remember a thing," he said. Then he reached for her hand. "Honey, how could I forget?" he added, smiling warmly.

"Then you do remember the special rub?"

99

"Special . . . ?"

"Then you *didn't* know what I was doing?"

"No. Guess not. What did your pretty mind lead you to do?"

She laughed softly. "Instead of the usual whiskey rub given for fever, I rubbed you down with champagne."

He raised his eyebrows quizzically. "You used the champagne?"

She laughed again. "I knew that if the alcohol in whiskey could help lower a temperature, the alcohol in the champagne should do the same. . . ."

Wesley's sudden fit of laughter caused Serena's eyes to widen with wonder. "Wesley, what—?"

Wesley continued to muffle his laughter with the back of his hand, then said, "Darling, don't you know the alcohol content in champagne?"

"No, I never thought much about it."

Wesley's eyes showed a keen amusement. "There's not enough to even compare with what's found in whiskey," he said, watching her growing perplexity.

"Meaning . . . ?"

"If you believe your champagne lowered my fever, you're mistaken," he laughed further.

Serena's face reddened. "Then, why *did* your fever lower after I rubbed you down with it?"

"It's as I remember telling you. A fever just doesn't last long with me. It's the Wyndham in me."

"But so quickly . . . ?"

"Until I was shot, I was a specimen of strength and good health. This alone makes for resistance build up and quick recovery."

"And you are okay, today?" she asked, moving her hand to his brow. "Are you truly feeling better? Last night you said you were, then before I knew what was happening, you were delirious with fever."

"I don't want to admit to feeling so much better to your father," he said, moving back down onto the bed.

"Why not, Wesley?"

"Do you think I want to be moved to the jail where I won't be able to be with you any longer?"

Serena's face paled. "Don't even think of it," she said.

"Then I must act sick for a bit longer, right?" he laughed.

"Well, I don't think you'd have to do much acting right now," she said firmly, realizing that he did have quite a bit of fever still.

"Yeah. I know," he said thickly, licking his parched lips. He looked sideways at her, smiling once again. "Tell you what. I could sure use some of that champagne or something stronger again this morning. Thirsty as hell. I guess from the fever."

"I'll take care of that pronto," she said, rising, going from the room. She glanced quickly around her, seeing that Edward had been moved to the upstairs room, and that her father was also out of sight. She reached inside a medicine cabinet and pulled an unopened bottle of whiskey from inside it, then gathered some fresh linens in her hands and hurried back to Wesley's bedside.

"Here. I've come to give you a whiskey rub, but I've brought fresh whiskey, so you could take a swig or two."

"Swig? My, my. How you do talk, my lady," he chuckled, accepting the bottle. He looked around, hoping not to be noticed, glad to find that most were turned from him, either asleep, or watching the activity in the hallway. He took a quick drink, then handed it back to Serena.

"There. Does it feel good, having it burning your insides so?" she teased, pouring some onto a cloth, then taking long, smooth strokes across his brow.

"Does burn a bit," he said, chuckling. "But tastes mighty good. Haven't had even a decent cup of coffee since coming to this north country."

"Oh? Do the southerners make coffee even better than us?" she said, setting her jaw firmly. "Why, I would have thought tea would have been the more appropriate drink for ones who live in mansions on plantations."

Wesley laughed, covering her hand with his. "One day I will show you just exactly the way we *do* live on Folly Island."

Her eyes widened, feeling the hammering of her heart against her chest. Once again . . . he had mentioned taking her to Folly Island. Oh, if only he would be serious. "What I'd like to know, Wesley, is when will you be well enough to have another nightly visitor, namely myself?" she whispered, still caressing.

"Tonight," he said thickly. "Can you truly arrange to come again tonight?"

"I will try," she said, glancing sideways. "But no champagne this time," she giggled. "I got into a bit of trouble over that champagne."

"Oh?" he said, raising an eyebrow. "Did your father discover it gone?"

"No, not exactly," she giggled. "I'll tell you about what did happen tonight, when it is just the two of us."

Her mind was whirling with other plans. If he was so well now, he might even be better by eleven o'clock. Maybe he needed exercising. Maybe he needed to take a trip to an upstairs room . . . her room . . . where they could indeed have privacy . . . and talk. . . .

"I've just thought of the craziest thing," she blurted, stroking his chest now.

"What? You look a bit wicked in the eyes, darling," he said thickly.

"I will tell you. Tonight," she said. "I think you will agree that it will be a lot of fun."

She was already puzzling over how she would secure the key without her father's knowledge. To get Wesley to her room, she would have to remove his shackles, and to remove them, she would have to steal just one other item from her father. . . . The key. . . .

Chapter Six

"Priscilla, do you think you'll truly be able to sit here all night with Edward?" Serena asked, with growing admiration for her sister. She would have never thought her sister capable of such fortitude. Priscilla had sat beside Edward, watching him for any signs of movement in his lips or eyes, since that morning.

Serena looked around her, seeing the rattan sewing basket that still sat as a memorial to Julita Kate beside a thickly upholstered chair that had been her favorite while mending. Serena closed her eyes and quickly looked away, feeling a deep inner sadness, so missing her mother.

"I'll be all right, Serena," Priscilla answered, pulling a knitted shawl more snugly around her shoulders and slouching down into the chair that was to be her bed for the night.

Serena leaned down, touching Priscilla softly on a cheek. "Is there anything I can get you? Aren't you hungry?" she asked softly, remembering how little Priscilla had eaten that day.

"I'm famished," Priscilla drawled, licking her lips. "But when beside a sick bed, I cannot hold food inside my stomach too well. You know that. I'll eat later. . . ."

"Okay, then," Serena said, stretching, yawning, feigning a sleepiness she did not in truth feel. She knew what the next hour would hold for her. She was going to Wesley. She was going to invite him to her room. Oh, if she got caught . . . !

She strolled over to Edward's bedside and touched his brow. He wasn't feverish, but he hadn't regained consciousness either. His breathing was coming in slow, even rumbles, though, which was encouraging.

She studied him a bit. Now that he was wounded, she could see the child in him that even men were capable of showing when lying helpless. She had thought over what he had done to her. She had come to the conclusion that most men needed women in many ways. He wasn't to blame for what nature had instilled in his mind. She could vividly remember Wesley and how his hunger for her had shown in his eyes, the same as it had in Edward's. The difference was that Serena loved Wesley, not Edward. She now knew that to be with the man you loved meant to surrender your all . . . even your body. . . .

"He will be all right, won't he?" Priscilla asked, disturbing Serena's train of thought. "Edward will be himself soon, won't he?"

"Yes. I'm sure he will be all right," Serena murmured. "Just give him time. He did get a nasty blow on his head."

"I don't understand these people who caused the train wreck, southern sympathizers as Father called them," Priscilla hissed. "How could anyone sympathize with the enemy? If I was a man, I would go and fight and shoot as many of those Johnny Rebs as I could find. I sometimes even think I should take a gun and finish off those who are downstairs taking up our beds and eat-

105

ing our food. . . ."

Serena felt a swirling in her head as she turned on a heel to stare in astonishment toward her sister who was saying such terrible things. How could she? It wasn't at all like her. "Priscilla!" she said firmly. "You hush with such talk. I can understand your feelings for Edward at this moment, your worries, but you must not talk of such things as shooting men. Why, you are usually so gentle. Why would such things come to your mind? Don't you know the southern men are the same as northern men? They have the same blood, the same feelings. The only difference is that one has been branded Johnny Rebs and the other Damn Yankees. Don't you see? Neither can help what has happened. They pick up guns and fight, because they have no other choice."

Priscilla's eyebrows tilted, and her face paled. "Serena, listen to you," she murmured. "You sound as though you don't believe in what Lincoln stands for. If Father would hear you say such things, he would disown you for sure. How could you? Lincoln means salvation to the white people as well as the Negroes. Slavery is sinful. Just sinful. This is why the war. Surely you understand this? Those people of the South are all sinners. And they should be shot if they don't obey the law. Our President Lincoln's law."

"Priscilla, I must go. I think I'm in more need of rest than I had thought earlier," Serena said, feeling numb inside. She hadn't meant to spout off at the mouth so much. When talking of the war, she had always watched her words so carefully. She understood quite well that her beliefs clashed with all those around her, but she hadn't revealed it yet.

She rushed from the room in a nervous sweat, then on

to her room, readying it for Wesley's arrival. She had stolen two white candles from the kitchen cupboard and had placed them in candleholders on the one nightstand in her room. She had also chosen a vintage bottle of wine that had already been opened, knowing that a few more glasses poured from it wouldn't be noticed. Two thin-stemmed wine glasses sat sparkling beneath the shimmerings of the candles, waiting to be filled, to be shared with the man she loved.

But now, she had to do the dreaded. She had to secure the key which would unlock Wesley's ankle chains. Surely her father as well as the rest of the household were fast asleep now—all except for Priscilla, who wouldn't budge from Edward's side.

"Yes. The time has come to make my move," she said, holding her kerosene lamp high, inching her way out into the hallway, glancing from side to side. The only lights visible besides her own were the pale golden flickerings from inside Edward's sickroom.

Tiptoeing, lifting the skirt of her dress above her ankles, Serena moved hurriedly up the staircase, stopping to check around her once again when on the third floor landing. When no sounds could be heard, she opened the door to the sitting room and crept to the corner where her father's huge oak desk sat. She fell to her knees in front of it and placed her lamp on the floor beside her. With trembling fingers, she slowly opened the bottom drawer, immediately seeing the shine from the keys reflecting upward into her eyes. Something grabbed at her heart. "So many?" she gasped. "Which one . . . ?"

She lifted the keys into the palm of her right hand, studying them, then noticed faint markings on each. She lowered the keys to the light and one by one read the imprints. She hadn't only found the keys that led to the ankle chains, but also to the supply of guns that her father so boasted about owning. She knew that they were kept in the privacy of his bedroom, where he felt they were safer than anywhere else in the house. He had always said, "If any Johnny Reb chooses to fight his way into this room of mine to get himself a gun, he will find more than a gun waiting for him."

"Well, I most certainly don't need a gun," she laughed absently. "All I want is the key to Wesley's lock. Surely, oh, surely it is here somewhere. I don't want to carry this whole collection of keys with me. The noise of their rattlings would most assuredly awaken Father."

Trembling even more, she continued to study each individual key, then smiled triumphantly when she found the one marked "prisoners."

"This has to be the one," she whispered. She noticed its size, envisioning it to fit into such a lock that secured each of the men's chains. "Yes, it is surely the key."

She worked it around the ring that held the keys, then was able to slide it off the end. When it was safely in the palm of her hand and the rest of the keys back inside the drawer, she lifted her lamp and inched her way back to the door. She peered out, relieved to still see no activity on either side of her.

"It's safe. I shall now hurry on. I shall go to Wesley. Oh, what a surprise I have for him," she giggled to herself. Her heart thumped wildly inside her, both from fear of being caught, and from the thought of having Wesley all to herself. A bit of apprehension invaded her being. What if he wasn't well enough? What if the fever had returned in full force as fevers often did in the evening?

"But I can't think about that," she said, moving past the second floor landing, on to the first. "I'm sure he will want to go to my room with me and share a glass of wine. Didn't he say that Wyndhams were hardy and healed quickly? He is a Wyndham. Maybe one day *I* will be . . . a . . . Wyndham. . . ."

A brief recollection of other Wyndhams whom he had vaguely spoken about entered Serena's thoughts. His sister Dorlisa May—she didn't sound as hardy, nor did his brother Truman Firman.

Now that the lower floor had been reached, Serena tried to screw the wick even lower on her lamp, knowing that her father had probably hired a more alert night attendant now that Terence had let him down so. But she had to laugh when she looked toward the desk and saw that even this attendant was snoring noisily as his bent head bobbed on his shoulder with each loud snort. *Won't Father be furious if he finds out? But only Father can please Father. He knows that.*

Tiptoeing further, Serena entered the room where Wesley lay waiting. Barely breathing, she glanced from side to side, afraid that eyes would be following her, discovering her midnight flight once again. But to her relief, all were asleep . . . fitfully . . . but asleep. Then her gaze settled on Wesley. He was sitting upright and to Serena's surprise, he had a shirt pulled on, hiding the ugliness of the bandage-covered wound.

Hurrying now, she fell down onto the floor beside him, all wide-eyed. "Wesley, you look almost well," she said. Fear of him being moved to the jail made tears surface at the corners of her eyes.

"Do you like my shirt?" he asked, squaring his shoulders.

"Where on earth did you get it?

"I talked this new night attendant your father has hired into finding me one among the pile of discarded ones. He found this one that didn't have even a trace of blood on it. Like it?"

"I think you look good enough to eat," she giggled. "You're even beautiful," she sighed, lifting a finger to his lips, smoothing it over them.

He laughed a bit hoarsely, reaching up to caress his whiskers that were growing thicker each day. "Sure would like to have a shave. Then you'd get your first true look at this southerner."

"What I see is quite good enough," she whispered, feeling the same flames flickering at her insides as he continued to look at her with his dark, beguiling eyes. Her gaze moved to his chin, seeing that its cleft was becoming hidden by his beard. It did make him different . . . even more handsome. But one day soon, surely she could be allowed to hand him a razor, or better yet, be allowed to shave him.

"And what are your cheeks so rosy for this night, darling?" he asked, lifting his lips in a sensuous smile.

"I have plans," she giggled. "Do you feel like traveling upstairs? Are you strong enough?"

"What?" he gasped, growing serious, his eyes resembling two dark coals as he studied her. "What do you mean?"

She giggled wickedly, lifting the key before his eyes. "I've stolen something else that belongs to my father," she said. "Are you interested in knowing why?"

"Serena," he gasped further. "Is that the key to . . . these . . . chains around my leg?" He inched his way toward the edge of the bed, groaning a bit when his shoulder pulled. "I can't believe that you daring," he said, laughing.

"But I am," she said flatly. "Maybe one day you see that I'm just as daring as you are, my sweet."

"But after you loosen the chains from my ankle, what then? Why did you mention stairs? Do you plan to aid in my escape from this place?"

Serena's face drained of color. "No," she quickly blurted. "Nothing like that. I could never do that. . . ."

"Then what the hell, Serena?" he said, eyeing her questioningly.

"I didn't even think of the possibility of your escaping, Wesley," she said. She curled her fingers around the key, worried now about her plan. Would he take advantage of her? Would he make her appear foolish in her father's and sister's eyes? She couldn't take the chance.

He laughed throatily. "Serena, don't you know that I couldn't now, even if I wanted to?" he said, reaching for her hand.

"And why not?"

"I may appear healthy to you, but I know my limitations," he said. "I know that to move out into that snow in my weakened condition, without a gun, with no horse—I wouldn't even get to the edge of town."

"I suppose you're right," she murmured.

"I am," he said. "So what were you planning for me? To take me upstairs? Isn't that where your . . . bedroom is?" He smiled knowingly now. He knew what was on her mind.

"If I unlock the chains, will you promise not to try to escape from this house?" she said, placing the key to her lips.

"If you unlock the chains from around my ankle,

ag, I will be yours. Forever," he said, reaching to all her face to his, kissing her softly, then more demanding as he held her tightly to him. The blood was rising inside him. Oh, to possess her in the way a man should possess a beautiful woman. But was his shoulder going to cause him too much pain to enjoy such a rendezvous . . . ?

"All right. I'll go ahead and do it," she said, moving from his arms, trembling. She inched her way to the foot of the bed, feeling as though she had a mass of burning embers inside her, with the need to have them turn into full-blown flames. She desired him so. Never had she felt such a feverish excitement.

She cursed lightly beneath her breath as she fumbled with the key, then with a low, snapping sound the lock flipped open; the chain fell onto the bed in a heap. "Darling, you are free," she said, bright-eyed, looking quickly around, hoping that no one had heard. She reached for the curtain and circled it around the bed to hide herself and Wesley, hoping she wasn't too late in doing so.

He lifted the leg, rubbing his ankle. He sighed quietly. "I can't believe it," he whispered. "I am at last free."

Serena's heart froze inside her, having heard him actually say it. "Now let's try to get upstairs without being seen," she said hurriedly, needing to know that he was going to keep his word. Oh, if he did escape, it would be *she* who would be sent to the jail and possibly even shackled. She would be tormented over and over for betraying her country, her beloved President Lincoln. . . .

"Can you really pull this thing off?" he whispered, scooting to the edge of the bed, letting his legs dangle

112

from it. He lifted the edge of the curtain and let his gaze move around him at his fellow-prisoners, then looked quickly toward the door. It would only take one person to see them, and utter chaos would erupt.

"We must hunker low as we pass by the men in this room," Serena said, blowing her lamp out. "In the dark, they won't even notice if one should wake up. Are you able to hunker, Wesley? Will the tension on your shoulder cause you too much pain?"

He let the curtain ripple downward, seeing her profile in the darkness. "Darling, I can stand anything to get out of this hellhole for a few hours," he said thickly. He moved from the bed, then to his knees beside Serena.

"And to be with me, Wesley? Are you anxious to be with me?" she asked, suddenly doubting his true intentions. She didn't want to play the fool. She had never played the fool, not even with Edward. With Edward, she had been forced. . . .

His hands sought her out in the dark and touched her heaving bosom. "Darling, how could you ask such a question?" he whispered.

"Then first I'm going to fluff your blanket atop your pillow, to make it resemble a body in case someone glances in here. Now, move along beside me," she whispered back. "We must move slowly . . . cautiously. . . ."

Serena felt herself to be in another world, as though this wasn't truly happening to her. She had been bored, and so restless for so long; but now she was actually deep into a reckless venture, the result of her own scheming. She turned and smiled sheepishly as Wesley moved along beside her. Then as they reached the doorway, she placed her hand before Wesley, stopping him. She looked cautiously toward the desk. Again she could smile. The night attendant was still snoring noisily as he sat cross-armed with his head nodding.

"It is safe. Now," Serena said, taking Wesley by the hand. "The steps are only a blink of an eye away." She urged him onward, tensing when she heard him let out a soft moan as they began to move up the steps. She turned her eyes to him, seeing only a shadow. "Are you all right?" she asked, squeezing his hand. "Can you truly make it?"

"It's just this damn shoulder," he grumbled. "Certain ways I twist my body, it hurts like hell. And, yes. Keep moving. Do you think I want to turn back now? Not on your life."

Exhaling heavily, she moved on up the steps, then stopped suddenly when she heard a noise above her. She pulled Wesley to the side of the stairs, leaning against the wall, as closely as possible, watching as Priscilla moved back into Edward's room. "Whew!" she said, wiping her brow with the back of a hand. "It was only Priscilla. Now that she's back in Edward's room, I doubt if she will leave again all night."

"Edward? Priscilla? Who are they?" Wesley whispered, moving along with Serena now, stepping up onto the second floor landing.

"Shhh," Serena encouraged. "I'll tell you later."

She tugged at his hand then moved on to her room, not stopping to even hear if her father was snoring. No matter if her father would happen to be awake, she knew that she had no choice now but to take Wesley on into her room, and as quickly as possible. Once there, they would be safe until the time came for Wesley to return to his bed. She had to smile, though, remembering how her father had said that no man could escape from his hospital quarters. Well, she had just proven him wrong!

"In here," she said. "This is my room, Wesley," she added as she opened the door. She felt wicked, utterly wicked. What would her mother have said, if she had been alive, to witness such shameful behavior? But her mother wasn't alive. And if so, maybe her mother would have even approved, knowing of Serena's sudden longings for this man whom she had fallen so desperately in love with. Serena's mother hadn't known such love. She had been too dominated by only one man.

Wesley moved on into the room, glancing quickly around him as Serena closed and locked the door behind them. His lips lifted into a soft smile when he spied the soft light from the burning candles and the two wine glasses beside the tall bottle of wine. He turned to Serena. "Please put that damn lamp down, Serena," he said thickly, reaching for her.

"Your shoulder? Does . . . it . . . hurt much?" she murmured, placing the lamp on a table beside her. "Did the stairs weaken you, Wesley?"

"I'll show you how great I feel, darling," he said, then he had her in his arms, kissing her with light, feathery kisses, first on the lips, then her nose, and down to the hollow of her throat. His fingers went to the buttons of her dress and began to release them one at a time, making Serena tense a bit. He was in too big of a hurry. She didn't want to think that he was only with her because of what he could get from her. She couldn't help but remember Edward. Oh, how horrible that experience had been. She wanted more from Wesley. She wanted his arms to become paradise. . . . She moved away from him, securing her buttons once again.

"I have some wine, Wesley," she said, breathing hard. It was most difficult to control her own hungry desires. She had never known such pressures building up inside her. They were painful, but beautiful. She knew that Wesley had to have some way of quelling such feelings. But not too soon.

He laughed a bit clumsily as he sauntered toward the table. Serena watched him, truly seeing him for the first time. His gray uniform breeches were wrinkled and dirty, and the blood spatters were black spots. He was tall, over six feet, and he carried his well-muscled and masculine body gracefully.

His borrowed shirt was tight across his shoulders and back; his breeches also showed a tightness—at the buttons, where a bulge presented itself to Serena, making her look quickly away.

"Does look cozy, darling," he said, settling down onto a chair, wheezing a bit. He eyed her closely, realizing that he had been too hasty in his approach. He knew that she had her own reputation to uphold, especially if this was the first time she had ever done anything like this. From all appearances, it was. She showed to be the picture of virginity, innocence, even though she had chosen to wear quite a low-cut gown for this night's performance. God, how beautiful she looked in her pale lilac velvet gown with its clean, simple lines, mainly emphasizing the fullness of her bosom. The gown moved from her slender waist in many gathers to settle around her ankles in yards and yards of material.

He hadn't noticed this before, but the petticoats now rustled voluptuously as she moved to the table to lift a long-stemmed glass toward him. "My father chooses only the finest of port," she said. "Please do share some with

116

me tonight. I've heard that wine is good for the blood."

"And for many other things," he laughed, accepting the glass. He watched her feverishly as she poured a glass for him, then herself.

"To us," she purred, clinking her glass against his, then settling down onto a chair across from him.

"Yes, to us," he said, laughing suavely. "May we share many more such glasses of wine." He tipped his glass to his lips, not taking his eyes from her and her sensuous beauty. In the soft light of the two flickering candles, her hair looked almost the color of the wine he was drinking, and hung in thick massive curls around her face and down her shoulders. Her large, seductive eyes were teasing him as her lashes fluttered like butterfly wings over them. The slight dusting of freckles across her nose was cute, making her appear very young—ah, such a picture of innocence!

"Now this is much nicer than even your own private room on Folly Island, isn't it, Wesley?" she said, smiling charmingly at him. She had the need to keep reminding him of his island, hoping that he would still want to take her there. Didn't it sound just too grand? An island all to themselves. . . . No—she had to remember. He had family. They would also be there. She and Wesley wouldn't have such a paradise all to themselves, if they would even ever have the chance to have *themselves* all to themselves.

Wesley winced as he moved his shoulder in an awkward position, then scooted more down onto the chair, stretching his bare feet out before him. He wiggled his toes, feeling as though the circulation had returned completely, relishing in the freedom that had been handed him, even if for only a short time. The chain had cut into his ankle, making it throb even now, as though the chain was still draped across it. "Ah, my island," he said dreamily. "If only we were there now. I would show you huge oak trees laced with Spanish moss that would clean take your breath away. It is more beautiful lace than one can buy to sew onto a dress."

"I've seen pictures of plantation houses that had such trees around them," Serena sighed. "I know that it has to be breathtaking. Tell me more, Wesley." She took another sip of wine, and felt she was in a dreamland.

"I have a residence in Charleston, too," he boasted, missing home so much, his heart ached.

Serena leaned forward, eyes wide. "You do? Your family owns more than one house? Your family must be rich."

Wesley's gaze moved around him and took in the grandness of her bedroom's furnishings. With the rosewood chairs and the great mahogany bedstead, and the plush beige carpet in which to curl one's toes, and the beige velveteen drapes at the window, it appeared that the Calvert family were not paupers. "Yes," he answered at last. "But I'm sure no more than your own father. He does sport quite a large house here in Illinois, you know."

Serena's gaze moved around her. She frowned, then took another sip of wine. "I'm not impressed," she finally said. "You see, I have grown so tired of my way of life. This town has nothing to excite me." Her lashes fluttered once again as she peered toward him. "Until you, Wesley. Until you . . ."

Wesley lifted his own thick lashes as he sat his glass on the table. "Serena, damn it, I must kiss you," he said, rising. "Don't you see? We don't have much time to be

118

together. I'll have to return to my bed soon, or my absence might be discovered." He went to her and pulled her up into his arms and kissed her hungrily while his hands caressed the small of her back. She leaned a bit away from him, as though in a daze. "Wesley, your wound . . ." she murmured. "I don't want to be the cause of . . ."

"Forget the wound," he said thickly, crushing his lips against hers. He worked his body against hers, letting his hardness tease her into wanting him. "I want you. Now," he said, reaching for her buttons again. "Please tell me that it's all right. Serena, the time. It's passing so quickly. Please let me have you. This one night. I love you. I want you. . . ."

Feeling the fire building inside her, Serena couldn't say no. She wanted him as badly as he wanted her. She knew that this wouldn't be the same as with Edward. She hadn't felt this excitement with Edward; Edward had left her cold. Wesley had turned her into a boiling sea of passion and desire. She now knew that she was a woman with needs, some of the same needs as a man. . . .

"Yes, darling," she whispered, leaning away from him. She encouraged him to release her from her dress. "I want you. Please teach me how beautiful it can be between a man and a woman. Please show me that it can be. Please."

Wesley's eyebrows tilted. He heard such a pleading in her voice. And the way she was talking, it was as though she had been with another man, and that it had been most unpleasant for her. What if she had? He wanted her to be a virgin. Marriage had even entered his mind. But he wanted to marry someone who had been a virgin before him.

Before, marriage had been far from his mind. He thought he would never wed. His troubled thoughts of his sister's condition had made him think it better not to wed. What if his own children . . . ?

But Serena had helped to push these doubts from his mind. She was, oh, so lovely. . . . Could he truly leave her behind, now that he had found her?

His fingers busied at releasing her from all she wore, then encouraged her to move to the bed where she stretched out on it, waiting. "I won't remove my shirt," he whispered. "I won't remind you of my wound while making love, darling. But I will have to remove my breeches. That is quite necessary, you know." He laughed hoarsely, fumbling a bit in his haste.

Serena turned her head away, once again remembering Edward. Would she ever be able to put him from her mind? She was with the man she loved now. He should be the only thing on her mind. But yet, she was afraid. Edward had hurt her. Edward had made her hate him for what he had done. And now? It seemed Wesley was about to do the same, except that she was wanting this from Wesley. She had such a storm building inside her, only Wesley could quell it. Only Wesley. . . .

When he climbed on the bed beside her, Serena turned to him with arms outstretched, sighing leisurely. "Wesley, darling, I can't believe you are truly here with me," she whispered. "Please kiss me. Please hold me."

Wesley winced as a sharp pain shot through his shoulder, but the pain in his loins was even stronger, as the heat rose to such heights, he felt he might explode. His mouth sought hers out, then let his tongue enter, teasing, probing, as his hands began to trace her body, feeling a trembling in her flesh as he touched each spot anew. Then when his fingers circled a breast and squeezed, she moved her body next to his and worked its fullness against his, moaning softly.

"My mind is swirling, Wesley," she said sweetly. She reached down and touched where she felt him throbbing against her flesh. She felt brazen, daring, but couldn't help herself. Her mind was out of control now. Her body was speaking for her, thinking for her. Her hand began to caress his hardness, amazed at its ability to grow even larger the more she caressed. Then when his fingers sought out the soft spot between her legs while his lips were sucking on a breast, she felt as though she were soaring, climbing, like a bird, weightless above the clouds, losing her senses as his tongue continued to attack her flesh, moving across her stomach, then down where she throbbed between her thighs. When his tongue made contact where his fingers had just been, she pushed him away, gasping for breath.

"No, Wesley, you mustn't do that."

He breathed wildly, trying to not feel the pain in his shoulder. He was so close to having her completely. He wouldn't give up now. "Why not?" he asked, reaching to capture a breast between his fingers once again.

"I'd just rather you didn't," she whispered, urging him upward. "My head is already spinning enough. Please don't do anything like that. Though it felt delicious, it doesn't seem the right thing to do."

He laughed hoarsely, smoothing his hands over her once again. He sighed, then positioned himself over her and watched her expression reflect agonizing ecstasy as he entered her. He tensed and his heartbeat skipped as he realized that he . . . wasn't . . . the first with her . . . wondering who. . . .

121

But then he closed his mind to such thoughts as he felt her vaginal walls close around him in a warm wetness. He began to thrust in and out, slowly at first, then more quickly as she began to lift her hips to move with him.

"Wesley, oh, Wesley," she cried, never having felt anything so marvelous in her life. It was as though she was one mass of swirling warmth inside, and the largeness of his manhood was fulfilling the longing inside her. Her heart was pounding so wildly, she thought she might not survive the rest of the lovemaking. She clung to him, rode with him, sighed his name over and over again, caressed his back, reached down to try to touch the part of him that continued to pleasure her, but only found her fingers touching a part of her own self that was throbbing in unison with her heart. Her fingers began to move over this spot, causing her to see small explosions in her brain, all the colors that she had ever seen in her lifetime, and with one last thrust of wildness inside her, she felt Wesley's body begin to spasm. Wesley's body continued to jerk wildly, over and over again, and when he cried her name, it frightened her, as she thought her father might even hear.

Then groaning, Wesley moved from her, clasping onto his shoulder, where a crimson red had appeared on the outside of the shirt.

Serena saw this, then bolted upright. "Wesley," she cried, covering her mouth with her hands. "You're bleeding anew. Oh, what have I done?"

He laughed a bit hoarsely, checking his shoulder. "What have you done?" he said, looking her way again. He raked his eyes over her, seeing her nudity once again, wanting her even more. "I believe we did this thing together, don't you, darling?"

Then his face darkened in shadows, remembering his discovery upon his first entrance into her. He hadn't been the first. There were ways of telling. His eyes searched the bedspread upon which their union had been made for the talltale signs of her virginity, but, no. No sign of blood. . . .

He moved from the bed, suddenly silent. Serena joined him, not at all conscious of her nudity. It seemed natural to be standing nude next to the man she loved, would always love. Even his nudity didn't embarrass her. Her eyes lowered, exploring his body. She would always desire him, only him. Her hands reached for the part of him that had suddenly become so small, but he moved quickly away from her.

She covered her mouth with her hands, wondering what could cause such a reaction, after such a beautiful experience together. It hadn't been the same as with Edward. She had experienced pleasure right along with Wesley. Oh, she would live for his touches, caresses. Why was he acting so cold . . . so distant . . . ?

"Wesley, darling, what's the matter?" she asked, reaching for his hand, but even this was denied her as he reached for his breeches and stepped into them. He strolled to the table and poured himself a glass of wine, which he downed with one quick swallow, then another, stopping to stare questioningly at her in between each fresh drink.

"Wesley, please tell me what's the matter," Serena whispered, suddenly being made to feel wrong to be undressed in front of him. What was she seeing in his eyes? Such—what was it—*contempt?*

She shivered and reached for a nightrobe, hiding herself quickly beneath it as she slipped her arms into it.

Then she took a quick intake of breath when she heard a movement outside her door, then a light tapping. When she saw the knob being turned, she grew ashen with fright. She placed her hands to her throat, first looking at Wesley, then the door, then took a step backwards when Priscilla's voice broke through the strained silence.

"Serena? Why on earth do you have your door locked?" Priscilla whispered loudly. "I have to talk to you. Open the door."

Serena looked desperately around her. She then hurried toward the wardrobe and opened it, making room for Wesley as she scooted her clothes quickly aside. "In here, Wesley," she whispered. "I have to open the door for my sister Priscilla, or she will know I'm up to something. I never lock my door."

Wesley's eyes had grown wild. "Serena, if I'm caught in here, I'll most surely be shot," he said. His shoulder was truly throbbing now. He winced as he bent into the small space of the wardrobe, then sighed heavily as the door was closed in his face.

Serena swallowed hard, then spied the wine and accompanying glasses and candles. "Just a minute, Priscilla," she said, hurrying around the room. "Let me slip into my robe. It's mighty chilly in here." She struck a match and lit her kerosene lamp, then blew the candles out and thrust them, along with the wine and glasses beneath her bed.

Sighing heavily, she rushed to the door and opened it a crack, leaning out into the hall. "What the devil do you want, Priscilla?" she grumbled, rubbing at her eyes, acting as though she had been awakened from a sound sleep.

"Let me in," Priscilla demanded, moving on past Serena, looking quickly around the room. When she discovered Serena's dress and underthings lying in a heap on the floor in the center of the room, she knelt and scooped them up into her arms. "This is no way to treat your things," she accused. "Mother would frown on this if she were here." She moved toward the wardrobe. "I'll hang them up for you," she said leisurely.

Serena's breath caught in her throat as Priscilla swung the wardrobe door widely open. But when Wesley couldn't be seen, Serena slumped down onto a chair, exhaling deeply. She further watched as Priscilla hung the dress on a satin padded hanger, then placed the underthings on an upper shelf, starting to ramble on about being so tired.

"I truly can't stay awake the full night," she said, swinging around to face Serena as she closed the wardrobe door behind her. "I beg you to help me. Please? It looks as though you've had a few winks of sleep already," she said further, gazing toward the mussed up bed with a raised eyebrow. "Though I didn't know it was your habit to go to bed before removing the bedspread. Serena, your habits have become even more sloppy than mine." She moved to the bed and began to toss the bedspread back, but was stopped by Serena's strong grip to her wrists.

"Priscilla, I'll relieve you from your assigned duty if you'll give me a chance to freshen up a bit," she said quickly, worrying about Priscilla discovering what was beneath the bed, and wondering how on earth Wesley had managed to get so well hidden in the wardrobe. But she had to remember. Her things were mostly floor-length. He had probably hidden himself deeply beneath a velvet dress, or possibly even her velveteen cape.

"Oh, will you?" Priscilla sighed, clasping onto Serena's hands. "You will be a doll, if you will. And I promise, I won't sleep long. Just a little while. I feel as though my lids are going to drop off, I need sleep so badly."

"If you will go back to Edward's bedside and promise not to move from the room again until I get there," Serena said flatly. "Only then will I promise to relieve you of your tiring duty."

"I promise," Priscilla said, swinging the skirt of her dress around, moving toward the door.

"You must *not* leave his bedside until I get there. Do you hear?" Serena repeated.

"I understand."

"You know how important it is for someone to be there at all times, Priscilla," Serena said, guiding Priscilla on toward the door.

"You won't take long, will you, Serena?"

"It will take me longer now that you've put away my things," Serena fussed. "Now I will have to take the time to remove them from the wardrobe again. Then it will take me some time to brush my hair. Things like that. You know." She hoped she was sounding convincing enough. She needed time . . . time to return Wesley to his bed and the shackles around his leg. She didn't wish to do either, but had no choice but to do so.

Priscilla turned and frowned at Serena. "You don't have to fuss so. You don't have to be that carefully groomed to just sit at Edward's bedside."

Serena laughed, raking her eyes over Priscilla. "And who are you to talk? You look as though you have stepped from a magazine's page."

"Isn't that what you wished for me for so long, Serena?" Priscilla snapped. "Now that I have taken pains with my appearance, you tease me even more. I shall never understand you. Never."

"Well, never mind about that," Serena urged, moving to open the door. "You just don't listen to my ramblings. You get back to Edward. While we are having a sisterly argument, he could be choking to death."

Priscilla's eyes widened. "Really? Oh, Serena, I never even thought about something like that happening."

"Then on with you. I'll be there as fast as I possibly can," she said, shooing Priscilla off with the flick of a wrist.

"Thank you, Serena," Priscilla said, then rushed on down the hall and into Edward's room.

Serena closed the door behind her, leaning heavily against it. She sighed with relief, then laughed a bit as Wesley emerged from the depths of the closet with a lace handkerchief draped foolishly over his head. He pulled it away from him and let it drop to the floor.

"Too damn close for comfort," he grumbled.

"But the coast is clear now, darling," Serena said, rushing to pull her dress and underthings from the closet. "As soon as I dress, I must get you back downstairs, and then you heard what I must do later."

"Yes. I now understand who Priscilla is, but this Edward fellow. Who is he?"

"Darn. I was going to explain about him," Serena said,

127

pulling her petticoat beneath her dress. "But I will later. In fact, I must. There is something you need to know about him."

Wesley's eyebrows tilted upward. He had to wonder if this Edward fellow was the one who had slept with Serena. A veil of gloom settled over him, again remembering that she hadn't been a virgn. He moved toward the door without even waiting for her.

"Wesley—" she whispered.

"I'll be careful," he said, moving on ahead of her, out into the darkness.

Serena gasped as he disappeared from her sight, then hurried on after him, looking at him questioningly as she reached him and they moved side by side into the ward. In her haste, Serena had forgotten the lamp. She knew that she would be risking much by working in the dark. But it wouldn't take much effort to fit a key into a lock. Oh, God, how she hated locking him back to that bed. And, oh, God, she could tell something had changed between them. He was being too distant. Too cold. Why had he grown so quiet? Surely he hadn't been disappointed in the way she had made love with him. . . .

"Darling, I love you," she whispered, as they moved to his bed. "I don't want to lock the chains around your ankle, but I must. Please understand."

"I'm a prisoner," he grumbled. "All prisoners must be shackled. I'm no different than the next man in this prison, am I, Serena?"

Even though it was dark, she could feel his eyes on her, cutting through her. What was he implying? She didn't understand. But she couldn't take the time to question him about it now. Priscilla was waiting. Serena had already taken too much time.

"Remember, Wesley, I love you. With all my heart," she whispered. She touched him briefly, then moved from his bed toward the staircase. What had she done wrong? His body had responded to hers in such a beautiful way. But she could question him tomorrow. Hopefully, they would have many more tomorrows before he would be moved to the jail. And after that . . . ?

Chapter Seven

A low moan drew Serena from her deep sleep. She awakened to a stiffness in her joints, then looked around her, now realizing where she had slept the full night. Priscilla had failed to come to awaken her. Priscilla had slept leisurely in her own bed, leaving Serena to curl up into a chair next to Edward's bed.

Serena stretched and yawned. "I should've known she'd do this to me," she whispered to herself, then tensed when she realized that it was Edward who had been moaning. She looked his way and saw that his eyes were fluttering a bit, as though they might be ready to open. Moving quickly from the bed, Serena moved to his side and took one of his hands in hers and began to rub it briskly. "Edward. It's me. Serena," she said hurriedly.

She felt awkward being left in this position, after having gone through so much with Edward that no one would ever know about. But she was at his bedside and he was awakening. She had to encourage him to try to awaken fully. It wasn't only her duty, but the human thing to do.

"Serena, is that you?" Edward whispered thickly, licking his parched lips, opening his eyes to two narrow slits.

130

Ripples of fear traveled up and down Serena's spine. She had to get Priscilla. And quickly. When Edward *did* fully awaken, it must be Priscilla's hand that he would be holding. But how?

Then Serena saw that luck was on her side. Edward's eyes had fallen shut once again, and his hand had released hers. She could tell that he was breathing evenly, even peacefully, so knew that she had time to rush to Priscilla's door and tell her sister the good news. It was even more important to Serena to inform Priscilla before even their father. Edward *had* to believe that it had been Priscilla who had stayed faithfully at his side. He had to think it was Priscilla who cared this much for him, that she was ready to sacrifice everything for him.

She placed his hand on the bed, then rushed from the room, stopping at the door to glance one more time over her shoulder to see if he was all right, and when she saw that he was, hurried to Priscilla's door and tapped lightly on it.

"Priscilla," she whispered, glancing from side to side, not wanting to awaken anyone else. She had to guide Priscilla to Edward's bedside. She must. Serena had other things on her mind this morning besides Edward and Priscilla. Serena was remembering how quiet Wesley had become after their lovemaking. She had to go to him. She had to talk with him before the day's activities began. In no way could she wait an entire day before seeing him, to question him.

The door creaked open, revealing a still fully clothed, yet rumpled, Priscilla. Priscilla stood, wiping her eyes, then gasped loudly. "Oh, my God, Serena," she said. "I went to sleep and didn't wake up. I'm so sorry." Her gaze moved to Edward's door. "Edward. How is he? I must go to him." She moved on past Serena and into Edward's room.

Serena followed after her and told her what had happened. "Now you must take his hand, Priscilla," she encouraged. "He must see you when he awakens again."

"And do you think he will? Soon?" Priscilla asked anxiously.

"Yes. I am sure," Serena said, glancing toward the door, anxious to take her leave. She would have to go to Wesley before awakening her father. Edward's condition was improving. Edward could wait a while longer before having her father's attention. Right now, Wesley was of prime importance to Serena.

She took Priscilla's free hand in hers and squeezed it. "Honey, I have something to do," she said. "I'll be back shortly with Father."

"Then you are going to go and inform Father of Edward's awakening?"

"Yes. Soon," Serena murmured. "Just be patient."

"Where are you going, if not right to Father's room?" Priscilla asked, her dark eyes full of suspicion. She had noticed so much about Serena these past few days. There was something even aglow about her face this morning. Did it have to do with what Priscilla had seen in the bedroom the night before? Priscilla hadn't said anything. She would later, when it would be more opportune for her.

And there was something in Serena's eyes. They were so troubled. This wasn't like Serena. Serena wasn't known to worry about anything. "First foot forward and proceed," was Serena's usual way of approaching things.

"Just some business to attend to," Serena said, then rushed from the room. She had to wonder just how long she was going to be able to keep her feelings about Wesley to herself. She knew that her actions would reveal a great deal to a close observer. And what would everyone think and do when they found out that she was in love with a wounded enemy? Shoot Wesley? Or maybe even herself? She shuddered as she began to rush down the stairs, finding the lower floor to be a mass of activity.

Daybreak always brought out the worst groans and moans from the wounded. Oh, if she could only get away from these hospital quarters! She needed to escape the looks of emptiness that followed along with her as she passed by most of the beds. But in Wesley's eyes . . . oh, how different it was! She had seen so much more. . . .

With a pounding heart, she rushed onward to Wesley's bedside, finding him lying on his back in a deep sleep. She glanced over him, loving him even more, but aching inside when she saw the dried blood on the outside of his borrowed shirt. His thick lashes looked heavy as they rested against his cheek, and what she could see of his lips beneath his mustache were curled downward, as though in a pout.

Serena stooped and touched his lips with hers, not caring about the heads that turned to witness her show of affection. She knew that they had noticed that her presence at Wesley's bedside was more frequent than usual. So far, they hadn't teased or tormented her. But she knew why. They had seen her father, they had heard the severity of his words. . . .

When Wesley's eyes opened, Serena smiled warmly down at him and caressed his brow with her fingertips. "Good morning, darling," she whispered. "How are you? Did you rest last night?"

Wesley turned his eyes from her, still remembering his

doubts about her. When he had thought of taking her to Folly Island with him, he had thought to be taking a lady, one he would be proud to present to his family. He knew that she was high-spirited and even a bit reckless, but he hadn't imagined Serena to be one who would give her body so freely to more than one man. But she had. He had been able to tell. A woman's first time was supposed to be painful, and there was supposed to be at least a trace of blood, the full proof that he had been the one to have made first entrance.

No. He couldn't greet her cheerfully this morning. He wasn't sure now if he even wanted to ever talk with her again. He didn't want her thinking that he would take her with him to be his wife. If he ever were to feel he could think of marriage, he wanted a decent woman, who had loved only him. A man could have as many women as he desired, but it wasn't the same for a woman. She was to remain faithful to one man, or she would be justly labeled a whore.

"Wesley, what's the matter?" Serena whispered, taking her hand to move his face around so their eyes could meet. Something froze inside her. She could see the coolness in his eyes, even something resembling dislike for her. There wasn't anything warm about his expression this day. Why? What had she done? Would he even tell her? She didn't know men well enough to understand how their minds worked, except that she knew that sex played an important role. Well, she had shared this part of life with him. What else would he want from her to make him love her even more?

"Nothing, Serena," he said sullenly. "Just tired, I guess." He closed his eyes, trying to force them to stay shut. Then maybe she would leave. Maybe she would find another man's affections to toy with. There were plenty from which to choose in this damn northern hospital.

"But, Wesley—" Serena began, but was interrupted by the stern voice of her father as he moved to her side.

"Serena Kassia Calvert," he boomed. "What is this? Why are you here so early in the morning? Your duties don't call for this. Can you explain this?"

Serena felt the furious pounding of her heart, knowing that the inevitable had happened. She had been discovered. Her face paled as she rose upward, face to face with her father. "I . . . was . . . just . . . uh . . . worrying about Wesley's welfare," she stammered. "You know. His temperature? It was a bit out of hand yesterday morning."

Hiram's thick eyebrows tilted upward. His fingers moved around his mustache, curling, twisting, as his gaze moved from Serena to Wesley. "Before even eatin' breakfast, Serena?" he growled. "You have never been anxious to move to these hospital quarters this early before. It's hard to believe that you would suddenly have a change of heart about these things."

"But, Father . . ." she stammered further, reaching for him.

He began to walk away, still scowling. "But never mind about it now, Serena," he stormed. "It is Edward who is now asking for you. Come along."

Serena felt Wesley's eyes burning a hole through her. She turned and began to speak, but her father's further shouts drove her away from Wesley's side. She glanced across her shoulder as she moved along with her father out of the room. To her, her paradise had just been shattered. She had the feeling that she would never be with Wesley, maybe not even see him again.

"Serena Kassia," Hiram grumbled as he guided her by the arm up the stairs. "Your behavior is questionable, you do know this, don't you? You must remember, handsome though that Wesley lad is, he is still our enemy. That is the only reason he is here with us. He is our enemy, wounded. You must focus your thoughts elsewhere."

She set her jaws firmly and straightened her back. "On Edward," she said stiffly. "You mean focus my thoughts on Edward, don't you?"

"Seems that it has to be that way. At least for the time being," Hiram grumbled, stepping heavily from one step to the next. His attire was jet black, from pants to shirt. Even his eyes appeared to be the same color this morning as his anger guided him to his next words. "And as for Priscilla, you can go to her room later and apologize to her," he boomed.

Serena's face became a mask of confusion. "What about Priscilla? Why would I have to apologize? What have I done?" she stormed right back.

"She was with Edward a minute ago and when he awakened, he spoke your name," Hiram said. "Then when Priscilla whispered that it was she who was there, not you, he began cursing her, calling her vile names, saying that only your presence by his side could make him become well again."

Serena's face reddened. "Father, why would I have to apologize to my sister for that?" Serena hissed. "It is Edward who has done her wrong. Not I."

"You have done her harm by leaving her there to have such an embarrassing thing happen to her. If you hadn't been with that Wesley lad, you could've been at Edward's side. Then he wouldn't have had to humiliate your sister in such a way."

Serena sighed disgustedly. "Father, I just can't believe you," she shouted. "I just can't. How can you come to such crazy conclusions as that? Do you like Edward so much that you will take it out on me? I can't help it if Priscilla has fallen for Edward, and not I, and that Priscilla wanted to be by his side, not I. I have nothing to apologize to Priscilla for, and she knows it, and doesn't expect it. I flatly refuse. And I don't even think I will go to Edward's room with you. You seem to have everything under control. Or at least you think you do, if only in your mind."

Hiram stopped and grabbed her by the shoulders and held her at arm's length. "You listen to me, Serena Kassia," he grumbled. "I don't like it one damn bit what Edward has done to Priscilla, but right now, we have to think of Edward and his full recovery. Don't you see, girl? He didn't even know he was talkin' to Priscilla in such a way. He was delirious. So we must play along with him. You see, these head wounds are tricky things. He may never even be right in the head again. You have to do a few things in life you don't like, and Serena Kassia, you are about to do a few. I order you."

"Father, please," Serena said, squirming, trying to release herself from his tight grip. "You are hurting me."

"I won't take one more step until you agree to help me with this patient of mine," he said flatly.

"Father, what do you want me to do? I don't understand."

"You have to go to Edward. Pretend you care. If you even have to, tell him you will wed if that is what is needed to make him recover."

Serena felt a tightening around her heart and a weak

feeling encompassing her. "What?" she gasped. "Father, I cannot do that. I just can't."

"You can . . . and you will."

"But what about Priscilla? Her feelings for Edward are true. Don't you know what this will do to her? Then I *would* have reason to apologize to her."

"I'll explain the necessity of this plan to her," Hiram said, quieting his tone of voice.

"Nothing will convince her that what you are asking of me is right."

"No matter. She will get over it. He's much too old for her anyway."

"For her? Father, what about me? Priscilla is only two years younger than I. I am also too young for him. You insult my intelligence, Father."

"You are matured in many ways that Priscilla isn't and never will be. And you must remember, I am only asking you to play a game. Then when Edward is on the road to recovery, Priscilla can do as she wishes. If she truly cares for him, then I will give her my blessing to approach him in any way she wants."

Serena groaned inwardly, but felt so trapped, she had no choice but to do as asked . . . until she and Wesley . . . *Oh, Wesley,* she thought sadly to herself, *what can I even say to you . . . ?*

"Then it is agreed?" Hiram said, smiling.

"Only until Edward begins to recover. . . ."

Hiram leaned over and surprised Serena by giving her a wet kiss on her cheek. "That's my girl," he chuckled. "I knew that you would see it my way. Come. Let's go to Edward's room."

Serena moved along with her father, hating each added step, and when they made their entrance into Edward's room, she tensed, seeing that he was wide awake, watching her entrance. *Darn him,* she thought to herself. *I can see the triumph in his eyes. Why can't Father?* But she knew that her father wouldn't want to see this. Her father didn't want to think anything at all bad about this man he so wanted his older daughter to marry.

"Edward, how good it is to see your eyes open widely," Hiram said, moving to Edward's side, to take a wrist between his fingers, checking his pulse. "And now that you've awakened fully, you can see that I've brought you the best nurse in this Mattoon hospital of mine." Hiram turned his head and motioned for Serena to move to his side.

Stiffly, Serena did as she was bid, forcing a smile. "Hello, Edward," she said between clenched teeth. This was too quick a recovery. In no way had he been speaking out of his head when he had cursed Priscilla. He had darn well known what he was doing. Well, she would play along. But for not too long. She couldn't neglect Wesley. He needed her in more ways than Edward ever would.

Edward licked his lips, then mumbled, "Serena, I'm so glad you came. You always bring a bit of sunshine into a room."

Serena glanced toward her father, wondering if he hadn't yet noticed just how recovered Edward was. Was her presence even still necessary? Then she winced when Edward began to groan and grab at his head. Serena didn't know if he was pretending to be in pain, or if he actually was. No matter, she now knew that her time would be long at this man's bedside. If he wasn't in pain, he would pretend, especially while Hiram was in his presence.

"Hey, there, ol' boy," Hiram said, leaning down over

Edward. "Settle down. Some pain is expected. Just try to go along with it. Soon it'll dissipate. Then you'll be your old self." Hiram turned to Serena, frowning. "Come here, Serena. Take Edward's hand. I must go eat a fast bite of breakfast then see to the other wounded."

Serena slowly extended her hand, then draped it over Edward's. "And myself? What about my breakfast?" she asked.

"I will see to it that yours and Edward's will be brought to you. You may even have to assist Edward with his first few meals. Eh, Edward? Sound all right to you?" he said, leaning down into Edward's face.

"Yeah. Sounds all right," Edward said, between groans.

"Then I'll take my leave, Serena," Hiram said, taking a pocket watch from his front breeches pocket, checking the time. "Seems the mornin' is passin' me on by. You see to it that Edward gets all he asks for. Hear?"

"Yes, Father," Serena said, thinking that Edward had already gotten all that he had wanted from her that night . . . oh, how she hated the memory of that night! She tensed when Priscilla crept into the room, looking downcast.

"And, Priscilla, get along with you," Hiram boomed, moving past her. "You have to help me downstairs this mornin'. It's a mad rush down there. You know that. And while Serena is seein' to Edward, you don't have any choice but to help. Come along."

Priscilla glared at Serena, showing her humiliation in the depths of her dark eyes, then swung the skirt of her dress around and left beside her father.

Serena turned her gaze back to Edward, who smiled toothily up at her. His walrus mustache twitched a bit as

140

he laughed a bit beneath his breath. "Edward, you are pretending much of the pain, aren't you?" she hissed, glowering.

"No. I'm full of pain," he said. "But mainly around my heart, Serena. And you know the reasons why."

"There's not one darn thing I can do about that pain, Edward," she hissed, dropping his hand with a thud. She swung around and settled herself down onto the chair, refusing to stand near him. He was playing games. His recovery had been fast and full enough to satisfy her. But as long as Edward chose to play this game with her father, Serena had no choice but to play along with him. She knew that her father wouldn't believe her if she told him what Edward was up to. Agree to marry such a man? Never! No, never! Not to even guarantee his full recovery, because Serena now knew that would not be necessary! She would once again have to plant Priscilla at his side. She would have to find a way!

The late hours of the night awarded Serena some privacy. She was now free to creep down the stairs to have a few moments with Wesley. The day had seemed like a year, and now that Edward was asleep, Priscilla had been allowed to take Serena's place at his side.

Serena crept from her bedroom, looking up the staircase, hoping that her father would be relaxing in front of the fire. He had said that he had been too wound up to go to bed at his normal time, that even though it was nearing midnight, sleep would have to come later . . . after he had sorted things out in his mind.

Serena had said that she would keep him company until he decided he was ready to retire, but had instead said that she had needed some rest, that the long day had tired her. She had seen a look of distrust in his eyes, knowing that he had indeed grown suspicious after having caught her at Wesley's bedside so early in the morning. She knew that even now she was taking chances, knowing that he might even have informed the night attendant to watch for anything out of the ordinary. But she didn't care. She still had things to straighten out with Wesley. And she had to do it now.

With only her dimmed kerosene lamp and her shadows accompanying her down the staircase, she rushed into the room, peering through the semidarkness, so anxious to see him, even possibly waiting for her arrival. Nothing would make her happier than to know that he was as anxious to see her as she him. But the closer she drew to his bed, the more apprehensive she became.

The outline of this man in the bed . . . was much larger . . . and he had bright red hair . . . and his wrist was shackled to the headboard of the bed!

Serena's heart sank. Where was Wesley? She looked at every bed, thinking that maybe her father had decided to move him. But Wesley wasn't there.

Her heart began to pound. Then she turned and raced up the stairs, past the second floor landing, to the third, then stopped to get her breath before entering the sitting room. She panted noisily, trying to make sure tears wouldn't surface. She had to confront her father with some degree of composure to get the right answers from him. She knew that only he would know where Wesley had been taken.

Oh, God, she prayed. *Not the jail. It is too soon for him to be taken to the jail. He wasn't that well. . . .*

But she knew that he had appeared to be. She was quite aware of it. Hadn't he managed to be able to make love in his condition? Had her father guessed the extent of Wesley's strength and had him ordered from the hospital quarters? Had her father thought Wesley well enough . . . or had he thought Wesley to be too much of a threat to his older daughter?

With her head held high and her jaw set firmly, she entered the sitting room, spying her father sitting before a roaring fire on the hearth with his face hidden behind the morning newspaper that he was enjoying, his first chance to read after the busyness of the day. She didn't know how to approach him. Would he see the flush on her face? Would he even suspect her to be upset after discovering Wesley's absence? She had to pretend that nothing was wrong.

She blew her lamp out and placed it on a table, then with a forced gracefulness, she glided to a chair and settled down onto it. She sighed loudly, trying to get her father's attention. When he didn't respond, she said, "Hello, Father. Seems the weather is changing a bit, isn't it? The warmer temperatures of the day have almost melted all the snow that fell yesterday." She watched the newspaper, wishing for it to be lowered. But, instead, he only began mumbling along with reading. It was obvious that she was of less interest to him than the news.

"Says here Sherman's troops are continuin' to move northward and Grant's troops are hammerin' at Richmond's doors," he said.

Serena let her back ease against the chair, as she rolled her eyes in exasperation. Only two subjects seemed of importance to her father. The welfare of Edward and the advancement of Sherman's and Grant's troops. She had to wonder what he would find to talk about once the war was over and Edward was wed. What then would occupy his mind? She grew restless, toying with the gathers of her dress, having to wait patiently while he continued to turn the pages of the newspaper. Tension was building inside her. Her heart and mind were heavy with thoughts of Wesley. What had her father done with him?

Hiram finally folded the newspaper into a neat square and placed it on the table beside him; then he lifted a pipe to his lips and lit it. Between his clenched teeth, keeping a firm grip on the pipe, he said, "Hell, will that Grant ever succeed? He's been at Richmond's door for almost a full year now. Sure thought it'd be over before now."

"Then you hate this war as much as I?" Serena asked, leaning forward a bit. Her heart began to pound. Maybe she could find a way to bring Wesley's name into the conversation.

"Always have," he grumbled. Then he turned his full attention to Serena, raking his eyes over her. "Serena, you look as though you've been fightin' a battle yourself. Why are you so pale? And I thought you had said you were going to bed. Couldn't you sleep either?"

"No. I couldn't. Did you ever think it might be a bit hard on me taking the full responsibility for Edward?" she said sullenly, settling back in the chair once again. "Why not Priscilla? I have better things to do with my time."

Her father's face seemed suddenly to become all shadows. "Like that Wesley lad? Eh?" he said with a lifted eyebrow.

Serena's eyes widened and she swallowed hard. "What do you mean?" she gulped, wondering just how much he knew. She had always known that he was shrewd. Maybe he had ways of finding out.

"You know that I've seen you makin' eyes at that

damn Reb," he growled. "Serena, don't you know he probably makes eyes at all available women?" He cleared his throat nervously, then added, "Serena, you ought to be ashamed of yourself. Don't you know that that man probably even shot some of our town's men and boys? How can you even take a fancy to such a man as a Johnny Reb? It sickens me. Purely sickens me." He paused, then added, "It's beyond me why you, or any—"

He paused once again, glancing nervously away from her, as though something else was troubling him, then continued, "Why you'd let yourself become so infatuated by that lad when there's Edward, and if not Edward, any number of our own heroes, wounded and whole, from which to choose if you need to take a fancy to a man at your age of eighteen."

Serena lowered her eyes, feeling many things. Confusion about her father's hesitation; she felt that he wasn't concerned about her alone, but about someone else, too. The only other person he ever worried about besides Serena and Edward was Priscilla, but Priscilla had nothing at all to do with this particular conversation. Serena felt such anguish over Wesley—fear of never being in his arms again; shame for deserting the northern cause by letting one of the southern men make love to her. But her eyes began to show fire as she remembered that if there were not a war, it would be perfectly acceptable. She was in love with a man, no matter if he was from the North or the South. And she had thought that he had also loved her back.

"What has become of Wesley, Father?" she asked flatly, at last, straightening her back even more, defying her father with her eyes. She even forced them to not blink under his steady gaze of accusing.

"Taken to the jail where all prisoners are supposed to be," he grumbled, rising to knock his pipe's ashes into the flames of the fire.

Serena's fingers went to her throat. He had done just what she had dreaded. "Father, Wesley isn't—he can't be—" she stammered. "He wasn't well. . . ."

He swung around, glaring. "He's recovered more than you think," he grumbled.

"What do you mean?"

He cleared his throat nervously, then quickly added, "I've seen men placed behind bars that were in much worse shape than that Wesley lad."

Serena's mind was swirling with confusion. If Wesley were in jail, their time together would be at an end. Even after the war's end, she had a feeling that he wouldn't think one moment about her, and the fact that she was waiting, eagerly, to travel south with him.

Then she pulled herself together. Even though her father thought he had succeeded at separating two people in love, he had *not*. No one, no, nothing would keep her away from Wesley. Not her father, nor the brick walls of the jail. "You are despicable," she said, rising. She went to the liquor cabinet and poured herself a glass of wine, already making plans.

"You are gettin' out of line, Serena Kassia," her father roared, striding to her side. He knocked the glass from her hand, spilling the rosy liquid down the front of her dress. She gasped, then twirled around and began to rush from the room, but stopped and shouted, "You'll be sorry, Father," she said. "For everything. You'll see. You'll be sorry."

She fled from the room, not able to keep the tears from wetting her cheeks. Never had she been so angry as she was now. Her father had dominated her mother until her death. Serena was not going to let him do the same to her. She had to flee soon. She had to find a way. And she had to include Wesley in her plans. She had to be with him. No matter how. . . . Even if it meant having to find a way of helping him . . . escape. . . .

From this moment, her loyalty was only . . . to . . . Wesley. . . .

Chapter Eight

Though the hour was late, Serena knew that she had to manage to find Wesley. She would see this thing through to the end. Her father would no longer be able to run her life. Her plan would not only set Wesley free from his bonds, but hers as well.

But she had many problems to face before those first breaths of freedom could be inhaled. How could she manage to get inside the jail, not once, but twice?

"Is a second time even that necessary?" she whispered, pacing the floor of her bedroom. Could she manage to get everything aboard her carriage to set Wesley free this very night?

Then doubts assailed her. Would Wesley be well enough to travel by carriage the many days and nights, possibly even weeks, that would be required to reach the Carolinas? And could they actually travel safely enough close to where battles might still be raging?

"I have no choice but to try this," she whispered further. "I must. To delay might mean losing Wesley forever, and to delay might even mean to lose my sanity." She stared downward at her dress and the way the wine had dried in purple blotches on its front. Seeing this made a determination flow through her veins.

"I will do it," she murmured. "And I *shall* succeed."

She rushed to her wardrobe and pulled a travel bag from a shelf. Then she began to choose the least cumbersome of her dresses and underthings. She pushed and shoved all these inside her bag, then changed into her heaviest riding skirt and blouse. She grabbed her hooded velveteen cape and placed it and her travel bag beneath her bed. Her mind was swirling with what else would be needed and how she might manage to secure it all and get it to her carriage.

"A gun is quite necessary," she said. "One of father's Springfield rifles. That's what I have to get from his room. And before he settles in for the night." She knew that he had been too upset for retiring, especially after their conflict.

She began to pace the floor once again as her fingers worked at securing her hair in a tight bun. "I must find a way to get the key to father's guns from the sitting room, and go to father's room for the gun, and all this while he is in neither room."

Then she heard his heavy footsteps on the stairs, realizing that he was going downstairs to take his usual last look at the wounded before going to bed. If she didn't move quickly, all would have to wait until another night, and this was not a part of her plans.

She lifted a kerosene lamp and went to the hallway and up the staircase, once again sorting through her father's keys. Once she had the proper key, she tiptoed back to the second floor and inched her way to her father's room.

Luck continued to be with her. Hiram was no where in sight. But she knew that at any second he could enter his room and discover her. If he found her stealing a gun—a

149

gun that would soon be in the hands of the enemy . . . !

She shuddered, thinking about the end result of such a discovery. But she banished guilt from her thoughts. Even when the gaunt, haggard face of Abraham Lincoln materialized hazily before her eyes as she opened her father's bedroom door, even then Serena was able to blink her eyes and make him disappear just as quickly.

"The war is almost over," she whispered. "Father and Edward have said so. Surely Wesley won't have a chance to reassemble a regiment. The gun will be used only for our own protection . . . not to shoot any of our own troops."

The lamp cast dancing shadows around Hiram's room. Something grabbed at Serena's heart when she saw the tall, glass-encased display of guns. There were so many from which to choose. But then she smiled smugly. But wasn't this in her favor? She doubted if he would soon miss just one.

She set her lamp down on a table and with trembling fingers turned the key in the lock and soon had the rifle. She searched quickly around her for ammunition and when she'd taken some, she closed and relocked the case.

She went quickly to her room and slipped the rifle beneath the bed and the ammunition in her travel bag. How was she to get all these things to the horse and carriage? And more than this was needed—bedrolls, food, a supply of water, and laudanum.

"Poured into a bottle of wine?" Her eyes brightened. "Yes! That's how I'll do it. The guards will never know what hit them!"

She went once again to the sitting room. Once she had returned the key to her father's guns, she stole another bottle of wine, one that was only half full. She needed room for the laudanum to be poured. . . .

She then made her way back to her room and entered it quickly, trembling even a bit at this stage of her escape into the world of freedom. It seemed that everything was going too smoothly for her. Surely it wouldn't continue to be so easy. And when Priscilla opened the bedroom door and peered inside, Serena turned with a start, smiling nervously.

"Oh, Priscilla," she murmured. "You startled me so."

Priscilla looked in wonder at Serena and the way she was dressed. "Why your riding clothes, Serena?" she asked, moving around Serena, lifting the heaviness of the skirt, then letting it drop back in place in deep folds around Serena.

Serena moved to the window and stared out, seeing the dancing shadows of the moon move along the surface of the ground. Very little snow remained. Serena was thankful for this. Escape would be easier without the hardship of snow to travel through. "Why the travel clothes?" she said, then swung around and studied Priscilla, wondering if this sister of hers was the answer to many questions. Could Priscilla help in her escape? *Would* she? And could Priscilla be trusted not to rush to their father and tell all? But surely she wouldn't. Priscilla had to know that with Serena out of the way, she would have Edward all to herself. Yes. Priscilla had to be the answer.

"Yes, Serena," Priscilla said, settling down onto a chair. "It's quite late. I don't understand. You have to know that no woman is safe riding alone at night with all the soldiers filling the streets and alleyways of Mattoon."

Serena wanted to say that no woman was safe . . . period! She just couldn't put Edward from her thoughts.

Maybe if she could be with Wesley both day and night, Edward would be finally pushed to the deepest recesses of her mind until drowned in the waves of pleasure Wesley aroused in her. "I don't plan to be alone, Priscilla," she said cautiously, settling down onto a chair across from Priscilla.

Priscilla scooted to the edge of her chair, clasping onto the arms, wide-eyed. "Then . . . who?" she asked. "Have you met someone? A soldier . . . ?"

Serena saw something in Priscilla's eyes, a wavering of sorts, as though Priscilla were being disingenuous . . . Was she playing a game? Did Priscilla truly know? "A soldier? Yes," Serena said flatly.

A smile flickered across Priscilla's face. "Oh? Who?" she said in an almost strained fashion. "Tell me. Where did you meet him? Is he as handsome as Edward?"

Serena groaned a bit, thinking Priscilla to be so blind. But maybe it was true love. Maybe Serena had been wrong to try to see something in Priscilla's eyes and smile other than love for a man Serena despised. Priscilla's face had become flushed. Serena didn't know if it was because of the excitement of finding out a secret about her sister, or because of finding out that she would indeed have Edward free to herself. Or was it something else . . . ? "Priscilla, what I'm going to tell you has to be kept between the two of us," she said, rising, beginning to pace back and forth.

"Serena, you are acting so mysterious," Priscilla said, as she rose and went to Serena.

Serena stopped and clasped Priscilla's hands in hers. "Priscilla, I have some plans that I must carry out," she said, setting her jaw firmly. "And I need you to help me. Can I depend on you?"

"What on earth are you talking about, Serena?"

"I'm not sure if I should really tell you," Serena said, dropping Priscilla's hands. She went to the window once again, wondering if she really could pull this thing off. Her true test was near. If Priscilla could be told without any problems, then she would have hope that in an hour's time she would be in Wesley's arms—traveling by carriage toward enemy lines. The thought excited but frightened her. She turned on her heel and stared questioningly toward Priscilla.

"Serena? What is it?" Priscilla said.

"His name is Wesley Alston Wyndham," Serena said, then stopped when Priscilla gasped. Serena tensed, seeing the flush on her sister's face replaced by pallor.

"Him?" Priscilla said in a near whisper. "I've heard Father speak of him. I think I've even seen him while Father was doctoring him . . . in the hospital. . . ."

"Yes. That was him," Serena said, straightening her back, swallowing hard.

"But, Serena, he is an enemy," Priscilla said. She sat down and looked at Serena in complete dismay. She began to fidget with the lace at her throat and grew suddenly silent.

"Yes. He was brought here wounded," Serena said, sitting down opposite Priscilla. She reached for Priscilla's hands and took them in hers, squeezing them. "But you see, he is no more an enemy than Edward. Yes, he has had to fight against everyone in the North. But only because he *had* to. Not from his own choosing. . . ."

"Serena," Priscilla gasped. "I've heard you speak this way before. It is *treason*. Pure . . . treason . . ."

"Please, Priscilla," Serena said more firmly. "Hear me out. Please?"

"I'm not sure if I should," Priscilla said, lowering her eyes. "It will make me look as though I have the same strange ideas and feelings that you do. I'm not so sure . . ."

"Priscilla, you have always known that you and I are entirely two separate individuals," Serena said. "Our thoughts have always been different. So why act so surprised when I say these things to you now? As children, you accepted my difference. Why not now? You see, it is more important now that you understand me than it was when we were children. Now we have more important things in life to be concerned about. For instance, there's Edward. . . ."

"Edward?" Priscilla murmured, pulling her hands free from Serena's. "Why do you bring him into the conversation? You don't care a thing about the man."

"That's the point," Serena said. "You do, and that's why you must listen to what I have to say. Because of the way you feel about Edward."

"I don't understand. . . ."

"You will," Serena said, clearing her throat nervously. "At least, I hope you will."

"Then go on. What's this all about? What about this man—this Johnny Reb—you have taken a fancy to? How does he enter into this?"

"I'm in love with him," Serena said.

"You're . . . what?" Priscilla exclaimed, wide-eyed.

"Yes. And I must be with him."

"But hasn't Father sent him to the jail?"

"So. You know more about Wesley than you led me to believe?"

Priscilla's eyes lowered. "Yes. He's . . . spoken with me on . . . uh . . . occasion . . ."

154

Serena's face flamed red, remembering how Wesley had questioned her about Priscilla when Serena had mentioned her sister's name. Had Wesley known all along? Had he even made eyes at Priscilla? A new feeling for her sister was surging through Serena. That of jealousy. . . . And hadn't Priscilla been almost radiant this evening? Could it have been because of *Wesley* and not Edward?

"And what was the conversation about?" Serena finally asked, growing tremulous inside.

"It most certainly wasn't about the war," Priscilla said firmly, tilting her chin up into the air.

"Then what . . . ?"

"It's not of importance. You know how I feel about him."

"And that is . . . ?"

"Oh, you know. As our enemy. I could never think of him as anything else," Priscilla said, blushing. "Not as you have let yourself do. You are foolish, Serena. If Father ever found out—"

"What are you trying to say? That Wesley made a pass at you?" Serena stormed, rising, pacing once again.

"No. Nothing like that—"

Serena swung around, glaring. "Then what, damn it?"

Priscilla began to chew on her lower lip. "Serena, must you use such . . . such language? Like I told you. Wesley didn't say anything much to me. Please don't worry about it."

"If he did, I need to know," Serena said, knowing that she couldn't set a man free if he had only been toying with her affections. If he had done the same with Priscilla, then Serena would just let him rot in that jail. She would never speak with him again, though how

155

unbearable such a thought was for her.

"He did not flirt with me, Serena," Priscilla said firmly. "He did not. We talked of the . . . weather. That's all."

Serena rolled her eyes with resignation. It was evident she could pull no straight answers from her sister. Serena would have to believe that Wesley wouldn't use anyone, especially when he had been so sincere in his lovemaking. But she had to remember how distant he had become . . . after their lovemaking. Would she ever understand men? Were they all so complicated?

She moved to the chair and slouched down onto it once again, sighing heavily. She had to get on with this. Time was fast getting away from her. "No matter," she said flatly. "What is important is that I get on with what I have to tell you. Priscilla, if I do confide in you, promise you won't breathe a word to Father?"

"How can I promise such a thing, before I've been told what it even is that I am to make such a promise about?"

"Priscilla, you must. If not, you can just leave my room. And don't you even remember the help you have received from me recently? Don't you owe me a favor?"

Priscilla's face softened. "All right, Serena," she sighed heavily. "What is it? What is it you have so desperate a need to tell me?"

"First, let me say that if you do love Edward, please remember that what I am going to tell you will be something that will make it even more possible for you to be with him. I know this. So please trust me. And knowing this, I'm sure you will be ready to go along with what I have to say."

"Serena," Priscilla said, exasperated. "Will you just

get on with it? Let me be the judge of whether or not what you have to say will help me with Edward. I'm not as dumb as you make me out to be. Being an older sister doesn't automatically make you my superior, you know."

Serena's eyes widened. She had never seen Priscilla anger so quickly. It indeed gave her a bit of color. Her personality was blossoming. "Then please just listen, Priscilla," she quickly said. "I have to speak to you in haste. Time is running out on me this night. If my plans are to work, I must move quickly."

"Plans?"

"I am leaving this house tonight," Serena said. "And when I do, I plan to travel quite far from Illinois. I may never even return. . . ."

"You are leaving? And traveling alone?" Priscilla gasped.

"I'm leaving, but not alone," Serena said guardedly.

"Then who . . . ?"

"I plan to set Wesley free from the jail," Serena said.

"Oh, my God," Priscilla said, pushing herself up from the chair. She turned and looked at Serena as though seeing her for the first time. "Serena, you wouldn't. You just wouldn't be that foolish. Father—what will he say when he finds out?"

Serena rose and moved toward the bed, stooping to pull her travel gear from beneath it. She glanced toward Priscilla whose hands had gone to her mouth. "Father won't find out until later," she said smoothly. "Unless, of course, you tell him."

"Serena, I just can't believe you would do this. And how *can* you? There's no way you can get inside that jail. The guards won't let you. And once in, how on earth

157

could you get that man free? You will be shot alongside him if you try. You just can't, Serena."

"I can, and I shall," Serena said firmly, placing everything on her bed.

"And . . . a . . . gun, Serena? Why a gun . . . ?"

Serena's lashes fluttered nervously as she moved to Priscilla and grabbed her by the shoulders and held on tightly. "For my protection. Only my protection for my escape from this dreaded life I've been born into. And you have to help me, Priscilla."

"Why would I?" Priscilla murmured, trying to be set free as she squirmed and yanked. "*I* don't find life so unbearable here."

"Because of Edward . . ."

"What does Edward have to do with this?"

"Don't you see, Priscilla? If I am gone, then Edward will turn to you. Eventually he'll surely ask you to marry him. Think of it. Even Father will be happy about this arrangement. He will hate me so much, he would gladly push you toward a man he seems to worship. You must help me, Priscilla. Doing so would be to help yourself."

"You think I can't win Edward on my own? Is that what you are saying?"

"You've seen how Edward reacts to you. That should be enough answer for you."

"He's been too ill to notice my change," Priscilla said, with her lips turned downward into a pout. "You see, the other men in the hospital quarters have noticed me. I can tell. I see it in their eyes."

Once again Serena was reminded of Wesley and her earlier worries about him. Surely he hadn't made eyes at

Priscilla. Not her own sister. He had to have known that they were sisters. But she had to dismiss this from her mind. She couldn't let anything cloud her thoughts of Wesley. She loved him too much. And her love was directing her to do things she had never thought herself capable of. Was her sense of adventure and her recklessness going to lead to disaster?

She released her hold on Priscilla and went to the mirror and checked her hair, knowing that only a few moments remained before she sought her freedom. No matter the decision of Priscilla. "Are you going to do as I request, or not?" she asked, furrowing her brow.

Priscilla sighed heavily. "I don't want to," she grumbled. "But I guess I will. I am so tired of bickering with you over every little thing. And especially about Edward."

Serena turned on her heel, her eyes snapping. "Do you forget who it was who even told you how to make yourself presentable enough for Edward? Didn't I even make your hair so pretty? How can you act as though I have caused you trouble with bickerings? I've tried to help you."

Priscilla lowered her eyes. "I'm sorry, Serena," she said. Then her eyes shot upward. "But all that you've told me tonight is so alarming. . . . How am I supposed to feel? Aren't you afraid of what you're about to do?"

"Maybe so, but I must do what my heart leads me to do. And my heart leads me to Wesley."

"And you are actually leaving the North with him if you do succeed at setting him free? You are going to go, as a southern sympathizer would, and join the enemy?"

"I have no other choice. If Wesley is set free, how can he get through the streets of Mattoon alone? He would be shot on the spot."

"It is shameful. Oh, so shameful, Serena."

"Call it what you may," Serena snapped. "All I need to know now is whether you will help me."

"I said I would."

"Okay, then. Here's what you must do . . ."

Chapter Nine

The low branches from the majestic elm brushed against the outside of the carriage, sounding ghostly to Serena as she sat on the seat, saying her last goodbyes to Priscilla. She clutched the horse's reins, feeling the need to shed a few tears, thinking this might be the last time she would see her sister. But she had to act brave, even though she felt nothing inside but tremors of fear. The excitement had deserted her for the moment. She knew the trials that lay ahead. She only hoped that she wouldn't get caught while releasing the man she loved.

Priscilla climbed onto the carriage seat beside Serena and threw herself into her sister's arms. "Serena, please don't do this. I so fear for your safety. You know the chances of you arriving at the Carolinas unharmed are slight," she sobbed, clinging.

Serena dropped the horse's reins and gently pushed Priscilla away from her to hold her at arm's length, to study her. Her sister so looked like an innocent child now with her cloak thrown across her shoulders and with the tears making a path down her cheeks. It was now that Serena knew the intensity of her love for her only sister. She had had many feelings about her in the past: sudden moments of hate, annoyance, joy, love, and, only moments ago, jealousy. They had shared many things, but mostly angry words that sisters were wont to do. But now? Remorsefulness flowed through Serena that there hadn't been more than these things between them. They could have had so much. They could have tried harder to make one another happier. But it was too late to think about these things now. They were parting. Possibly forever . . .

"Now, Priscilla," Serena said firmly, swallowing back a lump in her throat. "You know that I am a strong person. I can take care of myself. If I am determined enough to begin this daring venture, believe me when I tell you I will succeed and will be in the Carolinas possibly in a month's time."

"But . . . the war . . . ?" Priscilla asked, sniffing noisily.

"Wesley will know the best routes to take," Serena said flatly. "He's been a part of the war. You must remember that."

Priscilla lowered her eyes. "How can I forget? You are leaving . . . with . . . the enemy." Her gaze shot upward. "I'll never forget that. And Father? He will hate you for it. I just know it."

Serena released her hold on Priscilla and let her own hands drop to her lap. "Ah, yes. There's Father," she murmured. "He will rant and rave at first. Then after he has time to think about it, he will probably even be glad that I am gone."

"Serena, that's a terrible thing to say," Priscilla gasped.

"But it is true," Serena said softly. "You know how Father and I have become almost as rivals these past months. Ever since mother's death, it seems. Yes, when he's left with his more reserved daughter, he will probably be much happier." She set her jaw firmly. "But you will have to help him more than you have in the past, Priscilla," she said. "You must. For the sake of his health, you will have to help take some of his heavy load of duties away from him."

"Oh, no," Priscilla groaned. She hung her head in her hands. "I didn't even think about that. Oh, how I hate helping him in the hospital. I shudder even now when I think of having to be around armless and legless men. Oh, it so repels me. Any imperfection . . . repels me."

"But you must," Serena ordered. "I have done my share in the past, now it is time for you to do the same." She would never understand how Priscilla could be so disgusted by the maimed men. But Serena knew that it was only one flaw among the many in her sister's character.

"I'm sure I will," Priscilla said, lifting her head, her eyes heavy with sadness and weariness. "Knowing Father, I will have no choice."

Serena looked toward town, realizing the time had come to give her sister a farewell kiss. She needed to get on with this thing. "I do have to leave now, Priscilla," she said quietly, lifting a hand to Priscilla's cheek, pushing a loose strand of hair back. "And please don't worry about me. I will be fine."

"But how will I know?" Priscilla cried.

"When I arrive at Charleston, I will try my best to get a wire back to you. But if the city is in as bad shape as I think it is, this might be impossible. So just try to think of me as being with the man I love and very happy. Don't even let your mind wander to the dangerous side of my mission. I am doing what I want, for the first time in my life. What I am doing is what I need for my own salvation. Please understand."

Priscilla turned and looked through the small window of the carriage, eyeing everything that was inside it. "And do you truly believe you have everything you will need? Did I sneak enough food and water from the kitchen? Did you and I carry enough blankets from the spare bedrooms on the third floor?"

Serena laughed lightly. "Yes. Yes. We've thought of everything. I've prepared for this trip most carefully. I don't believe I shall freeze. I've always been a survivor. So shall I be now."

"Then you must truly leave? At this moment?"

"Yes. For if Father decided to take a late night stroll and discovered me with this carriage, with an extra horse tied to the back, he would come running for sure and put a stop to what I must do. So, Priscilla, please go on back to the house and wash your face with some cold water to clear up its redness. We don't need any telltale signs to arouse curiosity, especially since you must rush back to Edward's bedside for the rest of the night. Do you hear?"

Priscilla burst into more tears. She wiped at her eyes, then murmured a soft, "Yes. I do know what I should do." She threw herself into Serena's arms and clung desperately to her. "I shall so miss you, Serena," she sobbed more loudly. "Oh, what shall I do without you to talk to? Even though we have bickered, I have always depended on you. Oh, what shall I do?"

Serena swallowed hard. She patted Priscilla on the back and whispered soft words of comfort. "Priscilla, hush. You're a grown lady. Grown ladies don't weep so openly. What you must do is rush to Edward's bedside.

Let him be the one you depend on from here on out. He's a man. He will even transfer more strength to you than I have ever been able to do. Go to him. Make him love you. Do you hear?"

Priscilla turned her eyes upward to Serena, then she broke into a quiet smile. "Yes. That's what I will do. That's what I must do," she said, then added, even more softly, "And, Serena, I have a need to say I'm sorry. Don't ask what for, just . . . accept . . . my . . . apologies . . . ." She scooted across the seat, stopping to take one last lingering look at Serena, then fled from the carriage toward the house.

Serena's mouth opened in dismay, wondering what Priscilla could mean with her rushed apology? But this wasn't the time for more questions. She didn't stop to take another look at her sister. She flicked the reins and spoke a soft "Hah," glad when the horse lurched forward and began carrying her away from the Calvert house and all the miseries that she had found there. She had wanted to go to the grave to whisper a quick farewell to her mother, but felt that would steal too much of her precious time.

Serena continued to glance around her as she guided the carriage down one street, then another, tensing occasionally when she would catch a glimpse of a blue-uniformed soldier staring back at her. She pulled the hood of her cape more snugly around her face and moved to sit closer to the back of the seat, hoping to not draw too much attention to herself at this late hour. She had only one thing to truly worry about, though. How could she explain her arrival at the jail to the guards, since the hour *was* so late? She had to hope that the bottle of wine and the temptation that it would carry, would be her answer and the solution to all the problems that kept swirling around inside her brain.

Taking special pains to avoid Corral Road, Serena circled on around until she found herself traveling along the road that led right to the front of the jail. The closer she drew to it, the more she noticed extra commotion along the streets this night. She looked all around her. It was strange. It seemed as though the streets were filled with more nonuniformed men than uniformed. And it seemed that each was even noisier than the next.

She tensed, remembering another night shortly after the news of the war had reached Mattoon, when the Northern Draft Law had been instituted. Many men had gathered on the streets and had even set fire to some buildings. Even now, the draft remained an unpopular law. So many soldiers had grumbled that this war had become a rich man's war and a poor man's fight because a draftee was allowed to pay a substitute to serve for him.

In all states of the North, a draftee could pay the government three hundred dollars to avoid military service. And most men who had been even the least bit influential had managed to do this. This was the reason for the mobs and riots. Serena only hoped that tonight, the same wasn't about to happen. Hadn't the men even heard the news that the war might be drawing to a close? But she knew that most wouldn't believe that. And even if the war was about to end, most knew that it took only one day to be a part of a regiment . . . and to get themselves killed.

Oh, so many have been killed, she thought to herself. She would always think it to be a disgrace.

The war had not only caused death and heartbreak of all kinds, but also had caused many men to show the more ugly sides of their nature. It had been only recently that Serena had heard about the bounty system, for instance. Volunteers were known to receive a bounty, or payment, for enlisting, causing thousands of bounty jumpers to desert the North after being paid and then enlist over and over again using a different name each time just for the money. These men felt no duty whatsoever to the North . . . only to themselves. . . .

Well, I am finally going to make my move and get what I want, Serena thought angrily to herself.

The carriage wheels squeaked noisily over some deep ruts in the road; then she guided it to a stop next to a vacant lot, not wanting to move directly in front of the jail. To do so would raise suspicion, not only because it was now well past midnight, but also because it was the carriage of the town's most respected doctor, without the doctor's presence in it, and also because the carriage had an extra horse tied to it.

Serena climbed down from the carriage and secured the horse's reins to a low limb of a tree. Then she reached beneath the seat and pulled the wine bottle free and tucked it beneath her cape. She walked toward the jail, through the darkness, continually watching on all sides of her for any quick movement that might be a threat to her well-being.

She felt as though lost in the crowd when she moved into the thickness of the men who were rallying around the door of the jail. She swallowed hard, just waiting for someone to notice that a woman had just ventured into their midst, but their anger about their own personal problems was keeping them occupied enough for her to move on to the door without further notice. And when she tapped loudly above the door's heavy latch, she waited breathlessly, sighing with relief when the heavy oak door swung suddenly open. But when she saw the large muzzle of a gun pointed in her direction, she stepped back, gulping hard.

"Oh, it's only you, Miss Calvert," the guard said, lowering the gun. He leaned forward and looked toward the crowd, showing the depth of his worry in his eyes. "Hurry on in with you, though," he quickly added. "Seems we might have some trouble brewin'."

Serena hurried inside, relieved when the door was closed swiftly behind her and secured with a heavy, sliding bolt. She turned and eyed this young guard cautiously. Then she smiled seductively when he moved to her side.

"What are you doin' out this late at night, Miss Calvert?" he asked, resting the barrel of his gun in the crook of his left arm. "I'm sure your father knows the dangers."

Serena pulled the bottle of wine from beneath the confines of her cape. She handed it to the guard, whose name, she now remembered, was George Hedrick. "My father wished for me to present this bottle of wine to you for all the troubles you bear on your shoulders each day and night," she said smoothly.

George looked at the bottle, doubt showing in his eyes. "This was your father's idea?" he said, hesitating about accepting such a gift.

Serena lowered her lashes, blinking nervously. "I was supposed to do this earlier in the day," she murmured. Her gaze moved upward. She forced an appearance of innocence. "But you see, I forgot. I got so busy and all. And my father. He has such a temper. If he were to find out that I hadn't done as he requested *when* he requested, you just don't know the trouble I would find myself in."

"Well, hot damn," George chuckled, taking the bottle, eyeing it hungrily. "Awful nice of good ol' Doc Calvert. Awful nice." He paused, then lifted an eyebrow. "But, Miss Calvert, it *is* so late. . . ."

"This is the only time I could have brought it tonight. I had to . . . uh . . . wait until my father retired for the night," she answered, then quickly added, "You won't tell him that I brought it so late, will you?" She fluttered her lashes even more. "Please?" she asked meekly.

George winked at her as he placed his gun on a desk next to him. "Ain't one to get a beautiful female in trouble with her pappy," George chuckled. He moved the bottle next to a lantern and watched its colors of ruby twinkle back at him. "Guess it can't hurt to take a swig now, can it?" he said quietly.

"No. I'm sure it can't," Serena said, looking slowly around her. Leading out of this large room were hallways to the many cells, each barred and locked. Serena shivered, worrying about how she would secure the key, then Wesley. She moved toward a large, potbelly stove that sat glowing orange in a corner, then put her back to it, rubbing her hands together behind her. "You won't mind if I get warmed up a bit before going home, will you?" she murmured, smiling sweetly toward George once again.

"Take your time," George said, settling down onto a wooden chair behind his desk. He placed his feet on top of the desk, then flipped the cork from the bottle and drew a large swallow from it then licked his lips hungrily. "Very good. Tasty. Maybe a few more swallows," he said, winking toward Serena.

She eyed him carefully. His blue uniform was a bit

rumpled and his copper-colored hair seemed to stick straight up from his head on all sides, as though a comb had never been introduced to it. His eyes seemed to be constantly roaming all around him, as though cautious of any passersby. Serena examined the room more thoroughly now: the racks of rifles leaning against the walls; the stucco of the walls streaked with brown beneath the barred windows, showing that the rain always found entrance on the most blustery of days of spring and summer; the flooring of a faded gray oak and tracked heavily by mud. Serena then spied the nail that showed a heavy ring of keys hanging from it. Her heart raced as she realized that on that ring, she would find the key that separated her from Wesley.

She pulled back the hood of her cape from around her face and licked her lips seductively, smiling coyly as George continued to drink from the bottle. Then her attention was averted when another guard entered. Serena wanted to hurry, to seek Wesley out, to tell him of her plans. But she had to work slowly. She had to make sure this other guard began sharing this bottle of wine with George.

She listened intently as they began a quiet conversation, glancing occasionally toward Serena, smiling, as though they had more on their minds than the tasting of wine. But she stood her ground beside the stove. She knew there was enough laudanum in the bottle to take care of both of them. She only hoped that there were no more guards around. And if there were, that they would either be asleep, or too occupied to notice her.

She turned her gaze back to the two guards, smiling triumphantly when she saw the sudden heaviness of their eyelids. George's head was bobbing a bit and he began to speak incoherently, and when the other guard crumpled to the floor in a neat pile, George didn't even have the strength in his limbs to assist his fallen associate. Then George turned to her, his eyes accusing her; Serena's hands went to her throat—perhaps the laudanum hadn't been strong enough for him. But then she breathed a sigh of relief when George slumped his head atop the desk and fell into a deep, drugged sleep, snoring noisily.

Some measure of guilt followed along with her as Serena went to the nail that held the keys. Suddenly she heard some loud bangings on the outside door. The crowd had suddenly come to life, and it seemed that they had chosen to take it out on the jail and its occupants. Serena had to wonder if their purpose was to release the enemy. They had done so in the previous uprisings. No matter which way they were planning to move, she knew that she had to hurry.

Grabbing the ring of keys, she slipped the ring onto her arm beneath her cape, then moved cautiously into the other area of the jail, breathing easier when no signs of other guards were in evidence. When she began to make her way between the rows of cells on each side of her, she wanted to close her ears to the beggings to be released and the outstretched arms and hands reaching for her through the bars. She had come for only one Confederate. She in no way was going to be any more disloyal to the North by letting more than one gray-uniformed man free. If she did that, she would never be able to forgive herself.

She continued to think of Wesley as other than an enemy. He was the man she was in love with. He was in love with her. They were meant to be together. And in a time of war such as this, what Serena was now doing was the only way possible to guarantee their life together.

Her pulse raced when she heard his voice when he spoke her name. She turned her eyes in the direction of the voice and thought she would melt inside when she saw the darkness of his eyes gazing back at her from the narrow space of a cell only footsteps away. She rushed to him and placed her fingers over his as he held onto the bars. "Wesley," she murmured. "Oh, darling Wesley."

He looked peaked, even through the thick set of whiskers that was marring his handsomeness. Her gaze moved to his wounded shoulder. The blood seemed to have saturated his shirt even more. She now knew that her father *had* acted in haste by placing him in the jail cell, and she hated her father even more.

"Darling, what are you doing here?" Wesley whispered, glancing quickly around him, seeing all eyes on them. He feared for Serena and her safety. She never ceased to amaze him. Was she even more reckless than he had at first guessed? Then he remembered his feelings about her after they had made love. Had he been wrong? Had she been forced the other time she'd been with a man? Surely Serena didn't make it a habit of bedding up with a man—then visiting him at the jail. . . .

"I've come to set you free," she whispered back, leaning her lips to the bars, so wanting to taste his sweetness.

His eyes widened. "You've . . . what . . . ?" he gasped.

She looked quickly around her, then whispered again, "Wesley, we don't have much time. I don't know how long the laudanum will last. We must find the key that will fit your lock."

"Key? Laudanum? Lord, Serena, what is this all about?"

Serena pulled her fingers from his and let the ring of keys drop from her arm, to her fingers. "I have drugged the guards," she whispered further, beginning to sort through the keys, trying one, then another into Wesley's lock.

"You can't get away with it, Serena," Wesley said thickly. "We will be caught. It's impossible. Do you hear the crowds outside? They sound angrier than hell."

"The crowd is truly a work of the Lord," Serena said, sighing when a key finally made a turn, causing the lock to snap free. "The crowd will give us perfect cover." She looked down the full length of the hallway, smiling almost wickedly when she spied a back door. She knew where it led. Right onto the property next to where she had left her carriage.

The loud shouts from the men in the cells on all sides of her made Serena tense. "Hurry, Wesley," she said, motioning with her head as she held his cell door open. "Believe me. I have it all planned. We will make it. But before the crowd attracts the soldiers from their beds all across town, we must make haste." She dropped the ring of keys to the floor as she reached for him.

Wesley looked on all sides of him, feeling guilty for having to leave his many comrades imprisoned. But something told him that they soon would be released anyway, if the crowd had anything to do with it. He had heard the men speak of such crowds of the past. There seemed to be many southern sympathizers in the North. The thought made him proud. Damn proud. Maybe it was such actions as this that could make the victory lean more toward the South once again. No matter, though; he had to do as Serena was suggesting. She did seem to have it all under control, but he had to wonder how she had managed to pull this off, especially with such a father to have to deal with.

He ducked his head and let Serena wrap her arm around his waist, trying not to see nor hear the men as he and Serena moved on past them. Then when they reached the back door and Serena finally managed to find the latch to push it aside, the night air and the darkness was glady accepted when the door was closed behind them.

Serena tightened her hold on Wesley's waist, smiling upward at him. "I so want to kiss you, Wesley," she purred. "But even that will have to wait. I must get you to my carriage."

Wesley laughed raucously. "My little vixen," he said, admiring her anew and the way she was handling herself. "I cannot believe any female could be as daring as you. You should have been under my command. Damn. We could have set the world afire." He cringed when pain shot through his shoulder as he tripped over a rock. His hand went to his shoulder. He felt the renewed wetness of blood and began to worry about whether or not it would ever heal. But now that he was with Serena, surely even his wound would be forgotten. He was anxious to hear of her further plans.

"My carriage. It's close by," she murmured, licking her lips nervously.

"Do you plan for us to make our escape in a carriage?" he asked, peering through the darkness, now making out a stately black carriage led by a sleek black mare, and then could see a spare chestnut mare tied to the rear.

"We have to look the innocent couple, Wesley," she said. "And maybe a carriage might even give us some warmth on our long journey."

174

"And where do you plan to travel to?" he said, furrowing his brow. "I will be caught for sure if I try to hide out in these parts."

Serena held her head high and set her jaw firmly. "We are headed toward the Carolinas," she said determinedly.

"You plan to go with me, now, to Folly Island?"

"We will make a serious attempt, my love."

"It is so . . . far. . . ."

"You know the way," she purred. "Didn't you say you were responsible for making daring raids before being captured?"

"Well . . . yes . . ."

"Well, we are about to travel the country you made your raids in."

"How in the hell . . . ?"

"I have a carriage filled with all necessities. Even my father's Springfield rifle."

"Even a gun?"

"Yes. I knew what would be needed for our safety."

"Your father, Serena. What do you think he will do when he discovers what you've done?"

"Shout, shout, shout," she said, laughing.

Wesley tensed, hearing shouting all right. But it wasn't from Serena's father; it was from the crowd that still persisted in trying to enter the jail. Then he saw something in the far distance. There was a redness to the sky. It was a fire. . . .

"Serena, it looks as though your town of Mattoon has gone crazy. Don't you see the flames licking at the sky?"

Serena's insides froze. She looked in the direction of the flames. She knew exactly from where they were materializing. The railroad station. "They've done it again," she hissed. "Those darn crazy men and boys have set fire to the piles of coal that are stored for the trains. Anything to cause trouble. When the war is over, what will these bored, angry men do? What will things come to?"

"Who does this?"

"Bounty jumpers, mixed in with delinquent youngsters who are too young to go and fight the true war. Up until this war started, the town was so quiet and peaceful. Then once the fighting got into everyone's blood, there seems to have been no end to violence."

"It's that way all over, Serena, in fact, I'm sure it is at Charleston. But on Folly Island itself? There aren't enough plantations to have to worry about such a thing there, thank heavens." But he did have to wonder if anything had been left at Folly Island by the hands of the raiding bluebellied Yankees. His insides flamed, just thinking about his father's mansion that would one day be his. He hoped that he and Serena could make it to Folly Island. Oh, how anxious he was to see how his family had fared through this hellish thing called war.

"We've made it thus far, Wesley," Serena said, laughing triumphantly. "You get inside the carriage. You will find a change of clothes. Priscilla helped me sort through some men's clothing at the hospital quarters and we've found several that might fit you. They are civilian clothes. I hope you don't mind."

Wesley's eyes wavered. "Priscilla? Did . . . you say Priscilla . . . ?" he stammered.

Serena's heart quickened. Was she reading too much in the way he reacted to the name? But she surely was. She knew that she could be so foolish at times! "Yes, Priscilla," she said. "And the clothes. Do you truly mind?"

He laughed a bit nervously as he climbed on inside the carriage. "Mind? Why, I'd wear anything if it meant leaving these northern states behind me."

"Then I will guide the carriage until we get to the country, where no one will be the wiser when you take the seat beside me," she said, releasing the reins from the tree's limb. She climbed aboard the carriage, smiling through the small window at Wesley. When he had the door closed and was slumped down, where even she couldn't see him, she spoke softly to her horse and urged her on with the flick of the reins.

Thinking it wiser to move away from the swelling crowds, Serena turned the carriage in a semicircle, then urged the horse onward, tensing when anyone would stop and stare at her. Serena knew that most townsfolk knew her because of her father. But she couldn't worry about their thoughts at this moment. It would take them a while to figure out what was going on.

She clucked to the horse and smiled as it carried the carriage on past the rows of houses, then onto deeply rutted country roads, until they came to a thick grove of trees, where Serena could feel safe to stop and see how Wesley was faring.

With anxiety filling her veins, she jumped from the seat and secured the horse's reins, then opened the door of the carriage and crawled inside, next to Wesley, who was fully clothed in dark breeches and shirt. She moved into his arms and let him swallow her in his embrace. This was only the beginning. They had many nights ahead of them to share the comforts of the carriage interior. She had succeeded. Thus far . . . she had set him free . . . she had set herself free. . . .

Chapter Ten

Clasping tightly to the reins, Serena yelled another "Hah" to the sleek black mare. Relieved to feel the sun on her face, she glanced toward Wesley to see if he was faring as well. She had seen how he continued to grab at his shoulder when the carriage would bounce in and out of potholes in the road. She had wrapped fresh bandages around the wound their first night out of Mattoon and had felt a bit of hope when she had seen that the rougher edges of the wound had adhered so well. Now, only small blotches of red continued to seep through the bandage. But she knew there was no longer any danger of infection. Knowing that she no longer had this to fear had lifted at least that burden from her shoulders.

She turned her gaze back to the road and the countryside around her. She saw fresh greens in every direction. The narrow road they were traveling on had been cut through low hanging branches of massive oak trees, which seemed to be alive with birds' chatter.

She inhaled deeply, savoring the aroma of freshness, like new-mown grass, which leaves the pleasant odor in the air, for all to feast upon.

They hadn't yet reached Confederate territory. But

Wesley had told her that the border between Kentucky and Tennessee could be reached by the very next day. Then her worst fears would surface. She would no longer feel as though she could turn back, if needed. Once she was in the Confederate states, she knew that Wesley wouldn't let her retreat. He would be in his own territory. He would feel that home couldn't be that far away.

Serena knew that his every heartbeat was a countdown to the day he would arrive at his Folly Island. The worry was etched across his face. She knew that he feared for his family. Serena hadn't heard that much about them, but she even feared for them herself. She had been wondering about them quite often the past several days, wondering if they could like her . . . even though she was from the North . . . a hated word in the South.

"You don't mind that I don't take the reins quite yet, do you, Serena?" Wesley asked, reaching over to take her hand.

"No, darling. I wouldn't want you to rush into anything that could be hard on you," she said. Her eyes softened as she glanced toward him. "But you will feel like taking over tomorrow, won't you, Wesley?" They would be in Confederate territory. She didn't want to worry about the possibility of having to make a fast getaway if soldiers would suddenly confront them. She was speedy enough on horseback, but not by carriage.

"I feel it important that I do," he said, now only patting her hand. He reached inside his jacket pocket to pull a pipe from inside it. He chuckled, sticking it between his teeth. "You thought of everything for this trip, darling," he said. "Even a pipe and tobacco." He pulled a small pouch of tobacco and a match from his other pocket, then lifted the pipe from between his teeth

179

and filled it.

"I'm glad I remembered the razor and shaving brush," she giggled, glancing back toward him to see how smooth his skin was. The only whiskers that he had left were in his neat mustache. It wasn't thick and bushy as her father's had been, but thin, revealing his full lips. She now enjoyed his kisses even more.

Her face reddened a bit, remembering these past nights of lovemaking. It had been easy enough to manage on the seats of the inside of the carriage. She had welcomed Wesley even more because of the coldness of the night. When he had covered her with his body, the heat from him had filled her with more than his sperm. She had hated even moving from beneath him.

She sighed to herself, remembering the intensity in which he had taken her. Her earlier fears of something being the matter had been quelled. His fervor had erased all her doubts. She knew that his love was true. But . . . he hadn't mentioned marriage again. She had to wonder why. . . .

He puffed on the pipe, resting his full weight against the back of the carriage. He stretched his legs out leisurely in front of him, but continued to watch on all sides of them. He wasn't dressed as a Rebel, but closer inspection by anyone would reveal that he had been wounded. When questioned, it would be hard not to reveal his true loyalties. He could never say that he was fighting for the Union cause, even knowing that to do so would keep him out of jail. No. Never. So he had to hope that their travels would be free from questioning strangers.

He folded his arms across his chest, furrowing his brow. "Now the most important thing to do is to avoid those damn Appalachian Mountains," he grumbled. "The route I've charted should help us succeed at doing that."

"After Kentucky, where did you say we would travel, Wesley?"

"We shall travel through Tennessee," he said, then frowned deeply. "But we must avoid Fort Donelson and Fort Henry at all costs. They're deeply infested with your Yankees. I'm sure even the woods encircling the forts would be swarming with Bluebellies, just like ants that swarm around a nest."

Serena's lips moved downward into a pout, always feeling almost criminal when he spoke so freely of Bluebellies in her presence. She knew that it was a nasty nickname for the men who fought so faithfully for the North. She knew that she should say something in a condescending manner back to him, in an effort to defend her people, but she knew, too, that she had made a choice. Her loyalties were no longer with . . . the . . . North.

Oh, what was her father thinking? Had she broken his heart? Or had her absence made him even a stronger person? When his wife had died, it hadn't seemed to make him any less strong-willed. It seemed that such a loss had even strengthened him as a person. Serena couldn't understand this, but had to think that this second loss would do the same.

But she had to think that such outward appearances were to only hide his inner torments that had to eat away at his insides when he continued to lose the ones he loved. And, oh, how he had loved Serena. His constant bickerings and goadings were the true evidence of his love. If he didn't shout or hound someone, it was because he didn't care about them.

Oh, Father, please understand, she thought to herself. *Maybe one day I will be able to explain.*

She turned her attention back to Wesley. "And then? Where shall we go? Aren't you afraid of coming in contact with a battle area? Aren't you afraid for someone to see you traveling along so nonchalantly?"

Wesley lifted an eyebrow, smiling confidently. "Darling, will you just trust me? Remember, I was the one who made so many raids. I know every stitch of the land from Tennessee clear to the Carolinas," he said, then spread his arms out on each side of him on the back of the seat. "And where shall we go? Well, beautiful, we'll travel right through the middle of Alabama and across Georgia, then on to Charleston."

"Wesley, can we truly make it? That's such a long way."

"Darling, you had to think we'd make it, or you wouldn't have started this thing. Now, aren't I right?"

"At first, it seemed so simple," she said. "But now? I can only think of the days and nights ahead of us in this darn old carriage. My bones are already aching." Her gaze shot around her, checking the area for any movements, then back toward Wesley. "And you? My poor darling. How your shoulder must ache." Each time she looked his way, it was hard not to keep staring at him. It was unbelievable that they were together and alone. She was afraid that if she looked away from him for too long at a time, and then looked back in his direction, he would be gone. What if she were only dreaming and would soon wake up?

She continued to study him and how handsome he was. His dark brown eyes seemed always to be dancing, except while making love; then they would become as two dark coals, burning through her, causing her insides to flame and become raging fire. When he was thinking about her, she could always tell. His thick lashes would grow heavy and his eyes would grow dreamy, always causing her to turn her eyes away from him, for fear that she wouldn't be able to control herself from rushing right into his arms and devouring him with her hands and lips. Her gaze lowered. Oh, how she loved the deep cleft of his chin. What fun it was to run her tongue over it after having made passionate love. . . .

"Me?" he chuckled, chewing on the stem of the pipe. "I've never felt more alive. I feel as though I'm leading a regiment into battle. Only this time, my regiment is full female."

"Oh, Wesley," Serena said, giggling a bit. Then she tensed when she saw movement in the brush ahead. She tightened the reins and glanced at Wesley, then back in the direction of where she had seen the movement. She glanced once again toward Wesley, seeing that he had scooted down and had placed a hand on the rifle that was hidden beneath a blanket at his feet.

"Just keep on moving, Serena," Wesley said thickly. "Kentucky at first remained neutral in this war, and even now, to our benefit, most are southern sympathizers, even though the Confederates were expelled from their occupation of Columbus by a military force created by the State Legislature after Grant occupied Paducah. These actions placed Kentucky on the Union side of the war."

He looked quickly around him for any other movements, hoping they hadn't come across a regiment of Yankees who were possibly on their way to Fort

Donelson. He knew that they weren't that many miles away from that damn fort. He wished now that he *did* have a full regiment of soldiers with him. He would succeed this time at capturing that fort back for the Confederate cause.

But he had to worry about the safety of Serena. She had risked her neck to save him, and he was sure as hell not going to let anything happen to her. His finger went to the trigger when the movement in the brush increased. Then Wesley let out a loud sigh of relief and he began to laugh when several small children rushed out onto the road, chasing a rabbit.

"Damn kids," he said, chuckling still. "Scared the hell out of me."

Serena's brows tilted. She had never heard Wesley use the word "scared" before. She had never thought him to be afraid of anything. But he was human. She knew that everyone feared something sometimes. And with him wounded and the possessor of only one gun, he had reason to be afraid. "Darling, what if it had been . . . well, you know," she murmured, feeling prickly fingers of fear traveling across her skin.

"Well, I'd first try to talk us out of any situation we might find ourselves in, and if that didn't work, shoot like hell," he said thickly. "And if that didn't do it? Well, you know the rest."

Serena was truly afraid for the first time. She knew that at any moment a regiment could surround them. "Wesley, I do hope you know the proper routes to take," she said softly. "Ones that will truly take us away from any signs of the fighting. I don't think I am brave enough. . . ."

Wesley placed the gun back beneath the blanket then

184

scooted to her side. He placed his arm around her neck and squeezed her shoulder affectionately. "It's only natural that you would get frightened at such a thought as running across some fighting," he said. "It scares the hell out of me, too. You see, when I've fought in the past, I had a full regiment of my own around me. Now? I feel naked. So, you have to know I will, at any cost, move away from signs of action. I sure don't want anything to happen to you."

Serena leaned her head back and rested it on his arm, sighing heavily. "When should we stop for the night, Wesley?" she said weakly. "I am suddenly tired. Oh, so tired."

Wesley's gaze moved all around him. He had seen a few caves along the way. He had been silently searching for one for their night of rest. Even though it was cold, and the interior of a cave would be that much colder, and damp, they could build a nice cozy fire and truly stretch their legs out. The carriage was too cramped for his long legs. He had made it thus far, but this night, they would be sleeping elsewhere. Yes, a cave would be the perfect place for them to share another night of lovemaking. "Soon, Serena," he finally answered. "I'm watching for a cave. We'll be sleeping out of the carriage tonight."

Serena's eyes widened. "A cave?" she said, moving her head from his arm. "Won't there be wild animals in a cave?"

"Maybe a few bats," he chuckled. "But there aren't too many wild animals in these parts. Maybe an opossum will visit us with its pouch full of babies. But other than that, only an occasional fox is known to wander these parts."

Serena shuddered. "Bats? Foxes? Wesley, please say

no more." The sun was hurrying toward the horizon in reddish oranges, and as Serena guided the horse from beneath the cover of the trees, she was relieved once again to see the slight hilly slopes on each side of her. The noise of water splashing from one of these slopes drew her quick attention, then she was staring, wide-eyed, toward the rippling waters of a creek that looked as though filled with fish dancing beneath its shallow surface.

"Here. This is the place," Wesley said suddenly. "I see just the cave I have chosen for our resting quarters for the night."

Serena looked quickly around her and discovered the limestone and rock opening in the side of the hill. On the far side water trickled from a small crack and then onward into the larger stream. She could see where the constant trickle of the water had eaten away at the stone, possibly even causing the cave's formation in the very beginning of its existence. She guided the horse to a halt next to the cave opening, then climbed from the seat, puffing with exhaustion. This had been the hardest day yet. They hadn't even stopped to eat. While traveling onward, they had shared the last remaining fruit that she had stolen from the Calvert kitchen. A few hard biscuits had been washed down with the last drops of one of the many bottles of wine that she had chosen to place in the carriage, all of which had been stolen from her father's liquor cabinet. She had stolen so much. She only hoped that one day she could repay him, if he even would let her.

"It's quite beautiful here, Wesley," she said, securing the horse's reins to a tree's lower limb. She clasped her hands together in front of her, taking it all in. Ferns

186

appeared to be green lace as they clung to the hillside, where yellow buttercups bloomed in the thickness of many other different-colored wildflowers. A raccoon scampered through the brush, like a masked bandit making its escape.

Wesley moved cautiously into the cave and looked around him, checking for any signs of what could be other nightly visitors. The steady trickle of the water at his side sounded like a hollow echo next to the dead silence of the rest of the cave. A dampness, smelling of wet moss and limestone, entered his nostrils. He moved his boot around in the loose rock beneath him, relieved when no signs of a recent fire could be found.

He lit a match and held it up high, searching even further around him, looking into the deepest recesses of the cave, seeing only the round roof of rock that extended even further than his eye could see. He moved onward, barely breathing, still thinking maybe someone might be hiding in the darkness beyond. Wouldn't this cave make perfect cover for a deserter? He flinched when the match burned down to his fingers and nipped at him, then very determinedly struck another one and held it even higher, looking, admiring what he had found. This cave's deeper interior roof was an exhibit of beautiful stalactites, and as the flickering flames from the match danced along these beautiful rock formations, their colors seemed to be constantly changing, first from goldens to even that of pale blues. It was an impressive underworld. A perfect place in which to take shelter, if even for only one night.

He blew the match out and rushed back outside, where Serena was already unloading supplies from the carriage. He went to her and pulled her into his arms. "Darling, this place we've found is just what I've been searching for, and even more," he said, kissing her fully on her lips.

She gazed into his eyes, enraptured all over again. But then she had to remember where they were. Until they had safely reached the Carolinas, surely she shouldn't let her guard down. Even though their lovemaking would make her mind leave her, she still had that feeling of having to be cautious, ready, in case someone would suddenly be upon them, causing them untold dangers. "Is it safe, Wesley? Truly safe? Will we be even able to go to sleep, without feeling we should keep one eye open?" she murmured.

"As safe as can be," he said, moving away from her. He stooped and began filling his arms with supplies, carrying these toward the cave. "Come on. Let me show you." He turned, smiling. "But bring a lantern. I have something to show you that will take your breath away. You will surely forget about danger. In this cave, only the innocence of creation is represented."

Serena lifted her skirt and the tail of her cape and stepped upward into the carriage, moving the rest of their nightly supplies closer to the door within better reach. She then hurried out of the carriage with a lantern, on toward the cave. "Wesley? Where are you?" she said, looking around her as she entered.

"Darling, light the lantern. Then you shall see."

Sighing in exasperation, she did as she was asked, then inched her way into the cave, until she saw him standing with a backdrop of the most beautiful rock formations she had ever seen. She gasped and rushed to his side, all eyes. "Wesley, I've never seen anything like this. Can this be real?"

"Quite, darling," he answered, taking the lantern and

lifting it even higher. Then he moved quickly away from Serena to the earthen wall to hold the lantern next to it. "Serena. Look here," he exclaimed.

Excitement was building inside her. It was the first time since their escape that she was actually beginning to feel lighthearted. She felt as though she and Wesley were explorers, discovering a long lost underworld.

"These paintings and drawings. They must have been put here by man, possibly even before written history," he said, tracing the pictures with his forefinger. "It looks quite prehistoric, don't you think?"

"Yes. I do," she answered, also studying. "I've read books about such discoveries."

"Then don't you think we can enjoy our stay in here for the night?" he asked, placing the lantern on the floor so he could pull her into his arms to hold her next to him. "Think of all those who have stayed before us."

"I even believe I can feel safe," she said, pursing her lips into an invitation for his to seek hers out. She did feel safe. As always, when in his arms, she did, and would always, feel safe.

He kissed her sweetly, but swiftly, then said, "I only wish we could pull the carriage inside. By having to leave it outside, it's an open invitation for any passersby to come searching."

"We will have to take our chances, Wesley," Serena said, straightening her back. "At least we will have a chance to stretch ourselves out and even take the time to eat a decent meal."

"Well, then, let's get to it. I'll try my luck at catching some fish, while you start a fire, and if you're lucky enough to get a fire going, a cup of coffee would sure hit the spot."

Serena giggled. "Yes, sir, coming up, sir," she said, lifting her skirt, going to the supplies.

"And if you're that eager to please, I shall also ask for something even sweeter after our meal," Wesley teased, moving from the cave.

Serena yelled after him, feeling ripples of sensuous delight rushing through her. "Yes, sir, anything, sir." She watched him as he began to make a spear with which to catch the fish, then she began to rush around right outside the mouth of the cave, until she had an arm full of twigs, enough to get a nice-sized fire going; then she arranged them in a neat pile and set a match to them. Somehow, the evening ahead was going to be not as all others she had known with Wesley. This cave and its prehistoric writings made her even feel a bit less civilized. She felt as though she could love Wesley with more intensity. . . .

She would be ready to try anything this night. Anything. . . .

Serena stretched out on the blanket next to the fire, feeling wickedly content. She had miraculously turned this cave into a home of comforts for this night. The aroma was that of fried fish and steaming coffee, and two bedrolls lay spread, waiting. She sipped on her tin cup of coffee, gazing rapturously toward Wesley who was also spread out next to her. She placed her tin cup on the ground beside her then ran her fingers through his thick hair.

"Darling, you've enchanted me again. Did you know that?" she purred, feeling feverish inside because of his closeness. She hungered so for him. She let her fingers travel downward to trace his facial features, then to rest on the fullness of his lips. She jumped when his lips suddenly opened and captured her finger between his teeth.

He looked toward her with dancing eyes, then suddenly had her in his arms, lowering her downward, sliding his body snugly next to hers. "I want to bite you all over," he said thickly, reaching to remove the pins from her hair. When he had succeeded at doing so, he combed her hair with his fingers until it lay around her face in a massive crown of red.

She lifted her arms around his neck and pulled his head downward, peppering his face with soft butterfly kisses. "I've never been so happy, Wesley," she purred, running her hands along his shoulders, then down his back, feeling the rippling of his muscles and the curve of his back. Urging him gently away from her body, she brazenly moved her fingers to his trouser buttons and slowly began to loosen them, one by one, all the while smiling seductively at him. She licked her lips to moisten them, the fever inside her causing a dryness in both her throat and mouth.

Wesley's hands began to move over her, traveling from her freed hair, to the tip of her nose. "Such sweet freckles," he laughed hoarsely. "Just enough to make you look a child." His lips went to her nose and acted as though he was going to kiss them away.

"And your eyes," he said further. "First I see browns, then goldens. They seem to change as fast as your personality, darling." He began to breathe harder as her fingers continued to undress him from below. He could feel the heat rising in his manhood and watched her expression as he positioned his member where her hand was still exploring his body after having scooted his breeches down, to rest just above his knees.

He smiled as her fingers circled his throbbing member and began to move on it, making Wesley's heartbeat almost consume him. With quick movements of his legs, he had his breeches completely removed and then began working with her clothes: first the buttons of her blouse, then her upper undergarments, exposing the two swells of her breasts and the dark nipples that had swollen to sharp peaks, inviting his lips to envelop them.

Lowering his mouth, he devoured first one breast, then the other, all the while very masterfully continuing to disrobe her, with the assistance of her lifting her hips, as his hands pushed first the skirt, then all her undergarments down away from her.

Wesley closed his eyes and groaned as her fingers continued to work their magic on him. "Serena," he said thickly. "You'd best slow down, or it will all happen too quickly for me."

Serena giggled wickedly, scooting from her pile of clothes and slipped her blouse and upper undergarments away from her, then wiggled her way beneath him as he leaned up on an elbow. "Are you sure what we are about to do won't get your shoulder throbbing too much, Wesley?" she asked, circling his nipples with the sharp points of her fingernails.

"You've got something else throbbing," he laughed. "That's all I can concentrate on right now."

"Then make me become as one large mass of throbbing, my love," she said, arching her hips upward, enticing him to move into her, take her to the realms of passion that only he was able to stir inside her.

"I love you," he said deeply, cupping her face with his hands. He lowered his lips to hers, moaning rapturously

192

as he made contact inside her with only one thrust. Then slowly, leisurely, he began to take her, as his body began to move in her, thrusting, aching so to release, but he wanted to wait for her. He could tell by the way her body was working with his, that she was coming close, oh, so close.

"Wesley, oh, Wesley," she groaned. Her body was flooded with desire for him. Her flesh burned where his lips and fingers touched anew. Though it was cold and damp in this cave, she felt the hotness of her face as she shivered from both anticipation and exposure. His lips continued to smother her with hungry ecstatic kisses. She lifted her hips and ground them into him, savoring each and every assault of his body into hers. She could feel the pressure mounting and the haziness of her mind as it began to reel.

As his hands continued to move over her, squeezing, pinching each breast, lifting her hips even closer to him, she felt the fire building, knowing that it was going to be over, way too soon, but she didn't care. She could only think of now. How the sensations were leaving her groaning, moaning, for completion. Then she saw the burst of colors exploding inside her brain as the pleasurable warmth flowed through her body and seemingly into his as their bodies united in torrents of mind-soaring blasts of passion, leaving her panting and limp in his arms.

"Serena, my Serena," Wesley murmured, then leaned down over her and began to trace her body with his tongue. "I must have you again, darling," he said further, then continued to move with his tongue on her body, leaving her even more limp, mindless, as the desire for him began to mount inside her once again. She closed

193

her eyes and savored these caresses of his tongue, sighing deeply as it moved from one breast to the other, then on downward.

His tongue circled her navel, then moved on downward across the more sensitive part of her abdomen; she twisted and squirmed, then lay barely breathing, in suspense, when she discovered where his tongue was now lapping. She began to draw away from him and urged him upward and accepted him when he entered her again with his manhood.

"I love you, Wesley," she whispered. "Oh, how I love you."

Her body tremored slightly, then became as a volcano erupting, her insides the lava, all hot and trembling, as she was absorbed in the heat of another triumphic reunion with the man she would always adore. Then when she felt his spasms of delight, accompanied by his groans of pleasure, she knew that she had made him just as happy as he had just made her. Then when he rolled from her, laughing lightly, she joined with him, knowing that they probably could never be as carefree and happy again, even with danger lurking ever so closely as she knew that it was at this very moment somewhere outside the confines of the cave.

"You are my vixen," he said thickly, reaching for his pipe, filling it, lighting it. He lay on his back, leaning onto a raised arm, puffing leisurely on the pipe. He even crossed his legs, not caring about his full nudity. "Yes, you are my vixen," he sighed once again.

"And you are my knight in shining armor," she sighed, moving to cuddle next to him. She shivered a bit from the chill, but still wanted to feel his flesh against hers.

"We've a good bit to go yet, Serena," he said, taking on

a serious note.

"But we shall have all the nights to share in such beautiful embraces," she murmured. "At times like these moments, I sometimes even wish for Folly Island to be years away."

Wesley's expression turned a bit somber. "Serena, I—" he began, but hesitated to go further, knowing that to do so could spoil this moment together. But he had waited . . . and waited . . . and didn't want to wait any longer. "Serena, who is Edward?" he suddenly blurted, watching her out of the corner of his eye, tensing when he could see her eyes lower and could even see a blush creep onto her face.

She cleared her throat nervously and moved to a sitting position, circling her knees with her arms. Then suddenly she felt a deeper chill and began to search around her for her clothes. Was the chill worsening because the flames were lowering on the spread logs? Or was it because of the mention of Edward? She had hoped that to leave Mattoon was to leave the hated memories behind her. Why would Wesley even ask about Edward? She had only mentioned Edward's name in passing in the presence of her father. But then she remembered another time. . . . She had told Wesley that she had something to disclose to him about this man named Edward. . . . But she had thought Wesley had forgotten. *She* had. . . .

She moved quickly back into her clothes, then murmured, "Why do you ask about Edward, Wesley?" She stirred the fire, then added a few more twigs and settled more closely to its warmth.

"I must know who he is . . . and his connection to the Calvert family," Wesley said, pulling his breeches on. He settled across the fire from her, watching her with smoldering eyes.

"You probably heard my father mention his name after the train accident," she said, pouring herself a cup of coffee, needing its warmth in her blood stream. She didn't like the direction in which this conversation was headed. "You see, Edward was injured quite severely," she quickly added.

"So that's why he was on the second floor or even the third floor of the Calvert house?" Wesley said. "I thought all hospital quarters were on the lower floor. Or is this Edward fellow someone special? Possibly an uncle? Or even a brother?"

Serena's heart palpitated with the mention of brother. She now felt the opportunity had arisen to speak of her sister. She had yet to question Wesley about her, and if he had even spoken much with Priscilla while laying wounded in the hospital bed. She could just see him watching her . . . hungering after her . . . even though Priscilla had looked so dowdy until Serena had helped with her appearance. But Serena now knew men well enough to know that no matter the appearance of a female, if without one long enough, any would look desirable. It was the desire for the flesh. A never-ending hunger, it seemed. . . .

"No. He is not my uncle nor my brother," she snapped, her eyes suddenly all browns. "But you do know about my sister Priscilla, do you not?"

Wesley quickly filled his pipe with fresh tobacco, avoiding eye contact with Serena. "Priscilla? Yes, I do remember her flitting around the beds, helping your father, though she had considerable pain in her eyes while doing so. But I only saw her that one day. The day I was moved to the jail."

196

"And you thought her attractive, Wesley?" she further snapped, spilling her coffee her fingers were trembling so.

Wesley's eyes wavered as he looked toward her. "At first I thought her a simpleton, probably even like my sister Dorlisa May, but then she took the time to tell me of the many novels she absorbs in a week's time and my feelings changed about her."

A jealousy began an ache circling around Serena's heart. She hadn't wanted Wesley to share anything with Priscilla. Not even conversation. And now to know that her interest in novels had taken his fancy? Oh! That even made her more furious. "So she talked quite freely of her silly romantic novels, did she?" she said stubbornly. "Did she tell you that that is all she ever does? Just sits lazily beside a fire and reads? I think her quite foolish and boring."

Wesley laughed throatily. "I think I see something new in your eyes, darling," he said, reaching to pour himself a cup of coffee. "I do believe you are jealous. And of your own sister. I'm glad to have you jealous over me." Then as he began to sip on his coffee between occasional puffs from his pipe, he studied her more intently. "But you have managed to evade my questions about this Edward fellow long enough," he added. "I'd like to know exactly what this man means to you. Your father seemed so fond of the man. . . ."

Serena placed her tin cup down on the ground, then rose and moved to the cave's entrance, looking outward, watching the moon's reflection moving along the stream in twinkling goldens. Then the night was disturbed by the lonely cry of a bird that was unfamiliar to Serena, making her hug herself, while trembling anew. She tensed when

Wesley moved to her side and placed his arm around her waist.

"Does it disturb you so to speak of this man?" he asked, leaning his nose into the thickness of her hair. "Want to tell me about it? I will try to not go into a fit of rage if you have something to confess to me. Damn it, Serena, I need to know, or I shall never sleep a wink tonight."

Serena moved away from him and out beneath the stars, letting them guide her way to a rock beside the stream where she positioned herself, still trembling, but more inside than out.

"Serena, damn it," Wesley persisted, settling on the stream's edge, tossing pebbles into it, watching circles moving, to many added circles, then to only ripples that moved toward the shore on both sides.

Serena moved a hand to Wesley's cheek and caressed it tenderly. "Darling, I just don't like to think of the man, much less speak of him," she confessed, tightening inside, knowing that he was going to succeed at pulling all the truths from inside her brain. She just knew it. He had ways with her that no one else would ever have. He was a magnet, drawing her and all her feelings toward him.

Wesley studied her eyes. He could see much. He was beginning to be afraid of what his persisting to question her might reveal. Maybe this Edward had— Then he remembered their first night together. God, it probably had been. And it had to have been rape, for it to pain her to talk about it. But why would Serena's father treat Edward as a special person—after . . .

Damn it, he thought further. *The only reason that makes sense is that she didn't confess this terrible thing to her father.*

198

She has been harboring it inside herself like some terrible plague!

Why hadn't he seen it before? He should have known that Serena wouldn't give of herself so willingly, unless she truly loved the man.

"I think I now know, Serena," he said, rising, pulling her up into his arms.

Her eyes widened and her heart hurried so, she thought she might suffocate from its poundings. "You do?" she whispered. "How?"

"God. Serena, it is true, isn't it? This man . . . raped . . . you. . . ."

Tears sprang from her eyes. "Wesley, I don't understand . . . how . . . you . . ."

"How I knew?" he said, sealing her lips with a forefinger.

She nodded her head yes, still watching him with hazing eyes, so near to breaking into massive tears.

"That first night? I knew I hadn't been the first," he said, then felt her tightening in his hold and her eyes reddening even more. "I thought at first you had made this thing a game, you know, moving from one man to the next. But then I knew I was wrong when you came and helped in my escape. You wouldn't have taken such chances unless for the man you truly loved. It was then I knew of your deep love for me, Serena. It was then that my doubts began to leave me. But I had to question you to find out the whys of my not being the first man." He kissed her tenderly, then added, "I'm sorry if I have caused you any embarrassment by talking of this terrible thing to you tonight. Please forgive me?"

"My love, you have done nothing to be forgiven for,"

Serena murmured, and leaned her head heavily against his chest, feeling as though she had to forget her own troubled jealousies of Priscilla. Hadn't he been so generous to forgive her of her one time with Edward . . . even though he now knew the reason behind this one night . . . a night of hated seduction.

But Serena would always remember that Wesley hadn't flatly denied hungering for Priscilla. . . .

At least now, though, Serena was free of Edward and her father. *Oh, Wesley. I never want to be free of you. Never. . . .*

"We must get some sleep, Serena," Wesley said, leading her back to the cave. "Tomorrow we move into Tennessee, and Tennessee speaks of . . . danger. . . ."

Chapter Eleven

Now deeply inside Tennessee's boundaries, tension mounted as each mile was traveled. In city and country alike, wherever regiments had fought, the land lay desolate. Fields everywhere lay untilled, or where any crops could be found, most had been uprooted. The stench from livestock, spread across the farmlands after having been uselessly slaughtered, had seemed to cling to Serena's clothes. The fresh rainfall that had just begun was welcomed, but the bright flashes of lightning that were shooting from the sky as long, straight arrows into the ground, made Serena scoot more closely to Wesley's side to cling to him.

"Darling, why don't you get inside the carriage? There's no sense in both of us getting soaked to the bone," he said, snapping the horse's reins, urging the horse to hurry onward.

"I am not a sweet thing that will melt, Wesley," she said stubbornly. "As long as you will continue to sit in the rain, so shall I." She looked toward his wounded shoulder, wondering what the cold wetness was doing to it. She lifted her hood and unfastened her cape at the neck, and threw the one side around his shoulders, keeping the other securely around hers. She jumped in fright as a loud crash of thunder reverberated through the air around her.

"Getting a bit darker," Wesley grumbled, eyeing the black rolling clouds overhead. "We should try to find shelter. And fast. I don't like the way that lightning is dancing all around us."

They were now on a barren stretch of land where only the earth met sky, this only being disturbed by an occasional upward slope of land topped by groves of trees. As the wind began to whip around her and the rain became hard and driving, Serena began to tremble.

Her eyes searched further around her through the semidarkness, then she grabbed Wesley by the arm, pointing. "There! I think I see something over there," she shouted. "Beside that small grove of trees. Isn't that a house?"

Wesley followed her gaze and slowed the horse's pace. He feared any houses. A house meant possible inhabitants, though along this stretch of travel hardly any signs of life had been found. Inhabitants meant possible trouble. Only by finding a vacated house could he feel that least bit safe.

He stared even more openly for signs of life. There were no lights at the windows, and there was no smoke circling upward from the one lone chimney. Then he studied the house fully. It was a small, faded-out frame house with a smaller outbuilding only a few feet from its back door. It was surprising to him to even find these intact. Most that he had run across these past few days had been completely reduced to ashes. Doubt assailed him. Why hadn't this particular house been among the ones destroyed? Had it been by chance? Or on purpose?

"Wesley," Serena said, clinging. "The rain. It is one solid sheet now. Mustn't we go to that house and see if we can stay the night?"

"Only if there are no people living there."

"And even if there are," she argued. "You don't look the role of a soldier any longer. We are just two poor people in search of another way of life because of the war. Can't we tell anyone this, who might ask? Surely people would welcome us in out of the blinding rain."

Wesley laughed hoarsely, wiping the rain from his eyes and mouth. "Do we truly look poor, Serena? Don't you know that this carriage speaks of certain wealth? And we have two horses. I've been even considering leaving the carriage behind because of these things."

"I never thought of that," she said, coughing as the rain continued to splash in solid sheets against her face.

"Then what we must do is approach this house very cautiously," he shouted above another rumble of thunder. "If all is well, we will stop. If not, I will move like hell away from this place and hope they don't have a gun that will shoot at a range of two-hundred-fifty yards."

Serena sat stiff-backed as Wesley guided the horse and carriage toward the house, then up a narrow path, until they were only a few feet away from the leaning front porch. It was quite visible that this house had been deserted. The front door hung precariously on one hinge and the glass of the windows had been broken out.

"Well? Is it safe enough, Wesley?" Serena asked, wiping the wetness from her face once again. "Can't we enter? I'm getting so cold."

"Yes. I think it's all right," he said cautiously. "But let me check it out. You stay put while I go inside and see what's there. If I come running, you take the reins and get the carriage to moving fast. I'll be able to jump on as you're moving."

Fear surged through Serena's veins. She had known that times like this would surface while on this journey of daring. Up to this point, Wesley had used his skills to maneuver them around possible dangers. She had to believe that he was being just as skillful this time. "All right," she said, moving behind the reins as he jumped from the seat. "I'll be ready. No matter what." She wiped at her eyes again, needing to see every move that Wesley made. But even now, her hair had fallen from its pins and was continually draping down in front of her eyes in wet, stringy masses. She coughed a bit more and continued to watch, then breathed a deep sigh of relief when Wesley stepped from the house and began motioning with his arm for her to come ahead, that the coast was clear.

Only stopping to tie the horse's reins to a hitching post, she hurried on inside to Wesley's side and clung to his arm. Her gaze moved around her, seeing the desolation they had found. It was a house of one room, with a half room visible above where they stood, this being accessible by a ladder.

Then her eyes moved on around her. It was apparent that others than Serena and Wesley had made their visits inside this house. Most of the furniture had been broken into scattered pieces, and evidences of it being used as firewood lay in the grate of the fireplace as a remaining, unburned leg of a chair lay in black charred ruins.

The interior of the house was half filled with fallen plaster from the walls and rubbish where family portraits peeked up through the filth of the floors. A lone table had been left standing, with signs of someone having eaten a complete meal.

Serena watched as Wesley moved to the table and picked up a cup to study it, then cautiously looked around him, focusing his eyes on the opened door. "I don't like it, Serena," he whispered. "It seems this might be a stopover point. For whom, I don't know. But I'm sure it's not for an innocent victim of the war."

"Cavalrymen, do you suppose?" Serena asked, tensing her shoulder muscles.

"Probably," he said, slamming the cup back onto the tabletop, splashing the coffee out, around it. "You stay here. I've things to do outside."

Serena went to Wesley and clung to his arm. "What?" she whispered. "What are you planning to do?"

"I must get my gun, that's for damn sure," he grumbled, brushing her hair back from her eyes. "Then I'll make several mad dashes to get us some comforts for the night."

"Then we are staying? Even though it might be dangerous?"

Wesley laughed. "Darling, my life has become one of danger ever since the first gunshot at Fort Sumter. I've learned to live with it. If you are to be my companion, so must you."

"I understand, Wesley," she gulped, looking quickly around her once again, calculating just how much danger they might be in. Would she even be able to close her eyes when the time arrived to sleep? She doubted it. She melted into Wesley's arms as he wrapped them around her.

"I'll only be a minute, Serena," he said thickly. "I even think that I should check the outbuilding, though, just in case. And then if I find it suitable, I shall take the horses in out of the rain."

"Shouldn't you hide the carriage?"

"If there is room," he said, then moved briskly from the room, leaving Serena shuddering both from the cold and fear.

She knew what had to be done. She had to make some space in the debris for her and Wesley to try and have some comfort for the night. She only hoped that Wesley would think it safe enough to start a fire on the grate. They had refrained from having too many fires once they had entered Tennessee. They had managed to live by eating everything cold, mainly the salt pork that Serena had managed to steal from the Calvert kitchen, along with wild, spring berries they had found along the sides of the road.

Serena's stomach ached for some regular food. She had begun to wonder if that day would even arrive. She turned on her heel as Wesley rushed back into the room. Her eyes widened when she saw something unfamiliar in his two outstretched hands.

"I found a cellar out back," he boomed. "Damned if I can figure out how the soldiers overlooked the likes of these." He handed Serena two jars, one filled with canned peaches and the other with green beans.

"Wesley, we shall have a feast," she laughed. Then she eyed the ashes on the hearth. "But do you think we might have a fire to heat the beans? Just think how marvelous it would be to have warm food in our stomachs for a change." She eyed a stray coffeepot that sat at the edge of the hearth. "And even warm coffee? Don't you think? Just this one night?" They hadn't shared such luxury since that night in the cave. . . .

Wesley's brow furrowed as he ran his fingers through

his hair. "You do know the dangers," he said, looking toward the door.

"Please?" Serena said, going to him, begging with her eyes. "We haven't seen any signs of life for miles and miles. Surely there won't be anyone out, especially now that the storm is so fierce."

"Well, all right," he said, moving toward the door. He turned and eyed her warily. "But you know that I don't fully approve. We could be asking for trouble before the night is out."

"I don't think so," Serena said, sighing heavily. "I still believe the storm will keep all away."

Wesley took one step forward. "Did it keep us away, Serena?"

Serena's pulsebeat raced. "No. . . . It is what actually attracted us to this house, isn't it, Wesley?" she murmured, placing the two jars of food on the table top. But then she said more stubbornly. "But I still want a fire. Darn it, Wesley, I'm cold as hell."

He laughed gruffly and went to pull her into his arms. "Hey, there, darling," he said. "Such language coming from between such beautiful lips? Am I teaching you things besides making love?"

She giggled and lifted her lips to his, suddenly feeling contented, even though it was freezing cold and her clothes hung in wet shreds from around her. "I do love you so, Wesley," she said.

"And I you," he said, kissing the tip of her nose. "But for now, we must think of securing ourselves for the night. Let me continue to get things settled, then we can chat, even into the wee hours of the night, if you wish."

"I believe I will want to do something besides chat," she said with a wicked glint in her eyes, shaking her head, pushing her hair back from her face.

He patted her on her behind and then moved away from her. Serena moved quickly around the room, gathering pieces of furniture that were small enough to break apart for the fire. Her thoughts were with the family who had at one time lived here. A trace of guilt for what she was doing to their possessions made her hesitate for a moment, then she shrugged, knowing that all was lost to this family anyway, no matter where they were at this moment. She went on her way until she had a roaring fire blazing on the grate.

Turning her back to the fire, she watched as Wesley brought the last of their things into the house and began to unbutton his shirt. "I'll place this across the window," he said. "Though the smoke from the chimney alone could attract passersby, it still is best that we keep as much light from escaping the window and door as possible."

Serena went to the door and tugged and pulled on it until she had it at least leaning against the entranceway. She then moved back to the fire and held her hands over it. "It's kind of fun, Wesley," she said, turning her smiling face to him. "And won't it be fun, having a place of our very own once we're married?" She tensed when she saw traces of shadows fall across his face. Had the word "marriage" been the cause? She suddenly realized that the word hadn't been mentioned, not even once, on this trip. Not even since the night she had helped remove him from the jail. A sense of foreboding suddenly chilled her. Wasn't he planning . . . to . . . marry her? Was she being a fool even hoping for it? But he had spoken of it while still on his back in the hospital. Then she thought hard. He had, hadn't he?

She turned her eyes back to the fire, feeling suddenly not so sure of herself. She felt as though he was a stranger as he still stood there in silence, not yet having answered her. She forced a nervous laugh as she swung around and headed for the table, sorting through all that Wesley had placed on it. "Well, if we're going to get comfortable for the night, I must first get things warming over the fire," she said. "Then I feel I must change from these wet things." She eyed him warily. He still hadn't spoken. He had moved to the fire and was warming his hands over the heat.

"Honey, you've suddenly gotten so quiet," Serena said, moving to his side, wrapping her arms around his waist, admiring his bare chest and the way the muscles rippled.

"I still don't feel comfortable here," he said thickly. "I feel something is amiss here. Don't you feel it?" he said further, turning his face quickly to hers.

Yes, she felt something amiss all right. But she would not speak of it. "You're just imagining things," she said, flipping her skirt around, moving back to the table. She poured some coffee into the coffeepot, then some water from their dwindling water supply, and hurried and placed the pot over the fire that had turned to orange coals.

"Well, Serena, I have one thing to say to that," he grumbled, moving to pull on one of the dry shirts that Serena had managed to steal from the hospital quarters. "I won't be able to relax this night. Not for even one minute. And anything that you might hear that I don't happen to, you alert me to it right away. Do you hear?"

"You don't have to worry about that," she laughed lightly, straining to remove the lids from the two jars.

She squeezed and twisted until her hands stung. She sighed with relief when he came to her side and with two twists had them opened.

"Serena, I think before you do anything else, you had best change into some dry clothes," he said, letting his eyes travel over her. "We sure don't need you coming down with a cold. There are many more nights ahead of sleeping beneath the moon."

She held her limp skirt out away from her then reached behind and unbuttoned it and let it fall to the floor. "I know you're right," she said, moving to her travel bag which had luckily remained untouched by the rain. She bent and began to scramble through it, but stopped when Wesley moved up behind her and leaned his body into hers.

"Vixen, you should never bend over so, revealing the curves of your buttocks to these wandering eyes," he laughed. He swung her around, then consumed her lips with his.

Feeling the warmth seize her brain, she leaned her body into his and wrapped her arms around his neck, moaning lightly as his tongue sought entrance into her mouth. Through her thin undergarment, she could feel the hardness of his manhood and began to move her body in seductive circles, teasing him into an almost tormented madness. He pulled his lips away and gazed heavy-lidded toward her. "Darling, I must have you. Now," he whispered.

He unbuttoned her blouse and began to explore inside it, cupping a breast, but a swift movement of noise behind them made him turn with a start, then quickly withdraw from his moment of passion when he discovered that two men had managed to move the door aside with such ease, only faint noises had been heard above the passionate whisperings and kisses.

"Well, what have we here?" one man chuckled, pointing the barrel of a Springfield rifle toward Wesley and Serena. His wide-set eyes were dancing and his buck-teeth gleamed beneath the light of the one kerosene lamp that had been placed on the one lone table.

"Looks like we've disturbed a little love nest," the other said, leering, as he held his rifle also poised, with hands trembling and his dark eyes smoldering with hungry lust.

Serena's hands went to her mouth as she gasped. Wesley's gaze moved from the men to his own rifle that was only a few feet away, hidden partially from the intruder's sight behind the stack of bedrolls and blankets that Wesley nor Serena had yet had time to get readied for their night of rest.

"What the hell do you two want?" Wesley grumbled, standing his ground. He knew that to move could mean that one bullet fired at this close range would mean a quick death. He had to act confident, though. He couldn't for one minute act alarmed, though the color of their breeches was enough to cause his heart to racing. The navy blue was enough proof as to where these two men's loyalties lay. But why weren't they with a regiment if they were indeed loyal? Wesley looked toward the door, listening intensely. There weren't any noises of other horses advancing toward the house, and there wasn't the loud garble of conversation as there would have been if these two men hadn't been traveling alone.

Smiling to himself, Wesley now knew why these two were alone. By the filth of their matching blue shirts and the leanness of their flesh, it was apparent that they had possibly been traveling alone for some time now. They were deserters. There was every indication of it. And they were headed north, as Wesley and Serena were headed south.

"What do we want?" the bucktoothed man said, spatting onto the floor beside him. His wide set eyes moved quickly around him and his thin lips widened in a grin. "Everything there is to get, mister," he added, laughing throatily. His gaze stopped at Serena and traveled her figure up and down, then up again. "Especially what she was offerin' to you," he said further, motioning with the barrel of his gun.

Serena was suddenly aware of her half-nudity. She tried to cover herself where her blouse gaped open in front and she crossed her legs, hoping this to keep their eyes from seeing too much of what lay beneath the thinness of her lower undergarments. Her gaze moved to Wesley, wondering what he could do. Then her gaze moved to their own gun, knowing that for this moment, it had to stay hidden. She swallowed hard, so wishing her heart would stop pounding at such a fast rate of speed.

"Just try," Wesley sneered, taking a step forward. In one swift movement, the butt of the dark-eyed man's gun snapped across Wesley's head, causing Wesley to fall backwards in a heap atop the stack of bedrolls and bedding.

Serena screamed and attempted to move toward Wesley whose eyes were closed and whose head was bleeding, but she was stopped by the rough, bony hands of the dark-eyed man. He dropped his gun and crushed his mouth against hers as he began moving his hands over her body, causing her to want to wretch. She kicked and clawed at him, but he only tightened his hold.

The bucktoothed man laughed and said, "Want to get your pleasures 'fore gettin' food, eh, Floyd?"

Floyd pulled his mouth from Serena's, leaving a cold wetness on her lips, only to then tear her blouse from her breasts, to circle a now exposed nipple with his tongue. "Yep, Lawrence," he said thickly. "Ain't had such a beautiful wench since leavin' Mattoon."

Serena's eyes widened with alarm. "Did you say Mattoon . . . ?" she gasped, looking from one man to the other, trying to recognize even a little something about them. Were these disgusting men truly from her own town? She felt a bitterness rising into her throat as this Floyd's hands searched lower, touching her between the thighs, probing, hurting her with his fingers through her undergarment.

"Yep. Hometown," Floyd snickered, busying himself at ripping the rest of her clothes from her body.

"My God," she gasped, growing limp as his fingers made contact with the flesh of her abdomen and then even lower. "Please stop," she then begged, squirming, trying her best to be set free. "You are ready to rape a woman from your hometown. I . . . also . . . am from Mattoon," she shouted. "Please let me go. My father. He will find you and kill you, if you don't."

The man who was still holding the gun and enjoying the scene before his eyes suddenly lowered his gun a fraction. "Your name? What might it be?" he said quietly.

"My name is Serena Kassia Calvert," Serena said, panting as Floyd was struggling to get her to the floor. "My father . . . is . . . Doc Calvert. . . ."

"Floyd, that's Doc Calvert's daughter," the bucktoothed man stammered. "I know Doc Calvert. He'll look us up until doomsday if need be if'n she blabs about this to him."

Floyd positioned himself over her as he pushed her atop the rubbish on the floor. "Think about it, Lawrence," he panted, unbuttoning his breeches. "What is she doin' in these parts? Huh?"

"What *are* you doin' here?" Lawrence asked, inching his way toward Serena.

"Never you mind about that," Serena cried. "Please tell this man . . . to . . . stop. . . ." She cringed as she felt his manhood move along her leg, then close to where she was being forced to open up to him. Through a mist of tears, she watched as Lawrence made his way to Floyd, reaching for him.

"God damn it, Floyd," Lawrence shouted. "Get up off'n her. Do you hear?"

When Lawrence grabbed Floyd by the collar and began to jerk, two shots rang out, echoing over and over again in Serena's brain, then she screamed when Floyd's body flinched and then went limp atop her. She screamed over and over again when the heat of his blood began to swirl across her stomach, and when she looked toward Lawrence, she grew silent as she watched him clutch at himself and fall limply to the floor, also in a pool of his own blood.

Serena pushed and squirmed, still screaming, until she saw Wesley bend over her and kick Floyd from atop her and reach for her to rise to his waiting arms.

"God, oh, God, Wesley," she cried, clinging, still hearing the sounds of the shots ringing in her ears. She hadn't even heard the screams of the two men who now lay in silence next to her. But she could still feel the blood on her abdomen and the way it was trickling downward,

214

even mingling with the bright red hairs of her pubic area.

"There, there," Wesley murmured, comforting her as he ran his fingers through her hair, then down her back. "You're safe. Darling, you're safe."

"I've never seen men shot before," she sobbed further. "Wesley, it's so . . . horrible . . ." Then she pulled away from him and reached upward, touching the flesh wound of his scalp. "You're all right," she sighed. "I had thought . . . I had . . . thought . . . you . . ."

"No. I have more than nine lives, don't you know that?" he laughed, then moved away from her, eyeing all around him, knowing that they had to get away from this place but fast. The sound of the gunfire could have attracted anyone within hearing range.

"What are we to do?" Serena said, inching her way from the two bodies. She refused to look at them again. She had seen much blood while assisting her father in the hospital quarters, but she had never been anywhere near where blood had been spilled in such a way as she had just experienced.

"We've got to get out of here," Wesley said, gathering up as much as he could in his arms. "And, Serena, don't put your skirt on."

"What?" she gasped, looking down at the way in which she had been left after the shooting. Blood was fast drying on her flesh . . . and in her pubic hair. She moved quickly to their water supply and began pouring it desperately onto the blood, rubbing frantically until it finally disappeared.

Wesley continued to make his way around the room, filling his arms with travel equipment. "In your travel bag, where you've deposited some of the clothes you brought for me—find yourself a pair of breeches and a shirt and put them on. And hurry. We don't want to stick around here. We don't have a lot of time to mess around," he said.

"Wesley, why—?"

"We are no longer going to be traveling by carriage, Serena," he said flatly. "We are traveling by horseback. And I am no longer going to have to worry about men attacking you. You are going to look like a man. For as long as is needed."

"But, Wesley, I—"

"Get your hair pinned up tightly atop your head. Maybe there will be a hat somewhere here in this rubbish that we can shake the dirt off to use to cover your hair."

"Oh, Wesley," Serena groaned. "Is this truly necessary? And to leave the carriage? To leave it behind will be to have to leave most of our luxuries behind."

"The further south we travel, the more suspicious that carriage will be," he said, moving to her, grasping onto her shoulders. "Now you do as you are told. Pronto."

"Oh, all right," she said sullenly. She searched through the travel bag until she found a pair of breeches that appeared to be a bit smaller, slipped into them, and sighed disgustedly when she held the loose-fitting waistband out away from herself. But with her jaw set firmly, she ripped a piece from her petticoat and tied it around the waist, realizing this was the only way the breeches wouldn't slip from her hips.

Then she put on a loose-fitted shirt. She buttoned its front and searched for a hat, finding one beneath a pile of debris in the far corner. With haste, she hit it across her knee, knocking the dust and filth from it, then forced her hair beneath it, knowing that to take the time to pin it now would be a waste. She had to leave this place as quickly as possible. And when she heard the neighing of the horses right outside the door, she closed her travel bag, secured it in the crook of her left arm, then hurried to the porch. She sighed resolutely when she saw Wesley loading the horses' backs with the bed gear and as much of the supplies as the horses could hold.

"At least it has quit raining, Wesley," she said, looking into the sky, where the dark clouds were being whisked away by a brisk wind.

"But we are once again in search of a place to stay for the night," he said. "Give me the travel bag, then climb on the horse. We must make tracks."

Serena tossed the bag toward him and watched as he secured it behind him, then pulled herself onto the horse, grabbing the reins. She was glad that Wesley had chosen the chestnut mare for her to travel on. It had always been her favorite. It had a more gentle nature than the sleek black mare. Even now, the black mare was snorting and digging at the ground with its front hoof, while the chestnut mare stood, almost poised. "Do you have everything, Wesley?" she asked.

"All that we can take," he said, positioning the Springfield rifle close at hand. "We'll travel for a while, then settle in for the night at the most closed-in area of trees that we can find for shelter."

"Things will still be damp and uncomfortable," she said, flicking the reins as Wesley moved away from her.

"Yes. It will be," he shouted. "But at least we are alive, darling."

"Yes, we are that," she answered, trembling. *But will we be tomorrow, and the day after that, and the day after that . . . ?* she thought to herself.

She gently thrust her knees into the side of the horse

and shouted, "Hah," not wanting to linger too far behind Wesley. She had chosen this way of life—but she had only done so because of him. Had it been a wise choice? Would the next few days reveal the answer to her? She shrugged and traveled onward, holding the reins with one hand and the borrowed hat atop her head with the other. . . .

Chapter Twelve

Serena pulled her horse up next to Wesley's and motioned for him to stop. A full week now on horseback, with only bits and pieces of sleep grabbed whenever shelter could be found, had just begun to take its toll on Serena. She felt bone-weary, and there seemed to be a continuing trembling inside. Fear had begun to be her constant companion. They had come close to being confronted by passing soldiers, but Wesley and she had skillfully fled at the first sound of horses' hoofbeats thundering against the ground in the distance. She leaned forward, shoulders slouched and head bent.

"What is it, darling?" Wesley asked, taking her reins, holding them for her.

"I don't think I can go on, Wesley," she said, licking her parched lips. Not having their own water supply handy at all times, nor a bottle of wine to warm her insides, she continued to thirst for liquid to apply to her cracked lips.

"You must," he said flatly. "You have no choice but to continue. Take a look around you. All that is surrounding us now in this part of Alabama are forests of pine, oak and red cedar. Do you really want to take up housekeeping in such a forsaken land? No. We must move on to Folly Island. Once there, you can sleep for weeks, if you wish."

"But, Wesley, I am so tired and thirsty," she whined. She felt as though she was acting the way Priscilla would act in such circumstances, and not wanting to be compared to someone who had never shown much character, she forced herself to straighten her back and set her jaw firmly. She quickly said, "I'm sorry, Wesley. I know I'm behaving like a child. Let's move onward."

Wesley handed the horse's reins back to her, smiling softly. "That's my girl," he said. He peered into the distance, running his fingers through his dark hair. He could see a clearing up ahead, and knew that shelter was probably near, since in many such clearings he had seen inns. He didn't want to admit that he was just as weary himself. His fatigue surprised him, having spent week upon week with his regiment, hardly ever leaving his horse. But he knew his wound had drained him of much of his strength.

He reached upward and probed his shoulder. Feeling no pain, he smiled, knowing that it had completely healed, and that he could expect to soon be his old self. Then nothing would stop him. He even was dreaming of the day that he could gather together another regiment. Once he checked on his father and Wyndham Hall, he would leave Serena there, then head on out. No man would ever get the chance to shoot or capture him again. He would be faster. He would be bolder.

"Wesley, you look as though in dreamland," Serena said, reaching to touch his cheek. Upon their continuing days and nights of journey, he had failed to shave. He looked like the man she had first met, all stubbly with whiskers. But nothing took away from his handsomeness. Nothing. His dark eyes were a magnet, drawing her to him.

Wesley laughed nervously as he turned his gaze to her. "I was thinking about the future," he said. And now that he was directing his thoughts elsewhere, with her at his side, could he ever leave her once they had reached his beloved island? Even though she looked so tattered and worn in the men's clothes that were twice her size, there was something about the way she could look at him, with the passion in her eyes and the fullness of her lips. He felt the heat in his loins now, even though dangerously stopped in the middle of a raod that could be suddenly swarming with Union cavalrymen.

"Were you thinking about us?" she asked, fluttering her lashes nervously. "About our future, once we reach your beautiful island? About the day we will be wed?"

Shadows fell across Wesley's face as he let his eyelashes fall to cover the doubt in the depth of his eyes. He loved her, but he was filled with renewed doubts. He wasn't sure if he could make her into a southern lady, one that would be acceptable at all functions. He loved her spark, her reckless nature, but somehow, now that he had studied and thought about it, that wouldn't fit into what he might want as a wife. A lover, yes, a mistress he might place in one of his townhouses in Charleston. But not a wife.

And then there was always the reminder of his sister, her . . . oddities. Should he wed? Would it even be fair? What if a child he would bring into the world would be . . . ?

"We'd best be on our way, Serena," he said thickly, thrusting his knees into the side of his horse. "I think we

221

might even entertain the thought of seeking out an inn for the night." He glanced quickly over at her, hoping that she would overlook the fact that he hadn't answered her. As he saw her eyes light up, he knew that he had been wise. But how long would he be able to evade such a question? Damn. He wasn't even sure himself. One minute, he could think of nothing but her and how he would like to have her as his wife. Then he would think of his mother and her acquaintances, of his sister and her . . . ways . . . and feel pinpricks of doubt enter his brain.

The Wyndham name. Ah, how he did want to be the one to carry it on. But even if he decided to do so, would Serena want to be burdened by a child? She didn't appear the type. Yet, all these decisions could be reached once they did reach Folly Island, if, indeed, they did.

"Truly? An inn?" Serena shouted. "Wesley, what made you decide to become so daring?"

"I see the weariness in your eyes, darling," he said, keeping the horse at a slow pace at her side. "Maybe one night on the softness of a feather bed might do you a world of good." His gaze moved upward, at the hat hiding her beautiful hair. "And you might even enjoy washing your hair with real soap and letting it drape across a pillow for a full night."

He could envision himself burrowing his nose in its depth. Ah, how it stirred everything to raging fires inside him just thinking about what the evening could bring, if indeed they could find such an inn. They had passed by many that hadn't been disturbed by the war. But so far, in Alabama, not too many signs of war had been seen. Only an occasional burned farmhouse. But the inns had been kept intact. Wesley had to wonder if it was because the Union officers frequented them themselves, possibly seeking out pleasures of the flesh. Well, he would have to check this out first. If uniformed men were strolling around outside any inn that they might come across, then he and Serena would have to just move onward and sleep once again beneath the trees, while dreaming of finding something suitable the next day.

"It would be heaven," Serena sighed. She gazed around her as they moved on through the trees. It was her first experience of seeing the moss-draped live oak trees. It was as though she was moving beneath fine, green lace. "This countryside is heaven," she quickly added. "It is so beautiful."

"It seems this state has been spared most troubles of war," Wesley said. "Did you know that it's begun to be called 'The Yellowhammer State'?"

"No. Why on earth would it be called such a funny name as that?"

Wesley chuckled. "The nickname originated when a company of Alabama soldiers paraded in fancy uniforms trimmed with brilliant yellow. They reminded people of the birds called flickers or yellowhammers, which have yellow patches under their wings, so they began calling the soldiers Yellowhammers. Then the state picked up the name, as a sort of lightness, something to smile about during these hard times of war."

"You speak of the war with such a longing in your voice, Wesley," she said, seeing his brow furrowed. "Do you miss fighting?"

"I miss the excitement," he exclaimed. "I hate the killing."

"I'm so glad to hear you say that," she sighed. "I would hate to think that the man I love would enjoy shooting a man." Her thoughts went to the two soldiers that they had left in the house while still in Tennessee. These men had even been from her own town. Though they were attacking her, she still felt a deep pity for them and even more so for the families who would never know the truth behind their deaths.

She glanced toward Wesley once again. "Wesley, those men? You know, the two you shot at the house?" she said, feeling a coldness surge through her veins, hating to have to remind him of those two men that he had shot so quickly. But he had had his reasons. . . .

"What about those two bastards?" he grumbled, flicking the reins of his horse, urging it a faster pace.

Serena frowned, then did the same, moving to his side once again. "I was wondering how the family would know of their deaths? You know, they are from my town of Mattoon. I would hate to think of two families there, wondering. . . ."

Wesley's eyes narrowed as he looked quickly toward her. "Why would you even care, Serena? The one was raping you, and you have to know the other one would have done the same, given the chance."

"I was only thinking of their families," she said. "The town of Mattoon is family-oriented. I'm sure they were from a good family. You know how the war changed many men. These were probably two innocent farmer boys before the war started."

He laughed sarcastically. "Yeah. Two farmer boys who were deserting their side and who didn't bat an eye at knocking me in the head and raping my woman," he said. "Sure as hell can't make myself care about their families."

"I would like to know how all these men who have

been killed are identified for family," she persisted. "It has always puzzled me."

"If you need to know, a dog tag of sorts was devised at the first of the war," he said. "A soldier letters his name and address on his handkerchief or on a piece of paper and pins it to his uniform before going into battle. This is how. Now, damn it, will you please talk of something else? I don't like being reminded of my dead comrades—"

Serena quickly silenced his remaining words by shouting, "Wesley, see! Just ahead. It is an inn." In the sudden clearing, a two-storied brick dwelling stood at the side of the road with green ivy decorating its walls. Serena's heart began to pound at such a speed, she had to draw a quick intake of breath.

"By George, it is," Wesley said. He reached for Serena's reins and yanked them hard. "We must approach cautiously," he added. "If there are any signs of soldiers, take off through the brush."

Serena tensed, letting Wesley guide both his and her horse. The set of his jaw was so tight, his lips had narrowed to straight lines beneath his mustache. She then looked ahead and gazed cautiously around the inn, seeing only horses and a lone stagecoach tied to the inn's long, narrow hitching rail.

"Does it look safe, Wesley?" she whispered.

"From here, I'd say yes," he grumbled. "But I guess I'll have to ride ahead and check out its insides. If it looks good, I'll go ahead and get us a room. Thank God, you brought some money with you."

He handed her back her reins. "Now move over to the edge of the road. You mustn't be too conspicuous," he said, laughing a bit. "You look like hell. Did you know that?"

She set her jaw firmly. "Yes. I know that," she hissed. "How else could I look in these darn clothes and without proper baths? I don't only look like hell, but I feel like hell. Wesley, will you just go on ahead and check out that inn? I can take care of myself. Just you be sure and do the same for yourself."

"Yes, ma'am," he laughed, then moved away from her in a cautious trot.

Serena guided her horse into the thick brush at the side of the road. She felt the pounding of her heart, just imagining what it would be like to stretch out on a bed once again. And maybe even some decent food. . . . Oh, how her stomach ached. . . .

Wesley tied his horse's reins to the hitching rail, looking cautiously around him, so far not seeing any uniforms of any color. The only man that he had seen had been dressed in civilian clothes—breeches and a loose cotton shirt. They had exchanged a quick glance before this man had climbed onto his horse and had galloped away in the opposite direction from where Serena sat on horseback, waiting.

Then, with rifle at his side, carrying it as casually as possible, Wesley moved to the entrance of the inn, stopping once again to study the surroundings. The inn was quiet, but filled with comfortable chairs positioned around a roaring fire on the hearth. At one end of the room a group of men stood around a counter, chatting among themselves, then stopped when Wesley moved toward them. Wesley knew that his appearance was cause enough for these silent stares. As Serena, he wasn't the cleanest. He ached for the warm water of a bath as much as she did. And he was anxious to shave at his leisure to remove the itchy whiskers from his face.

"Good evening, gents," he said, moving to the counter, placing his rifle atop it. "Got a room to spare? Mighty tired, these legs."

One moved to stand behind the counter, lifting his gold-framed spectacles to study Wesley even more closely. "Always got rooms," he said. "If you've got the green to pay."

Wesley glanced sideways as the group of men moved away from him, beginning to chat amongst themselves again. "I've got the green all right," he said, tensing inside when he caught a few of the words being exchanged. They were discussing the war—but what had he heard? He turned his gaze back to what he now figured to be the innkeeper. "The war," he said cautiously. "I believe I just heard one of those gentlemen say—"

The innkeeper replaced his spectacles on his long, severe nose and pushed them back into place with the tip of a forefinger. His green eyes and his pudgy face seemed to empty of color as he answered. "Ain't heard, eh?" he said, handing a pen toward Wesley, then shoving a journal toward him.

"Heard what?" Wesley said in a near whisper. Had he actually heard right? *No. It just couldn't be.*

"Where the hell ya been? The war's over," the innkeeper grumbled, reaching inside his front shirt pocket to get some chewing tobacco. He placed a plug into the corner of his mouth and began to chew angrily.

Wesley leaned his full weight against the counter, paling of color. "And by the way you're acting, and from what I heard that gentleman say, the South is not the victor," he said, feeling an ache circling his heart.

"You heard right," the man said, spitting into a spittoon at his side. "Damn bluebellied Yanks won all right."

Wesley's shoulders slumped heavily. Even the wound began to ache, a harsh reminder of how hard he had fought, only to now find that it all had been in vain. All the lives lost, all the miseries of seeing wounded men bleeding to death on battlefields . . . Wesley had seen so many casualties at once, there had been no way to get to them all before their life's blood had drained from them to stain the ground red.

"How? When?" Wesley said, feeling his eyes burning, wanting to cry for the very first time in his life.

"A date I'll never forget," the innkeeper said, spitting once again. "April ninth. Just a few days ago. Lee surrendered to Grant and settled it all in a farmhouse at a little country settlement of Appomattox Court House in Virginia. It's been said that Lee realized that continued fightin' would mean useless sacrifice of life. He wrote Grant, askin' for an interview to arrange surrender terms. Of course, that damn Grant, he swelled up like a balloon, thinkin' he was the only one responsible. Thinks he's a god, he does. Been said, though, that Lee was in full dress uniform with a jewel-studded sword at his side, while Grant was in a private's blouse, unbuttoned at the neck. Shows which one has real class, don't it? Our man Lee. He'll always be the better of the two."

"And since you know so many of the details, might you know the terms of . . . surrender?" Wesley said, almost choking on the word.

"Sure as hell do know," the innkeeper said, spitting once again, tilting an eyebrow. "Grant thought he was bein' generous by offerin' our Confederate soldiers a full

228

day's rations, and then released them on parole," he scoffed. "After what our men went through? And this was all that was left? Bah! But they were allowed to keep their horses, and the officers were able to retain their sidearms. I guess there weren't too much room for complaints when you think about it."

"And Jefferson Davis? What has happened to him?" Wesley asked, tensing even more. Though most hadn't liked Jefferson Davis, Wesley had. When Davis had been inaugurated into the Provisional Presidency of the Confederate States of America, standing for the right of a state to choose and maintain its own institution, Wesley had been all for him. Jefferson Davis had done his best, but it seemed that that hadn't been enough. Wesley had to wonder whether, if more people had backed Jefferson Davis and his way of handling the war, it might have been Grant surrendering his sword to Lee.

"Davis?" the innkeeper said. "Taken prisoner and is now imprisoned at Fort Monroe. Hear tell he's goin' to be tried for treason. Damn shame. Damn shame."

"Oh, God," Wesley said, leaning his head into his hands.

"I just have to ask," the innkeeper said, leaning closer to Wesley. "Why ain't you heard any of this news? Why is it you're just findin' out? Where the hell you been? In a cave, or somethin'?"

Wesley straightened his back and swallowed hard. He knew that it was now safe to reveal his true identity. Even though all was lost, he was free to speak of his identity and his feelings about the war. "I'm Colonel Wesley Alston Wyndham," he said loudly, thrusting his chest out.

Many loud gasps surfaced from all sides. He looked quickly from man to man and saw looks of recognition in their eyes. Had the news continued to travel about his raids? Was he still the hero, as he had been called before his capture? Did being captured make him any less a hero? No—it seemed not. He could see it etched across their faces and in their eyes.

"Well, I'll be damned," the innkeeper said. "Are you *the* Colonel Wesley Alston Wyndham? The colonel who all thought was dead after the attempted raid at Fort Donelson?"

"So it's been rumored I am dead?" he said, furrowing his brow, wondering what his father—his entire family— were going through. If they had thought him dead, surely they had been attempting to have his body returned for a proper burial. He was reminded of Serena's words about the men whom he had shot and left unattended. Guilt sprang through him.

"It's no rumor that you are a hero," the innkeeper said, moving from behind the counter to clasp Wesley's hand. He began to shake it heartily. "It's a damn *fact* that you're a hero. And alive? Congratulations, Colonel Wyndham. Congratulations."

Besides Serena's brief references, Wesley hadn't heard himself referred to as colonel since that night of the last raid. God damn, it felt good! He smiled widely when the men circled him and all began patting him on the back and shaking his hand. Then he remembered Serena. He had to go to her. Tell her the news. Not leave her waiting any longer, knowing that she was still scared as hell, believing she could be captured at any moment by the Union cavalry, and she had even worried about being taken back to Mattoon and tried for treason, herself.

"Tell us about it, Colonel Wyndham," all exclaimed in unison.

"Where've you been?"

"Were you captured?"

"How'd you escape?"

"Were they rough on you?"

"We've heard that the Yankee prisons are hell. Pure hell."

Wesley looked from one man to the other, then laughed heartily. "Listen, gents, I'd love to answer all your questions, but I've got someone waiting for me," he said. "Let me go rescue her from her plight, then I'll tell you more about my adventures after I get her settled in a nice room, with nice soapy water, if you don't mind."

The innkeeper rushed back behind the counter, lifting his pen. "I'll sign you in, colonel," he said eagerly. "You'll get the best room in the house. Next to the bath. Your missus can have all the warm water and suds she wants." He chuckled, winking. "And even a bottle of champagne for the colonel and his missus."

Wesley chuckled, loving the attention, though inside his heart was aching, because of his discovery. But he thought it best to prepare them for Serena's appearance. While speaking of "his missus," he could see sparkles in their eyes, probably expecting someone in a beautiful velveteen dress and matching hat. Yes, he'd best alert them, before she came in.

"Gents, about my female companion . . ." he said, pacing back and forth, kneading his brow. He laughed hoarsely as all eyes followed along with him.

"Yes? What about your missus?" the innkeeper asked.

"Well, uh, you see," Wesley began, still chuckling a bit. "I have recently escaped from enemy lines"—gasps echoed all around him again—"and my female friend helped in my escape. In fact, she is from the North and

231

escaped right along with me."

"Damn it you say," the innkeeper said, grabbing another plug of chewing tobacco from his pocket, thrusting it into the corner of his mouth.

"And she's not that lovely to look at right now," Wesley continued.

"Eh?" the innkeeper said, tilting an eyebrow.

"You see, she's wearing breeches. . . ."

"Breeches . . . ?"

"A lady . . . wearing . . . breeches . . . ?"

"Unbelievable. . . ."

"But once you see her after she changes, you will see, ah, just how lovely a wench I have chosen to travel with me," Wesley shouted over his shoulder as he rushed from the room.

He rode to Serena's side, wondering how to tell her the news. How would she react? She had in a sense deserted the Union cause. Would she be jubilant? Or would she be sad, because he was sad?

"Wesley, what is it?" she said, seeing something different in his eyes. "Was there someone at the inn who troubled you? Tell me. What's the matter?"

"First, let me say, we will be spending the night at the inn," he said. "Come on. We shall return together." He nudged the horse's side with his knees and when Serena moved alongside him, he swallowed hard, then said, "Darling, the war is over. It seems the South lost the battle."

Serena was stunned. "Wesley, are you sure? Who told you?"

"There were men at the inn, speaking of it when I arrived. They told me that Lee surrendered to Grant. It is indeed a truth."

"Then the North *did* win?" she shouted, suddenly realizing she had all along surely felt a true loyalty to the North. If not, why would such news make her feel so jubilant? She felt an inner excitement, thinking about her town of Mattoon, and how they must be celebrating at this moment. Did she truly miss being there? Oh, surely not. She loved Wesley. She wanted to be with him. She would go anywhere he asked. Forever. Always. Then her thoughts moved back to the war.

"And President Lincoln," she sighed. "Maybe the dark circles can be erased from beneath his eyes. He had come to look so haggard. I didn't believe as he did, but I did so admire the man."

"You only do so because he is from your state of Illinois," Wesley grumbled. "If you were from South Carolina and didn't have any reason at all to admire the man, your heart would turn to stone as mine does whenever I think of that man of all legs."

"He is a man of heart," Serena argued.

"Well, whatever," Wesley grumbled. "But the good news that I have carried to you is that I have secured for us the best room in the inn."

"The best?"

"Once the news of the war was revealed to me, I was able to reveal my true identity to the gentlemen at the inn," he said. "Seems I've returned home a hero."

"They knew of you?" Serena gasped.

"They address me as Colonel Wyndham," he boasted, straightening his back. "It sounds mighty good to my ears. Mighty good, even though I shall never use it again while in command of a regiment."

"Well, then, Colonel, my Colonel," Serena said. "Is it truly safe for me to enter into that inn at your side? Me

233

being a girl from the North and all?"

"The only thing that is going to cause eyebrows to tilt, is the way you're dressed," he replied. "But we will soon make a change there."

"But, Wesley, besides these breeches, I only have the flimsiest of cotton dresses in my travel bag. I didn't have room to carry any of my better things. What shall I do? Now that you are a returned hero, you will want someone beautiful at your side."

"Though I didn't see any women present at the inn, I am sure there are some accompanying the men that I've become acquainted with. Surely among these women, I can bribe one of them to make a loan of one of their extra dresses until we arrive at Folly Island, when I can then wire them enough money to pay for their generosity."

Serena felt jealousy creep into her veins. "I don't wish for you to speak to any of these women," she snapped jealously.

"Darling, don't you know how anxious I am for this night, when you will be smelling of jasmine? It is only you I plan to crawl next to, to explore with my mouth and fingers."

"Wesley, please stop," Serena blurted, feeling the stirrings between her thighs. Suddenly everything in life was becoming as it should be. The North had won, she and Wesley no longer had to remain hidden from the world, and they would be sharing a real bed. But she could see something new in Wesley. Was it arrogance?

Wesley moved his horse toward the hitching rail, studying Serena closely. "At least remove that hat," he grumbled. "Even toss it into the bushes. You will no longer have any need of it."

"You act as though you may be ashamed of me,

Wesley Alston Wyndham," she snapped. "If you wish, I shall travel onward without you. Is that your wish?"

"Now, now, Serena. Control that temper of yours," Wesley groaned, jumping from his horse. He secured his horse's reins, then took Serena's reins and secured them, lifting his arms upward, to help her from the horse.

"Well, not even in a dress yet, and you treat me like a true lady," she snapped again. "What next, Wesley?"

"Just you watch your mouth when you enter the inn," he said flatly, lifting his fingers to her hair, removing the pins from its tight confines. "And shake your hair, so that it will fall across your shoulders. Show the men that and that alone will clean take their breaths away."

Serena sighed resolutely, then did as she was asked and then went on into the inn next to Wesley, tilting her chin up into the air, when all turned and stared in silence at her.

Wesley moved to the counter. "Which room?" he asked, glancing quickly around him, amused at the look of shock in each of the men's eyes. But he knew that once Serena had been transformed, then not only their eyes would bug out, but their tongues would hang from their mouths, while their hearts would follow along with her.

"The top of the stairs," the innkeeper said. "The room clear to the end of the hall, on the right. Looks out over a garden of red camelias. The bath? Right next door. I'll have a maidservant prepare the bath." He chuckled gruffly, then added, "And I'll have her add some considerable amount of bubble bath to the water."

Serena's eyes flashed in golden browns as she stomped away from the watchful eyes. She didn't even wait for Wesley to secure the key from the innkeeper. She pulled at her breeches, feeling them slipping a bit at the waist,

235

then like man might, took the steps two at a time, hearing loud gasps surfacing from behind her. Once she was on the landing of the second floor, she tore into a fit of laughter, knowing that she had shocked these gentle Southern gentlemen, but when Wesley joined her on the landing, she could see more than shock in the depths of his dark eyes. She was seeing even more than annoyance.

"Wesley, maybe I shouldn't have done that," she said, smiling nervously. "But those men. They were staring holes through me. And that darn innkeeper! Did you hear that remark about adding more bubble bath to my water? Oh! I just couldn't help myself."

"Serena, that temper of yours. I'm sure that all your life it's gotten you in more trouble than you'd like to think about," he said, thrusting the key into the keyhole. He hurriedly turned the knob and jerked her into the room.

"You are treating me like a daughter . . . not the woman you love," she snapped, eyes flashing even more. "You just release your hold on my arm. I am capable of moving on my own." She squirmed until he released her, then smiled coyly when she saw a grin break out across his face, then his sudden loud laughter caused her to throw her arms around his neck.

"I knew that you couldn't be mad at me," she purred. "I just knew it."

"Vixen," he said thickly, then covered her lips with his, anxiously reaching up beneath her shirt, growing breathless when he found and clasped onto a breast. "Go and ready yourself for that bath, darling," he panted. "And make room for me. I'm going to take one with you."

Serena stepped back a bit, staring wide-eyed at him.

"Wesley, you will take . . . a . . . bath with me?" she gasped. "Why, colonel, what will the guests at this inn think?"

"Who gives a damn? And, besides, who will even know?" He needed to avert his mind from the emptiness he was feeling at the moment over the loss of the war. Yet, he wondered if the numbness of defeat could be replaced even by Serena's talents.

"Then a bath it shall be," she giggled. She tiptoed out into the hallway and opened the bathroom door, sighing with relief when she saw a maidservant busying herself with filling the tub with water.

"I'm Serena Kassia Calvert," Serena said, extending a hand. She giggled when the maidservant turned and grew ashen in color when she saw Serena and the way in which she was dressed.

"Annie. Just call me Annie," the maidservant said, ignoring the extended hand of friendship. "Your bath is ready, ma'am." Annie moved her eyes up and down Serena's full height, then took herself and her two hundred pounds from the room, tidying up the gray locks that had fallen from a tight bun that circled her head.

Serena rushed back to the room, where Wesley stood staring in silence out the back window. She could see sadness in his eyes. She knew that he was thinking about Lee's surrender. She understood. But she knew ways of making him forget. She went to him, placed a forefinger to her mouth, wet it, then placed it inside his ear, causing him to jump. "Darling, the water is ready, if you were truly serious," she whispered, wrapping her arms around his neck, gazing with hunger into his eyes.

"Is there a lock on the bathroom door, Serena?" he murmured, pulling her even closer.

"I do believe so," she giggled.

"Then what are we waiting for?" he said, guiding her by the elbow out into the hall, stopping to look quickly around them. "The coast is clear. Let's go," he whispered, then pushed Serena into the bathroom, laughing softly as he bolted the door.

"This is scandalous, simply scandalous, colonel," Serena said, hurrying out of her things, as he did too. She looked all around her. The bathroom was neat and clean, with a gilt-trimmed mirror over the basin reflecting Wesley's back at Serena as he moved behind her and circled his arms around her waist.

"Is the tub large enough?" she whispered, sighing in ecstasy as his breath warmed her neck.

"For what?" he teased. "One doesn't need much space to wash dirt from one's body."

"But, Wesley, I thought you had other things on your mind," Serena purred, turning, forming the nudity of her body into the nudity of his, already feeling the strength of his desire for her in the hardness of his manhood.

He lifted her up into his arms and eased her down into the water, then climbed in with her, blowing some circling bubbles away from one of her breasts, then leaned his mouth over it and began sucking.

Serena lifted her hair and scooted all but her head beneath the water, teasing Wesley further.

"Do you think you can get away from me like that?" he asked, thrusting his right hand into the water, searching.

"I'd certainly hope not," she whispered.

Wesley's fingers continued to hunt beneath the thick layer of suds and laughed hoarsely when he found the softness between her thighs. With ease, he began caressing her there, causing her to close her eyes and moan with intense pleasure.

"Search me out also, darling," he whispered, moving down over her, kissing her gently on the lips, continuing his assault with his fingers.

"I feel so drunk, Wesley," Serena sighed. "Your fingers. They . . . are . . . magic." She moved her fingers along his abdomen until she found his throbbing hardness, then began to work her fingers over it, smiling almost wickedly when she saw his look of complete rapture.

"I need release. Now," he said, then moved his fingers to guide his hardness into her.

"Wesley," she sighed, now laboring with him, relishing the feel of his manhood slipping so easily inside her, and the way his body moved against her with the softness of the suds lathering even more as they moved faster . . . and faster. . . .

"I cannot wait, Serena," Wesley said, now supporting his body by holding on to each side of the tub, as his body began to tremble along with hers.

"I love you, Wesley," she whispered when through, tracing his face with a forefinger. "Please always love me as much as you do this moment."

"I will, darling," he said, rising, stepping from the tub, brushing clinging suds from his body.

Serena watched him gather his clothes together and step into his breeches. She could tell by his eyes that he had forgotten about the Confederate's loss for the moment of passion, but now that their shared intimacies were over, he was once again dwelling on the failures of the South.

"Wesley—" she began, but he began speaking also.

"Serena, you go ahead and enjoy the bath," he said, securing the buttons on his breeches. "I shall go find you that dress promised, and check into means of travel that will get us to Charleston.

"But what about our horses?"

"The money secured by the sell of the horses will be spent for securing our passage to Charleston. I'm sure it will be by stagecoach. After seeing so many train rails burned and twisted, I'm sure the chances to travel by train are indeed poor."

"When shall we go, Wesley?"

"Tomorrow. After breakfast."

"Maybe tomorrow the burden of the news of the war will be lighter. Surely nothing else will come of the war to upset you so again. It's over. Now maybe life will find some level of sanity."

"Until I get to Folly Island and see that things are all right, I doubt if I will be able to relax. Sometimes when a war is over, even worse problems arise because it *is* over. . . ."

Chapter Thirteen

"Are you all right, darling?" Wesley asked, leaning closer to Serena.

"Fine," she answered quietly. "Just fine."

Wesley began to toy with his mustache, gazing around him at the four other passengers, all of whom were men. The crowded interior of the stagecoach made privacy impossible. Wesley hardly even had room enough to stretch his legs out occasionally before him, much less cross them as he was so wont to do.

His gaze raked over Serena. She had sat so prim and proper since having boarded the coach. And didn't she look the picture of a southern lady in her russet-colored silk dress? He could hardly keep his eyes from staring at her bosom where the pink of her skin showed through many gathers of lace. But he had to frown at the many times he had caught the other men's eyes assessing her with admiration.

When the stagecoach wheels fell in and out of a pothole, Serena tensed and grabbed for the lace-trimmed hat that had been loaned her along with the dress. She clamped her lips together in aggravation. The stagecoach seemed to bounce her around even more severely than when traveling by horseback. And there was the dress she now wore. She hated it and the itchy lace that constantly grated across her skin. She most certainly wouldn't have chosen this dress for herself, if having been given the opportunity to enter a stylish dress emporium to do the choosing.

But anything is better than my own cotton dresses, she thought further to herself. She had months, even years ahead of her to dress beautifully for Wesley.

She glanced his way, to wonder at his handsomeness again in his loaned black waistcoat and tight breeches. But when she caught him staring back at her, she looked quickly away and placed her hands on her lap.

She smiled demurely, realizing that each day carried them closer to Folly Island. She wanted to feel excited about reaching their destination, but just when she would allow herself this pleasant luxury, she would have reason to feel guilty, when another burned-out city would be traveled through. Serena knew that it was sinful to feel happy when so many had lost so much and would never be carefree and joyful again.

Wesley leaned down further and whispered into her ear. "This damn gun," he said. "I should have kept the rifle. I hate wearing a gun at my waist."

"And you still believe a gun is even needed?" she whispered back, nervously smoothing the gathers of her dress.

"I've heard rumors that there are still many who haven't heard of the war's end. The idiots would probably shoot at anything moving."

"I can understand them having not heard," Serena sighed. "We hadn't heard. And even the two men you shot hadn't."

"Try to forget about that, Serena," Wesley grumbled, crossing his arms angrily. "I did what I had to do."

"It's just so sad that news travels so slowly," she said, sighing.

"If Sherman and his men hadn't been so anxious to destroy the telegraph wires all over the South, then everybody would be able to keep up with the news. Even daily."

"I know," Serena said, remembering the ugly sights that they had come across. Since Atlanta and the desolation they had found there, it hadn't seemed to have improved. Atlanta's streets had been almost impassable, being so deluged with debris. Gaunt skeletons of chimneys rose above the blackened devastation, and where so many houses had stood, there had been only beds of cinders remaining.

Serena would never forget the people. Widows and helpless orphans were wandering in poverty and exile, stopping only wherever chance or charity afforded them shelter or food.

Then there were the former slaves wandering empty-eyed from street to street. They were free at last. But free to do what? Most were uneducated. None had ever owned land, and few had ever worked for their own wages. And now that Confederate money was worthless and United States currency almost nonexistent in the South, most of the former owners couldn't even pay freedmen wages if the Negroes did beg to work again.

Also, though land remained, the seeds and agricultural tools had almost disappeared.

Serena knew that times were bad. She only hoped that Wyndham Hall hadn't been as struck badly as what she would never forget witnessing while traveling through

Atlanta and Savannah, Georgia. She knew that now that they had traveled many days and nights, Charleston had to be near. Oh, so very, very near.

She reached and took Wesley's hand, tilting her chin up into the air as she noticed one of the men staring at her outward show of affection for her male companion. She even scooted closer to Wesley, leaning her shoulder into the solid steel of his arm. She was hoping that this night they would be out of this stagecoach and safely at Wyndham Hall.

Oh, darn. She just couldn't quell the excitement building inside her. But then she tensed when she heard a low rumble surface from between Wesley's lips. She followed his gaze and tensed inside, seeing some railroad tracks not far from the road they were traveling on. They were twisted around a tree as though they had been rope. "My God, Wesley," she uttered. "How . . . ?"

"I'm sure in one of the many bonfires set by Sherman," he growled. "You see how they have ruined the South? Do you even see the telegraph poles along this road? Completely destroyed!"

"Maybe there are still some communications to Charleston," she encouraged. "You must remember there are many roads that lead into your city. This one is just a continuation of the one that led from Georgia, where the devastation was the worst that we have yet encountered."

"Do you even know the beauty that was destroyed when Atlanta was taken in such a way? It was a city of mansions and it was the heart of industry. God. How I fear for my city of Charleston."

"Shall we soon be there?" she whispered.

"Darling, I even see signs of its outskirts now," he

said, leaning to look from the window. "And what I see isn't encouraging. I'm afraid it is the same. It will probably be another Atlanta."

All grew silent in the stagecoach as it rumbled along the road, passing many more farmhouses and outbuildings reduced to ashes. The crops had been uprooted and there were signs of more livestock slaughter as carcasses lay buzzing with flies and throwing a stench into the wind that caught at Serena's throat.

Then as the stagecoach entered the city, Wesley's face drained of color. He scooted to the edge of the seat, staring in silence all around him. Naked chimneys and charred ruins met his eyes as each street came into view. Bricks and burned timbers lay everywhere, with only a fugitive flower, or a bit of grass struggling for life among them. The lovely gardens had been trampled, neglected and gone. Charleston was a city of ashes. What the huge fire of 1861 hadn't destroyed, the bombardment of the Union forces had succeeded at completing.

"It's as I feared," Wesley said, reaching for the handle of the door as the stagecoach pulled to a stop, where at one time a railroad station had stood. Only a pile of brick and rubble now lay in its place.

Wesley stepped on from the stagecoach and lifted his arms to Serena, then helped her out onto the street. They hadn't carried many belongings with them. What they hadn't sold at the inn, they had stuffed inside the one lone travel bag. Wesley pulled it from the top of the stagecoach and began walking, as though blind, through the charred remains along the walkway.

"Wesley, I am so sorry," Serena said, going quickly to his side. "So very, very sorry."

"We've got to find a carriage that will take us to the

Kiawah Landing, where a ferry usually accommodates my comings and goings from Folly Island."

"What if it isn't there any longer, Wesley? What if the ferry was destroyed as most everything in this town was?"

Wesley frowned darkly and looked around him at the people on the street. Hardly anyone was on horseback and few carriages made their way through small paths in the street. Everyone here appeared to have been made homeless by the war. Their clothes were hanging in blackened shreds from around them. There were more Negroes than whites, and Wesley could see the bitterness etched across the white people's faces when a Negro would walk next to them, as though an equal.

It will never work, Wesley thought bitterly. *Never*.

A slow ache moved through him. His homecoming. He had never thought it could be like this. He had left in glory with never that first doubt of returning home the victor. Now he knew that he was lucky even to be one of those returning, humble though it made him to think of those who hadn't. Suddenly pride was a word far removed from him.

"We must keep searching until we can find a carriage," he finally said, slinging the travel bag across his shoulder, carrying it by a rope tied to it.

Serena lifted the skirt of her dress, stepping through the debris, feeling strangely detached from all of this. It wasn't her hometown. She knew that she wasn't filled with bitterness as Wesley had to be. But what she had dreamed of going to had suddenly become a nightmare. When she had thought of Charleston . . . of Folly Island . . . she had tried to not let herself even connect it with the war. But now that she had witnessed Charleston, she had to wonder what they would find once they set foot on Wesley's beloved estate.

"This city of Charleston is acres of pitiful and voiceless barrenness," Wesley shouted, raising his free hand in despair. Then he remembered his other places of residence beside Wyndham Hall. Seeing so much desolation and being in a state of semishock had caused him to push his townhouses from his mind. He hurried his pace and rushed from street to street, now seeing houses that had been spared the ravages of the war, left standing, vacant.

He looked anxiously toward the ocean front, where his townhouses sat side by side, overlooking what used to be a bay of ships coming and going at all hours of the day and night. Hopefully his townhouses had been spared. But he doubted it. He couldn't be that lucky.

"Wesley," Serena pleaded, panting. "I can hardly keep up with you. Where on earth are you going at such a pace?"

"My townhouses," he said. He felt the pulsebeat quicken in his throat when he spied the wrought-ironwork that fenced in his two buildings, one of which had always served as a place to rendezvous with women once he had discovered his fondness for a female's flesh at the age of seventeen.

His father, being a free spirit himself, had given Wesley the key and had encouraged him to use it, but to choose the women with discretion, not wanting him to bring an unmentionable disease home to spread among the Wyndhams.

Wesley smiled to himself, remembering so many delicious skins that had beat against his own during moments of heated passion. It had been fun. But now that he had Serena, surely these pastimes of his youth would be forgotten.

He opened the gate that led to his favorite of the two-storied townhouses. "Serena, it seems I've been spared," he shouted. "My townhouses still stand." His gaze raked over them both, seeing some bricks missing at the corners and a few broken panes of glass. But the ironwork had been left untouched and the balconies that led from the doors of the second floors showed only bits and pieces of cement missing from their undersides.

He went to the door and tried the knob and then almost fell inside when the door moved quickly open, revealing a small Negro boy, whose eyes were wide with fear and wonder. "Well, I'll be damned," Wesley said, then looked on past the boy and grew sick inside when he saw the ruins of the interior of his dwelling. The furniture had been treated as the furniture that he and Serena had come across in that house in Tennessee. It had been broken up and used as firewood. And as he pushed his way on into the living room, his heart ached when he saw the velveteen curtains that had at one time hung so clean and majestic, now hanging in twisted shreds.

"What's happened?" he murmured, kneading his brow. Then he watched as four more Negroes, both male and female, inched their way into the room. "Why are you all here?" he blurted, paling even more.

"Nowheres else to go," the oldest of the five said, twisting her long, jet black pigtail between her fingers. Wesley could guess that her age would be probably fifteen.

"Where is your family?" Wesley said.

"Gone," the same girl spoke in a sullen voice that showed no pity, and even less caring.

"Where to, by God?" Wesley stormed, growing more angry. His house . . . his belongings . . . and *slaves* living in it, ruining it?

"Don' rightly know," the girl said, lowering her heavy dark eyes.

"Well, you get the hell out," Wesley stormed. "Now. This is my place of residence, and by God, I plan to make it livable again."

"Where does we go, massa?" the girl said, blinking her eyes nervously at him as a child of about four moved to her side and began to cling to her faded, limp cotton skirt, his lip quivering and his eyes lowered.

Serena moved to Wesley's side and took his hand. "Wesley, don't push them out just yet," she whispered. "Where would they go? They've probably been abandoned. They were probably children of slaves, and the older, even a slave herself. Let's leave them be for now, then return later and maybe find someplace for them. Please?"

"Serena, this is my townhouse," he stormed, swinging his arm around him, dying a slow death inside once again as he saw the walls that had been marked on and even scraped of wallpaper and paint.

"Wesley, your first interest now should lie with Folly Island. Your father. Your family. Let's come back later. Please?"

Wesley knew that she was right. And the large eyes of this young girl would always haunt him if he threw her out into the charred streets of Charleston. "Well, all right. But only until I return. Do you hear that, young lady?"

"Yes, massa," she said, even more sullenly, lowering her eyes humbly.

Wesley hit his brow with the palm of his hand and hurried from the house. "God. What next?" he grumbled, stopping to look at his other townhouse. His eyes wavered a bit when the thought of what he might discover inside it made him choose to not enter. It would probably be the same, maybe even worse. Instead, he walked through the gate and closed it behind him as Serena moved to his side.

"You did the right thing, Wesley," Serena purred, taking his arm, clinging.

"I don't want to even discuss it," he said, looking up and down the street. His eyes widened when he caught sight of a horse and carriage moving along where there was less debris. He grabbed Serena's hand and began to run and when he caught up with the carriage, motioned for the lone driver to stop. His heart dropped when he saw that it was also a Negro. Where were most of the whites? Would they return if they had chosen to flee?

Wesley's mouth flew open in rage when the carriage pulled away from him, after the Negro occupant, a man with graying hair, huge bloodshot eyes and rumpled clothes, had stared openly at him for a moment and then had broken into song as the carriage rolled on.

Wesley listened, glancing quickly at Serena as she stood panting at his side. "What's he singing?" she asked, brushing some loose curls from her eyes, repositioning her hat.

"Damned if I know," Wesley said, listening still. . . .

The Negro's voice carried after him as his carriage moved around the street corner, still singing, over and over again:

"De massa run? Ha, ha!
De darkey stay? Ho, ho!

250

It mus' be now de kingdom comin',
An' de year ob Jubilo!''

"He sounds happy as hell that the Negroes have nearly taken over this city," Wesley growled. Then when another horse, and a much smaller, scuffed-up buggy moved beside him, Wesley stopped in front of it and swore to let it run over him if it didn't stop and listen to what he had to say.

He breathed a sigh of relief when he found that this buggy was occupied by a white man. "I'm needing a lift to Kiawah Landing," Wesley shouted, wiping his brow free of nervous perspiration. He looked the man over carefully, seeing remnants of clothes that had at one time been fine. The white lace of this man's shirt lay ripped at its edges where it gaped open at his throat and his black breeches had a satin stripe along each leg's edge. His face was heavily lined and his head balding, and in the seat of the buggy next to him, he had placed a small bundle of what had probably been the only valuables saved after the demolition of the city.

"Your name?" the man said flatly, cautiously looking from Serena, then back to Wesley.

"Colonel Wesley Alston Wyndham," Wesley said, putting emphasis on the Colonel, and knowing that all who lived in Charleston were well-acquainted with the name Wyndham.

The man's face lightened with recognition. "Young Wyndham?" he shouted, reaching a hand in friendship. "You're home? I'd heard tales that you'd been killed. It's so good to see ya, lad."

"And your name, sir?" Wesley asked, shaking the man's bony hand anxiously.

"Charles Teague," the man said, then looked toward

Serena, frowning a bit.

Wesley pulled Serena to his side, seeing the wonder in Charles's eyes. Wesley knew that Charles had to be wondering at Serena's and his own attire, clean and stylish, while all else moving along the streets looked no better than beggars.

"And this is Serena Kassia Calvert," Wesley then said cautiously. "She aided in my escape from the North." He immediately knew that he shouldn't have revealed such a truth to a southern gentleman. It wasn't the time to introduce a northern lady to anyone in the South, no matter if she *had* risked her neck to rescue *the* Colonel Wyndham.

Charles ignored her. "Hop in. I'll be glad to take you to Kiawah Landing," he said. "But I'm not so sure it isn't in charred ruins like most everything in Charleston that was made of wood."

"Hope the ferry is working," Wesley said, helping Serena onto the buggy. "Otherwise I don't know how I could make it to Folly Island. And with father not knowing I'm coming, he sure won't have a johnboat waiting."

"Haven't seen your father for several years now," Charles said. "Too much on my mind to be running to Folly Island. Sure hope all fared there better than here in the city."

"Yeah. Me too," Wesley sighed heavily.

Charles slapped the horse with the reins. "Sure was chuckling this morning about the news that finally reached us here in the Carolinas," he said.

Wesley leaned forward. "News? What news? I'm not sure if I'm ready to hear anymore news. The last bit of news that was handed my way was about the bluebellied

Yankees succeeding in this war."

"You haven't heard of Lincoln's assassination?" Charles asked, wide-eyed.

Serena's heart thundered wildly and her stomach lurched. "What . . . did . . . you say?" she gasped, throwing her hands to her throat.

"Thought you'd have such a reaction, you being from the North," Charles grumbled, looking Serena's way with a deeply furrowed brow.

Wesley smiled a bit nervously. But he couldn't let Serena see how jubilant this news could truly make him. But why couldn't it have even happened sooner? Then the power behind the Union would have been quickly nipped in the bud. "So Lincoln was assassinated?" he asked, glancing sideways at Serena who had begun to sob at his side. It was the first time that he had ever seen her cry. But he knew why. She had spoken so highly of Lincoln. Yes, he could understand her feelings. But he just couldn't share them with her. "When? Who did us the favor?" he added, then tensed and grew silent when he felt Serena grab his hand and squeeze it.

"Some fellow called John Wilkes Booth. Seems Lincoln was attending a function at Ford's Theater in Washington. This Booth fellow managed to get past the guards and just one shot behind the president's ear was all that was required. The next day, Lincoln was pronounced dead to the country."

"How horrible," Serena said, shuddering. It was as though she had heard the news of a relative's passing, she had admired Lincoln so. "I can't believe it. Lincoln was . . . so . . . good."

"That isn't something you'd best speak of while here in the South, Serena," Wesley said softly, yet placing his

253

arm around her shoulders, trying to comfort her. "You have to know that the feelings in these parts are completely against Lincoln. Please refrain from showing such feelings or we will have trouble on our hands." He glanced over at Charles and saw just how correct this assumption was. Charles's face had become streaked red with apparent anger.

"Ma'am," Charles said gruffly. "Maybe you'd best move back up North so you can stand along the railways to greet this dead Yankee's body. Seems that's what's happening. His body is being taken back to Springfield, Illinois, where he should have stayed in the first place instead of taking over the responsibility of the Presidency."

Serena's heart was full of so much at this moment. The mere mention of Springfield was making her homesick, and she so ached to get a glimpse of Lincoln's casket as he returned home, since she had seen him the day he had left. She almost choked as she tried to stifle her tears. She had always been strong. She had to be even more so now. She was among strangers. Even Wesley seemed as a stranger at times.

"And what has happened to Booth?" Wesley prodded. "Given a medal by the Confederacy?" he said further, chuckling, and remembering Serena, he felt as though he ought to bite his tongue.

"Says he's being hunted down. I hope he gets away. Hate to see a man cut down in his prime like Lincoln, but he just would've gone on and on causing hardships for us here in the South. I know it. Now it's up to President Johnson to make things right for us. Let's pray that he has the know-how."

Serena was glad when the buggy came to a halt next to

a lagoon veiled in Spanish moss dipping into the water's edge. Wesley helped her from the buggy and began moving around, frantic.

"You were right, Charles," he shouted, gesturing with his hands, dropping the travel bag to the ground. "Nothing left. Not even burned rubble. When they decided to do away with the ferry, they took care of the whole damn mess, landing, stakes and all."

"Then how shall we get across?" Serena asked, going to his side. She looked around in wonder. It was a lovely scene, so tranquil. She was so relieved to have moved away from the city and its ugliness to the peaceful atmosphere that now lay around her. Cattails lined the water's edge, pushing upward, through the green marsh grasses. A brown pelican splashed along the water in front of her, ahead of the snout of the sudden appearance of an alligator. Serena grabbed at Wesley's arm, suddenly feeling that this area was not all that tranquil after all. She looked into the distance and could see a larger body of water and knew her geography well enough to know that she was looking at the vastness of the Atlantic Ocean. Ah, it was so blue, a thing of beauty, but so restless. . . .

Wesley moved on away from her, searching in the tall weeds. "There has to be a johnboat or a canoe here somewhere," he grumbled.

"Should I wait and maybe take you back to the city with me?" Charles asked, scratching his bald head.

"What's in the city?" Wesley asked, swinging around, glaring. "I'd best risk what I'd have here for the night than what the night brings to the streets of Charleston."

"Just thought I'd ask," Charles asked, flicking the reins, speaking a soft command to the horse. "You take care, Colonel Wyndham and give your father my best regards," he added, saluting clumsily, then drove off, leaving Serena and Wesley searching together for what they might find in the marsh grasses. Serena, though, couldn't keep her eyes off the large, bulgy eyes of the alligator that kept moving, as though on wheels, along the water's edge.

"If we do find a boat, will the alligator attack us once we're out in the water, Wesley?" she asked, shivering.

Wesley laughed. "If the truth be known, he's as scared of us as we are of him," he said, slapping his hands noisily together, watching the alligator make one wide dip downward to the bottom of the lagoon. He strolled away, laughing, then let out a shout of triumph when he began to tug and pull on something that he had found beneath the thick palms of a dwarf palmetto tree. "A johnboat and oars!" he shouted. "We will make it to Folly Island after all."

He dragged the boat along the edge of the water to where the water was more clear and more accessible for a boat's entrance. "Come on, darling, climb aboard," he urged, now tossing their travel bag into it.

"Are you sure there is no leak in it?" she asked, stepping cautiously into it.

"Serena, where has your daring nature gone? Has this trip stripped you of your finest quality? The girl I first met wouldn't have feared a small hole in the bottom of a boat."

Serena gasped, searching around beneath her feet. "Then there are holes in this horrid boat?" She sat down in the boat, clinging to the sides. She was glad that it wasn't nightfall. The sun's rays were seeping in through the thick vegetation above her. If the boat wouldn't make it, at least she wouldn't be thrown into the water. But still, there were the horrid alligators. She knew that if there was one, there probably would be many more.

She tensed when she saw Wesley pull his pearl-handled pistol from beneath his coat and place it on his lap. "And why the gun on your lap, Wesley?" she asked, tensing her back muscles even more.

He began to move the oars in unison, each stroke a strain since he had been away from the water so long. "You never know who might be lurking at the edges of the lagoon," he panted. "I don't plan to let anyone surprise us. Who knows? There may still be a bluebellied Yank thinking the war is still raging."

Serena's eyes grew wide and she sat in silence, continuing to watch all around her, while Wesley put his muscle into the oaring of the boat, now and then feeling his wound as pains would shoot through his shoulder. But he just gritted his teeth and continued to heave and pull, growing more worried as the boat moved closer to the shore. He just knew what would await him. He knew that Folly Island was just too close to Fort Sumter for the Yankees not to have taken full advantage of it. He knew that Wyndham Hall, and the way it sat back amid the hanging Spanish moss, would be a perfect place to take refuge. He knew that was the reason the Kiawah Ferry Landing had been destroyed. The Yankees had destroyed all visible means by which to reach Folly Island.

Serena's heart skipped a beat when she caught her first glimpse of the majestic mansion. If not for the grown up marsh grasses, the house would appear to not have been disturbed by the ravages of the Civil War. The three-story mansion seemed to be emerging from the forest like a tall magnolia. Serena was hoping that the insides of the mansion weren't the color of the bright red seeds of the magnolia, having shown that it had known bloodshed and death. . . .

"There it is," Wesley said beneath his breath. "Home. God, it's home." His heart ached when he saw how badly the grounds had been neglected, but the house itself was the most important thing to be concerned about. He had expected the fields to be in ruins. He knew that once the Wyndham slaves had been introduced to freedom, they wouldn't be able *but* to take advantage of it, to get a taste of this thing that up to this point in their lives, had belonged only to the white race.

"It doesn't appear to have been damaged, Wesley," Serena said, straightening her back. "In fact, I think it is breathtakingly beautiful. Just look at the way the Spanish moss drapes over the house. Like a sheer netting of green. Ah, Wesley, I cannot wait to see the inside of your house. I bet it will just take my breath away."

"If Father sees our boat approaching, he will soon be on his way to bid us welcome," he said, feeling almost breathless now from the excitement of being so close to the moment when he could clasp his arms around his father. During the war, he had dreamed of this. Though Wesley had been daring and had even come close to death many times, he was sentimental about his family. That had always been the way of the South. He had often wondered about Serena and how she had deserted her northern family so easily. Would she one day desert him as well? Was this another reason he chose to evade the subject of marriage?

"I don't see anyone, Wesley," Serena said, peering even more intensely toward the house. She wondered if he had noticed how the shutters were pulled closed on all the many windows of the house. If his family was present in the mansion, why would they have these shutters closed before nightfall? Wouldn't it be a waste of kerosene for the many lamps that would be needed to light such a house?

"The paddles of the boat move silently, Serena," Wesley said, struggling even harder to move toward the shore. He had seen the closed shutters. There suddenly was a feeling of doom lowering over him. The house was too quiet. Everything on the island was too quiet. All that could be heard were the birdsongs and the splash of the fish as they moved away from the advance of the boat.

Wesley gazed toward Serena and saw how she was studying the mansion. His gaze also moved back to the house, as he let memories travel through his mind, as through a picture book being flipped quickly from page to page. He could remember the many evenings spent as a child on the wide porch that was supported by brick arches on the main floor. It faced the ocean to the south, whence came the sea breezes that cooled the evenings from early spring to late fall. Ah, how he had loved to romp back and forth along that porch, pretending even then that he was a soldier.

Then on the north, facing the wide vista of the Kiawah River marshes, was the formal portico that ran the full width of the entrance hall, where Wesley had watched as the women would move gracefully from carriages in their wide-hooped ruffled dresses into the house. From his vantage point at his bedroom window, he had enjoyed the view of these ladies' bosoms, and how each seemed to differ, from one lady to the next. It had become as sort of a game with him to remember which bosom matched which face when he would arrive at the sitting room where all had been asked to tea. Even now, he could put faces to bosoms. . . .

He had grown up at Wyndham Hall, and he had always hoped to have the opportunity to raise his own children there. He loved the house and its two main floors, and its garret where he had hidden many times as a child when his father threatened to give him the lashing of his life for whatever prank he had been accused of.

Would he one day have a son who would choose the garret for his hiding place? He *did* want children. Oh, God, he *did* want children!

One more stroke and he felt the boat hit land. "Serena, you stay put while I secure the boat, then be careful as you step out. There's slippery moss at the bottom of the boat that could cause you to fall," he urged, slipping his gun back inside the waist of his breeches. He then jumped from the boat and pulled it, along with her, onto the land, then wiped his brow and waited for her to follow.

"My eagerness to see your family has been over-shadowed by Lincoln's death," she said, lifting the skirt of her dress, then stepping onto the sandy shore.

"I know," Wesley murmured. He turned and looked toward the house, hoping that he wouldn't have any more bad news.

He held a hand toward Serena, and together they began to make their way through the knee-high marsh grasses.

"I don't like it one damn bit," Wesley grumbled, slowing his pace. "Father should have known of our landing by now. He was always observant of the comings and goings from this land. I fear that he may be ill. Let's make haste, Serena."

What had at one time been gardens were now weeds, but the tall ailanthus bushes, with their pinnate leaves and ill-scented greenish flowers still surrounded the house. They had been planted many generations ago because it was said that the ailanthus bush was able to dispel tempers and torpors of the dreaded malaria fever.

In the distance, Wesley could see the ruined fields that had at one time grown indigo, then later cotton and rice. But as the outbuildings that dotted the land, all had been left to ruin. Wesley was growing ill, seeing his worst fears becoming a reality.

Then Wesley saw something else . . . something that had been added to this island. There was a difference in the way the land lay in the square of the private family cemetery plot alongside the far back corner of the house. There was an added mound and a makeshift tombstone made of a jagged rock. Something grabbed at his heart as he hurried his pace and moved inside the decorative iron fencing that enclosed the graves of the Wyndham ancestors.

"Wesley, what is it?" Serena asked, moving to his side, seeing how ashen his face had become.

Wesley fell to his knees and buried his face in his hands after having discovered the writing on the stone. "God," he whimpered. "No. Not Father. *No!*"

Serena felt a numbness as she read the name. It read:

Carvell Chatwin Wyndham
Died
August 1863

"Oh, Wesley," she said, stooping beside him, placing her arms around his shoulders. "Darling, oh, darling." He leaned into her embrace and she held him there, cooing to him as though she were the mother, and he the

261

child. But when she heard something from somewhere behind her, she turned her head with a start and saw a massive, dark-eyed Negro approaching.

Serena screamed and clasped Wesley's hand.

"Massa Wesley," this Negro exclaimed in a deep southern drawl, stopping, bowing his head in humility as Wesley rose and moved quickly toward him.

Wesley was relieved to finally see a familiar face. His overseer Tobias had been one to have apparently remained faithful to the Wyndham plantation. "Tobias, it's so good to see you," Wesley said thickly, embracing the Negro, standing face to face, shoulder to shoulder.

"Massa Wesley, I thought you be dead fo' sho," Tobias said, eyeing Wesley with deep affection, making his eyes soften a bit. "But I've been watchin'. Day an' night. Just hopin' you'd come back in one piece."

Wesley released his hold on Tobias and looked toward his father's grave once again. "My father, Tobias," he said, kneading his brow nervously. "How?"

"One day dem men with the big guns came," Tobias said, stooping to pluck a tall weed, which he thrust between his teeth to chew on as he spoke. "Massa Carvell, well, he done got mad and ordered dem off this here property. Fo' long, all's I knows is Massa Carvell is shot. All's I can tell you, Massa Wesley. You see, I hightailed it out of here and hid in the low-country marshes until I sees dem big guns all leave the island. But not befo' I gets the chance to sneak yo' valuables from the place."

"You did what?"

"Whilst there were only a few of dem big guns here, befo' Massa Carvell tried to order dem from the island, he asked me to take your valuables to Kiawah Island, back deep into the swampland, where the one tribe of Kiawah Indians remains. To this day, all's I can tell you is that your silver and the jewelry of your mother and sister are there. Safe and sound. Halona gave her word to watch over them."

The familiar name of Halona gave Wesley a twitch in the groin. Even though he hadn't seen her now for four years, he could still feel the magic of the beautiful Indian princess's tongue on his body. Dare he even venture to her hut to rescue the Wyndham belongings? To do so would lead him into a temptation that Serena would never understand.

Then his gaze moved swiftly to the mansion, once again seeing the shuttered windows. "And the rest of my family, Tobias?" he said weakly. "What was their fate?"

"Massa Carvell sent dem away to relatives in Boston," Tobias said, still chewing on the blade of grass. "He succeeded in doin' this befo' de big guns moved onto the island. He had thought de guns would come. We heard the gunfire all de time. Massa Carvell felt he should stay and defend his plantation, and Massa Carvell had hoped to talk the Wyndham slaves into not runnin' away once word reached dem that freedom was theirs, if they wanted it."

Wesley looked toward all the outbuildings. He could see their neglect and emptiness. He knew that it was true that Tobias was the only one left on this corner of the island. And without slaves, how could Wesley ever expect to get the crops planted and the weeds removed? His breathing was coming in shallow whispers as he moved to Serena's side.

"Let's move on into the house," he said. "I know you are tired. And I am exhausted. Both mentally and

263

physically. The war seems to be handing me tragedies. One upon the other."

"I'm truly sorry, Wesley," Serena said, leaning into his embrace as they left Tobias standing alone, all eyes, and made their way up a narrow path made of embedded bricks into the earth, but now seemed to be more grass than brick. "Maybe we can console one another, darling. We have ways," she added softly.

"Not tonight, Serena," he said thickly. "There's too much sadness burdening my mind."

Serena felt something squeezing the life from her heart. This had been the first time ever that Wesley had refused to accept the fact that their bodies could push all unhappiness aside, if only for a moment. Would he be a different person now that he had arrived on his island and at his mansion? Would he cast her aside? Had she even been a . . . fool? She climbed the steps next to him, clinging to his arm, but no longer certain that she would one day be mistress of Wyndham Hall. . . .

Chapter Fourteen

"Serena, since I've now become master of Wyndham Hall, I've many things to attend to today," Wesley said as he took the last stroke with his razor, then splashed aftershave on his face.

"Do you think you should work so soon?" Serena asked, moving toward him in a pale blue silken chemise that Wesley had given her from his mother's belongings. She yawned and stretched. "We only arrived yesterday. Don't you think you should take a day to rest? It's been hard on you, traveling so far so quickly after having been wounded."

Wesley combed his hair in quick strokes, then turned to Serena, frowning as he buttoned his red plaid cotton shirt. A drop of aftershave twinkled back at Serena from the depths of the deep cleft in his chin. "Under ordinary circumstances, the Wyndham fields would be filled with slaves planting our spring crops of cotton," he said, scowling even more. "Serena, do you see any slaves? This land has never before been neglected since the Wyndhams first set foot on this land in the late sixteen hundreds after their long voyage from England."

"Wesley, I understand how distraught you have to be

about all of your recent discoveries," Serena said, going to him, wrapping her arms around his neck, savoring the sweet smell of him and his closeness. The night before, they had gone to bed, only to have slept apart, each with their own thoughts separating their bodies. Oh, how she ached for him now. She needed him. She missed him. "But you can't rush into things. You must think this all through," she quickly added. "Haste makes waste, so the old saying goes."

He reached up and took her hands and moved them from his neck, then moved away from her, securing his pistol in the waist of his breeches once again. "It's important that I go to Kiawah Island and claim all of my valuables," he grumbled. "There won't be any other means of raising capital for the planting. You know that the northern money will take forever to drift South—if even then they will loan any to us 'Rebels,' as they chose to call us."

"You'll use all of your valuables? That will be your means to raise some money?"

"Just my mother's jewels. Nothing else. The rest belongs in this house. It will be a slow climb, but my plantation will become self-supporting once again."

"So you must travel to Kiawah Island this morning? You won't change your mind?"

"I don't need rest," he said angrily. "If you do, then return to the bed."

"I don't need rest either," Serena spat, placing her hands on her hips. "I shall show you just how much I can do in a day's time. When you return from Kiawah Island, you will see the beginnings of a shine in this beautiful mansion. I will throw the shutters back and let the sunshine become a welcome visitor in the many rooms of this house."

"You will do this for me?" Wesley said, moving to her, lifting her red curls from her shoulders. He laughed, seeing what the damp ocean breezes had done to her natural curly hair. It was a mass of frizz. But, ah, such beautiful frizz. He leaned and buried his nose in it, inhaling deeply. It even smelled of the ocean breezes. He suddenly wanted to postpone his journey of the morning. He could feel the heat rising now . . .

But several reasons had stood in his way last night. And even now, his thoughts were turning to Halona . . . now that he was so close to seeing her after so long. Would Halona be able to erase Serena from his mind? Did he even want her to? Now that he was home, did he even truly need Serena any longer? He lifted his eyes and felt them wavering a bit as she gazed back at him with a passionate longing. He pulled away from her and strolled toward the door. "I truly must leave," he said. Then he turned on his heel. "But you shouldn't do work that a slave can do," he said flatly. "Maybe some will return. Then maybe we can find among them one that can be your personal servant, and others to handle the other household duties."

Serena rushed to him and took his hands in hers. "I have a perfect solution," she said, beaming.

"What kind of solution? What are you talking about?"

"Do you remember the Negroes you discovered living in your townhouse complex?" she said anxiously.

"How could I forget?"

"Last night, while laying, unable to sleep, my thoughts went to them and their plight," Serena said. "I then remembered how your slaves had fled and had left you with no workers, and thought that maybe, possibly, these that you found at your dwelling might want to come to Folly Island, to work for you."

Wesley laughed hoarsely. "Work? Serena, you speak as though I would have to pay them wages if I even *did* agree to bring them back here. Pay a *slave?* Never."

Serena moved away from him, doing a slow burn inside. Would Wesley always show such an outwardly contempt for the Negroes? Maybe Lincoln had been right! Serena hadn't ever witnessed such contempt before when being around one who spoke of the Negroes. In the North, the Negroes had always worked as maids, servants, but had never been treated as inhuman, as Wesley seemed being capable of doing. They had been paid wages. Just as the whites.

She turned, her eyes flashing. "Wesley, there are no longer any slaves. Don't you see? The war has ended, the North has won, and Lincoln, though dead, has also won. He set the slaves free long ago. And now that Lee has signed the papers of surrender, there should be no question about slavery any longer. They are free. *Free.*"

"Damn it all to hell," Wesley shouted. "Your mouth is working mighty freely this morning. Have you got anything else political to say before I take my leave? Serena, I can do without your outbursts of loyalty to the Negroes. I didn't bring you to Wyndham Hall to listen to you ranting and raving about who is free and who is not."

Serena's face reddened in further anger. She stomped to Wesley's side, her eyes flashing. "And just why did you bring me to Wyndham Hall, Wesley Alston Wyndham?" she snapped, circling her hands into two tight fists at her side. She had seen how he had withdrawn from her only moments ago. She had felt the distance he was now placing between them, erasing what had at one time been touches of ecstasy. She understood his pain, but that gave him no just cause to ignore her, even shun her.

Wesley's face paled a bit and his eyes wavered. He turned and jerked the door open and began to leave, but was stopped when Serena reached and took his arm, digging her nails into his flesh. He turned and raised a hand to slap her, but then stopped when he saw how beautiful she was when angered even more. He gazed first at her hand that still held him almost powerless, and then up at her and the way her lips were quivering and how her freckles had turned a pale red instead of their usual brown. He threw his head back in a fit of laughter, then composed himself, but chuckling still, when he felt her release her hold on him.

"So you think this is all funny? Huh, Wesley?" she said, turning her back to him, so wanting to cry. But she wouldn't. She would not show that she was a foolish woman hungering after a man. She was strong. She would show him!

When she felt his hand cover hers and swing her around to pull her into his arms, all signs of her anger disappeared into feelings of rapturous ecstasy. She closed her eyes as his lips found hers in a warm wetness, and when his tongue sought entrance and explored slowly inside her wet cavern, she felt herself go limp in his arms.

"I love you, darling," he whispered. "I do love you. I don't know what gets into me at times. I guess this has all been a bit too much for me."

She nibbled on his earlobe, sending electrical currents through his body, down into his throbbing manhood. But he still couldn't guide her to the bed. He had much to sort out in his mind.

"Then delay your trip?" she purred, reaching down, touching him. She began to unbutton his breeches, but was stopped when his hands brusquely shoved hers away.

"No. I cannot," he said, clearing his throat nervously. But he quickly added, "And I tell you what. I'll send Tobias into Charleston. I'll have him vacate my townhouses quite quickly."

Serena paled of color. "Then you won't have those sweet, innocent children brought here, where we can give them shelter?" she gasped. "You are going to put them all out on the street?"

Wesley laughed. "No, my darling," he said, lifting her hair, sniffing it again. "I'll have Tobias tell them to come to Folly Island."

"*Tell?*" she said, emphasizing the word with strength in her voice. "Don't you think *ask* would be more appropriate? Don't you think you should at least give them a chance to refuse? They are *free*, Wesley. . . ."

Wesley's face reddened and his lips compressed, then he stormed, raging mad. "Damn it, Serena, I'm leaving," he shouted. "And when I return, please watch your tongue."

"But you will still have Tobias go and see if the children would want to come to Folly Island? You will do this, Wesley?"

He threw his hands into the air in exasperation as he moved out into the hall, still shouting. "Yes! Yes! They will be *asked*. But I don't know why I'm doing this," he shouted further. "To make them leave one of my dwellings, to bring them to another? It doesn't make sense. But they will be placed in the outbuildings. You will be sure of that."

Serena giggled and closed the bedroom door, still

hearing his cursings and rantings as he moved on through the house. She moved to the window and threw back the shutters, inhaling. The cool morning air greeted her and the birdsongs made her feel, as though she were standing in the midst of a tropical forest. The sun was making its presence known in soft shades of orange filtering through the lacy moss of the many oak trees.

Another splash of sea breeze settled around her face, and she could even taste the saltwater as it settled on her lips. Then she looked downward, catching sight of Wesley as he moved toward the Kiawah River's edge. Her heart pounded with love for him. Their temperaments clashed quite often, but didn't that make for even more excitement when their time to be alone would arrive? Didn't that make their passion peak to such explosive climaxes?

She tensed when she saw Tobias approach Wesley and begin to chat. When Wesley gestured with his hands, looking toward the house, Serena had to wonder if he was speaking of Tobias venturing into Charleston to vacate his townhouses? Or was Wesley explaining Serena's presence to Tobias?

A sudden panic seized Serena. She was sorting through her mind the moments of having first met Tobias. Why, Wesley hadn't even introduced Tobias to Serena, nor her to him. Had this neglect been on purpose? What *did* Wesley have in mind for her?

She continued to watch, feeling so out of place now. She was an intruder, an outsider. She was even worse than that: She was from the North. She was a Yankee.

Her fingers went to her throat when, after Wesley had waved a goodbye to Tobias and had moved on toward the taller marsh grasses, he stopped as someone else emerged on the scene: a beautiful woman, an Indian, dressed in a short-skirted buckskin dress and moccasins. From further study, Serena saw how tiny the Indian was, so small in bone and facial structure, and her hair was pulled straight back from her tawny oval face, and secured into two pigtails that hung to the small of her back.

"Who—?" she whispered, then remembered a passing mention of—what had Tobias said her name was—the Indian princess who had hidden Wesley's valuables. . . .

The name came to Serena just as Wesley pulled Halona into his arms. "Halona," she whispered, growing numb inside as she witnessed Wesley kissing Halona and pulling her into his embrace so that they appeared to be one, instead of two.

Throwing a knuckle into her mouth, Serena clamped her teeth onto it, moaning with pain, a pain that circled and circled her heart, making it become as one large aching mass of throbbing inside her chest. Then tears blurred her vision. But she could still make out these two clinging figures and how passionately they continued to embrace. And when Wesley's hands began to travel across the curves of Halona's body, Serena slammed the shutters closed in a fit of rage. "Oh, how could he?" she screamed. "How could Wesley kiss me so sweetly one moment, then go into the arms of another. And an . . . Indian!"

She didn't want to let herself, but she had to see if they were still embracing, so inched one of the shutters back just a fraction and caught sight of Wesley and Halona just as they moved into a long, narrow canoe, where Halona positioned herself in its middle and began to move the paddles, while Wesley sat down on a far end and stretched his legs out in a leisurely fashion, watching.

"I don't know him at all," Serena whispered. "This is a man I don't even know, but risked my own life to release from that jail. God, I even traveled and slept with him nightly."

She swung around and began pacing the floor, trying to get her thoughts straight in her mind. "I'll show him," she snarled. "He won't get away with this. I shall show him that I *do* have a mind of my own. That I am still as strong-willed as when he first met me. The hardships of the journey haven't softened me. I'm even stronger for having experienced so much. I shall do as I wish. And if he orders me from this house, I shall decide on my own if I shall leave or not. Damn him. He brought me here. He shall see just what kind of woman he thought he had conquered."

She moved toward the wardrobe, her jaw set firmly. "Wesley Alston, you have once again become my enemy."

She swung the door aside and began searching through the dresses that Wesley had brought to their room before retiring the previous night, saying that these had been the ones remaining of his mother's. Serena's nose curled up, smelling the fragrance of some sickeningly sweet cologne, knowing that when she would finally meet this Lona Gale Wyndham, she would recognize her by her scent.

Finding a dress that wasn't covered with lace and ruffles, that would be more appropriate for her explorings of this house, she pulled a pale green, flower-dotted silk dress from a hanger and held it up to herself. She closed the wardrobe door, to study her reflection in a mirror that was set into the outside of it. She hated having to wear another's clothes. But with Charleston in ashes, how could one be expected to find a dress for months to come—until Charleston was at least partially restored.

She studied the waistline and the gathers at the bosom, and then the length. Yes, Wesley's mother was as small-waisted and of the same height. Serena knew that, if she chose, she could pull full-skirted evening gowns from the closet, to look alluring in for Wesley in the evening hours. But did she even now want to? Oh! She was so angry! She was so hurt! Would Wesley and this Indian maiden even do more than embrace and kiss when in the privacy of the Indian village?

With a silent rage building inside her, Serena pulled her chemise off and replaced it with the soft fabric of the dress, which seemed to cool her anger as it caressed the curves of her body. She buttoned it and smoothed her fingers over the low-cut bodice, proud that her deep cleavage was revealed, knowing this to be a way to entice Wesley back into her arms—if she would even allow him to draw near to her with the fragrance of the Indian maiden still on him.

Grumbling to herself, Serena began to brush her hair in quick, angry strokes, flinching when a witch's knot would tangle and pull. Then she found a ribbon among Lona Gale's other personal belongings that Wesley had left in a heap on a nightstand, for Serena to choose from. She lifted her hair high and tied the ribbon around it, letting her hair hang in shades of red in a long pony-tail down her back.

Stopping to look around her, she saw this room as though entering it for the first time. The Union troops had spared much of the furnishings of the house, though they had taken their hate out on the walls and draperies, and what had at one time been magnificent oak floors.

In this room, as in all the other bedrooms, the wallpaper was of a flower garden design. The bedstead and all matching pieces of bedroom furniture were solid mahogany, as were most furnishings in the house.

She went out into the hallway where, from the entrance hall on the lower floor, the stairs led along the west wall, then on to the third floor and the garret.

She moved from room to room, observing that rather simple wainscoting had been used in the main rooms, and all walls were plastered above the chair-rail. Ceilings were also of plaster, thick and grainy. The laths had been hand hewn and left rough. But each room was without drapes or carpets, and each table was empty, except for an occasional kerosene lamp, some with smoked chimneys, and some without.

Serena left each room's shutters and windows opened, letting the mustiness and dust filter outward, to be replaced by the sun and fresh air. On her only first day there, Serena had found that when there is sun, Folly Island seemed to be splashed with it. And when night fell, dark colors collided in even darker shades of blacks and swirling navy blues.

Serena stopped at the staircase that led to the garret, shrugging, not feeling the need to go among more dust, where she supposed the Wyndham ancestor's journals, clothes and odds and ends of furnishings would probably be stored. Instead, she decided to move on to the lower floors, into the drawing room, where she immediately threw the shutters back, then stood and gazed around her at what at one time had been the grandest room of the house.

Where she now stood, many sparkling jewellike prisms hung from the great crystal chandelier, breaking up the light into many colors of the rainbow. She thought it a miracle that this piece of work had been spared by the troops.

Serena moved to the wall opposite a magnificent stone fireplace and ran her fingers across the graffiti left on the plaster walls of the Wyndham mansion. The date was December, 1863, and the name of Lt. Marshall P. Harkins had been scribbled in bold black handwriting, along with many other scribbled names, and then alongside the name of the unit's—the 42nd New York Volunteers, someone had scrawled a Latin quote: *Veritas vincit,* which Serena had translated from her one year of studying Latin as meaning "Truth overcomes." Also, she read something else that had been written in a quick scrawl: How are you, Gen. Beauregard?

The evening before, when Wesley had discovered the vandalism and then had seen these scribblings, he had cursed the Union troops with even more vigor. He had explained that General Pierre Beauregard was the commander of the "Rebel" army in Charleston. Having put the emphasis on the word "Rebel," Wesley had then walked from the room in angry haste.

He had said no more, or less, about this General Beauregard, but Serena had wondered why. Wesley was disappointed that this general hadn't been able to do more for the South. And hadn't Wesley had to wonder why General Beauregard hadn't been able to keep the troops from such a remote place as Folly Island? Surely only a few of his troops would have been required. . . .

But it was apparent that no actual combat had taken place on this paradise island, and that not that much

276

damage had truly resulted from this possessing of the house. Drapes could be replaced. Walls could be replastered.

But then she remembered Wesley's father. Oh, how could she have forgotten? He had lost his life—guarding the Wyndham inheritance.

Feeling renewed sadness for Wesley and his losses, Serena moved on around the room, still opening shutters, glancing first at one piece of furniture, then the next, seeing that only some lemon oil polish would be required to recapture their luster. And the many upholstered chairs would simply need a good scrubbing with thick suds.

Serena moved on into an oval music room, where windows had already been opened onto a wrought-iron balcony. This room had been the first for Wesley to check, his father having left it double bolt-locked before his death. As now, the inner wall of the music room was enhanced by a pair of windows with mirrored panes. They seemed to reflect haunting images caught by time and eternity. . . .

She looked further around her, sighing when her gaze settled on the two musical instruments in the room. Because of the bolt locks at the door, the large baby grand piano hadn't been molested, nor the golden harp that sat by its side. She had to wonder who of the Wyndham family possessed a musical talent.

Serena moved from the room, suddenly exhilarated. *It will all be just as beautiful once again, Wesley,* she thought, lifting the skirt of her dress, as she walked toward the door that led down to the basement. Wesley had said that the Wyndham wine cellar was one of special distinction. Well, she would just go and get one of his finest bottles of wine to have ready for his return home. She would not give him up so easily. If she had to fight for him, then a new Civil War would begin, but only between the Indian and herself. No matter what, Serena would win him over for keeps. Jealousy made Serena's determination to win even stronger. Yes, she would win.

She swung the basement door open and began to make her way down the steps, but felt ripples of fear travel through her, seeing the darkness of what lay below the stairs. She found and lit a kerosene lamp, then moved again onto the steps, making her way down them, slowly, one at a time. She held the lamp higher, casting light more around her, then tensed when she heard a scraping noise from somewhere down below her.

Stopping, her heart pounding so hard she could hardly breathe, she peered cautiously down below her, seeing only shadows of more furniture and the reflection of the wine bottles that had been arranged along a side wall.

Feeling a bit foolish, she moved onward, taking another step. But another noise made her heart skip a few beats. She swallowed hard, now thinking that maybe someone had been occupying this house, even last night, when she and Wesley had been sleeping. Had a soldier hidden away in the cold depths of this cellar? Or had their sudden arrival caused a soldier to flee to the darkness below and he just hadn't yet had the chance to escape?

But Serena knew that if it was a stray soldier, he would have to realize the risks of trying to escape from this island, now that the owner had returned and could see in all directions from the many windows of this three-storied house.

Serena continued to stand there, mulling over her next move, then felt foolish, this time for letting her mind

278

wander so.

Breathing more evenly, she scooted on down the steps and placed the lamp on a table, going to the wine bottles, choosing one. As she reached to pull it from its resting place, she felt icy cold hands move around to cover her mouth, then her waist. She tried to scream, but the pressure was too strong on her closed mouth. She then tried to kick at her attacker, but couldn't make contact since he was behind her.

"Don't try anything stupid," the voice whispered. "I've killed enough during this war to not care if I have to kill someone else, even if it is a beautiful wench."

Serena tried to speak again, but could only manage low mumbles. And when she was eased around, to face the intruder, she saw a burly man, whose face was so fat it seemed swollen, and his pale gray eyes bulged almost from his head beneath bushy brows. Serena wrestled more with him, but succeeded at only getting slapped across the bosom, causing her breasts to begin a slow ache. She then became quiet, watching him as his eyes began to assess his catch. She could see his raw hunger by the shine of his eyes and the way he was beginning to lick his thin lips. Black whiskers matched the coal black of his shoulder-length hair, and his clothes were soiled Union blues.

Then he released her just as quickly as he had grabbed her. He began laughing throatily. "Don't know what the hell I'm doin' holdin' you so tight," he said, beginning to move and make circles around her, looking her up and down. "I've seen enough through the basement windows this mornin' to know that you're alone in this tomb of a house."

Serena eyed the staircase, then him, swallowing hard

when she saw that he had caught her doing so. "You are mistaken, sir," she said, tilting her chin up into the air. "My husband is upstairs. The ones you saw leave were our overseer and our hired hand that has arrived to this island to help renovate our lovely home."

The man laughed raucously, placing his hand on his holstered gun. "Tell me more jokes, lady," he said, laughing still. "I saw you arrive with that man who left with the Indian wench. I've just been waitin' for that nigger to leave the island, too, before makin' my move. But seems your snoopin' has caught me red-handed." He began to finger his whiskers, tugging at them, eyeing her even more hungrily. "And whil'st I wait, I might as well entertain myself," he said.

When his mouth moved to Serena's, she could smell the strong aroma of alcohol and knew that this man had busied himself by tasting the Wyndham wines. When she refused to offer him any kind of encouragement, he pulled away from her, giving her the opportunity to spit in his face.

He wiped at his face angrily, then slapped her across the face. "Now, you wench, you, Goddamn it, don't do anythin' like that again, do you hear?"

He jerked her to the floor and ripped the skirt of her dress and then her underthings away as his hands began to move greedily over her. "I plan to get me a bit of ass before headin' out, and you won't stop me."

She tried to remain calm, even though his hands had already found the soft spot between her legs. She had found that force on her part was in vain. She had to try a different approach. She began to speak softly, reaching up to run her fingers through his greasy hair. "I'm not going to fight you, you big lug," she purred. "Don't you know I like to have a man show force?"

Her fingers worked over his face, touching his lips, discovering that they were parched and cracked. "Give it to me, Yank. Give it to me," she encouraged, even lifting her hips, teasing him.

"I ain't never run across anyone quite like you, lady," he said, unbuttoning his breeches with trembling fingers.

"And why are you even hiding in this basement, Yank?" she purred, creeping her fingers lower, having her eyes now on the gun. In his haste to rape her, he had forgotten that his gun was readily available, if she could get brave enough to pull it from its holster.

"Got separated from my regiment, damn it," he said, pulling his manhood from the tight confines of his breeches, lowering it against her, where her undergarments now lay in shreds. "But damn glad that I was. Bet none of the other regiments has found someone as beautiful and willin' as you. They're probably too busy shootin' filthy Johnny Rebs to see that there's more to life than shootin'."

Serena suddenly realized that this man didn't even know the war was over. If she told him, would he be so shocked that he would quit his assault? She started to speak when his mouth crushed hers into silence. Serena felt sick to her stomach when his tongue entered between her lips. And his hands. He seemed to have ten, instead of two. If they weren't on her breasts, they were caressing her between her legs. Then when his mouth finally lowered, to secure a nipple between his teeth, she said hurriedly, "Yank, didn't you know that the war is over?" She heard a low throaty laugh as his tongue circled and continued to wet the full mound of her breast.

"Tell me more that I can laugh at," he finally said,

grabbing his manhood, beginning to guide it downward.

Serena gasped as she felt the hard steel of his member make contact, then enter her in a downward thrust. "Please. Stop. I'm not lying. The war is over. I'm from the North. I'm from Illinois. You're raping a girl from the North. . . ."

He laughed once again, saying, "Do you think I even care where a woman is from?" He began to work his body in and out, groaning like a wounded animal.

Serena was remembering another rape. When she pictured Edward in her mind, she reached for the gun in earnest and just as she had her fingers clasped around its handle, a single gunshot rang out, causing her to drop her hands to her side, realizing that blood had begun to seep over her arm and hand, and that the attacker's body had lunged one more time, even harder than before, but not because of the pleasure he was getting from her body, but from a bullet having just entered into his back, causing his body to spasm in short jerks, then come to a halt.

Serena looked anxiously around her, feeling hysteria growing inside her. She worked and shoved until the man was free from his entrance into her body and was now lying next to her. Then she peered through the semidarkness, thinking to find Wesley. Had he returned for her? Had he felt guilty about the embrace he had shared with the Indian maiden? But then her heartbeat consumed her when she found that it was another stranger in the basement with her. And he still had his gun poised—pointing in her direction.

She covered her mouth with her hands, muffling a scream, then began to inch herself upward. As the man moved closer and was in full range of the kerosene lamp's glow, Serena began to see some resemblance to Wesley, in the beguiling glint to this younger man's dark brown eyes, the straight nose, and smaller cleft in his chin. His shoulders were more narrow and his height not as great, but it was quite evident that this man was Truman Firman Wyndham, Wesley's younger brother. Serena could guess his age as now being twenty.

"Who the hell are you?" Truman asked, lifting the thickness of his eyebrows, then curving one downward.

"Serena Kassia Calvert," she said, sighing deeply. She was relieved that Wesley's brother had arrived on the scene when he had. But how? When did he arrive on the island? Did this mean that the whole family had arrived back from Boston? Then she suddenly remembered the state in which she had been found. The color drained from her face as she looked down and saw the dress that was not even hers, ripped, blood-stained, and rumpled. Was she going to have to meet Wesley's family in this state? Oh, she just wished she could hide. At least until Wesley arrived back to Wyndham Hall and could help explain her presence.

"And what are you doing in Wyndham Hall?" Truman blurted, glancing first from Serena, then to the dead soldier, lying now in a pool of his own blood. "I can only figure what that damn Yankee was doing. He was a deserter. One who didn't know the war was over." He laughed cruelly. "Well, that's one damn Yankee that won't be returning North."

Serena didn't know how to answer Truman. She wasn't yet properly betrothed. Wesley hadn't even spoken of marriage for weeks now. And wouldn't she look the whore when they discovered that she had taken residence in Wesley's room . . . and bed . . . ? "I'm a friend of your brother Wesley's," she finally stammered.

"How did you even know my brother's name? And how did you even know I was his brother?" he stormed, reddening in the face. "I come up on two bodies writhing in lust on the floor of my basement, and then you have the nerve to say that you even know me? If I hadn't stood for a while and watched you enjoying the man's assault, I wouldn't know the kind of person you are and would possibly believe what you say. But I *did* see you lifting your hips to him. I saw you intertwine your fingers in the man's mangy hair. I had hoped that one bullet would kill the both of you."

Serena gasped, putting her hands to her throat. She was standing in the presence of a maniac. Wesley had said that his younger brother was a sissy . . . and that his sister was a bit odd. Well, what she was seeing was no sissy. He was a young man with a twisted mind. "You stood watching? You actually let this man continue with his rape? You are despicable. Even worse than that. You enjoyed watching that man humiliate me in the worst way a man can humiliate a woman. And you had to have known that I was leading him on purposely, that my hand was inching toward his gun. What else could I do?"

He laughed sardonically. He moved toward her, still holding his pistol erect. "No matter. I got my enjoyment for the day, it seems. You put on a good show. Maybe you'd even like to continue? But with me?" He moved to her and lifted her hair with the long, narrow barrel of the pistol.

She slapped the pistol away, trembling. "You?" she hissed, lifting her chin haughtily. "You wouldn't have the guts. Do you know why?" She placed her hands on her hips and spoke into his face, feeling more brave, since the pistol had been lowered to his side.

He laughed, but this time Serena could tell that it was with less force. She was tearing down his wall of defense . . . one that made him look less a man of the world. Maybe he wasn't only a maniac but also a sissy as Wesley had said. Hadn't he escaped to Boston instead of fighting for the southern cause? Hadn't he just shot this man in the back?

A slow smile surfaced on Serena's lips, as she glanced toward the dead soldier, then back to Truman. Why, she now knew why he had been so eager to shoot the northern soldier. Not to defend Serena. If it had been to defend her from such an assault, Truman would have done it way before the man had plunged his manhood deeply inside her.

No. He had received his pleasure from watching, then had chosen to shoot himself a Yankee before the soldier had had a chance to pull away from Serena to catch himself being observed. Yes, Truman Firman Wyndham had finally shot himself a northern Yankee, but he had done so in the back, and after the peace treaty had been signed. And she realized that brothers had killed for her, but for entirely different reasons.

"Would you like to explain why you think I wouldn't have the guts to take you sexually?" he finally said, moving away from her, avoiding her accusing eyes.

Serena's gaze raked over him, seeing the impeccable, sleek, finely pressed breeches and waistcoat. White ruffles billowed at his throat and down the front of his shirt. She laughed coyly. "In the first place, noticing how clean you keep yourself and your clothes, you wouldn't think to dirty yourself by touching me where another man just had," she said. "Secondly, if you *did*, Wesley Alston would beat you senseless."

Truman turned quickly on his heel, having grown ashen in color. His thick lashes had grown heavy over his eyes. "This is the second time you have made mention of my brother," he said, stammering a bit. "Who *are* you? Why are you here? And how do you even know Wesley's middle name?"

"I am Wesley's betrothed," she snapped. She had finally said it. Now what would Wesley say or do when he found out? But he had brought her to Folly Island because he loved her and planned to marry her. She had to keep believing this. Then her thoughts would travel to . . . Halona. . . .

Truman dropped his pistol and staggered a bit toward Serena. "It can't be," he whispered. "You're lying!"

Serena scowled. "Why? Only because you caught me being raped? Does that make me too dirty now to become a Wyndham?" she shouted, narrowing her eyes.

He began to knead his brow nervously. "None of this can be true, because . . . because . . . Wesley is dead . . ." he finally managed to say. "I am now master of Wyndham Hall. Not Wesley Alston." He stood shaking his head, looking confused. "No. Wesley can*not* be alive. He cannot." He went to Serena and grabbed her by the shoulders, shaking her. "Tell me he's dead. Do you hear me? Tell me he was killed by the Yankees." He then released her and went to a chair and sunk down onto it, holding his face in his hands, sobbing.

"My God," Serena whispered, inching away from him. "You want Wesley to be dead. Oh, my God, Truman." She turned and rushed to the stairs that led upward, then stopped, staring once again at the dress and how so much of what had just happened to her was revealed by the stains, rips, and tears.

"I must get to Wesley's room before meeting his mother and sister," she whispered. "I must get myself ready to meet the rest of my future in-laws." She took one final look at Truman, hating, but yet pitying him, then crept quietly up the stairs. When she reached the first floor landing, she stopped and stared cautiously around her, barely breathing. Then she heard a loud gasp from beside her and whirled around and found herself face to face with a woman of her same height and build but much older, with a tight bun of brown hair swirled severely atop her head. She inhaled the familiar perfume. . . .

"My word," the lady gasped further, paling. "Who are *you?* What are you doing at Wyndham Hall? Why was there gunfire? Where's Truman Firman?"

Serena's pulse quickened. She had just met Lona Gale Wyndham, Wesley's mother.

Chapter Fifteen

Since childhood, Wesley had admired Halona's gracefulness. And when they had discovered that there was more to life than sharing fun and games, he had never had enough of her, though it was taboo for him to marry into the Indian race.

As now, he watched in a silent hunger as Halona so gracefully pulled the oars through the water. Each stroke was managed with quiet ease, even though she was tiny and frail. But it was the Indian maiden's way. She would never let the man take charge. She was superior to him. Always.

Wesley's sadness over the loss of his father was slowly slipping away to be lost in the moment of tranquillity as Halona continued to guide the canoe into the depths of the swampland, where the land of the Kiawah waited. Only a small village of Indians remained of the many thousands that had been on Kiawah Island when the first white man had set foot on the tropical paradise. The Kiawah, neither understanding nor liking the ways of the white man, had at first fought them in an attempt to frighten them away. But the big guns had slaughtered too many of the Kiawah warriors, leaving only a handful to keep the race in existence.

Though the hatred for the white man had never diminished, Wesley had always been welcomed to the land of the Kiawah, after he had rescued Halona from the fury of an alligator when Wesley had only been seven, and she five. When he had carried her to her father's waiting arms, bleeding and pale, Wesley had been made Halona's blood brother. But that had changed in time. Now the Kiawah continued to pray to their God for Wesley to leave Folly Island to move to Kiawah Island to become as one of them, to become Halona's husband.

Through the years the Kiawah had waited patiently for Wesley to come to his senses, as Halona's older brother Wolfram had so crudely put it. Wolfram had even thought that the Wyndham valuables that had been brought to Kiawah Island by Tobias had been gifts for Halona, preceding Wesley's request for her hand in marriage.

Wesley had read the disappointment in Halona's eyes when he had had to deny this to her this day, even though Tobias had said that he had taken special pains to assure her that this was not true on the very day she had agreed to keep these possessions until the war's end.

Wesley hadn't meant to lead Halona on through the years. He had explained the impossibility of ever becoming her husband, that his future lay with Wyndham Hall, knowing that it and the Wyndham Plantation would be his responsibility once his father had "gone to join his ancestors," as Halona had put it today when Wesley had told her of his father's passing.

But to Wesley's knowledge, Halona still remained faithful to him. With lowered eyes, she had said that she continued to refuse to let any other man enter her hut.

289

She had told Wesley that she would wait—for eternity, if it was necessary. It had been written in the stars that Wesley would be hers. And she knew that one day he would, if she saved herself for him long enough.

Wesley hadn't mentioned Serena and her presence at Wyndham Hall. He hated to think of what Halona or Wolfram would think about the possibility of him taking Serena as his wife. Wesley hated to think of never ever being allowed to be with Halona, and knew that would be the case if word of his possible marriage would leak out and travel to the Indians of Kiawah Island.

Sighing with the heaviness of his thoughts, Wesley began to gaze around him, having so missed all of this while being a part of a different world, carrying out his raids, his so-called victories. And now he listened to the rustling of the tiny fiddler crabs as they played their mating games. With a quick glance toward the mud flats that lined the Kiawah River banks, Wesley could see the fierce-looking claws of the fiddler crabs as they scurried around trying to entice their female companions to their burrows in the mud by waving to them with their "fiddles."

Gazing upward, Wesley spied a broadheaded skink, a member of the lizard family, sunbathing high on a bare branch of a dead tree. This particular skink was one foot long, and with its olive brown coloring, swollen jaws, and orange red head, it was quite impressive, though not poisonous. But now that Halona was continuing to row the canoe on into the thickness of the back-country bush, Wesley knew to keep his eyes ready for a poisonous snake that might drop from the limbs of the huge cypress and oak trees that shaded these banks. But Wesley allowed himself the pleasure of enjoying the camellias and other

290

flowers that were scenting the air with a sweet, heady fragrance. Around the boat, the massive trunks of the hundred-and-fifty-foot high cypress trees tapered upward from wide, flaring bases, where even larger roots combined to form supporting buttresses, roots that formed knobs protruding above the surface of the water.

When an alligator slithered from its resting place in the mud, to plunge to just below the surface of the water next to where the canoe kept moving along with its graceful, steady pace, Halona turned and smiled warmly at Wesley, showing her straight white teeth against her tan skin, as though she would always think of their first meeting when seeing an alligator.

Smiling confidently, Wesley placed his arms on each side of the canoe and continued to stretch out in a quiet leisure, knowing that his times with Halona were the only times of his life that he had been free of worry and frustration. Ah, how tempting it had been at times to stay with her, hide away from the world, let her teach him her ways, and shower him with forbidden love. But the call of the Wyndham blood surging through his veins had made him always return to his world.

The echoing of the birds that were perched in the many trees above the canoe grew no less when one final turn in the river brought Wesley face to face with the small Kiawah reservation nestled beneath the moss-covered oaks. He had been there so often, he felt as though he was returning home. The round huts, frameworks of saplings covered with slabs of oak bark, were clustered close together, and around these Wesley could see the familiar scene of women at work.

The women were outside the doors of their huts, some making cedar-back baskets, with designs woven on the outside with colored grasses gathered from the depths of the forest, and some were weaving, or spinning yarn. All eyes turned in the direction of the canoe. No one moved, but Wesley could see the joy etched in the deep lines of their leathery faces. He had become as sort of a god to them. As far as he knew, he was the only white man allowed to enter.

"We are here, Wesley," Halona said, maneuvering the canoe next to another group of tied canoes, then stepped from the canoe and secured it with a rope. She reached her hand toward Wesley and held his in hers as she watched his long legs move over the sides of the canoe. "My people welcome you among them again, Wesley," Halona added, smiling affectionately. "As I do, my love," she then whispered, sidling next to him as they moved toward her own private wigwam.

"Everything seems as usual," Wesley said, straightening his back, smiling at first one Indian maiden, and then the next. None were as pretty as Halona. She had been gifted, it seemed, with tinier bones and a more pleasant face. Many of the Kiawah women were heavy and even smelled bad. But Halona didn't abide with the Kiawah custom of fearing that a god would grab them to the depths of the river if they dared to enter it for a bath. Halona bathed daily. She was the head warrior's sister. She had privileges that no one else was allowed.

But no one else had been so daring. Halona was special. She was radiant with her special ways. Wesley had thought no one could match her beauty . . . until Serena. Now he didn't know which way to turn. He didn't want Serena to continue entering his thoughts while with Halona. He had plans for this day with Halona before gathering together his valuables to leave, never possibly to return again.

Ah, he had so much that was waiting to be done. He had to restore his plantation. He had to find some slaves, some that were still willing to be . . . slaves. . . .

Maybe Tobias would encourage the Negroes that had invaded his townhouse to return and work as his slaves. They had nothing better in life. They were mainly children, except for the oldest, but children were energetic. Children grew up.

He gazed downward at Halona. In her deerskin moccasins, with designs of embroidered porcupine quills and beads, she stepped so softly on the packed dirt, she might have been stepping on a cloud. Her dainty features were framed with pitch black hair that had been pulled severely back into two pigtails. Her dress was made of buckskin and was trimmed with many fringes that bounced as she moved on toward her hut, with head held high, not stopping to smile to all who still watched her in silent admiration. Her white man had returned. She was proud.

"Wesley, please," Halona said, gesturing toward her opened door. Then when she moved on in behind him, she closed it, meaning their privacy would be assured from any passersby for whatever length of time Halona would choose.

Stooping, in an effort to keep his head from scraping the low roof, Wesley glanced quickly around him. A low fire glowed in the center of the hut, where smoke spiraled upward through a small, round hole in the roof. Beneath this dim glowing, Wesley immediately spied the glitter of his mother's jewels and the shine of the silver that Halona had placed neatly in a corner next to where Halona slept on a pile of colorful blankets.

Wesley went to the valuables and checked through them, seeing that all was there, then turned and smiled when Halona sat down next to the fire, crossing her arms and legs.

"Halona glad Wesley here," she said softly.

Wesley took one of her delicate hands in his, smiling back. "Wesley glad to be here," he said. He wanted to pull her into his arms, but knew the custom of offering food before pleasures of the body.

"Wesley hungry?" Halona asked, blinking her wide eyes upward at him, reaching for some carved wooden dishes and some bread and berries that she had already arranged on another wooden platter and had left waiting for her return, knowing that Wesley would be with her. She had been watching, waiting, for months. But this day, she had spoken with Tobias. Tobias had said that Wesley had arrived safely home and that he would be ready to receive his valuables. She knew that she could have brought them to him, but to do that would have been to have given up being in his arms.

"Cassava?" Wesley asked, accepting a dish.

"Cassava. Bread made from bitter cassava," she said, laughing softly. "I don't have tapioca today. Sorry, Wesley."

Wesley had learned of this cassava his first day at the Kiawah reservation. It was a small shrub, from whose roots were made tapioca and bread. The bitter root would be ground and thoroughly washed to remove the prussic acid that it contained. Then the sweet cassava roots were eaten and fixed like ordinary potatoes.

Halona leaned over the fire and pulled a steaming mug from the coals. "Tea, Wesley?" she asked.

"Sassafras or wintergreen?" he asked, familiar with both.

"Sassafras," she murmured, widening her face into another smile.

"Yes. Please, Halona," he said, beginning to hate this ritual that postponed his moments of passionate embraces with her. He could see the heaving of her tiny breasts and knew that she was also experiencing the moments of anxiety between when they would eat and then make "love of the heart," as she had named it. Wesley hated the way *his* heart wouldn't give him any peace. It had been too long between Halona and himself. War! So many things had to be postponed because of war.

Wesley accepted the small ceramic cup offered him, seeing the beautiful paintings on its sides, knowing that this was probably one of the things that Halona had done while waiting patiently for his return. His heart ached now, thinking that this was probably going to be his last time with her. But could he even bear it, if it were? Maybe Serena didn't have to find out about Halona. Maybe Halona didn't have to find out about Serena.

Could he have them both? He doubted it. He had to think that Halona would finally grow tired of waiting and finally accept a Kiawah warrior inside her tent. She had to have needs such as his. How had she even waited so long without it? His eyebrows tilted upward. Maybe she hadn't. Maybe he had only been fooling himself into believing this. She was young. She was vital. She had needs.

"I feared the big gun's bangs, Wesley," Halona said, scooting closer to him, partaking in her shared feast with him. "Even here. I was able to hear the loud noises of white man's war. Did you hate it, Wesley?"

Wesley stretched out, leaning sideways on one elbow, sipping his tea. "War to me holds much excitement," he said, thinking back to his victories and how it had made his blood surge wildly through his veins. It had almost been the same feeling as after having made love to a woman.

"How? I remember my grandfather's tales of the white man's big guns that they brought to Kiawah Island long ago," Halona said, frowning. "Many brothers and fathers were killed by those big guns."

"Those deaths of your tribe weren't necessary, Halona," he said darkly. "The white man just wanted to scare you off. Show their superiority. And I guess you might even say the same about this war that has just been fought between the North and South. Deaths weren't necessary there either. The North and South just wanted to scare each other into believing as they each did—at first by threats, signed documents and such. But then one cannon fired against the wall of Fort Sumter and the war had begun. Just as quickly as that."

"Does this Fort Sumter still stand?"

"Just barely," Wesley grumbled. "Just barely."

"Maybe we Kiawah should have built a fort around our village," Halona said in a low whisper, her face shadowing in thought. "Then maybe we would have had more people spared. It so saddens me to think about my ancestors and how they suffered at the hand of the white man."

Wesley's heartbeat faltered, thinking about what he might soon be putting Halona through when he denied her his presence. Again, though, he had to think there had to be a way of having both women. The blood was beginning to pound in his manhood, even now, thinking of the possibilities of having two beautiful women at one time. He placed his bowl and mug on the ground and inched his fingers toward Halona's dress, touching the fringe, teasing her.

"How long are you going to sit there eating and drinking, when we could be doing other things, Halona?" he asked thickly.

"Are you finished, Wesley?" she asked softly. "I want to be sure you have finished with your food I have served you."

"Halona, I didn't even need food. I need you. Don't you know that? Through the years, you should've known that I never came for food. Only you, my sweet little Indian maiden."

Halona rose and stood before him as she began to undress, all the while smiling seductively toward him. Wesley in turn began to unbutton his shirt and when he pulled it from his shoulders, he saw her eyes move to the wound and the way it lay in creases around where the bullet had entered. She didn't say anything, but only frowned and continued to step from her things until she was standing nude before him, showing him the fine, lean, graceful lines of her body, where only small swells of breasts thrust out in tiny peaks. She kneeled down before him as he continued to disrobe. He kicked his breeches and underthings aside as she touched him ever so gently on the area of his wound, circling it with a forefinger, then bending to press her lips against it. He now knew that if she had been present while his wound had been healing, her lips would have probably been the only thing required. He closed his eyes and stretched out on the ground and let her fingers and tongue awaken him

297

even more than he already was.

"Wesley, I love you," she murmured. "My Wesley. I see your wound. I will make you forget it. My love, I will make you forget everything except Halona."

She stretched her lithe body atop his and began moving it, a caress itself, all the while her lips were tracing his eyes, his nose, his trembling lips, downward to his nipples. And when she scooted even lower, he found his body jerking in rhythm with her tongue as it circled inside his navel, then even downward. When her tiny fingers circled his manhood and led it slowly into her mouth, Wesley tensed and let out a soft moan. It was as he remembered. She had shown him the way of the tongue long ago. He knew that only she knew such art, though he had thought to teach Serena how. This was a part of lovemaking that was special. Oh, how he had missed it.

He reached down and guided her head, relishing in the continued caress of her fingers as she moved them over his body, causing ripples in his skin wherever they touched anew. And when the full tension was about to be released from his body, he urged her upward atop him once again and entered her. He became almost as a madman, thrusting, over and over again, until he felt his release come in sudden wild bursts of pleasure. His body spasmed, over and over again, then he lay panting, clinging to her, holding her.

"It felt good, Wesley?" Halona asked, kissing him softly on the lips, wriggling once again, trying to ready him for more.

Wesley circled his arms around her tininess and kissed her with such force, she let out a gasp for air. Then he withdrew a bit, letting his hands search for her breasts.

And when he found them, he couldn't help but compare them with Serena's. Halona was the same as a boy there in comparison to Serena.

"Want Halona to make you feel good again, Wesley?" Halona suddenly asked, as though she had known that he had been thinking of another woman, though still in Halona's tender embrace.

"No. I want to make you feel good," he said, easing her from him, to stretch her beneath him. With a skilled gentleness, he began kissing and fondling her until he could see her writhing and arching her hips upward, an invitation for him to enter her again.

"Halona is so pretty," he whispered. "Oh, so pretty." He moved inside her and took his time, watching her expressions changing from what seemed to be that of hurt to then be a pleasure so intense, she bit her lower lip until blood was drawn. This was when Wesley chose to hasten his thrusts inside her, and together they climbed a mountain of passion, jerking in unison as they moaned out their love for one another, until it was over and Wesley lay, sated, by her side. But yet he couldn't keep his hands from the smoothness of her body. It was as a piece of tan velvet, so smooth, so hard to leave behind.

Having seen Halona's deep pleasure, Wesley felt he knew that she no longer remained faithful to him. Such pleasures couldn't have been denied this Indian maiden for as long as Wesley's absence added up to. And since she was Halona, he knew that she would be allowed to have as many warriors as she chose without causing a stir among the other women. He remembered how she had explained what the women of the Kiawah had said about her—"If Halona dared a god, that was good . . . that was permitted." So he knew that they had probably said, "If

299

Halona wishes many warriors, that is good . . . that is permitted." She was the head warrior's sister. No one would argue what Halona would want.

But still, she chose to wait to make Wesley the special man in her life. What would she do if he continued to disappoint her? Wesley had grown to be a bit frightened of Wolfram and the long bow and quiver of arrows he always carried. Would Wolfram sneak onto Folly Island and sink one of those arrows into Wesley's heart if he continued to evade marriage? Wesley shuddered, thinking about it.

"Wesley cold?" Halona whispered, moving to cling to his side in an effort to give him some warmth.

"No. Wesley has to leave. I must get back to my plantation. I found it in a shambles upon returning home from the war."

"I haven't heard any big guns for a while. Are they no more?"

"They are no more," he said, rising. He searched out his breeches and pulled them on, then just as quickly had his shirt on and buttoned.

Halona moved to him and wrapped her arms around his neck, leaning seductively into him. "Wolfram should be home soon from long hunt. Wesley no wait to share long pipe with Wolfram?" she asked, pursing her lips to give him a brief kiss.

"Wesley doesn't have time," he said, feeling the thundering of his heartbeat as she released a button and reached a hand inside his shirt, smoothing her fingers over him in butterfly motions.

"Please, Wesley?" she begged. "We have more fun till brother arrives?"

"Halona, I could make love to you all day and night,"

he said thickly, framing her face between his hands, moving his gaze over her features, as though memorizing them. "But I've come for the Wyndham valuables and must return. These things mean money to me now, something even more important, it seems, than sharing secret moments of passion."

"I no made you feel good enough?" Halona pouted with her eyes cast downward.

"You've never made me feel better," he assured her, wrapping his arms around her, holding her tightly to him. He was thinking of when he would hold Serena and how he would always love burying his nose into the depths of her strawberry-colored hair. He suddenly missed her. Guilt pangs shot through his heart.

"You love Halona?" Halona whispered, resting her head on his chest.

More guilt pangs for Wesley. He did love Halona, but not in the way he should to ever have her as his wife. The forbidden part of their togetherness was where most of the excitement lay for him, if he would allow himself to be totally honest. The thrill of danger, the constant risk of what Wolfram might choose to do? Surely that was a big part of it.

How could he answer her? "Yes, Wesley loves Halona," he finally murmured. What else could he say? If he refused her, what could he even expect?

Halona sighed heavily. "Halona always love Wesley."

He pushed her gently away from him. "But I do have to go. We don't want to wait until the sun is replaced by the moon," he said, turning on a heel to move toward his belongings. "Halona cannot bring the canoe back to Kiawah Island alone, only being guided by the shadows of the moon."

"Halona can do that," she said stubbornly.

"Halona *not* going to do that," Wesley said. He eyed her hungrily, feeling the pressure building inside his manhood once again. Well, he couldn't have this. He had to leave. "Get dressed, Halona," he snapped.

Halona went to him and dug her fingernails into the flesh of his arm. "Wesley does not order Halona around," she hissed.

Wesley turned his gaze to meet hers and saw something different. It was a challenge. What had caused this sudden change? He had never seen this in her before. She had always been gentle, considerate of *his* wishes.

"I'm sorry, Halona," he said thickly, fear suddenly riding his spine. Had Halona seen his and Serena's arrival on Folly Island? Had Halona known through their entire lovemaking that he had a woman living with him at Wyndham Hall? Had Halona just tried to make him forget Serena by her magical ways, and seeing that she hadn't succeeded, chosen to treat *him* differently?

"That better," Halona snapped, moving to her clothes, quickly hiding her suppleness beneath her fringe-trimmed dress.

Suddenly Wesley was more than eager to leave the Kiawah reservation. If Wolfram would arrive back at the island before Wesley's departure, would Halona rush to her brother and tell him that Wesley no longer could make her as happy as she wished?

In haste, Wesley circled the sheet around the Wyndham silver and jewels, then tied it in a tight knot and swung it over his shoulder. When he turned and found Halona standing cross-armed in front of the closed door, blocking his way, further fear swept through him. "What are you doing, Halona?" he grumbled, moving

302

cautiously toward her, seeing how the fire danced in wavy shadows over her face that no longer showed a gentleness. She appeared a tigress, ready to pounce.

"Wesley no go," she said haughtily.

"Wesley *has* to go," he said firmly. "Stand aside, Halona."

"I no step aside."

Wesley had to push thoughts of Wolfram from his mind. He now realized that he would be leaving Kiawah Island under his own power. Not Halona's. Then he would have to learn to watch for any sudden movements in the brush from then on, knowing that he had now become only another white man to Halona, another enemy. But he had faced many enemies. He now had the skills with which to deal with enemies. Any enemy.

With quick movements, he jerked her roughly aside, hating it when she let out a whimper of pain, remembering what they had just shared.

He swallowed hard, knowing that it was over. He rushed from the hut with Halona close on his heels and when he secured a canoe and was already in it and paddling away, he listened to her ravings:

"You betray Halona. You take white woman to your wigwam. I loved you, Wesley!"

Her words tore at his heart. He now understood. She had seen Serena. She had even seen Serena's beauty and had thought to make Wesley forget.

"You choose red-haired she-devil over Halona?" she continued to scream. "Halona only able to make your mind fly as a bird from your soul. Remember this day. My spirit will haunt you, Wesley, when you take red-hair to bed at night."

Wesley's heart ached even more as he saw her from a

distance. She was so beautiful. But this day had been coming. All the years they had known one another, Wesley had known it would have to end.

He stretched his shoulder muscles as he made wider strokes with the oars, feeling suddenly sad. He had lost his father, and now he had also lost Halona. Who else . . . ?

Chapter Sixteen

After hiding Halona's canoe in the deepest recesses of the marsh grasses, Wesley hurried toward his mansion, occasionally glancing across his shoulder, up the full length of the Kiawah River, wondering just when Wolfram would make his move. Wesley didn't doubt for one minute that Wolfram would avenge his sister's honor. He only hoped that no others besides himself would be involved when Wolfram did decide to make his appearance on Folly Island.

The evening sunset was crowning Wyndham Hall in pale oranges. Wesley looked toward his house, smiling when he saw the golden flicker of lamplight at many of the windows. He hadn't thought to worry about Serena's safety earlier. He had let other things rule his mind. But now he could think of many things that could have happened to her, since Wyndham Hall had stood empty since the soldiers had vacated.

There were lights on in only two upstairs rooms, their bedroom, and the other—why had Serena left a light burning in Dorlisa May's room? What would be Serena's attraction to his sister's bedroom with all the other rooms to choose from?

Maybe she wanted to find out why I called Dorlisa May odd, he thought to himself, then felt a silent rage, not appreciating Serena making herself that much at home at Wyndham Hall.

He moved quickly up the back stairs and on into the kitchen, placing his heavy pack of Wyndham treasures on the kitchen table. Then he tensed, furrowing his brow. The voices echoing back at him from the drawing room were those of his family! But how? When?

He rushed to the drawing room, all eyes. "Mother?" he gasped. "My Lord, Mother. When did you arrive?"

Lona Gale's hands flew to her mouth, her dark eyes filling with tears. Then she rushed to Wesley and embraced him, clinging tightly. "Son, oh, Wesley Alston," she cried. "I had thought—Oh, Wesley, we had been informed of your death while in Boston." She didn't want to mention having just learned differently from that hussy Serena. Lona Gale didn't want to bring Serena's name into the conversation so soon, to spoil the uniting of the Wyndham family. She would take care of Serena later. She would be sure that the Northern Yankee bitch would not be a part of Wyndham Hall, no matter how Wesley felt about her. It was obvious that she was a tramp. Hadn't she already shared Wesley's bed? First the Indian called Halona taking her son from her, and now, this other woman who was no better than trash? Poor white trash. That's what she was. No. Serena would not be a Wyndham. There were ways. . . .

Wesley clung to his mother, shedding a quick tear also. "Rumors have a way of spreading falsehoods, Mother," he said hoarsely, swallowing hard. "Especially in times of war." His gaze moved across the room, settling on Truman Firman. Ice water filled his veins as he saw the

306

hate in his brother's dark eyes. Truman didn't even seem glad to see him. Did Truman hate him that much? But hadn't Truman always hated him? Why, it made sense that Truman hated him more now that he had seemed to have returned from the grave. All through life, it had been this way between the brothers. Truman had begun hating Wesley as a child simply because Wesley had managed to have been the first born to the Wyndham household.

Wesley forced his gaze from his brother's icy stare, then gently held his mother at arm's length, studying her. Her dark hair, tied into a severe bun, was still a nice shiny brown, not the salt-and-pepper texture that he had expected to find at her older age. But her eyes were different. They showed a sadness that she had probably acquired from the knowledge of her husband's death and the thought of having lost her eldest son. Her wrinkles had deepened, but yet he could still see the beauty she must have been as a young woman by the way her jawline was still so smoothly curved and the tilt of her nose yet so cute.

Her dress was as usual when not entertaining guests— as severe as her hairdo—a dark brown with only a trace of lace at the long cuffs of her sleeves and at the staid, high neck. Ah, it was so different when a ball had been held at Wyndham Hall. It was then that she had worn her most beautiful, low-cut gowns and the flashiest of her jewels. She had always been like a chameleon, changing, ever changing. He never knew what to expect from her. First she could be lovely, as a princess might be, then she could be dowdy, as a simpleton might be. Her personality was also as changeable. First she would be high-spirited, gay, colorful, then she would be cold, heartless, shrewd.

"You look quite well, Mother," he said, smiling warmly. "Seems Boston has done you fine."

She forced a shiver. "But the weather. I so longed for the warm breezes that blow from the Atlantic here on Folly Island," she said, tsk-tsking.

"But your color is quite good," Wesley said, releasing his hold. "Are you truly well?"

"As well as age allows me. But you, Wesley?" she said, moving to him, placing a fragile hand on his arm. "What about you? Don't you have anything else to say about yourself? The war. Was it terrible? I saw the devastation on my journey from Boston." She shook her head in despair. "All the beautiful houses all over the South. How could the North do this to us?"

"Houses?" Wesley said thickly. "Mother, what about the people?"

Lona Gale's eyes showed a quick coldness, the kind that Wesley had seen so often in his youth. He loved his mother, but she did have her way of being misguided in her thoughts. This had caused many a rift between them. She seemed to mostly think of herself and *her* comforts. No one else's. Then the light strummings of a harp drew his quick attention. He glanced toward the staircase that led upward. It was the family harp. The harp had been moved back to its rightful place. Now Wesley understood why the soft glow of a light in Dorlisa May's bedroom.

He listened for a few more seconds, then asked, "And my sister? How is she faring these days?" He watched the color draining from his mother's face as she pulled a lace handkerchief from beneath the lacy cuff of her left sleeve. She began to tap the tip of her nose slightly with it, sniffing.

"The journey to and from Boston was quite taxing for

me, Wesley," Lona Gale sighed heavily.

"Taxing? Why, Mother? Are you saying this because of Dorlisa May?" Wesley asked hoarsely, already knowing the answer.

"Yes. Because of Dorlisa May."

Wesley glanced toward Truman then back to his mother. "Mother, I hope you didn't embarrass that poor girl while on that trip," he growled. "I hope you didn't treat her as lower than yourself, as though she wasn't even your daughter. I know how you are. I know your damn southern pride. It has been almost the downfall of my sister. And you know it."

"Wesley, don't you speak to Mother that way," Truman said, taking wide steps toward Wesley with doubled fists at his side. "If you might notice, I've grown to almost your height and weight. If need be, I can take you down a bit. You must remember your respect for Mother. Respect for mothers comes before respect for sisters."

Wesley threw his head back with laughter. Then he met Truman's approach and held him by his shoulders, glaring into his eyes. "So he does speak, huh?" he said, chuckling. "My little brother has grown up a mite? Well, maybe in outward appearances. But I'm sure you're still the same coward as you've always been. You couldn't run fast enough when the need for men was announced here in the South."

Lona Gale moved toward her two sons. "Boys, boys," she pleaded. "Please. None of this. Not so soon after having just arrived back home."

Wesley released his hold on Truman. "And when did you arrive," he said, moving a forefinger around his shirt collar, clearing his throat nervously.

"We left Boston just as soon as we heard that travel was safe. And once we reached Charleston, we hired a man to secure a carriage and then a boat to bring us to our island," Lona Gale said, sweeping the fullness of her skirt into a chair, settling back against its tall back.

"I would have thought you would have waited a while longer," Wesley grumbled, pacing the floor. He was now worrying about Serena. Had they yet seen her? If so, why was she not present? Had his mother already done her homework and made Serena feel beneath the Wyndhams?

He turned on a heel when Truman came to him and grabbed him by the arm. "You just called me a coward, Wesley," he said, straightening his back. "When I tell you what I did today, you won't call me a coward any longer."

"I can't think of anything you might do to prove that to me," Wesley said between clenched teeth, jerking free. "Growing doesn't automatically make you into a man. You should be smart enough to know that."

"Follow me," Truman said, beaming, showing the usual mischievous wickedness in his dark eyes that he developed as a small child of even two. He moved toward the kitchen, glancing back furtively, making sure Wesley was following him. When he reached the kitchen, he lifted a kerosene lamp, screwed its wick to its uppermost position and moved toward the staircase that led to the basement.

Wesley followed, growing more and more suspicious, now truly wondering what his brother could be up to. The basement only held odds and ends of pieces of furniture being stored, and then there were the Wyndhams' vintage wines. But nothing else. Why was

Truman continuing down the stairs, still glancing back at Wesley with the most wicked glint he had yet been able to muster?

Then at the bottom of the staircase, Truman guided Wesley's way with the lamp across the basement floor, close to where the bottles of wine always lay as in peaceful slumber. Wesley's heart plunged downward when he saw the ruby reds that had been spilled across the basement flooring. It wasn't the ruby red of wine. It was blood. Something tore at Wesley's heart. His first thoughts were of Serena. He went to Truman and grabbed him by the throat, causing him to almost drop the lamp. Wesley's heartbeat was so rapid, he could hardly get his breath to speak, but he did manage to force the words between his lips.

"You didn't . . . you couldn't . . . have hurt . . . Serena . . ." he gasped.

He was taken aback when Truman began to laugh loudly. Then Wesley's gaze followed lamplight to where Truman had dragged the body to lay sprawled clumsily on his back.

"My God, Truman," Wesley shouted. "Who? Why . . . ?" He rushed to the man and felt his pulse, quickly withdrawing when he felt the coldness of the skin. He didn't have to check further. The man was dead. He looked over his body for the wound. There was much blood, but no wound. Then, ever so gently, he turned the man onto his stomach, gasping when he found the wound—in his back.

Wesley looked toward Truman, mortified. Then he glanced back at the man, studying his attire. It was that of a northern soldier. He would never forget this color of blue that the northern soldiers wore. In fact, Wesley knew that he now could never purchase a blue dress suit to wear. It would always be a reminder.

"Truman, you have killed yourself a northern Yankee," Wesley said, rising, scowling toward his brother.

"I know," Truman said, laughing shrilly. "See? I told you I was no longer a coward."

Wesley laughed nervously. "Coward? Truman, you shot this man in the back!" he shouted, gesturing with his hands, swinging them in the air angrily. "And the war is over. You knew that the war was over."

"He was in our house. He had no right."

"Truman, don't you see? He probably didn't even know the war was over. Why in hell would he have been here, obviously hiding, if he had known the war was over? Truman, what you have done here is cold-blooded murder. You could even be hanged. . . ."

"I doubt that," Truman said, chuckling, moving toward the body, kicking it so that it would flip back onto its back. He pointed with the toe of his shoe. "Notice something about this man, Wesley?"

Wesley fell to his knees, examining the body more carefully. "I see that the man's breeches are unbuttoned . . . and that—" he said, then stopped in midsentence when he did notice that the man's manhood was hanging from between the unbuttoned sheath of his breeches. But this could mean many things. He could have been relieving himself . . . and then, he could have . . .

Wesley's gaze moved quickly upward and he felt a numbness enter his body when he saw the cruel crooked smile on his brother's face. He rose quickly and went to Truman, grasping him by the shoulders. "Truman, what are you trying to suggest?" he murmured.

"I'm not trying to suggest anything, Brother," Truman said, stepping away from Wesley, shaking himself, as though his brother's touch had soiled him. "I'm trying to tell you that that soldier deserved to die. He was in *our* house, while . . ."

Wesley placed his doubled fists to his side, boiling with rage inside. "Truman Firman, damn it, spit it out. Whatever it is you have to say, say it," he shouted.

"Your brother shot the man who was consorting with the female you have chosen to bring into our home, Wesley," Lona Gale said suddenly, from behind Wesley. She had made her descent in utter silence, hoping this to be the opportunity to dirty Serena's name. She lifted the skirt of her dress and moved next to Wesley, her eyes flashing.

"You shot him while—?" Wesley gasped, paling, having the need to flee from this crazy situation. Serena? And this soldier? No. What they were saying was wrong . . .

"Wesley, I found the two of them writhing on the floor," Truman said, going to the soldier, kicking him once again, laughing bitterly. "Yes, they made quite a sight. I enjoyed it for a while, then thought the opportunity too great to kill me one of them Yankees for myself."

Wesley hung his head in his hands and turned and rushed up the stairs, not stopping until he had reached the landing of the second floor and headed on toward his and Serena's room. When he flung the door open, he found her standing there, waiting, wide-eyed, the picture of innocence with her strawberry-colored hair hanging in tight ringlets around her face and in a long mass of more curls down her back. Her wide lips quivered nervously as

313

she smiled at him. She had chosen a dress to make her look the southern lady, with its low-cut bodice revealing the magnificence of her bosom, and its full velvet skirt falling from a tightly fitted waist to hang over many yards of petticoat, held outward by a large, swaying hoop.

"Serena?" he said quietly, not moving.

"Wesley?" she murmured, afraid to move.

"I've been in the basement," he finally blurted, kneading his brow.

"Then you know—"

"What should I know?" he asked thickly, inching his way toward her. "What Truman Firman told me—"

"Yes, I'm sure he had fun with that," Serena said quietly, tilting her chin up into the air.

"And my mother—"

Serena laughed lightly. "And, yes, I'm sure your mother took full advantage of this situation. . . ."

"Please tell me what happened," Wesley said, suddenly moving to take her into his arms. "Serena, oh, Serena, are you hurt? I should never have left you alone. God, I should never have left you alone." He snuggled his face into the depths of her hair, now remembering Halona and feeling guilty.

"It was horrible," Serena sobbed. "This man—I found him down there—and he almost succeeded at completely raping me—"

"Almost?" he said, grasping her by the shoulders, eyeing her closely.

"He was raping me when Truman finally stepped forward," she said, lowering her eyes. "He hadn't yet found his complete pleasure," she said in a shallow whisper. Then she jerked her head up, staring at him, almost wildly. "I tried to stop him. I was even ready to

314

grab his gun to shoot him when Truman—"

"So Truman shot him in self-defense? Your defense?"

"Don't you truly think you could call it that, Wesley?"

"That's what we are going to call it," he stormed, whirling on a heel, pacing. "But why would Truman and Mother want me to believe the worst about you?"

"Wesley, need you even ask?"

Wesley went to her and pulled her back into his arms. "Honey, I'm sorry. My family. Well, they are quite hard to get to know. Please be patient." He believed her. He should have known to not suspect Serena of such a deceitful act.

"So you *do* want me to stay on here at Wyndham Hall?"

"I won't let you leave," he said thickly. "Not even if you want to."

Serena smiled to herself. She was now even almost glad that the attack had taken place. It had made Wesley return to her arms. She wouldn't even mention Halona. Not now. Now things had managed to work out better than if she had written the plot herself. After having met his mother and brother, she had known the impossibilities of this situation. But now? She had won Wesley over to her side. The Wyndhams had chosen the wrong way in which to fight this private war over Wesley Alston Wyndham. It seemed her loyalties were constantly changing, and her enemies as well. Wesley was once again her ally and his *family* the enemy.

She clung to him and met his lips in hungry passion when they crushed against hers. Then when he released her, he said, "Come. I have someone else I want you to meet." He began to guide her toward the door, squeezing her hand in his. "I doubt if Mother or Truman bothered to introduce you to the other Wyndham in this house. That's not their style, it seems."

"Another Wyndham," she murmured, having heard the beautiful notes surfacing from the harp. She had wanted to follow the driftings of the music, to discover who was playing, but had felt compelled to stay in the privacy of the bedroom until Wesley came to her. But Serena *did* know the one member of the family who hadn't been introduced to her. She had remembered Wesley speaking of Dorlisa May . . . and how *odd* everyone thought her to be.

As they approached the closed door that led into Dorlisa's room, Wesley tightened his hold on Serena's hand and stopped her, his dark eyes heavy as he stared downward at her. "Before entering, I must prepare you for what you will see," he said thickly.

"I don't understand, Wesley."

"My sister, well, she is . . . different."

Serena covered Wesley's hand with her free one. "Wesley, please let me be the one to see for myself what you might choose to call different," she said firmly. From her brief acquaintance with Wesley's family, she knew that what she would consider ordinary, they might consider different. They were from a different school of life. Serena had realized this right away.

"Then you just want to go on inside?" he said, lifting an eyebrow.

"Yes. Please," Serena said, now becoming more absorbed in the haunting melody that kept drifting in soft waves through the closed door. Anyone who could spin such magic with her fingers had to have much loveliness inside her. She was now even anxious to meet Dorlisa

May. Maybe they could find a liking for one another. Serena needed this. Wesley wouldn't be enough in this house of ice-filled veins.

Wesley reached for the doorknob and slowly pushed the door open, finding a room bathed in soft golden yellows from the low fire on the hearth of the fireplace at the far end of the room, and the steady dancings of a lighted kerosene lamp placed on a table next to where Dorlisa May sat.

Serena looked around the room, taking it all in. There was the harp, and Dorlisa May. Yes, how different she *was* from any of the other Wyndhams.

Serena put a hand on her throat, but when she realized Wesley's eyes were on her, watching her reaction, she quickly brought it to her side. "Why, she's such a lovely girl," she forced herself to say, unable to quit staring. She had never seen an albino before. She had read about them, but never, had she actually seen one.

Sixteen-year-old Dorlisa May was quite fragile in appearance, and her milky-white skin and white hair so contrasted with the purple velveteen dress that she had chosen to wear for her homecoming. Though fragile elsewhere, the low cut of the bodice of the dress revealed quite a swell of flesh, but even more white there than the skin of her face. But her eyes. They reminded Serena of a pet rabbit she had at one time held so precious to her. The pink, ah, the pink of the eyes . . .

"This is Dorlisa May," Wesley whispered, not moving forward or backward, but now gazing intently across the room at the magnificence of the harp resting on the floor and being held between the knees of his one and only sister. When her gaze moved and captured him standing there, her strummings on the harp became louder, less

317

controlled, having lost the haunting effect somehow.

Serena felt an ache circle her heart, seeing not even a trace of happiness on this young girl's face. Dorlisa May's pink eyes didn't even waver when Wesley began to approach her. Serena now was beginning to understand many things, and her hate for Lona Gale deepened.

Wesley moved to Dorlisa May's side and reached a hand to her, gesturing for her to rise. But Dorlisa May defied him with a quick twist of her head and continued to pluck and strum the strings, now once again filling the room with such soft melodies, Serena felt almost as though under some sort of a spell. She fluttered her lashes nervously, then moved on across the room to stand at Wesley's side. "Hello, Dorlisa May," she said, hearing the strain of her own voice, and hating herself for it.

Dorlisa May's gaze moved back to Wesley and held, and her thin, narrow lips stayed firmly sealed. There was now almost a challenge in her eyes as she began playing one tune, over and over again.

"Dorlisa May, I think you've proven your point," Wesley said firmly, suddenly covering Dorlisa May's tiny fingers with his hands, pulling them free, to clasp them tightly inside his own circled fingers. "You have proven that you don't have to become attentive when I enter, that you can play your harp anytime you damn well please. But I have a friend I would like you to meet."

Dorlisa May squinted her eyes as she moved her gaze to Serena. Then she rose upward and suddenly, without any forewarning, threw her arms around Wesley's neck, sobbing harshly. "Wesley, I'm sorry," she whispered. "I should have run to you when I saw you. I had been told you were dead. But when I saw you and knew that you

318

weren't, it was just like old times again. I wanted to defy you. Please don't be angry at me. You know that I mourned for you when I had heard that you were dead. Please love me, Wesley. Please?"

When Serena saw the gentleness with which Wesley held his sister, tears crept to the corners of her eyes. She could see the depth of his love. But why hadn't he spoken of it when having mentioned Dorlisa May earlier? Was it a love that he kept as hidden as Dorlisa May?

"There, there, Dorlisa May," Wesley crooned, lifting her chin to place a swift, light kiss on her lips. "It's all right. I understand. Truly I do."

"But, Wesley, I should've run to you the moment I saw you," she sobbed further. The tears streamed down her face.

"Honey, I said that it was all right," he said more firmly. "And how was your trip to Boston? Did you even have a harp to play while there?"

Dorlisa May's gaze lowered and she wiped at her eyes. "I hated it. Just simply hated it," she said, jerking herself free from Wesley. "Mother. Oh, how I despise her," she said, clenching her fists at her side.

"Dorlisa May, what did Mother do this time?" Wesley sighed in exasperation. She didn't have to answer. He already knew.

"While on the stagecoach," Dorlisa May said, "she . . . well . . . she treated me so horribly. And did I have a harp while at Boston? Yes. Mother rented one. How else could she charm me into the privacy of my room? How else could she be assured to keep me hidden as well while there, as here on Folly Island?"

Serena began a slow boiling inside. She now knew the answers to many things. She had read of the ways of the southern women. Most were too proud for their own good. Well, Serena had another way of putting it. Snobbery. Serena knew that Lona Gale Wyndham didn't want to reflect her weakness by revealing the daughter she had born into this world. Oh, just the thought of it made Serena want to take Dorlisa May by the hand and run outside with her, yell who she was to the world, tell the world how talented, and soft and sweet she was.

And I will, Serena thought further. *Darn it, I will. I will see to it that Dorlisa May is not made to feel as though she should remain in her prison of a room any longer.* Serena knew how she felt. She had been a prisoner herself, until Wesley. *Dorlisa May will not be ashamed of herself if I can have anything to do with it.*

Wesley's face was drawn as he turned to Dorlisa May. "I'm sorry," he murmured.

She swung the skirt of her dress around and moved to a chair to flop down onto it. "Oh, that's all right," she said. "Don't you think I'm used to it by now? Don't you think I even know that mother even hated to have tutors for me, so afraid they would rush to the busybodies in Charleston and tell them of the freak that was kept hidden? Don't you even know that I am aware of the money she paid—for these tutors' silence?" Her gaze moved to Serena and held.

Serena made use of this and made her quick approach. She positioned herself in front of the fire, with hands held behind her, facing Dorlisa May. "Dorlisa May, I'm Serena Kassia Calvert," she said, then swinging a hand around, offered it to Dorlisa May in a gesture of friendship.

Dorlisa May pushed herself up from the chair and slowly inched her hand toward Serena's. "I've been rude," she said, casting her pink eyes downward, but yet making a firm hold on Serena's hand. "Will you forgive me, Serena?" she added, moving her gaze upward once again, showing a quiet pleading.

"You've done nothing to be forgiven for," Serena said, dropping her hands to her side when Dorlisa May moved back to the chair. "I love the way you play the harp, Dorlisa May," Serena quickly added, seeing how this remark lit up the emptiness of Dorlisa May's eyes.

"Thank you. I play from the heart. Always. My heart guides my fingers. One can usually tell my mood by the way I play."

Serena tensed inside, remembering the haunting melody of only moments ago. Even now it created goosebumps across Serena's flesh. Her gaze moved to Wesley as he moved across the room to join them beside the fire.

"I think we should go downstairs," he said, looking briefly from Serena, then to Dorlisa May.

Dorlisa May began to fidget with the gathers of her skirt. "I don't think it best, Wesley," she murmured. "I must stay here. I must practice."

Wesley's face reddened. "Practice? For whom? For what? You know damn well why you won't go downstairs. Because of Mother. When, oh, when are you going to defy *her?* You always choose *me* to defy. Well, Dorlisa May, it's high time you chose to defy the one who has made your life so lonely and miserable."

"But, Wesley, don't you see? It's so easy to defy you. It isn't . . . Mother," she said, blinking her eyes nervously, revealing her white lashes that were as thick as Wesley's, the only resemblance between brother and sister. She rose and went to her harp and positioned herself behind it. "No. I prefer to stay here where I am wanted. My harp loves me. My harp needs me."

Serena swallowed hard as she glanced sharply at Wesley. "Wesley, can't you—" she whispered, trembling inside.

"After all these years?" he said sullenly. "I truly gave up trying long ago. Come on. Let's go downstairs. I feel my family needs to meet you in the appropriate fashion."

Serena's face drained of color. "What does that mean, Wesley?"

He straightened his back and offered her his arm. "It is about time for my family to meet my fiancée," he shouted, glancing over his shoulder, making sure Dorlisa May had heard. He broke into a wide grin when he saw her smile of approval before she began strumming the strings, creating a soft, sweet melody, one that trailed along after Serena and Wesley as they moved down the staircase.

Serena's heart was pounding erratically; she wondered if she had heard right. Did he dare? Especially after seeing how the Wyndhams so obviously hated his choice?

Wesley's heart was pounding, too. Had he actually said it? Did he dare?

But then his smile widened. Having just witnessed his sister's torment once again and being reminded of his mother's brutality had sealed it for him. He would show his mother. Lona Gale could shame Dorlisa May into a corner, but not Wesley Alston. Never. And as for the other fears that had plagued him since the first time he had thought to take a wife—he would have to brush those worries aside. He had something to prove to his mother, and, by God, he would do it!

"I love you, Wesley," Serena said, cuddling to his side

as they made their last step onto the first-floor landing only footsteps away from the drawing room. She was still trying to push the Indian woman from her mind. She was still trying to forget the hate she had felt for Wesley at that moment, when she had seen him caressing, kissing, holding another woman. She must not have meant anything to Wesley. He had chosen to ask Serena Kassia Calvert to be his wife. Not Halona. But she would always wonder if he would sneak off to be in Halona's arms even after their marriage vows were spoken. Would he? For now she would brush such thoughts aside and would relish the thought that one day soon she might become Mrs. Wesley Alston Wyndham. Oh, how beautiful a ring that had to it!

"I'll always love you, darling," Wesley said, scooping her into his arms for an ecstatic kiss before moving on into the drawing room. Then when they were fully composed and went to face Lona Gale and Truman Firman, Wesley guided Serena in proudly beside him and began to make the announcement when a sudden clamor erupted at the other far end of the room, stopping him.

"What the—?" Wesley said, looking toward the door that led into the kitchen. His mouth dropped open in dismay when Tobias entered the drawing room with the five Negro children that Wesley had sent him to bring back to Folly Island.

Lona Gale rushed to Tobias with her arms held tightly to her sides. "Tobias, what in the world are you doing bringing . . . these . . . these . . . slaves into my house?" she screamed. "Never, never, have I allowed slaves in this house. Only my chosen servants. Take them away. This minute. Do you hear? Or you shall be dismissed from your duties. *Immediately*."

Serena rushed to Tobias's side. "No. You cannot do that," she snapped, turning to glower at Lona Gale. "I asked Wesley to send for these children. We shall keep them here. I especially will request that the older child be my personal maid." She crossed her arms in defiance and lifted her chin haughtily as she saw the color drain from Lona Gale's face.

"Why, you . . . you . . . northern Yankee, how dare you," Lona Gale hissed. "The Yankee soldiers come into my house and desecrate it. Then *you* come into my home. You cause blood to be shed. You sleep with my son. And then you think you can tell me how to run my household? I have been the mistress of this mansion for way too long to let someone like you come in here and try to take charge." She turned to Wesley, eyes flaring. "You tell your hussy to move aside," she ordered.

Wesley chuckled and stood his ground. "No, Mother, I don't think I will," he said smoothly, lifting his eyebrows in amusement. "You see, we need these children. We have no slaves left on our plantation. These children will have to do for us until we can find help. Now it is you who has to step aside. Need I remind you who is in charge here since Father's death?"

Lona Gale spun around and began to leave the room, stopping only long enough to turn to Truman Firman, who had remained quiet during this latest outburst between Wyndhams. "You come with me, Truman Firman," she said flatly. "It seems the only true Wyndhams aren't needed here. We shall retire to our rooms and tomorrow you and I will plot our strategy." She glared first at Serena, then Wesley, then hurried on her way.

"I think you've done it this time, Wesley," Truman

Firman said, laughing oddly. "Mother will never forgive you for this. It is I who shall in the end be the master of Wyndham Hall. Just you wait and see. Mother will see to it."

"That's the only thing you've ever truly wanted, isn't it?" Wesley said sullenly. "All your life, you never thought of trying to get your way by loving. Only by hating. And your plan has always been to degrade me and get me out of the way. Well, Truman, just try it. Just you try it."

Truman Firman rushed from the room, laughing loudly.

Serena moved to Wesley and placed her arm through his. "Wesley, maybe I shouldn't have . . ." she said softly. Her mouth! Her father had always told her the trouble it caused. "I'm sorry if I've caused a rift between you and your family."

"You? Ha!" he exclaimed. "This is the way it's always been. Poor Father. He witnessed it until it even caused his first heart attack. By God! I shan't let this continue to happen to me, or Dorlisa May."

Serena's gaze moved to the children, all brown-eyed and clinging to one another. Their clothes were in filth-laden shreds and their cheeks were empty of flesh. She went to the smallest, possibly aged four. She bent and touched the smooth brown skin; this was the first time she had ever come in personal contact, flesh to flesh, with someone who had been born into this world a slave. Seeing the deep sadness in his eyes, she was reminded of Abe Lincoln and the sadness that had always been in the depths of his eyes when he had spoken so against slavery.

Something compelled Serena to fall to her knees, to pull this child into her arms. She felt the bones beneath his flesh and smelled the strong aroma of filth, neither a fault of the child, and suddenly understood Lincoln's compassion for the slaves and his deep commitment to do away with slavery.

She gently pushed him from her, holding him by his tiny waist. "And what might your name be?" she asked, trying to force a cheerfulness into her voice.

His voice was as frail as he was. "Bubba," he murmured.

Serena laughed softly. "I love your name, Bubba," she said, then pushed herself up and went to the oldest, the only female of the small family gathering. "And your name?" she asked.

"Francine," was her answer in a slow southern drawl, while Francine twisted the gathers of her soiled cotton dress around her fingers.

"And the rest, Francine? What are your brother's names and ages?"

Francine broke into a bashful smile, then spoke even more slowly. "Toy, he's eight, Elijah, he's six, and Martin, he's five."

"And your age?" Serena asked, lifting a black pigtail.

"Fifteen, ma'am. Be sixteen in a month."

"Did Tobias tell you why we wanted you here with us?" Wesley said, going to Serena's side, thrusting his hands deeply into his rear breeches pockets.

"Yes, Massa," Toy blurted. "And we be powerful hungry. Can we have somethin' to eat right away? Bubba here, he's already too skinny."

Wesley chuckled. He couldn't understand how he could have ever been angry at these children. Weren't they so helpless and innocent? Somehow the word "slave" didn't match their innocence, though he had had

326

many slaves born into the world at his plantation. These children seemed special. But these children had become suddenly special when they had been forced out onto the streets of Charleston and made homeless.

"Yes. I think we can scrape something up," Wesley said, eyeing Tobias.

"Yassa, Massa Wesley, while in town, I gathered up what supplies I could get my hands on."

"Then, Francine, you wash up and try your skills in the kitchen," Wesley said, trying to not let his words sound like an order, though this was not his way. He had ordered too many slaves in the past, to suddenly be forced to show a different side to his character. But he would learn. He had no choice.

Francine's dark eyes sparkled as she clasped her hands together. "Yassa, Massa," she sighed. She gathered her clan into her arms and shooed them ahead of her until they had all disappeared into the kitchen.

Wesley moved to Tobias and placed an arm around his massive shoulders. "You did good, Tobias, ol' boy," he said, cheerfully. "It's good to be home."

"I'll get on to the outdoor living quarters and ready spaces for the chillen to stay," Tobias said eagerly. He then lowered his eyes a bit and mumbled, "And, Massa Wesley, Tobias so glad you home."

Wesley chuckled a bit. "You do that, Tobias," he said. "And see to it that tomorrow you begin to search for more adult . . . uh . . . help."

"Yassa, Massa Wesley," Tobias said, then scampered away.

Wesley had noticed that Tobias didn't refer to the outbuilding as the "slave quarters." Yes, Tobias was up on things. He had hated his past friends having to be slaves, even though he had never considered himself one. "An overseer is not a slave," he had so often argued to Wesley. Wesley had always shrugged and let him have his way with things as he would continue doing now.

Serena moved to Wesley and placed her arms around his neck and pulled him to her. "You see? That wasn't so hard."

"What? I don't know what you're talking about," he teased.

"Oh, Wesley Alston," she said. "Just kiss me and shut up." As his lips crushed hers with a fierce intensity, Serena suddenly remembered that the announcement of their marriage had been postponed. . . .

Chapter Seventeen

It was a period of precarious existence for the Wyndhams, a life made possible by the availability of oysters, fish, shrimp and other seafood from the creeks and rivers. The revival of the Wyndham estate as a cotton plantation had been slow, but now that August had arrived, Wesley could stand at his bedroom window and gaze proudly at row after row of large and bushy cotton plants.

It wasn't the huge crop that it had been before the war, but with the return of most of his faithful slaves, who were now referred to as freedmen or field hands, they had been able to plant at least half the amount as before. It took about a bushel of seed to plant an acre, and four acres were generally considered work for one field hand. With the family jewels used as collateral, enough bushels of seed had been acquired to cover the wide spaces of three hundred acres of land.

Wesley leaned out of his window, seeing some stirrings below him. His plantation always came to life with the rising of the sun, and even before noon, a nearly full day's work was done, enabling the hands a few hours rest while the sun was at its highest. Wesley's father had always allowed this during the hottest month of the year and the loyalty he had gathered from his slaves because of these leniencies was the reason that most slaves had chosen to return to Folly Island. When they had discovered that Carvell Chatwin Wyndham was no longer alive and the master of the Wyndham plantation, they had wondered about staying. The good massa was dead. How would the young massa treat them?

But most had stayed on because they had found that living from day to day away from this plantation that had always been their home had handed them nothing but hardship. Disease was sweeping across the country, the companion of hunger and lack of sanitation. Whites and blacks had struggled to survive in makeshift shelters.

Seeing these plights and struggles, Congress had passed a bill creating the Freedman's Bureau, whose responsibility was to look after refugees, freedmen, and abandoned lands. Agents of the bureau were expected to help poverty-stricken white people, but their major responsibility became that of serving as guardians for the freedmen. A rumor had even spread that every former slave would get "forty acres and a mule" as a Christmas gift from the government in Washington, because of the vague promise in that bill that said abandoned land would eventually be distributed among the freedmen. Freedmen accepted it as truth and, overjoyed at the prospect of soon owning their own farms, refused to work for the white South, causing the progress of the South to come once again to a halt because there was no one to do the work in the fields. The bitterness against the Negroes became worse than even before the war. And because of this growing bitterness of the white South against the freedmen, the plantation owners gathered together, wrote and enforced slave codes, insisting these codes were necessary to restore order in the South. These codes forbade Negroes to possess firearms unless licensed to do so; to appear on the streets or roads after sunset; to travel without licenses; and to assemble without the presence of white men.

The codes also prohibited Negroes from entering business, provided for tight labor controls, and severe apprenticeship regulations, and put restrictions on the renting or leasing of farm land by Negroes. And if any of these codes were not followed, the Negro would be fined, and to pay the fines, the blacks would be hired out. Many were forced to work without pay.

What the codes succeeded at doing was forcing the freedmen back into other forms of slavery once again, having to return to most plantations for wages so low, they could still hardly feed or clothe their families.

But seeing the importance of fairness, and having the need to be in as good a standing with the field hands as his father had always been, Wesley had taken a further step to assure himself of the best crops in South Carolina. He had subdivided his plantation into small farms, going against the slave codes, and had leased these to his field hands for not even a profit to himself, and had promised the best of wages once the first crop was in.

Since having done this, he had seen more energies around Wyndham Plantation than he had ever thought possible. Yes. He had won the freedmen's respect and he planned to keep it!

Wesley continued buttoning his shirt, inhaling the fragrance of the twelve-inch magnolia blossoms that still bloomed outside his window, though most generally May and June were the months this was usually enjoyed. The rainfalls had handed this extended pleasure to Folly Island, causing at the same time many other hardships.

Wesley furrowed his brow. Because of these rains, he and his field hands had fought a different kind of war this summer. Grass, generally referred to as "General Green," continued to plague his fields because of its quick growth after a sudden rainfall.

The hoes had kept at a steady pace all summer long. They were kept sharp as razors and a skilled hand could chop out grass and weeds within a quarter inch of the cotton stalk without harming the plant. Some days, more hoeing had been done than anything else, because this summer had been the wettest of any past years.

A wide smile suddenly lifted Wesley's mustache upward and Serena saw this as she crept from the bed and moved to his side.

"What are you thinking about, Wesley?" she asked, wanting to reach for him, but deciding not to since something unknown to her had seemed to pull them apart again. They had shared a bed the past several nights, but nothing more. Serena had again suspected Halona to be the cause. Wesley had made it too much of a habit to leave the island early each morning. He always had what appeared legitimate reasons, but hadn't he also on the one day Serena had seen him and Halona embracing?

He swung around, now slipping into his beige waistcoat which had a way of making his tan appear even darker. "I was thinking about the feast that is nearing for our field hands," he said. He moved on past her without showing even a notice of the sheer chemise revealing her nudity beneath. The more he had thought of marriage, the more he had pulled away from her. Now how could he truly explain to her his fears of the oddity of the

Wyndham ancestors, his fear of having an albino child, when she had grown so attached to Dorlisa May these past weeks? The argument wouldn't seem valid somehow. Serena didn't look down her nose at the different skin and eye coloring. But if she would bear such a child . . . a son . . . then would she feel the same?

Any way he looked at it, he felt that his indecision was causing him to lose her. He knew that he would have to make a move, and one day soon. God, how long ago had it been since he had actually told her that he was going to make the announcement to his family? How much longer could he even put it off?

He forced a deep chuckle. "You've not seen watermelons until you've seen watermelons grown at this Wyndham Plantation," he said, placing his holster and pistol at his waist.

Serena wrapped a robe around her and tied it. "Watermelons?" she said. "I didn't realize that your field hands had planted watermelons."

"During the last hoeing session, they planted watermelon seeds under the growing cotton plants, knowing that the vines will grow and the melons will be ripe around the cotton picking time."

"How clever," Serena giggled. "So while working hard, they'll have some nourishment."

"Sweet, juicy nourishment," he chuckled further. "But I've asked that many of this year's watermelon crop be taken to Charleston to sell at the Watermelon Market. We need all the money we can get our hands on. We're making it so far, but I want to see to it that Wyndham Plantation is *the* plantation spoken of in the South."

"I believe it already has the reputation you wish for, Wesley."

"Not until I can feel free to enjoy plantation life as it was in the past," he grumbled. "One day, Charleston will be revived as a flourishing social city and I want to be able to be a part of that social life. I want to acquire enough wealth to enjoy every aspect of life to the fullest."

"And myself, Wesley? Do you include me in this plan of yours?" Serena asked, inching her arms around his neck. She felt the familiar ache between her thighs, having so missed his caresses.

Wesley's eyes wavered, then he hugged her to him. "Yes, darling. I do," he said.

"And, Wesley, where are you going this morning, so dressed up?" she murmured, tensing, not lifting her head from his shoulder.

"Into Charleston. I'm going to see that complete repairs are being made to my townhouses. There is so much reconstruction going on, I don't want my residences to be neglected."

Serena jerked away from him, her eyes flashing in mixtures of golden browns. "I don't believe you," she snapped. "It's the same every day. You cannot be that loyal to your townhouses. You say I'm to be included in your future plans. But what about now? We've been together for months and we are still not married. I feel like a whore. Your mother treats me like a whore. I've begun to hate Wyndham Hall. It seems the only satisfaction I receive is when I am with Dorlisa May, and, Wesley, that is just not enough for me."

"First of all, Mother does not show her anger to you because of what she thinks of you sharing my bed with me," Wesley stated flatly. "Yes, she resents you being here, knowing that I am in love with you, but she has grown to resent you more deeply because of Dorlisa May.

334

Don't you know that? Can't you see?"

"But why, Wesley? No. I don't understand. I only have done what any person would have done. I have made friends with the sweet, gentle sister of the man I love."

"By becoming so close to Dorlisa May, you have threatened Mother's way of existence at Wyndham Hall. Even in Charleston," Wesley said. "She is afraid that you have accomplished what she has been unable to succeed at. To make Dorlisa May feel normal, part of the human race. By getting Dorlisa May out of this house with you, out of the four walls of her room, taking the long strolls along the beach and having picnics beneath the lacy moss. Mother never did any of these things. Never."

"She never tried. Now admit it, Wesley," Serena stormed. "The main thing now is that your mother feels I may introduce Dorlisa May into society. Isn't that it? What if this white-haired, pink-eyed young lady would enter Charleston's life of society once the balls had begun again? What would this do to your mother's reputation? She would probably be the one to have to hide away in a room. She would have to feel ashamed to have kept such a lovely daughter from her friends. Oh, Wesley, it's just horrid what your mother has done to your sister."

Wesley hung his head into his hands. "Yes. I do know. I have always known. But I just hadn't wanted to admit it to anyone . . . to speak all these truths out loud."

"Well, one day, the truth will be known," she hissed. "And one day the truth of your wanderings will be known also, Wesley," she said even more firmly.

His gaze shot upward. "What the hell are you talking about?" he stammered.

"Do I have to truly spell it out, Wesley Alston?" she

335

said, placing her hands on her hips. "Don't you think I know that you are having more than business on your mind these days? Is it the Indian, Wesley? Is that the one who shares your embraces?"

"Serena, what . . . how . . . ?" he stammered further, his face having lost its color.

"Wesley, I've known since that first day," she said. "I saw you and that Indian. How could you have? After what we had shared together from the moment we met? And how many times since, Wesley? Or do you dare to try to keep count?"

Wesley rushed to her and tried to pull her into his arms but failed when she jerked away from him and moved to the far end of the room, pouting. "It's not at all what you think, Serena," he said anxiously.

"Wesley, I have eyes. I saw. . . ."

"Yes. You saw us embrace," he said hurriedly, guessing. "But Halona and I . . . well . . . uh . . . we go back a long ways. Since we were children. We are like . . . brother and sister. Nothing more."

"You are a liar, Wesley Alston," she screamed. "I saw you and Halona kissing, and I saw how your hands wandered over her body."

"Why didn't you say something earlier, Serena?"

"I had hoped that I wouldn't have to. You had promised to marry me. I thought she would be forgotten," she said, then heard a break in her voice when she said further, "But you haven't forgotten her, have you? You probably go to be with her every day."

"I haven't. I truly haven't," Wesley said, moving to her side. "Believe me. Trust me."

She stomped a foot even more angrily. "How can you even ask me to trust you? Believe you? You have told me over and over again how much you love me, even talk of marriage, then the days and weeks pass and no wedding date is set. No. Wesley, I cannot believe you."

"Then what do you propose to do about it?" he said flatly, growing more angry by the minute. He felt trapped. Damned if he did, and damned if he didn't. But one thing for sure, he didn't like Serena shouting at him for the whole household to hear. This could drive him completely away from her. No man liked to be ordered or made to feel lower than the female. Especially in his own house.

"I don't know, Wesley," she said sullenly. "I just don't know."

He whirled around, heading toward the door, then said over his shoulder. "Then when you decide, let me know." He fled the room, slamming the door noisily behind him.

Serena doubled her fists at her side and stomped a foot again. "Oh!" she shouted. "Oh! Wesley, sometimes I hate you so." She began pacing the floor, wondering what to do next. She had hoped to get some answers. But all she managed to pull from him was anger. Frustration was beginning to eat away at her insides. She had to find a way to bring Wesley to his senses. She could no longer bear the thought of him being in that Indian's arms. She had to think of something. And soon.

A light tapping on her bedroom door drew her back to what she had planned for this morning. As most mornings, when rain wasn't a deterrent, she and Dorlisa May would move to the out-of-doors before the sun became too strong. Dorlisa May's milkish-white skin was always at risk of burning. And the brightness of the sun always made Dorlisa May's eyes ache, causing her to keep them in a constant squint.

Dorlisa May had explained that the reason for her having to squint in sunlight was because of a lack of pigment in the iris of her eyes, allowing more light to enter than usual. And she had also explained that the pinkish cast to her eyeballs was because the blood of the tiny vessels of the eye showed through the transparent parts of the eye.

Dorlisa May had further explained that upon first discovering her difference in appearance from all others around her, it had been Wesley who had taken time to explain the reasons why to her. But from the reactions of the rest of the Wyndham family, who treated her as a freak, she had grown to be ashamed of this difference. A bedroom had become her only way of existence, until Serena.

Serena had made her feel alive, wanted, loved. Wesley had tried during Dorlisa May's first years of life, but the strong personality of their mother had caused anything that he had accomplished to fail, because of her stronger need not to show this "weaker" side of their family to all who would stare and gossip.

Yes, Serena knew that if nothing else had been accomplished since having landed at Folly Island, she had at least made a young girl happy with herself. She flew to the door and opened it eagerly, smiling broadly when she saw Dorlisa May already dressed, ready for the outing, and carrying her ever-faithful blue-flowered parasol, her only protection against the rays of the sun.

"Serena, you're not even dressed yet," Dorlisa May sighed heavily, disappointment showing in the droop of her lips.

"Your brother and I, well, we had much to discuss this

morning," Serena said quietly. She gestured with her hand. "Come on in, Lisa. I won't be a minute." She watched as Dorlisa May moved on into the room, in an almost skipping fashion. She had dressed in a long, pale blue eyelet, fully gathered dress and had done as Serena suggested, made sure to choose a dress that had long, full sleeves and a high neck, to be assured of having more of her body covered from the hot rays of the sun that on occasion would peak beneath the opened parasol.

A cute, wide-brimmed straw hat made heavy shadows over most of Dorlisa May's face, but this was as necessary as eating, if Dorlisa May was to be able to continue with these daily outings. But even this didn't keep her eyes from constantly watering. Serena had begun to worry that maybe these things might in the end discourage Dorlisa May into moving back into the privacy of her room. But so far, it hadn't. Dorlisa May ate up this out-of-doors. She seemed to be in awe of everything she came in contact with. A simple seashell would cause her to stand immobile, to study it for moment upon moment.

How it warmed Serena's heart. And this day, they would travel to the beach and watch the loggerhead turtles' nests. Serena and Dorlisa May had been watching eagerly each day for the eggs to hatch.

Maybe today, she thought to herself, going to the wardrobe to choose her own outfit. She didn't have to be careful with flaunting her own skin to the sun. She ate the sun up as Dorlisa May did all these new things she was experiencing. So she chose a flimsy cotton attire, with the lowest of necklines and shortest of sleeves in which to be able to romp and play as a child along the long stretches of the beach. She would forget Wesley for the time being. Then later, she would question him, and would even have to tell him of her decision. Would she remain at Wyndham Hall, or would she return to Illinois? She had received a wire from Priscilla that their father had had a mild stroke. Guilt pangs had plagued her, knowing that she should indeed return to her father's side. But when Priscilla had then later wired of his having almost fully recovered, Serena had decided to stay a while longer with Wesley, still hoping that a wedding date would be soon set. Then, after she had become Mrs. Wesley Alston Wyndham, she would return at her leisure to check in first person on her father's well being. She had to smile, remembering the further words of the wire: that Priscilla and Edward had married, and that a smaller Carlson was on the way. *Priscilla a mother?* Serena thought laughingly to herself. *Well, maybe . . .*

Stepping behind a folded screen, Serena hurriedly changed into her dress, omitting the heavy froth of petticoats, wanting to feel the ocean breezes move like soft caresses up the inside of her dress. She had begun to have a love affair with the ocean. So often she would remove her shoes and run barefoot through the lacy effervescense left on the sandy shore after the lapping waves would recede and become as part of the greater part of the ocean once again. It was at these moments that she could push Wesley, and the pain he continually inflicted on her, from her mind.

"Do you think the baby turtles will hatch from the eggs today?" Dorlisa May asked, going to the window, but suddenly shielding her eyes from the brightness with the back of her hand.

"Let's hope so," Serena said. "It will be exciting witnessing new births."

"Let's not even stop for breakfast, Serena," Dorlisa

May said, rushing to clasp Serena's hand in hers as Serena stepped fully clothed from behind the screen.

"Should you?" Serena asked. "You aren't the strongest, you know. And once on the beach, we'll be there a while."

"If you can go without breakfast, so can I," Dorlisa May said stubbornly, turning from Serena, pouting. She was no longer as frail and didn't wish to be reminded of when she had been. Not even by Serena.

"I'm sorry, Lisa," Serena murmured, pulling her hair back from her face and tying a yellow bow around its thickness. "We shall sneak down the stairs like thieves in the night and rush from the house and enter a world of morning's awakenings." She moved to the door, whispering, "And are you even ready now, Lisa?" She had chosen the shorter name Lisa. It made the bond between Dorlisa May and herself even more affectionate, somehow.

"Yes. Yes," Dorlisa May said excitedly.

"Then silence must be our companion until we get past the kitchen," Serena murmured, opening the door, peering cautiously down the hall on both sides for any comings or goings from any of the many rooms that lined either side of the hallway. Then feeling like the girl she had been on those evenings in Illinois, when she had sneaked to visit Wesley at his bedside in the hospital quarters, she crept from the room, then down the stairs, until she and Dorlisa May were finally on the beach, laughing as gaily and as carefree as young school girls.

Serena threw her head back and stretched her arms out, sighing leisurely. The sky was such a brilliant blue, without even a trace of a cloud. Then she gazed across the wide stretch of aqua blue ocean, the waves restless as usual, lapping, ever lapping onto the sandy shore.

Then moving on ahead of Dorlisa May, she began to gather a bouquet of sweet myrtle that was growing from the sand dunes, and also that of another beautiful flowering plant called the sea oxeye. This flower reminded Serena of the Illinois daisy, with its yellow blossom.

After adding one more type of flower, the horsemint with its prominent pink tips, to her bouquet, she walked to where Dorlisa May had built a sand castle the day before while Serena had spread out beneath the sun's rays for a sunbath.

Serena smiled to herself. The tide hadn't removed the razor clam shells that had been used for the long French windows. The auger shells were still standing atop the corners of every parapet and the row of moon shells were still embedded along the side of the castle. "For protection against an invasion," Dorlisa May had said before having to retreat, parasol and all, to the shade of the live oaks.

Serena laughed softly, then joined Dorlisa May, to walk by her side. "Serena, I've grown to love you so," Dorlisa May said, softly kicking through the sand as they began searching for the turtles' nests that they had discovered a few days earlier in the depths of the sand. "You are like a sister to me." She stooped and began running her hands through the sand. She shielded her eyes from the sun when she gazed upward at Serena, saying quietly, "And when will you become truly my sister? When are you and Wesley to be wed? I'm so anxious. I've never attended a wedding, or any such function before."

Not wanting to answer, not even knowing the answer

herself, Serena inched away from Dorlisa May, feeling a deep sadness, not only for herself for Wesley's neglect of her, but also for Dorlisa May and the world's neglect of *her*.

Serena chewed on her lower lip for a moment, not answering; then when she saw the first signs of life on the sand below where she had just stopped, she squealed with delight. "Dorlisa! Lisa, come here," she said. "One has hatched and, oh, it's so tiny!"

Dorlisa May moved to Serena's side, gasping with her free hand covering her mouth. Her gaze moved up the full length of the beach. The sand itself appeared to have come alive as many hatchling turtles began to wriggle to the surface of the sand and begin to make their slow march to the water.

"What an effort they are having," Serena said, watching first one, then another, of the tiny baby turtles scooting on the flatness of their bellies. They were so clumsy, and when various varieties of birds made a sudden appearance and began to swoop down, to make their early morning's breakfast of these helpless babies, it was apparent that most wouldn't make it to the water. Serena dropped her bouquet in the sand, aghast.

She began to wave her arms and shout at the birds, but nothing frightened them. Their instinct told them to devour this food so accessible to them, as the hatchlings' instinct continued to draw them to their home—the ocean.

"What can we do?" Dorlisa May screamed. "The poor babies."

Serena began running along the beach, scooping up as many hatchlings as she could, holding the skirt of her dress up, like a large pocket, placing the turtles in it. But suddenly there was something on this stretch of oceanfront to fear besides the birds. Serena felt fingers of fear traveling up her spine when she caught sight of an Indian crouching behind a sand dune. She could see enough of him to recognize that he only wore the skimpiness of a loin cloth and his coal black hair had been pulled severely back from his face to lay down his back in a long, thick pigtail. He held a bow and a quiver of arrows and stared back at her with contempt in his wide-set dark eyes.

Dorlisa May's continued frantic screams drew Serena's attention back to her and when Serena turned and began to go to Dorlisa May, she found Truman Firman already there, guiding Dorlisa May quickly toward the house.

"Truman? Dorlisa?" Serena shouted, suddenly forgetting the Indian.

Truman turned and glared at Serena, shouting across his shoulder as he kept moving with Dorlisa May. "I knew no good would come of you taking Dorlisa May out of the house," he said. "Why can't you just leave this family alone? Don't you see how upset Dorlisa May is? You're trouble. Nothing but trouble."

Dorlisa May's continued sobs tore pieces of Serena's heart away. She wanted to shout back at Truman, defend herself, but felt it useless. She would have felt she was arguing with Wesley all over again. She shivered. Since Truman had decided to grow a mustache, the resemblance of the two brothers had become almost uncanny, but only in appearances. Truman would never, ever know how to be gentle. Even now, as he pretended an alliance to his sister, Serena knew that only selfish motives guided him. To show a caring for Dorlisa May now was only an effort on Truman's part to pull Dorlisa

344

May away from Serena. Serena knew this and she wouldn't let it happen. And it was so plain to see that Truman's hate for Wesley continued to grow as Wesley showed his skills at being the master of Wyndham Hall.

The steady flapping of the birds' wings on each side of her made Serena begin to turn in circles, not knowing what to do. All around her, life was coming to a halt. It was almost unbearable for Serena. It was becoming a vicious cycle. The turtles kept hatching . . . the turtles kept crawling . . . the birds kept devouring. . . .

Rescuing more hatchlings into the gathers of her skirt, carrying them to the ocean, over and over again, Serena didn't notice someone's fast approach. When Wesley's voice broke through her state of semishock, she turned with a start just as he grabbed her and pulled her into his arms.

"Wesley, what?" she stammered, trembling.

"You're all right?" he said thickly. "Serena, you're all right?"

"Yes, I'm fine," she said, gently pulling away from him. "Wesley, you act as though I'm in some sort of danger. Honey, I'm not in danger. These poor turtles are the ones in danger. That's why I've been rushing so frantically around. To rescue as many as I can."

Wesley gasped, grasping onto her shoulders. "Didn't you see Wolfram?" he said, now panting.

"Wolfram? Who is—"

"A Kiawah warrior," he said, quickly. "He was ready to reach out for you. Only moments ago. I saw him as I came down the front steps of the house, right after Truman Firman brought Dorlisa May into the house crying. My God, Serena, you didn't see him?"

Serena's face paled, looking quickly toward the sand

dune where she had seen the Indian, but before Truman and Dorlisa had reached the house. That meant that the Indian warrior had been ready to grab her after she had seen him that first time. "Oh, Wesley," she cried. "I simply forgot about him. I did see him. Before Truman came and got Dorlisa May and drew my attention away from the Indian."

"Well, he's gone now. When he saw me running this way with my gun drawn, he took off like a deer."

"Why was he here? Why would he even want to harm me?" She stepped back away from Wesley, eyes wide. "And, Wesley, why are you even here? You said that you were going to Charleston."

"Darling, enough questions for now," he said thickly, pulling her to his side, urging her toward the house. "Let's go to our room, where we can have a serious talk." *Wolfram. Damn that Indian*, he thought angrily to himself. He now knew that that Indian warrior was planning some sort of reprisal. Would he have truly kidnapped Serena? If so, what had his plans been?

Wesley pulled Serena closer to him, realizing once again the strength of his love for her. If Wolfram so much as showed his face on this island again, Wesley knew that he would track Wolfram down and make sure no future worries of that Indian would ever be necessary.

"But what about the hatchlings, Wesley?" Serena stammered. She stumbled a bit, glancing back over her shoulder. She grew a bit ill when birds continued with their feast. She moved her gaze forward once again, doubting if she could ever think a bird beautiful again.

"Serena, this is nature at its ugliest," Wesley said. "But it *is* an act of nature. No man can stand in the way of this cycle that's been a part of this oceanfront beach for eons."

"But the poor things," Serena murmured, moving up the front steps of Wyndham Hall next to Wesley.

When the front door flew open, Lona Gale moved onto the porch in a rage. "Wesley, you should see the state Dorlisa May is in," she said, narrowing her eyes when she stole a quick glance toward Serena.

"And you truly care, Mother?" Wesley uttered, his few words full of sarcastic overtones.

"Why, I never," Lona Gale snapped, crossing her arms in anger as Wesley guided Serena by the elbow on into the house and up the one flight of stairs to the privacy of their room. He closed the door and locked it, then went to Serena and kissed her ever so gently, then whispered into her ear, "Darling, will you marry me? Even one day this week?"

Serena's heartbeat hastened. All thoughts of hatchlings, the Indian, Lona Gale's anger, were swept from her mind as though by a warm, gentle breeze. "Did you say *marry*, Wesley?" she murmured. "We can be married . . . even . . . this week?"

He pulled her closer to him and held her. "Yes. I've been a fool," he said. "But when I explain, you will surely understand. Come. Let's go sit while we talk."

Still smelling of seawater and sunshine, Serena walked as though in a daze and sat down opposite Wesley. She listened intently, breathing hard with eager anticipation of finally going to become Mrs. Wesley Alston Wyndham, a dream that she had carried with her since their very first embrace.

"First, let me explain why my sudden return instead of going to Charleston this morning," he said, then laughed lightly, lifting an eyebrow. "And, yes, darling. I *was* going to Charleston. That *is* where I've been these past several days. The townhouses are looking beautiful again."

Serena lowered her eyes, blushing. "Wesley, I'm sorry," she murmured. "I've been a witch. I know I have."

"You've had reason to be," he said in a strain, lowering *his* eyes. "You see, I've been a bastard. That's why I decided not to go to Charleston after all this morning. I decided I was leaving you angry for the last time." He rose and removed his waistcoat, then unbuttoned his shirt at the neck. He turned on his heel, his thick lashes heavy over his eyes. "I'm apologizing and I'm once again asking you to marry me. Do you accept my apology *and* my proposal?"

Serena rose and went to him and circled her arms around his neck. She felt as though she were melting inside, she was so happy. "Yes, to both," she whispered. "Yes, yes, Wesley."

He traced her facial features with a forefinger. "I've put marriage off for one main reason," he said thickly, afraid of her reaction. He wasn't ashamed of Dorlisa May, he *wasn't*.

"What is it? Tell me, Wesley."

"It's been because I've been afraid of . . . fathering a child," he said sullenly, almost choking on the words. He watched her eyes grow wide with wonder.

"Why would you be afraid of becoming a father, Wesley?" The despair in his eyes caused despair in her heart.

"Don't you truly know? Can't you even guess?"

"No. I don't understand," she said softly. She lifted a finger and pulled it along the line of the cleft of his chin.

"Darling, please tell me. You should know that my love for you will make anything you fear magically disappear."

"No. Nothing can erase this particular fear from my mind," Wesley said, gulping hard.

"Wesley, whatever on earth can be bothering you so?" Serena argued. "Please? Tell me now."

"Dorlisa May," he stammered, averting his gaze as he pulled from her and moved to slouch down onto a chair.

Serena's breath caught in the depths of her throat. She went to Wesley and kneeled down before him, framing his face between her hands. "Wesley, what does Dorlisa May have to do with this? I don't understand."

"Dorlisa's condition is inherited," he said, swallowing hard.

Serena's face paled. "Do you mean . . . that if . . . we had a child, this child might be albino?" she said quietly. "Is that what you are saying? That you fear that we might have a child like Dorlisa May?"

"Yes," he blurted, reaching to clasp her hands in his. "Don't you see? If I had a son who wasn't as strong as . . . most sons . . . I would most surely want to die."

Serena was trying to understand Wesley's feelings. She was even experiencing small tremors of doubt inside herself. But it was wrong. She knew that it was wrong. Dorlisa May was such a lovely, gentle person. And hadn't she grown to love her almost as a mother would a child? Surely if she and Wesley gave birth to such a child, he would love her or him just as much. "It shouldn't be that way for you, Wesley," she murmured. "If you had a son, an albino son . . . you would love him. I just know it."

"Yes, I would love him," Wesley said thickly. "I love Dorlisa May. But not to be able to have a son of all muscle and brawn? Don't you see? Haven't you even noticed how easily Dorlisa May tires? It would be the same for a boy."

Serena rose with clenched fists at her side. She began to pace the floor angrily. "Wesley, if Dorlisa May had been encouraged to leave her room to romp and play along the beach as soon as she had taken her first steps, she would be just as strong as any boy. But your mother has chosen to keep her hidden." She swung around, glaring. "How can a child expect to develop strong leg muscles if kept in a square of a room? I know that if we had such a son as you are worrying about, you could see to it that he would be as strong, and eventually as virile as you. I just know it, Wesley."

"But the pale skin? The weak eyes? The sun's rays are a constant enemy to Dorlisa May. Sure. I could take a child out on the beach, but just how long could he stand the sun to beat down on him? How could we go on horseback for hours at a time? How could we take long voyages by ship if the sun is such an enemy?"

Serena fell to her knees before him once again, taking his hands in hers. "Wesley, this is foolish," she stated flatly. "Here we are discussing something that may never even be. Just how much of a chance is there that we might even have an albino child? How often have there been albinos born to the Wyndham ancestors?"

"Enough of them," Wesley growled.

"But will you just stop and think for a moment? Neither you nor your brother are albino. Only Dorlisa May. Surely the chances are small. Please don't let this stand in the way of our happiness. Let's just worry about

350

it when the time comes, if ever it does. Aren't I right, Wesley?"

Wesley chuckled, reaching to loosen the bow from around her hair, then combed his fingers through the thickness of the strawberry-colored curls. Her hair continued to frizz in the dampness of Folly Island's sea breezes. But didn't that make her even more beautiful? "You are so right, darling," he whispered. "I don't know why I hadn't straightened this out in my head sooner. I guess it took you to convince me that my life can no longer be guided by a fear of something that may never happen."

"Wesley, I now understand much about your moods that have plagued you since we first met. I now understand why you have continued to evade the conversation centering around marriage. I had . . . thought . . . it to be for other reasons," Serena said quietly. "But I now know you've been troubled for some time about this. But why have you chosen now to come to me? To decide to tell me?"

"Because I could see that I was in danger of losing you, darling," he said hoarsely. "I saw the hurt and the confusion in your eyes this morning. I knew that you were coming to the end of your rope. I am so sorry, Serena. I shouldn't have thought for one minute that you wouldn't understand my feelings. I should have confided in you long ago. But I thought even you might be too afraid of having an albino child."

"Even after seeing how I felt about Dorlisa May? How I have come to adore her?"

"That was when I was truly afraid to talk to you about it," he said. "I thought maybe you would be furious at me when I tried to explain my doubts. I thought maybe you might think me terrible for worrying about having an albino child, since you understood Dorlisa May so well, and didn't think for one moment that being an albino was a disgrace."

"I think your mother and her obvious feelings about Dorlisa May are a disgrace," Serena hissed, rising.

"Yes. I do also," Wesley said, rising, moving next to her. "But she is of the southern aristocracy. She is proud. One can't condemn her for what was instilled in her even when she was a child."

"But, Wesley, it is wrong. No matter how you glamorize your mother's behavior, it is wrong."

"Serena, I know that. You know that. But Mother will never see it that way," he said, then moved his lips to cover hers. "But back to the wedding. Shall we?"

"Yes, Wesley. Whenever you say," she murmured.

"I shall make plans," he said. "Maybe we can have Charleston's first ball since the war's end. How does that sound to you? An engagement ball? Then the next day— the marriage."

"Wesley, oh, Wesley, it sounds grand," she sighed. Then her brow furrowed. "But one thing. We will introduce Dorlisa May into society at this ball. The ball will be for two reasons. Our engagement announcement, and the first time for Dorlisa May to be a part of such a gathering."

"I don't think Mother—"

Serena's eyes blazed. "I don't give a darn about your mother, Wesley Alston," she snapped. "It is Dorlisa May that I am worrying about."

"Well . . ."

"The answer has to be yes."

He laughed lightly. "Then yes *is* the answer, my vixen," he said.

"Oh, Wesley, how I do love you," she murmured, as he lifted her into his arms and carried her to the bed. As he placed her on it, she giggled. "And in broad daylight, Wesley? Are you truly going to make love to me while the sun shines onto our bed?"

He began to unbutton her dress, then lowered it from her shoulders. He reached upward and circled a breast, panting hard. "Darling, the sun's caress will flame my desire for you even more," he said thickly. With ease, he helped her off with her clothes, then his own, then settled down next to her.

"What if someone should come to the door?" she whispered, feeling the tremors in her body as his fingers brushed lightly from spot to spot.

"If they do, we will pretend we are not even here," he said.

"But might they even hear our groans of pleasure?" she giggled, suddenly feeling drunk with happiness.

"Maybe that's just what this house needs," he said, laughing hoarsely. "Just a mite of excitement."

"Nothing could be more exciting than this very moment . . . with you . . ." Serena purred, trembling even more beneath his continuing caresses. When he stretched out atop her, she welcomed the warmth of his body. His lips went to the hollow of her throat, then to her lips, crushing them with raw hungry desire.

Running her fingers over his back, relishing in the feel of his tightened muscles, she spread her legs and let him enter her, oh, so gently, oh, so sweetly, making her want to cry out from the intense flames of passion licking their way through her. Desire flooded her brain. She felt dizzy . . . her flesh burned. . . . Her heart was beating now in unison with his thrusts inside her.

"Darling, oh, Wesley, darling," she whispered over and over again as his lips moved over her breasts, causing them to draw tightly and throb. Complete ecstasy was then theirs when together they climbed the highest reaches of mind-reeling feelings of love for one another, quivering against one another until their movements ceased and they moved apart, laughing softly.

"I'm not so sure if it *is* wise to make love beneath the rays of this South Carolina sun after all," Wesley said, wiping his brow, laboring for breath.

"Wesley?" Serena whispered softly, tracing his body with a fingernail.

"Yes, darling?"

"Do you think the next time we make love, it can be as . . . man . . . and wife . . . ?"

"You would make yourself wait?"

"It wouldn't be for long . . . would it?"

He scooted next to Serena and fitted his body into hers, kissing her softly, then said, "Whatever you want, my love, whatever you want. . . ."

Chapter Eighteen

The Wyndham mansion smelled of lemon-oil furniture polish and bouquets of azaleas that had been placed around the sitting room. Francine scampered around, humming, dusting the last of the magnificent pieces of furniture.

Serena entered the room, glancing quickly around her, smiling. Some wainscoting and trim of this room had been replaced, and fresh wallpaper, found in the garrett, had been spread to cover the graffiti that had been left by the officers of the 55th Regiment Massachusetts Voluntary Infantry. The woodwork had been covered with mustard brown, feather-grained paint, and the crystal chandelier sparkled.

"Looks beautiful, doesn't it, ma'am?" Francine said, stopping to twist the dustcloth around her fingers.

"Yes. And the ball should be very exciting, Francine," Serena said, smoothing the young servant's hair back that had fallen from her pigtails.

"Can I truly be present?" Francine asked anxiously, widening the dark of her eyes. "Can I?"

"You will even be wearing a new dress, Francine," Serena said, laughing softly. "We haven't been able to shop as one would for a ball because reconstruction is not yet complete in Charleston, but I have chosen one of Dorlisa's dresses for you, one that is of a reserved style, and with the new lace-trimmed apron that you have so deftly sewn, you will be quite an added attraction to the ball."

Francine giggled, then moved quickly away from Serena when Lona Gale moved into the room. Serena stepped to the blaze of the fire on the grate and leaned her hands down over it. The first of September had brought with it a bit of chill in the air. Serena tensed when she felt Lona Gale's presence at her side.

"So you are going to go through with this farce of a ball and wedding, are you?" Lona Gale snarled.

Serena turned her eyes to Lona Gale and tilted her chin saucily upward. "Yes. And don't try to stop me. Nothing can stand in the way of my marriage to your son. Nothing," she said icily. Then she quickly added, "And nothing will stop me from introducing your daughter into society." She could see the anger flashing in Lona Gale's dark eyes. Oh, she was still such an ostentatious southern hypocrite. Serena could only thank God that neither Wesley nor Dorlisa May had acquired such undesirable traits from their mother. It seemed that only Truman Firman had, and Serena had begun to pity, instead of loathe him. Truman was letting hate and envy ruin his life. Serena just didn't understand why the man couldn't accept life as it was and take what happiness he could from it, instead of plotting ways to make others miserable around him.

"No one will come," Lona Gale said, laughing bitterly. "Since it is not myself giving this ball, no one will come. You will see. You will open the door and no one will be there. And no one will feel it is the right time to put the deaths of their loved ones behind them. Everyone is too caught up in their troubles to think to stop to come to a ball, even if it is at Wyndham Hall."

"You are wrong, Lona Gale. On both counts. People think as much of Wesley Alston as they do you. And people will be relieved to have some place to go that will speak of some fun and excitement. Wesley has already received affirmative answers from many. The ball *will* be a success. You will see."

Lona Gale reached and grasped one of Serena's hands in hers. Her eyes had grown weary, even a bit dim of coloring. She cleared her throat nervously, then said, "You must at least reconsider what you have planned for Dorlisa May. She is not ready for such . . . excitement. It will not be good for her."

"Release your hold on me, Lona Gale," Serena snapped, feeling her heartbeat hastening from increased anger. "I've heard it all before. Nothing you say will change my mind. You know that what you ask is for your own self. Not for the welfare of Dorlisa May." She swung the skirt of her dress around and moved quickly across the room, heading for the staircase, wondering what was taking Wesley so long to dress for breakfast. She smiled to herself, remembering their last embrace of the morning. Even though she still insisted that they now wait to make love again only after their wedding vows were spoken, as sort of a game, to make Wesley look forward to the wedding as much as she did, they still enjoyed each other's caresses and kisses. But they always stopped just at the right point, when each lay panting, eager for their wedding night when they could truly say that they were each other's, forever and ever. . . .

"If things were as they were before the war, I would move my things to Charleston and stay in one of our townhouses for the winter months and become a part of the social season by myself. I wouldn't have to worry about you or my daughter embarrassing me," Lona Gale shouted, then paled of color when Dorlisa May entered the room, causing Serena to stop in her tracks, seeing that Dorlisa May had heard the outburst of her mother.

"Lisa," Serena said, taking one of her hands. "Your mother—she . . . didn't mean—"

Dorlisa May's mouth quivered as she glanced from her mother back to Serena. "Yes. She meant every word of it, Serena," she sobbed. "I've understood all these years. No need trying to smooth over what's been done or said—"

Just then, Wesley, smelling of rich cologne and dressed in a most impeccable brown woolen suit, entered the room. "What's this? What's going on? Why are you crying, Dorlisa May?"

"It's nothing, Wesley," she murmured, wiping at an eye.

"Wesley, where have you been?" Serena whispered. "I only wish you had been here a few moments ago, and heard your mother—"

"Just moving a bit slower this morning," he said. "Why? What was said here?"

A quick scramble of feet into the room drew the attention from Lona Gale and her face that had drained of color. Four-year-old Bubba ran on into the room, panting hard, his dark eyes seeming to fill his even darker face.

Wesley went to him and kneeled before him, grasping onto his small shoulders. "What is it, Bubba?" he asked. "Why are you so winded? What has happened?"

Bubba wiped his runny nose with the back of a smooth, black hand, then blurted between deep heavings. "It's Massa Truman—"

"What about my brother?" Wesley said, strengthening his hold.

"I found him . . ."

Wesley's pulsebeat began to race. "You found him? What do you mean? Where?"

Bubba lifted a finger and pointed toward the door, even more wide-eyed. "On the beach, massa," he panted. "Behind a sand dune. . . ."

Gasps filled the room.

"And?" Wesley stormed. "What about him?"

"Massa Wesley, Massa Truman had an Indian arrow stickin' through him," Bubba said, running his words together, having become almost incoherent from the fear that was etched across his face. "I come runnin' to tell you. He's dead. Massa Wesley, Massa Truman . . . be . . . dead. . . ."

Lona Gale began to wail and ran toward the door, with hands flailing. Wesley was numb inside, but he couldn't let his mother see Truman Firman now—not with an arrow piercing his body. Not on the beach, murdered, as though only a turtle hatchling himself, unable to defend himself. He moved quickly after his mother and grabbed her and pulled her into his arms.

"Wesley, I must go to Truman Firman," she screamed, trying to wriggle free from his hold of steel.

Wesley held her, as though in a vise, feeling her tremblings moving against his body. His love for his mother suddenly engulfed him. They had had their differences, but, oh, God, how he still loved her. And now? To lose her younger son? He knew how her heart had to be tearing to shreds. "Mother, you cannot leave this house," he said, caressing her back, trying to comfort her, as one would a child. "Please wait."

A loud shuffling of footsteps surfaced from behind Wesley, making him release his hold on his mother, to see who had come into the room. His eyes grew wet with tears as he saw Tobias coming into the room carrying Truman in his arms. Lying lifeless now and with such a quiet peacefulness to his face, Truman Firman looked the little boy he had been, oh, so many years ago, when Tobias had rescued him from the angry waves of the ocean. Truman had defied death that once and had won, but this time, he hadn't been so lucky. This time an Indian had killed him, an Indian whom Wesley would now have to seek out . . . and . . . kill himself. . . . .

"Massa Wesley, where can I put . . . Massa Truman?" Tobias stammered, tears running like torrents from his red-streaked eyes.

Wesley glanced quickly toward Lona Gale who stood now as though in a daze, chewing on the knuckle of a doubled fist. Then he glanced quickly toward Serena, seeing how quietly she stood, with lips partly agape, and how Dorlisa May stood with hands clasped over her mouth. He moved toward Truman and touched his brow, tensing when he felt the utter coldness, though Truman had been lying in the early morning sun. Then his gaze traveled downward, seeing the splash of red on the front of his white, lace-trimmed shirt. He could see through the blood, the perfect round hole that had been made in the shirt. *Thank God,* he thought to himself. *Tobias had the sense to remove the arrow before bringing Truman into the house.*

He wiped his eyes with the sleeve of his suit jacket,

then patted Tobias on the shoulder. "Tobias, will you please take Truman Firman up to his room and place him on his bed? I will see to everything else later," he said quietly.

"Yassa, Massa Wesley," Tobias said, and began to lumber off.

"And, thank you, Tobias," Wesley murmured. "For everything. . . ."

"Yassa, Massa Wesley," Tobias said over his shoulder. Then he walked up the stairs, straining the muscles of his shoulders and back with each step.

Lona Gale began to wail once again, running after Truman's body. "Truman Firman, oh, God, son," she screamed, over and over again, but once again was stopped by Wesley.

"Mother, please," he said thickly. "You mustn't. Let Tobias take Truman to his room. You come and lie down on the couch until you are more composed." He led her to the couch and eased her down upon it.

"It's the Indian maiden, Wesley," she said, crying still. "I knew that she would be the cause of Truman Firman's death. I just knew it. I tried to warn Truman Firman of the dangers of mixing with a savage. . . ."

Wesley was growing cold inside. Halona? Truman? What was his mother saying? He kneeled down before her. Though she was distraught, he had to know. He began to smooth his fingers over her brow. "Mother? What did you just say about . . . an Indian maiden?" he whispered, trying to not let Serena hear. But he had to get to the bottom of this. He had to know whom to search for, who would be responsible for his brother's death. Yes, he and Truman Firman had never fared well as brothers, but he would avenge his death. He had never hated his brother. It had only been Truman . . . hating him. . . .

His heart ached now for his brother. But something else inside him drove him onward to find out the truth about Truman and—had it been Halona? Wesley had never suspected. Never!

"I've so worried about Truman Firman," Lona Gale sobbed quietly. "He's been meeting that Indian maiden for as long as he's been aware that there is such a thing as a woman's soft skin." She pulled a lace handkerchief from the sleeve of her dress and coughed into it. "I kept it from you. I knew of your attachment with the same Indian maiden. There was enough hate between brothers. I didn't see just cause to make it worse."

"Then it was Halona? She was the Indian maiden of whom you speak?"

Lona Gale began to wail even more loudly now, turning her face from Wesley. "Don't even speak the name," she cried. "I don't . . . even want . . . to hear the name. . . ."

Wesley straightened his back and stormed toward the stairs. He had to change into proper hunting clothes. He was now thrown into another war, but this time a personal one. He would not need a regiment to help fight this battle. He would do it on his own. And succeed he would. . . .

Serena flew to his side and clutched onto his arm. "What are you going to do, Wesley?" she said, desperation seizing her.

Wesley turned and stared as though in a daze downward at her. "I must go in search of the one responsible for my brother's death," he said, wiping at his brow with the back of his free hand.

"Do you think Halona—?" She couldn't believe that two brothers could have been involved with the same woman. Surely one would have found out. But they hadn't. Halona had made fools of them both. And now Wesley? Would he be killed defending the brother who would have never defended him? Who had never even loved him?

"No. I think it is Wolfram whom I seek," he said darkly.

The name seized Serena by the gut. She now remembered the Indian warrior whom had been so close to possibly even abducting her. "Why would he—?"

"He has his reasons," Wesley said thickly. "To him, he has many reasons." Wesley didn't know if it had truly been because of Halona, or if Wolfram had shot Truman, thinking it was Wesley. As of late, Truman had begun to resemble his brother. Yes, the mustache and the tan— these had made brothers look even almost like twins.

Serena now felt her gut twisting. Was Wesley speaking of the relationship he had given up with Halona? Had the Indian warrior meant to kill Wesley because of this— having thought Truman was Wesley? Would Wesley be the next one found dead with an arrow piercing his beautiful, warm flesh? "You mustn't leave the plantation," she said anxiously. "Please don't leave the plantation grounds. Don't you see? The Indian's arrow is swift and sure. I don't know what I would do if anything happened to you. I would want to die myself."

"Serena, you know that I don't run from a fight. You must remember what I did during the war. I was chosen for my daring ways. Do you remember how I told you that I even had twenty-nine horses shot from beneath me? Doesn't that tell you something? This time I will travel by canoe instead of horse. And this canoe will not be shot from beneath me. Not by an arrow, not by anything."

"But, Wesley, our marriage is so near. Please think of me. Please . . ."

"Darling, I will return," he said, moving to pull her into his arms. "But you also must understand that the ball and the wedding must be postponed. This is not the time for gaiety around Wyndham Hall."

He had just the same as had pierced her heart with an arrow. Their wedding—postponed . . . "Oh, Wesley," she sobbed, clinging.

"I know, I know," he said quietly, burrowing his nose into the depths of her hair. "But I'm sure you understand. Things have quickly changed. It is my brother who gathers the full attention now." He choked back tears. "It seems he has only gathered this by his death. Oh, God, Serena, it is so terrible."

His shoulders heaved with his heavy sobs. Then he pulled quickly away from her and rushed up the stairs, stopping to inch his way into Truman's room, to take one last look before his trip began down the Kiawah River. When he entered the room, he became choked with even deeper emotions when he saw Tobias spreading Truman atop the bed so gently, then stopping to smooth Truman Firman's dark hair from his forehead. Then when Tobias kneeled at Truman's bedside and began to sob, deep, heart-rending sobs, Wesley crept on away, feeling that Tobias needed this final time with his younger master. Ah, as a young lad, Truman Firman had so idolized this massive Negro. Tobias hadn't been able to do anything wrong. Tobias had been the one person whom Truman had been able to get along with. Tobias would miss Truman even more than any Wyndhams would. . . .

Wesley went to his room and quickly changed into

traveling clothes of denim shirt and matching breeches. As he strapped his gun and holsters to his waist, he went to the window and stared upward at the sky. He furrowed his brow when he saw the gathering black clouds. He knew that a storm was near, but he still had to travel down Kiawah River in search of Wolfram, and while there, he would see Halona just one more time. He had to ask the question. He had to know just how much Truman had meant to her. He had to know that the arrow had not been meant for Truman. It had most surely been meant to pierce Wesley's heart for having humiliated the fairest of the Indian maidens of the Kiawah tribe.

"Wesley?" Serena whispered, entering the room.

Wesley turned, blushing, knowing that his thoughts shouldn't have been on another woman. He did so love Serena. He knew this now. There wasn't any doubt in his mind about it. But he still had to speak with Halona. "Yes?" he murmured, brushing his hair back nervously. "What is it, darling?"

"Can I even go with you, Wesley?" she whispered further. "I cannot bear to stay in this house and not know what is happening to you."

Wesley's eyes widened and his heartbeat hastened. "You want to travel with me into the depths of the swampland? Darling, you just cannot do that," he said, swinging around, putting his back to her. Now he was the one to be choked up with emotion. Had he ever known such a love before? He hadn't even guessed her true love for him. He should have. Hadn't she confessed this to him, over and over again?

"We've traveled with danger as partners before," Serena said, moving to his side. "I can shoot a gun. Please let me go with you."

Wesley's thoughts moved back to Halona once again. He had to speak with her. He couldn't let Serena travel with him. She would be in danger from too many things if she did. Not only from an arrow whizzing through the depths of the marsh grasses toward her, but from Halona's words. They would be sharper than any arrow's tip. He swung back around, glaring. "You cannot. And, Serena, you must stay with Dorlisa May. I'm sure the death of her brother has her very distraught. Please stay and do what you can here. Will you do that for me?"

Serena's face muscles slackened and her eyes burned with the need of tears to be released from their tight confines, but she moved on away from Wesley. "Yes. I guess my place is here. Maybe even your mother might want someone to talk to. Maybe I can help," she said, moving from the room, not looking back. Her heart ached with each beat. She knew that while Wesley would be in the Indian country, he would see Halona. Would he even fall into her arms for comfort, even after Wolfram had—? No. Surely not.

Wesley kept a constant eye around him, watching for any sudden movements in the marsh grasses. Most of the island alligators had already begun their disappearing acts, due to the approach of cooler weather, and a circling of ducks overhead was another true indication of cold weather's approach. They had migrated from the colder climates of the north country.

Pulling the oars through the water, Wesley had never felt so alone. He couldn't erase the memory of Truman Firman from his mind. He couldn't believe that he was truly dead. But he was, and this was why Wesley had chosen to travel to the Kiawah village once again. He had to wonder what sort of reception he would receive. Had Halona and Wolfram warned the tribe of the white man's possible arrival? Would they all be painted quite colorfully in the war paints of their ancestors?

The bend in the river drew Wesley's quick attention. Around the bend—what would await him? A bright flash of lightning moving straight downward from the sky only a few feet away from him and a loud drumlike clap of thunder caused Wesley to pull even more strongly on the oars. Then when the village came into view, he drew the oars from the water and let the canoe move on its own until it settled onto the water's edge, on land, in the thickness of the marsh grass.

Wesley tensed. There were no signs of life around the huts and all the doors were closed, except for . . . Halona's. . . .

Wesley gazed intensely toward her hut, seeing smoke spiraling upward from the small hole in the roof. He knew that Halona was there. Who was she purposely waiting for? Who had she left the door of her hut open for . . . indicating a welcome? Would she expect to see Wesley—or Truman Firman?

With hands positioned on each gun at his hips, Wesley moved from the canoe and inched his way across the ground, hearing the utter silence around him. Only when another rumble of thunder echoed through the trees did he tense even more. But when Halona moved to the doorway of her hut, Wesley felt many things. A remembrance of nights in her arms . . . a remembrance of how she could make his mind leave him . . . and now a remembrance of his brother . . . possibly having shared those same intimate embraces.

He set his jaw firmly and moved to stand with hands

still poised on each gun and spoke: "Where is Wolfram, Halona?" he said flatly, trying to ignore her savage beauty and the way her eyes worked magic on him. He was trying to remember the dark side of her nature, the side that he had discovered while with her that last time. But his thoughts were continually returning to the way her tongue could work on him, as not even Serena had ever known how to do.

"Wesley, it is you?" Halona asked softly, disbelief etched across the soft lines of her tanned face.

"Halona, my brother Truman Firman was killed today by an arrow," Wesley said darkly. "It had to be Wolfram who did it. You must tell me where he is. He cannot get away with murder. I am seeking my revenge." He knew the dangers of speaking so openly while in this Indian reservation, but he couldn't help but think that all warriors had disappeared along with Wolfram. If they had been here, Wesley would not have been. They would have tried to have stopped his approach. Long before now.

Halona's gaze lowered and her shoulders slouched a bit. "Wolfram told me of a death," she whispered. "Wesley, I thought it had been you. Not Truman. Wolfram still thinks it is you." Her gaze shot upward, showing concern. Wesley wondered if it was sincere. "You must run. Wolfram will kill you also if he sees that you are still alive," Halona quickly added, glancing from side to side.

"Then it was my death Wolfram sought?" Wesley growled. "Why, Halona? Because you told him that I no longer would see you? Did you hate me so much, Halona, that you wished me dead?"

Halona rushed to him and clutched onto his arm. Her

dark eyes were now wet with tears. "Halona didn't know Wolfram would come after you," she said anxiously. "Wesley, Halona is so sorry. Halona cannot believe Truman is dead. Halona thought it was you, Wesley." She suddenly rushed into his arms, hugging him tightly. "Wesley, oh, Wesley, Halona is so glad you are alive."

Wesley felt familiar stirrings in his loins, feeling the softness of her body next to his, but then he had to remember Truman. He pushed her away from him, glowering. "Halona, Truman is dead. Surely you must feel something for his death. I now know that you have also been with my brother. Halona, you lied to me. All those years. You said I was the only white man. . . ."

"Wesley, Halona always missed you. When Truman began making approaches at Halona, Halona just pretended it was you. Don't you see, Wesley? Halona only loved you. Only you."

"Halona is a she-devil," Wesley growled. "Halona doesn't know the true meaning of love. Halona is the reason my brother lies dead in Wyndham Hall. Halona, I hate you now. I shall always hate you."

Rain began to fall in sudden blinding sheets. Halona pulled at Wesley's arm. "Come. Come in by the fire," she said. "I make you no hate Halona. I make you love Halona again. Please come and sit by the fire with me. You get wet out here."

"Halona, I've come to find Wolfram, not sit by a fire with you," Wesley shouted, wiping the rain from his face.

"Wesley never find Wolfram," Halona shouted back at him. "Wolfram moved to deep swamp country, knowing white man would come searching for him. He and the other warriors are going to hunt while away. You

may as well forget Wolfram for now. Wolfram not here."
She glanced quickly around her once again, making
Wesley tense, not believing anything she said. Was
Wolfram near? Did she plan to trap this man she had
once called a blood brother who had become something
even more?

She grabbed him even more strongly. "Please? Come
into my dwelling. Get warmed by the fire," she said.
"Then you can go back to Wyndham Hall to grieve for
your brother. Wesley, Halona is sorry. Halona didn't
mean this to happen."

Wesley coughed as the rain continued to drench him.
He looked toward the river and couldn't even make out
where he had left the canoe. He did feel as though in a
trap. He seemed to always be setting traps for himself.
Always damned if he did . . . and damned if he didn't. So
he chose to follow Halona into the hut and welcomed the
warmth of the fire that glowed in soft reds at the center of
the dwelling. He stood there, shivering. He felt defeated.
He felt as he had the day he had been captured at Fort
Donelson. This time he had also been defeated. He knew
the impossibility of finding Wolfram if he *had* chosen to
travel to lands where no white man had ever been. But
some day, Wolfram would have to return, and then
Wesley would fulfill his revenge. Wolfram couldn't stay
away from the village forever. He was their leader. The
feeble-minded Kiawah women wouldn't be able to live
without their leader and the other warriors who had
apparently decided to go and hide with Wolfram.

Halona closed the door of the hut, then moved to
Wesley's side and began loosening the buttons of his
shirt. "Wesley is wet. Wesley must get dried before the

fire," she murmured.

Wesley pushed her away from him, furrowing his brow. "Wesley is just fine. And as soon as the rain lets up, Wesley is getting out of here," he grumbled. He knelt down before the fire and began rubbing his hands over its warmth. He tensed when he watched out of the corner of his eyes as she began to shed her clothing from her lithe body. He shot upward, banging his head on the ceiling of the hut. "What the hell do you think you're doing, Halona?" he shouted.

"Halona is going to make Wesley forget all his sadness," she whispered, stepping from her last garment, moving toward him with outstretched arms.

"You'll do no such damn thing," he said, but he was already hungering after her. His gaze moved quickly over her, the way her tanned body shone as though sleek velvet beneath the rays of the fire. Her breasts were taut, though small, and he felt his hands reach upward to cup one, then the other.

"Wesley, Halona knows you still care," Halona purred, wriggling her body into the shape of his. Her fingers traced the smooth lines of his face, then moved lower, where he bulged beneath the tight confines of his breeches.

"Halona, don't," he said thickly. "You mustn't. . . ."

Halona's lips reached upward and captured his and he couldn't help but pull her roughly against him as his mouth crushed against hers. Damn. He hadn't wanted this. He had wanted to get his revenge, not Halona in his arms again. Serena. Oh, God, Serena. What was she doing now? Comforting Dorlisa May, or even his mother, while he was here . . . beginning to ache inside for this

371

beautiful Indian who always managed to steal his heart away? He knew that he should stop, but he couldn't help himself. He even felt tears brimming his eyes, knowing the wrong that he was about to do. But he was under this savage's spell. He always had been. . . .

"Undress me, Halona," he ordered. He stretched his legs out on each side of him and lifted his arms, closing his eyes when her fingers began to move over his clothing, until he stood just as nude as she before the fire.

"Halona make Wesley forget," Halona whispered, dropping to the floor before him, consuming his throbbing hardness with her lips and fingers. Wesley moved to the floor and stretched out, growling with hungry lust, but when he heard a sudden movement outside the hut, he was suddenly drawn to his senses. He lifted a foot and kicked Halona back away from him and jumped for a gun just as the door opened and Wolfram moved quickly inside, with bow and arrow drawn, ready. . . .

Wesley lay on his back and without even having a chance to take another breath, he had pulled the trigger and was watching Wolfram crumble to the floor, clutching to his chest.

Halona's screams filled the interior of the hut. She fell to the floor, covering her brother's body with her own, clutching it.

Wesley felt the thundering of his heartbeat, realizing the immense danger he was in. What if all the other warriors were waiting outside the hut with arrows ready? He only had to hope that the constant outside crashing of thunder had muffled the sound of the gun's explosion and Halona's screams.

Wesley grabbed his clothes and went to the door and slowly peered outward. He was in luck. No one was near. He even could see far enough around him to see that no one was lurking in the brush. Though it was still thundering, the rain had ceased to fall and only a small steamy mist was rising from the ground. He moved as quickly as his bare feet could travel until he was finally inside the canoe.

Breathing hard, and feeling dumb as hell because of his nudity, he managed to get the canoe away from the shore. In between loud claps of thunder, he could still hear Halona's screams, but he couldn't see anyone around the other huts. The doors had remained closed. Wesley now knew the reason why. The other warriors hadn't returned with Wolfram. He must have sneaked away, wanting to be the only one to get the applause for murdering this one other white man.

Wesley smiled to himself. Yes. That's how it had to have been. But he still didn't forget to watch all around him as he continued to move from the inner depths of the swamp country. It was only when he had one more bend to round that he decided it best to stop and get fully clothed once again. He didn't want any telltale signs of having almost been unfaithful to Serena once again.

He felt a sickness at the pit of his stomach, realizing his weakness of only moments ago. He would have taken Halona completely—if not for Wolfram. Wesley had never thought himself capable of doing this to Serena again. He hated himself for it. But he would make it up to her. Though she would never know of his true weakness, he would make life so easy and beautiful for her, he would forget, himself, that he had almost let this savage

373

do this to him.

Halona knew that Wolfram would appear, he thought angrily to himself. *In fact, Wolfram and Halona had probably even planned this. Hadn't Halona been the only one with the opened door . . . meaning "welcome," "enter"?*

Wesley furrowed his brow. Would he ever understand why Halona would do such a thing?

Chapter Nineteen

It was mid-February. The swamp maples were turning red with seed, and large flocks of robins were arriving each day at Folly Island. Serena stood at her bedroom window with shutters thrown open, gazing outward. She was barely able to see the beach. But she did know that the ducks had departed for their long flights to the North and had been replaced at Folly Island by wading birds. Serena had seen many pelicans, herons, and egrets already involved in their annual nesting rituals.

She smiled with contentment, realizing that her own baby was resting snugly inside her womb. She had even felt its quiet flutterings—what a butterfly's wings might feel like—even though she could boast of being only four months pregnant.

"Penny for your thoughts, darling," Wesley said, creeping up behind her. He wrapped his arms around her middle, purposely resting them on her abdomen.

"You know, Wesley," she purred, "what's on my mind from sunup to sunset." She rested against him, sighing deeply. She shivered with delight when he leaned his mouth against her ear, breathing warmth into it.

"I'm as anxious, darling," he said softly.

She turned and gazed into his eyes. Since she had discovered that she was pregnant, she had watched for signs of his doubts. But thus far she had only seen a radiance that constantly seemed to flow between them.

Their wedding vows had been spoken in private following the appropriate period of mourning after Truman's interment in the private Wyndham burial plot, next to his father. Wesley had said that he needed Serena, in every way that a man needs a woman, to help brush all the ugliness from his thoughts. Thus the marriage had taken place beneath the lacy moss of the live oaks at Wyndham Plantation, with only Dorlisa May looking on.

The only signs of unrest on Wesley's part were the many times Serena had watched him pacing back and forth, stopping occasionally to stare from the window toward Kiawah River. She thought it was because he had begun to miss Halona after their meeting the day Wesley had shot and killed Wolfram. But Wesley had finally explained that it had nothing to do with the Indian girl, but that he had feared a possible Indian uprising after the Kiawah head-warrior's death.

But no one had seen any signs of Indians on Folly Island. Male or female. And now that Wesley was busy with the spring plantings, Serena knew that his mind was occupied with more than fantasies of the child that would be born to the Wyndhams in early June. The fields had been prepared for row after row of cotton. And then there had been the rice that had been planted to feed the many field hands.

The leased plots of farmland had worked out well for Wesley. His field hands were content. They had found their freedom, but still on the plantation that most had known as home since their first arrivals in South Carolina.

Yes. All seemed to be one big happy family, except for Lona Gale. She had moved to Charleston, to grieve in silent privacy for her younger son. She could no longer argue with Serena over who the true mistress of Wyndham Hall was. She could no longer argue about what was best for Dorlisa May. And now that things seemed to be going well on both Folly Island and in Charleston, Serena had decided that it was now an appropriate time to have that ball that she had been planning since Truman Firman's death. She had just completed addressing the invitations and had begun to decide which foods might be served for the large gathering of people who would be seeing Dorlisa May for the first time. Yes. Serena was finally going to make Dorlisa May part of the living. She could hardly wait. A ball at Wyndham Hall would give the beautiful mansion back its vitality, its life. Nothing could stop Serena from completing her plans this time.

"There's much more than the baby in that mind of yours," Wesley chuckled. "It's like a book. Each blink of the eye, a different chapter to be read."

"And do you like its contents?" she giggled, fluttering her thick lashes at him, as though still unwed, flirting with him for attention.

"Yes," he said warmly. "And the ending? When I get to that last page, will it be as happy as what I am reading right now?"

"There will never be an ending to our love, my darling," she said, lifting her lips to his, kissing him sweetly. "Don't you see? We are going to go on forever. There just can't be a last chapter to the happiness we have found here on your paradise of an island."

"Though I've only returned home for a bite of lunch, I just might have to take more time to partake in dessert," he chuckled, framing her face between his hands.

"Well? What are you waiting for?" she whispered, reaching to touch his hardness.

Just as he began to lift her into his arms, there were some chatterings that seemed to carry from the direction of the river. Serena tensed when she felt Wesley withdraw from her and watched him inch his way to the window. She guessed that he would always worry and wonder about the comings and goings on Kiawah River. She went to his side and secured her arm through his, also looking downward. Then her heart began to race, as she saw someone being helped from a johnboat.

"Priscilla . . . ?" she whispered, putting her hands to her mouth. "Is that . . . Priscilla?" she said aloud, glancing upward at Wesley, then back to the direction of this beautifully dressed female.

"Priscilla did you say?" Wesley murmured, paling a bit. He leaned closer to the window, feeling something similar to that of a twisting of his insides, having pushed Priscilla and their one time together from his mind long ago, having thought to never have to come face to face with her again. But now? She had come to Folly Island. Why . . . ?

Then Wesley's hands doubled into tight fists at his side, watching the massive man who was walking alongside Priscilla. It was none other than Edward— Priscilla's husband, but also the man who had taken Wesley's own wife's virginity.

"It *is* Priscilla," Serena squealed, rushing to the door. "My sister! She has arrived on Folly Island. Can you believe it, Wesley?"

"Serena," Wesley said, clearing his throat nervously, wondering if she was too excited about her sister's arrival not even to have noticed Edward's. Wesley wanted to remind her, but the name somehow stuck in his throat. Instead he quickly blurted: "Be careful of the stairs. The baby. Watch the stairs and don't get too excited—"

Serena stopped to turn, suddenly more radiant than ever before in her life. These last remarks of concern for their baby proved again that Wesley *did* indeed want it. His fears of having an albino child were behind him. And Serena had to know that it was because of her own earlier acceptance of his sister. She now knew that he was ready to accept any child that would be born between them. *No matter the color, be it pink or white, it will be a child born out of love.*

"Wesley, I love you," she whispered, blowing him a kiss, then moved to the stairs and stepped carefully from step to step, breathing hard, anxious, and even a bit fearful to see her sister. Why *was* Priscilla here? Why hadn't Priscilla wired ahead? Someone could have met her at the train. Why hadn't she wanted to be met by her sister? It just didn't make any sense to Serena. None whatsoever. Then a fear grabbed at her heart. Maybe it was bad news about their father, and Priscilla had felt the need to inform Serena in person.

Oh, the questions! They were circling around in Serena's head like a kaleidoscope!

She frowned deeply. She had to face the fact that to welcome Priscilla to the island was to also welcome Edward. Serena had hoped to never be forced to be in his presence again and now, this day, he was on her beloved Folly Island. Somehow, it didn't seem right. . . .

Just as she reached the lower step a light tapping on the front door caused her heartbeat to hasten even more. She placed her fingers to her brow, feeling a bit lightheaded from the anxiety, then stood, barely breathing, as Francine rushed to the door and opened it. When Serena heard her sister's voice, she rushed and fell into Priscilla's embrace. Their tears intermingled when they placed their cheeks gently together.

"Priscilla, I can't believe you're actually here," Serena said, moving gently from Priscilla's arms, holding her hands. "On Folly Island. Priscilla, why didn't you write or wire of your coming? I'm sure you would have been made more comfortable by knowing that someone you knew would be waiting to bring you to the island." She gazed in wonder at Priscilla. Marriage had done wonders for her. She was no longer dowdy. Her complexion was peaches and cream, and her brown hair was swept away from her face and hung in tight curls beneath her fragile satin-trimmed hat. Her dress was of beige satin and was low-cut, emphasizing the magnificence of her bosom and the smallness of her waist. The skirt flared fully, where dozens of petticoats rustled voluptuously when she moved.

"My business brought us to Charleston," Edward interrupted in his booming voice as his large, rough hands drew Serena away from Priscilla, to hold Serena at arm's length, while his eyes raked over her. "You've put on a few pounds, haven't you, Serena?" he chuckled amusedly.

Serena lifted her chin haughtily and jerked free from his hold. "I wired Priscilla of my pregnancy," she stated icily. She glanced toward Priscilla, seeing traces of jealousy in the depths of her dark eyes. She knew that

380

Priscilla was remembering whom Edward had loved first. But Serena also knew that Priscilla *had* to be remembering Serena's feelings of loathing of Edward. Jealousy was not required here. Serena's hate was just as strong now for Edward as it ever was.

Priscilla moved quickly to Edward's side and circled her arm possessively through his. "Yes. We've come to Charleston for Edward to be interviewed for a position at the railroad," she said quietly, casting Edward a quick, fleeting smile.

Serena's face drained of color. She was glad to finally be able to see her sister, but she didn't wish to have her, or Edward, take up residence so close to Folly Island. There were too many feelings among them all. Serena was now even remembering her earlier doubts about Wesley . . . and . . . Priscilla. "You are seeking employment . . . in Charleston?" she said meekly.

Edward's massive body filled in his black waistcoat and tight-fitted breeches to an extreme. He even looked a bit awkward with his white shirt collar almost choking him. It was evident that he had fully recovered from his head wound.

His thick, brown, walrus mustache bounced as his toothy grin broke through. "Damn nice railroad now that it's been rebuilt," he drawled. "They're needin' a top hand like myself. Thought I'd check into it first hand."

"You . . . would . . . make your home in Charleston . . . ?" Serena stammered, glancing anxiously sideways when Wesley moved to her side. She could see the hate he felt for Edward in the cool glint of his eyes. A bit of alarm rushed through her. This was not to be the normal family reunion. Tension was thick in the air. Serena was beginning to wish that Priscilla had thought further of this decision to arrive unannounced at Folly Island.

Serena turned her gaze back to her sister, remembering the past so vividly: a past of two sisters romping, playing, fighting, teasing. It had been a normal relationship, based on sisterly rivalry. Would it be so, forever and ever? She gave Priscilla a nervous smile as Wesley took a step forward, hesitating before offering a hand to Edward.

"If the job is profitable enough, I do believe we could make a switch of residence from Illinois to South Carolina," Edward boomed, his gaze faltering a bit in Wesley's presence. He had heard much of this Colonel Wyndham and he had always felt compelled to dislike even the ground he would stand on. Hadn't Wesley Alston Wyndham taken Serena away from him? If it hadn't been for this Johnny Reb, Edward just knew that he would have been sharing his bed each night with Serena instead of Priscilla.

His gaze moved to Priscilla, then Serena, comparing the two. He had decided long ago that if he couldn't have Serena, Priscilla had been the next best choice. In bed, Priscilla was a hellion! At least he had that in his favor!

"So you say you might become our neighbor, eh?" Wesley said in a subdued tone, quickly withdrawing his hand, having second thoughts about welcoming this man to his island. Edward James Carlson spelled trouble. Wesley knew it. He could tell by the way Edward's eyes kept appraising Serena, as though she were his, ready to move into a bed with him.

Wesley had finally met Serena's rapist face to face. He again doubled his fists to his side, feeling a strong urge to hit Edward, even now, but knew that such a force of

382

anger would only upset Serena. And in her condition, Wesley had to keep an air of calm around her at all times.

"Thinkin' on it," Edward chuckled, fingering his mustache.

"I think it unwise," Wesley stated flatly.

Edward's smile faded. "And why do you, Colonel?" he drawled, putting emphasis on that word Colonel.

"Well, Edward, Charleston is just now beginning to rid itself of vermin," Wesley said between clenched teeth. "Now if *you* would arrive there to make residence, I would have to think—"

"Please, Wesley," Serena said quickly, stopping the words that were causing Edward's face to turn crimson and his breathing to hasten. "Let's go inside where Francine can serve us tea."

"You can go inside if you wish, Serena," Wesley grumbled, giving her a reproachful look. "But I must get back to the fields. As you know, I only came home for the lunch hour. The hour is now past, I must return." His gaze flicked over Edward, then softened a bit as he looked toward Priscilla. He felt sorry for her, having to be married to such a bastard as Edward James Carlson. She did appear to deserve better.

"You entertain your . . . uh . . . guests without me," Wesley quickly added, then rushed down the front steps and beneath the lacy frills of the live oaks. Serena had to understand that to stay in Edward's presence would be to cause more stress for her than to leave. He glanced across his shoulder, seeing her look of perplexity, then hurried on his way. He also knew other reasons not to create a scene. To do so could possibly cause Priscilla's tongue to loosen too much. Oh, God, what would Serena do if she knew? What would she say? Their life had just become serene. . . .

Serena clasped her hands together in front of her and laughed nervously, gazing from Priscilla, to Edward. "You must forgive Wesley," she said. "He has much on his mind. This plantation is quite large. Almost too much sometimes for one man to see to."

"Serena, if our arrival has caused problems, I'm sorry," Priscilla said quietly. "But it has been so long. I just had to see you. Especially being so close to Folly Island once having arrived to Charleston."

"I'm only too glad to see my baby sister," Serena said, taking Priscilla's hand, urging her on past Edward. Serena gave Edward a cold stare, lifting her chin haughtily into the air. "Come, Priscilla. Into Wyndham Hall. Have tea and talk. Tell me about father. How well is he? What does he do with his time?"

"Coming, Edward?" Priscilla said over her shoulder.

"No," he grumbled. "I'll just look over the grounds. You two carry on your woman's small talk. I understand."

Priscilla giggled a bit as she moved on into the house with Serena.

The house was quiet except for Wesley's lazy snorings next to Serena. The moon was casting dancing shadows along the ceiling where Serena lay tense, unable to sleep. Seeing Priscilla . . . seeing Edward . . . had brought too much of the past to the present. The whole evening had been a disaster. Though having been served a fine meal by soft candles' glow, the air had been heavy with uneasiness. Once small talk had been used up, only an early retirement to their rooms had been the reprieve for all concerned.

But rest . . . sleep . . . was evading Serena this night. She had too much to think about. She was torn between feelings about this move of Priscilla's and Edward's. Serena had seen Edward's mischievous eyes on her all evening, even though she *did* show with child. Would he . . . ? Dare he . . . ? And to know that he was now only two doors away, under the same roof as she . . . !

And then there was Priscilla! It *would* be nice to have her sister so near, though still such rivals at heart. Wouldn't it even possibly mean that their father might make the move to the Carolinas if both daughters were there? Such a thought was cause for ripples of excitement to course through Serena's veins.

Though having done everything in her power to remove herself from his loud, authoritative voice, Serena still missed her father, knowing that he could never order her around again. She was married. Wesley was her barrier to be held between father and daughter. But she did have a need to see him, to love him. . . .

Wesley tossed awkwardly across the bed, mumbling in his sleep. Serena watched him beneath the bath of the moonlight and loved him so. But she felt the need to get some fresh air. A walk on the beach—that's what she needed. The fresh sea air would do many things for her.

She crept slowly from the bed and moved stealthily to her wardrobe. She pulled her cape from inside and threw it around her shoulders over her sheer chemise. Glancing momentarily toward Wesley, she then hurried from the room and down the stairs until she was out on the beach, walking barefoot in the sand.

Sighing leisurely, she lifted her eyes to the sky, seeing its sheet of black velvet speckled with sequins of stars. The moon was full, gathering the tide to move higher on the beach in large tumbles.

Serena combed her fingers through her hair, inhaling deeply the scent of the water and tasting the salt on her lips. Her every fluid movement drew her chemise and cape around her in a silken flutter, and the roar of the water as it crashed and tumbled on the one side of her kept all other night noises from her ears.

She went to a sand dune and settled down next to it, stretching her legs out before her, welcoming the effervescence of the water as it lapped at her toes.

She watched with intensity as the crests of the waves farther out in the ocean were being whipped into whitecaps. The crests glistened triumphantly, as this spring tide became almost as possessed by demon force as it roared even more loudly. Serena hadn't even heard footsteps approaching. But she did recognize the coarseness of the hands on her wrists and the drawl of the voice—

"Well, little darlin', all alone? I hoped I'd get this chance," Edward said, suddenly towering over her in only his breeches. He yanked her roughly to her feet and put his face down into hers.

"Let me go, Edward," Serena said from between clenched teeth. "What do you think you're doing? Wesley will kill you. Surely you know that."

"Wesley won't find out," Edward snarled. "You wouldn't dare tell him or I will be the one to tell him that it was *I* who first knew his woman's body."

Serena kicked and jerked, causing her wrists to ache. "You idiot," she fumed. "Wesley already knows. I've kept no secrets from him. Couldn't you see the hate he has for you in the depths of his eyes? He could murder you for the first time you forced yourself upon me. If it becomes a second, he would not hesitate to direct a bullet into your heart."

Edward guffawed noisily, drawing her even closer, so that his body was a brute force of steel next to hers. "You think I'm afraid of him? I could mash his face in with one blow from my fist," he snarled. "I should anyway. He took what was mine."

Serena's eyes narrowed into two slits. "Edward, I was *never* your woman," she hissed. "It was my father who wanted the relationship. Not I. And you raped me once. Damn it, release me! Surely you aren't low enough to do it twice. Think of my sister. Your wife. Think of the condition I'm in. I'm pregnant. *Pregnant!* Do you hear?"

Edward's reply was a deep rumble of laughter as his mouth bore down upon hers. "I'll teach you to turn turncoat," he grumbled, struggling her down to the sandy floor of the beach. "Not only because of your abandoning the Union cause, but also because of myself. You shouldn't have left me, Serena."

He pinioned her to the sand, holding her with one hand and lifting her garments with the other. . . .

"Edward, please," Serena cried, lashing her head back and forth, feeling the weight of his body holding her, as though in a vise. Tears swelled in her eyes, making everything around her become a massive blur. "My unborn child," she pleaded further. "I fear for my . . . child. . . ."

His tongue became as a branding iron, inflicting a heated, torturous pain everywhere it stroked. When it moved to her breasts, flicking from one to the other, Serena groaned with despair. She knew that her breasts had already begun to fill with milk—would she now even have a child to suckle this milk from her breasts? Would

387

Edward's assault cause her to lose this child she so longed to give birth to?

"Serena, I've hungered for you," Edward moaned. His free hand began probing between her thighs, his knees forcing them apart. "I have to have you. Seeing you again made such an ache inside me. You have to quell that ache. Only you, my little darlin'."

"I'm not your little darlin'," she snapped angrily, feeling the sand eating at the flesh of her back and legs. "I never was. I hate you. I've always hated you. Let me go." She tossed her head more frantically when she felt the heat of his hands digging into her flesh and the wet of his lips moving across her abdomen. . . .

Suddenly the air was filled with mind-numbing screams. Serena watched in mortification as Priscilla pounced on Edward, pulling him free of Serena by the hair of his head.

"You beast!" Priscilla screamed over and over again. "How could you, Edward?"

Serena crept back a bit on the sand, eyes wide, aching, and feeling a sudden spinning of the head. She watched Priscilla as she continued slapping and attacking Edward while Edward attempted to protect his face with his crossed arms.

"And you, Serena," Priscilla then said, rushing to stand over her. "You are at fault here. You couldn't let Edward be mine alone. I knew of your one other time with him. He told me about the night you went to his house and seduced him—"

Serena swallowed back a bitterness rising inside her throat. She gasped, "What—?" She pulled her garments down to cover her nudity. "Priscilla, it isn't—"

Priscilla angrily kicked sand on Serena and continued

388

with her verbal assault. "But I can boast of playing the same game," she screamed. "I was with your Colonel Wesley Alston Wyndham—"

Serena closed her eyes and began to shake her head back and forth, not believing any of this. "No. You're lying—" she cried.

"Ha! Lying? You ask Wesley about the night we made love," Priscilla boasted, placing her hands on her hips. "You'll see that not only you can get a man to bed up with you, but also myself . . . ."

Edward moved to Priscilla's side, glaring. He grabbed her wrists and drew her roughly to him. "What is this you're saying?" he grumbled. "You? And this Colonel Wyndham?" He slapped her angrily across the face and began half dragging her along the beach.

"Edward, please," Priscilla pleaded. "I'm sorry—"

"And you think I'm goin' to move to Charleston so you can have easy access to fornicate freely behind my back?" he shouted further. "Go get our clothes together, woman. We're goin' back to Illinois. Tonight."

"Edward, please," Priscilla sobbed. "I said I was sorry . . ."

"Damn right, you'll be sorry," he grumbled. "You're my woman."

"Edward. But, Edward. What *you* were doing . . ."

"I'm a man. A man has these privileges. . . ."

Priscilla's sobs faded into the night, leaving Serena lying on the beach, alone, stunned. What Priscilla had said about Wesley pained her even more than what Edward had done. She hung her head into her hands, sobbing frantically, feeling each sob wracking her body, causing her abdomen to tighten into a hard knot. She flinched as a pain tore through her womb, and when another pain quickly followed, she gasped and drew her legs up before her, to hug them tightly to her.

"Oh, no," she wailed. "Not my baby. . . ."

A warm spray of water settled on her face as another large wave crashed and tumbled toward her. The roaring of the water was suddenly deafening, causing Serena to cover her ears with her hands. The feel of the water settling around her bare feet made Serena aware that the tide was rising and that if she didn't move, she would soon become consumed by waves, like flames from a hungry fire.

Moaning, she straightened her legs and tried to push herself from the sand, only finding that moving sent more pains scorching their way through her.

"I can't," she whispered. "I . . . can't move." She lifted her face to the sky. *God, I beg you,* she prayed. *Don't let this be happening. Awaken me in my bed with Wesley at my side. Please let . . . this . . . only be a nightmare.*

Serena tensed and listened, suddenly hearing something other than that of the noise from the ocean. She was hearing her name echoing around her through the thrashing of the waves. Her sobs tore through her anew, recognizing Wesley's voice. She could hear his fear. . . .

"Wesley. Oh, Wesley," she began screaming, flailing her arms wildly into the air. "I'm here. Over here."

When he reached her, Serena lifted her arms to him. "Darling, I . . . I can't move," she cried. "I'm in pain. . . ."

Wesley bent and scooped her up into his arms and drew her to him. "God, Serena," he cried. "What has happened? Why are you here? I awakened and found you gone. It frightened me so."

Serena twined her arms around his neck and placed

her tearful cheek against his shoulder. "Take me to our bed, Wesley," she sobbed, clinging. "The baby. I'm so afraid."

His breath was warm upon her cheek as he leaned over her, protecting her from any further dampness. His footsteps were hurried as he drew her closer. "Darling, I don't understand," he said huskily. "Why did you venture from the house? You know how dangerous it is. You know I've worried about the Indians."

A frantic sob tore from the depths of her throat, knowing that even white men could be savage. She lifted her head and peered toward the house, seeing quick movements on the porch. And as the moonlight splashed on the two moving figures, Serena could see Priscilla and Edward, now heading for the river. She swallowed hard, remembering Edward's assault, and oh, so hating to remember Priscilla's words. . . .

"Well, I'll be damned," Wesley blurted, stopping short, also seeing the quick departures from the house. "Where are *they* going? What the—?"

Serena lowered her head to Wesley's chest once more. She had a deep hurt inside her, having the need to lash out at Wesley for his night of romance with Priscilla. But Serena's main concern now was for her child. She clutched her abdomen with her free hand when another pain unraveled through it.

"Please, Wesley," she moaned. "I must get to my bed. The pains . . ."

Wesley's heart hammered against his ribs when he heard the pain in her voice. He resumed his pace, only glancing quickly now as the two ghostly figures disappeared into the night. He clamped his jaws together tightly, just knowing that Priscilla and Edward had something to do with Serena's plight. But his main concern now was for the baby. God. Oh, how he *did* want this baby! It had only taken the magic words, Serena's announcement that she was with child, to ease his worries about the color of the eyes and skin. If it was his and Serena's child, any child would be loved.

But deep inside, he couldn't help but pray for . . .

"Wesley, I'm so cold," Serena said, suddenly chilling.

Wesley took the porch steps two at a time and soon had her stretched across their bed, stripped of wet clothes and exchanged for dry, and tucked deeply beneath heavy, warm blankets. He sat down on the bed next to her, tenderly caressing her brow with the softness of a warmed, dampened cloth.

"There. Do you feel better now?" he said softly.

Remembering anew, Serena turned her eyes from him. "The pain in my womb has slackened," she whispered. "But I doubt if the pain in my heart will ever go away."

Wesley leaned over her, forcing her gaze to meet his as his forefinger pressed beneath her chin. "Serena, you must tell me what happened," he said thickly. "Now. I have to know. Surely you see that—"

"Yes, Wesley," she murmured, almost choking on the words as she blurted it all out to him . . . what had been done . . . what had been said. . . .

"Damn it," he growled as he lunged from the bed. He flung his hands to his hair and fingered through it angrily. "Damn them both," he shouted further, angrily pacing. He halted his movements and swung around on a heel, glaring. "I'll shoot that bastard Edward," he snarled. "I'll shoot him—"

"And, Priscilla? You'll . . . shoot . . . her also?" Serena murmured, blinking tears from her lashes.

"What about Priscilla? Can you tell me, Wesley? Can you?" Again she turned her head away, flicking tears from her cheeks with her fingers.

When Wesley fell to his knees beside the bed, Serena let him lift her hands from her face and kiss each one of them.

"I'm so sorry, Serena," he whispered. "So damn sorry."

"How could you, Wesley? How could you pretend to love me, then share a bed with my sister? And when did you even get the chance? Did you plan it? Oh, Wesley, I can't believe this has happened."

"One thing at a time, Serena," Wesley said, his dark eyes showing his inner traumas. "First, I'll try to explain why I shared a few moments with your sister."

"I'm listening. . . ."

"It was even a surprise to me," he began, moving to the bed, sitting beside her. "This one evening, everyone was asleep. Even myself. Priscilla, well, she came to my bed. She didn't even talk. She removed her undergarment and lay down next to me and placed her body next to mine, a silent invitation. At first, I ignored her, afraid that it was a trap of some sort. You see, she had never even spoken much to me until that day. Then it had only been of the novels that she enjoyed reading. Even when she spoke of them being romance novels, she actually blushed. It was later that same night that she came to my bed. She smelled of heaven. And she looked an angel. When she placed my hand on her, well, you know, what could I do?"

Serena covered her eyes with the back of an arm. "Oh, Wesley," she groaned.

"And I had to think that maybe *she* would be a way out

of that place," he said thickly, clearing his throat. "I had no idea that you would do what you did for me."

"And you didn't even love me at that time, as you had professed?"

"I have always loved you. . . ."

"And this time with her was after . . . our . . . time together?"

"Yes."

"Wesley, oh, Wesley . . ."

"Let me finish," he said. "As I was saying, I had thought maybe either she or you might eventually help to release me from my bonds. I was the enemy. I had to resort to whatever I could to return to my regiment."

"But that night you went to my room with me, I did release your bonds—"

"But I also had promised you that I wouldn't try to escape," he said. "Plus the fact, that at that time, I couldn't have escaped. I was too weak."

"Not too weak to have sex with two women, sisters," she stormed, flinging her arm from her eyes to glower at him.

"Do you want to know why Priscilla came to my bed?"

"Do . . . you . . . even know? I can't even imagine her going to the hospital quarters for *any* reason without being forced. She always so hated the sight of blood. Your wound. You know how it seeped blood."

"She wasn't forced. Believe me. And she forgot about my wound once with me," he said quietly. "And after we . . . well, she asked if she was as pretty and as good in bed as you were."

"What?" Serena gasped.

"Yes. You see, that night that she came to your room and I hid in your wardrobe?"

"Yes . . ."

"She saw many telltale signs. Beneath the bed? She was able to get a glimpse of the wine and candles. . . ."

"So? She wanted to prove what, Wesley?"

"She said that you had acted as though superior, as though you could get a man to notice you, but that she didn't have such talents. She had something to prove to herself, it seems."

"And you fell for it, huh, Wesley?"

"I don't truly think I would have if I had been in a different frame of mind," he said darkly.

"And what frame of mind were you in?" she snapped.

"You and I had already shared your room—" he began, but was interrupted by her gasp of horror.

"Don't tell me, oh, no, Wesley, not *that* night," she said. She could so vividly remember how Priscilla had pleaded with her to sit with Edward so Priscilla could get some rest and how Priscilla had failed to return to Edward's bedside. Serena could even remember how crumpled Priscilla's dress had been the next morning. . . .

"No. The next night," he murmured. "You see, I was a bit disillusioned by something I had found that night when you and I had sex—"

"Disillusioned? Oh, God, Wesley. I don't think I want to hear any more."

"You must," he stated flatly. "You see, that was the night that I discovered that you had been with another man. You see, there was no blood, no resistance whatsoever when I entered you."

"Please, Wesley—"

"Darling, I now know, remember? You told me about Edward later. But that night? I had to think you had had

395

many men. When Priscilla offered herself to me, that was another reason I took her to my bed so willingly."

"The . . . very next . . . night . . ." she stammered.

"And, Serena. Not only that. You must remember. I was at war; I had to do what I could to return to the South. When your sister came to me, I thought that she would be weak enough to eventually set me free, you see, weak in her defenses about what I, a man, could supply her with. I know it sounds callous. But it is the way I had thought at the time. And you've got to believe me—"

"And I was the one who took the bait," she said, laughing sarcastically. "I was the one who acted the complete whore and went even against my father and country. I turned traitor when I turned you loose. I was then guilty of treason. I bet you were laughing your fool head off about it when I wasn't looking on our long journey to the Carolinas."

"Never. I always loved you," he said. "From the first moment I laid eyes on you. Don't you know how lucky I felt to have it be you to actually be the one to secure the key for my release? If it had been Priscilla, I truly don't know what I would have done with her. But your father? He caught me in my little game."

"What—?"

"Just as Priscilla left my bed, your father jerked the curtain aside."

"Oh, no—"

"But he didn't realize the full extent of my moments with Priscilla."

Serena was remembering her father's uneasiness that night of Wesley's move from the hospital quarters to the jail. Now she understood. But she *still* couldn't believe Wesley and how he could have truly been in love with her and then blithely seduce Priscilla.

"Wesley, I don't know what to believe. I am so confused," she cried, rising on an elbow.

"I wish that you would believe me," he said, rising from the bed. "But I do understand your confusion. Again, I say that I am sorry." He went to the window. The moonlight showed a johnboat inching away from the marsh grasses along Folly Island's shore. Wesley's fists doubled at his side. He had to hope that Edward would lose himself in the dark waters of the river, but if so, then Wesley would be robbed of his revenge. He swung around and moved in quick strides to the wardrobe. He reached inside and pulled out his holster and gun.

Serena's eyes widened. "Wesley, what are—"

He strapped his holster around his waist. "I'm going to kill me a damn Yankee," he grumbled. "Seems the war isn't over for me after all."

Serena inched her way from the bed, breathing hard, reaching for him. "No, Wesley. You mustn't," she said, clutching to her abdomen.

"Why the hell not?"

"Leave them be, Wesley," she panted, feeling nervous perspiration beading her brow. Her thoughts were filled with her sister's deceit. It *had* been Priscilla who had seduced Wesley. She had to . . . believe . . . that . . . now. Hadn't Priscilla even as much confessed this truth to her?

"What?" Wesley said in a near whisper.

Serena went to him and touched his face softly. "Don't you see?" she murmured. "They deserve each other. Leave them be. I'm sure their punishments are served every day, just living with one another. Don't you truly see, darling?"

"I want to," he said thickly, drawing her to him. "And you?"

"You have to understand. There will always be a corner of my heart that will ache a little when I remember you having been with my sister."

"Yes. I understand."

"And now. How do you feel, Wesley? About all of this?"

"I'm filled with regret," he murmured.

"Wesley, our only worry should be about our child. Only our child." She flinched and shot a terrified look toward Wesley. "Wesley, something—" She felt a spinning of the head and saw many faces of Wesley as she fell to the floor at his feet.

"Serena," he shouted. He bent and scooped her up into his arms, suddenly weeping. He placed her gently on the bed and loosened her chemise and began to caress her brow with the back of a hand. "I'm so sorry for all of this, darling," he whispered. "I'll make it up to you. Somehow . . . I'll make it all up to you. . . ."

Chapter Twenty

Spinning magic into the air, a string quartet was positioned at the far end of the room, playing a light and airy waltz. Serena frowned a bit when she spied the harp that still sat vacant. Dorlisa May hadn't yet volunteered to play for the crowd. She had said that the violins, viola and cello were adequate, that she would possibly spoil the effect of the four stringed instruments if she would add a fifth to the group. But Serena had to think it was because Dorlisa May didn't wish to be the center of attraction— having already been the minute she walked into the room. . . .

"And Charleston thought the social season had slowed?" Wesley chuckled, guiding Serena around and through the other couples on the cleared floor of the drawing room at Wyndham Hall. "We showed them, didn't we, darling?"

Serena beamed. "Yes. I believe we did," she laughed softly, though she felt a bit awkward with her swollen abdomen causing her to move so clumsily. But she had assured Wesley that just because she was heavy with child, that didn't have to mean that she would stand idly by, watching everyone else enjoy the ball that they had finally been able to give. The stressful night with Priscilla and Edward had been cause for Serena to be confined to bed for many weeks, but she was now feeling strong enough, and felt that the proper time had arrived that she could even relax with the new faces that she and Dorlisa May were being introduced to. Anyway, Serena loved having an opportunity to be daring, and Charleston society was thoroughly scandalized by the appearance of their very pregnant hostess. Nothing, however, could have kept them away tonight.

Serena let her gaze move around her, proud that she was in part responsible for the crowds having such a grand time. All the great pieces of furniture had been removed from the room except for the necessary chairs that lined the full length of each wall. The floors had been waxed, over and over again, so that they now shone as though they were a sheet of ice. Couples glided around the room as though on skates, so happy, so carefree, the women so beautifully attired in their many yards of silks and satins held out from their bodies by gently swaying hoops.

As Wesley continued to guide Serena around the room, he held his chin proudly high, and his back straight. He was attired in his perfectly fitted black waistcoat and breeches, with an abundance of lace at his throat and cuffs. He was once again proud to be a Wyndham and he had Serena to thank for this. Ah, how easily it had happened, the introduction of Dorlisa May to all who were present. He now wished that he hadn't waited so long. How much easier life would have been for his sister and even himself. . . .

Along with him, Serena scanned the crowd, then found Dorlisa May as she stood chatting with another girl of her own age. It had been Serena's hardest chore yet as a Wyndham to urge Dorlisa May from her room, to enter this large gathering of strangers, who had never met this "odd" daughter because she had never shown herself to people.

But now, since the formal introduction had been successfully made, with only slight gasps from the crowd, Dorlisa May seemed confident and poised in her lace-trimmed silken gown with its low-cut bodice, tight waist, and flared skirt that was held out by the most perfect of hoops.

Dorlisa May's hair—like that of most women and young girls at this gathering—had been arranged to fall from a center part into long coils of curls. She indeed did look lovely and had reason to feel confident. Though her skin was milky-white and her eyes were strangely pink, she had to be one of the most beautiful of the young ladies that had agreed to be a part of this coming-out party.

Then Serena had to smile smugly when she saw something else. She was watching Dorlisa May's eyes move to one among the gentlemen playing in the quartet. As Dorlisa May would talk, her eyes would settle on this one young man, Adam Taylor, whose skin was almost as fair as hers and his light blond hair almost as colorless, settling around his oval face in ringlets, as a girl's might do.

Then something made Serena's breath catch in her throat. This young man who was eagerly drawing his bow across the strings of his viola was returning this intent gaze and now even smiling at Dorlisa May. Serena glanced quickly back at Dorlisa May and actually saw her lift a hand and wave with a quick flick of a wrist toward this young man. Were they attracted to one another? Could it be possible?

Serena lifted the skirt of her blue satin dress with her free hand and held her head back, sighing heavily as Wesley made another turn on the floor. She was happy. She had never been happier. Things were finally working out for them all. If Dorlisa May could get the attention of a young man so quickly, surely she could find a future of true happiness. Could Dorlisa May even one day have a child of her own? Oh, the love she would be able to instill in that child. She had much, much to spare.

"Honey, are you sure you should dance this long at a time?" Wesley asked, furrowing his brow. "What if you would overdo it? The baby, darling. You have another full month to go. Oh, you do worry me so."

"Now, Wesley, just you quit fussing at me. Dancing is much easier on me than worrying over the menu or the arrival of more guests," she said, laughing. "We now have others to carry out such chores."

Her gaze traveled on around her, seeing the dark-skinned, eight-year-old Toy acting the houseboy for this night, white-gloved and in black knee breeches and jacket, carrying trays of food, offering fresh pompano prepared with a sherry-flavored sauce of lobster, scallops, and shrimp. It was being impeccably served with a cold smoked grouper appetizer, a hearty seafood bisque, and tasty salad, along with hot yeast rolls and mint juleps or punch, whichever was the individual's choice.

Fresh raspberries Romanoff had been chosen for the dessert, which Serena had herself supervised, having so often seen her mother prepare this for groups when life had been normal at the Calvert mansion in Illinois before the Civil War had even been mentioned in conversation.

Serena had to smile when she saw Francine enter the room, curtsying deeply before taking empty dishes or glasses from the guests. The five children who had been discovered in Wesley's townhouse on their first day in Charleston had emerged into quiet, polite children whom Serena hated labeling as servants. She would never be able to do without them.

Her favorite was Bubba. He was the smallest, but he had the most colorful of personality. He had a way of stealing one's heart with his large, pleading, dark eyes. He had begun to constantly be Wesley's companion whenever Wesley would enter the fields to inspect the crops. It warmed Serena's heart to see Wesley chat so openly with this young child.

A sudden commotion at the door drew Serena's thoughts to the present. She felt Wesley's hand grow slack in hers, and when she gazed quickly toward him, she found a look of dismay in his eyes. Then Serena followed his gaze and felt her pulsebeat quicken, seeing Lona Gale standing arm-in-arm with a gray-haired, but quite handsome and distinguished-looking gentleman. All eyes were now focused on this Wyndham who had yet to make an appearance at this fancy ball, though she had at one time been *the* Wyndham of all balls on this plantation.

Lona Gale held her chin haughtily into the air and light from the candles' golden flickerings from the many sconces along the wall and the magnificent crystal chandelier above where she now stood settled onto the diamonds at her throat and on her fingers.

Her dress was of black silk without the aid of a hoop and was cut quite low at her bosom—revealing that the eldest of the Wyndhams still held a part of her youth, and she brazenly flaunted it to all who now had ceased to waltz along with the ceasing of the music.

Lona Gale smiled toward Wesley, lifting her fingers to her dark hair that was piled in loose curls atop her head. Then her expression changed to one of mortification when the soft pluckings from a harp began to fill the room with a haunting melody.

A slow smile lifted Serena's lips as she watched Dorlisa May at the harp playing one of her own composed pieces, while staring icily toward her mother. As she continued to pluck at the strings, the melody took on a quality of triumph, as the force of determination moved her eager fingers briskly from string to string.

Serena placed her fingers to her throat, trembling a bit, seeing how victoriously Dorlisa May was now gazing at her mother. Serena knew what Dorlisa May was feeling. Serena had felt it herself, when she had turned the key in Wesley's jail cell. When releasing Wesley from his bonds, she had also released herself from her own—those of her father and the prison he had built around her by his overbearing ways and loud, authoritative voice.

Knowing that she had been readily accepted on this, her first move into society, Dorlisa May *had* triumphed over her mother.

Oh, why did it have to take so many years to happen? Serena thought to herself. Then she felt the absence of Wesley at her side and searched around her, finding him guiding Lona Gale away from her escort and into the privacy of the music room.

Serena lifted her skirt and hurried also to the room, stopping short when entering, when she heard Wesley's lowered voice while speaking with his mother.

"Mother, you shouldn't have come," he grumbled,

grasping onto her shoulders, holding her at arm's length. "Did you wish to ruin this ball for Serena? Didn't you see how everything stopped when you entered the room? Mother, how could you?"

"I have never missed a social function at Wyndham Hall," Lona Gale snapped angrily. "And I wasn't about to begin now."

"Had you thought about what it might even mean to Dorlisa May?" he said, then dropped his arms heavily to his side. "That was a dumb question. Of course, you knew perfectly well what you were doing."

Serena made her presence known as she went to Wesley's side. She offered a hand to Lona Gale, smiling stiffly. "Good evening, Lona Gale," she murmured. "I'm as surprised as Wesley to see you here. Why, I would have thought you would be too ashamed to show your face, knowing that Dorlisa May was finally being introduced into society. Or did you think that Dorlisa May would have crawled further into her shell, and refused to come out? Tonight proved many things to me and one was that you alone are a snob. I had thought possibly all southern ladies might be the same as you in their feelings for Dorlisa May's differences. But I was wrong. Thank God, I was wrong. As you can see, she's being highly accepted."

Lona Gale refused Serena's hand and instead pulled a lace-trimmed handkerchief from inside her sleeve as her face paled. "I must return to my escort," she said stiffly.

"Mother, who is that man?" Wesley asked, stepping to the door, peering outward.

"He's just recently moved to Charleston from Atlanta. He's putting money into some land for more townhouses. It even seems his plantation was spared in Atlanta, while

405

all others were being ravaged by the Yankee scoundrels."
Her gaze swept icily over Serena.

"Married?" Serena asked, smiling wickedly.

"Widowed," Lona Gale hissed.

Wesley moved to Serena and placed his arm around her waist. "Well, anyway, Mother, it *is* good to see that you're feeling better. When you left those few months ago, I was quite concerned about you."

"How could I have felt any differently? My one son was killed by an Indian savage and my other had . . . had chosen to ignore my presence at Wyndham Hall," she said. She visibly shuddered, then lowered her eyes. "I had to get away. I had to."

"But, you are happy, Mother?"

"Yes. Quite," Lona Gale answered, meeting his gaze now with a fixed determination.

Wesley bent and kissed Serena gently on the cheek, chuckling a bit when he once again noticed the splash of freckles across her nose. Though with child, she still was so often such a child herself. "We're all one big happy family here at Wyndham Hall," he said. "And soon there will be one more to add to our happiness."

Dorlisa May moved into the room with her arm locked through Adam Taylor's. Her eyes sparkled with even further triumph. "Wesley, Serena, and . . . Mother, I'd like you to meet Adam Taylor," she said proudly. "And doesn't he play such a beautiful viola?"

"Yes, he does," Wesley said, reaching a hand to Adam. He smiled to himself when he felt this young man's firm grip. It seemed that being a musician hadn't made him any less of a man. And was this young man actually taking a fancy to Dorlisa May? No one could have ever asked for any more than this from this ball.

"It's quite an honor to make your acquaintance, Adam," he said proudly, glancing at Lona Gale, seeing how her face had paled even more. This moment had been well waited for. Now, his mother was seeing just how wrong she had been by having kept Dorlisa May from having a social life.

He then glanced toward Dorlisa May. Ah, how composed she was, and never having been with a gentleman friend before. But Wesley had felt her eyes studying him and Serena and how they had been so openly affectionate with one another. Yes, she had been in the process of learning, as she had been all of her life, having had to teach herself even the most important values of life.

He then glanced down at Serena, suddenly seeing something new in her eyes. And why was she suddenly placing her hands to her abdomen, as though testing its strength? He watched her still, as she flinched. When her gaze turned and met his and held, he could only guess what was happening. His insides turned to mush, realizing that the child was a month early. If she was in sudden labor, what could it all mean—?

"Darling?" he whispered, leaning down, studying her eyes more closely.

"It's the baby, Wesley," she whispered, now panting wildly. "I don't know why, but suddenly . . . I'm in pain . . . and though I haven't given birth before, I know these pains are . . . labor . . . pains . . ." She closed her eyes as she was wracked with more intense pains.

Wesley's gaze began to move frantically around him. He studied his mother's expression and saw the knowing in the slack line of her mouth and the fear in the dark of her eyes, then he glanced over at Dorlisa May and saw that she was so absorbed in her gentleman friend, she had no idea what was going on. But Dorlisa May was the one Wesley had to depend on in such a situation as this. She had more experience with tenderness and even more so with inner strength, both of which would be necessary to ensure Serena's well-being. The hospital was too far away. Wesley didn't wish to go by boat with Serena across the dark, swampy waters of Kiawah River when a child might be born at any moment. So he reached for Dorlisa May's hands and took them in his, pulling her before him.

"Lisa, Serena is in labor," he said thickly.

Dorlisa May's eyes grew wide as she stared in disbelief at Wesley, then finally glanced quickly at Serena and, yes, saw the pain in Serena's eyes. "What can I do, Wesley?" she asked, moving to Serena, placing her arms around her, whispering soft words of comforting love to her.

"You must see if we have a doctor present," Wesley said, pacing back and forth across the room. "I know we sent an invitation to Doctor Templeton, but I don't think he ever did reply. Damn. I don't know what we can do. I've heard of a Doc Shaw in Charleston, but I've never made his acquaintance."

His gaze moved to Serena once again, seeing the perspiration beading her brow. He hurried to her and placed his arm around her waist, directing her from the room. "Now take it easy, honey," he said quietly, looking from side to side as the guests stepped aside to make room. "Darling, do you think you can make it up the stairs? I'm afraid to lift you. With your added weight, it makes you so awkward. I'm afraid I might topple backwards once on the stairs if I tried to lift and carry you."

"Yes, darling," she whispered. "I can make it. Just stay beside me, though. Please. I feel so strange. The pains are so severe at times, I feel as though I might pass out."

When a fresh pain shot through her middle then moved on downward, pulsating in even more pains, she wanted to pull her knees upward, but had to keep putting her feet forward onto the steps, until the upstairs landing was finally reached. She breathed heavily with relief when she was guided into her room and eased down onto the bed.

"I'll see to everything, darling," Wesley said, quickly removing his jacket, rolling his shirt sleeves up to above his elbows. "Dorlisa May is finding someone who might assist."

His fears were many. This was the time that he had feared since the first words of Serena's pregnancy had met his ears. He feared for her as well as for the child. Since it was arriving one full month early, he no longer cared that it might possibly be albino. He only wanted the child to be healthy, with ten fingers and ten toes. A shuffling of feet into the room drew his quick attention to the doorway, then he breathed a sigh of relief when a tall, thinning man moved into the room, already unbuttoning the shirt at his throat and removing his jacket.

"I'm Doctor Templeton," the doctor said in a deep voice. "Sorry for not acknowledging your invitation, ol' man, but I never know when I can be anywhere. Learned long ago to just ignore invitations until the last minute. That way, I don't disappoint no one but myself." He chuckled heartily then moved to Serena's bedside. "Time to have a little one, huh?" he chuckled further, reaching to feel her abdomen, pressing into it, then laughed softly.

"Hard as a rock, this one," he said.

Serena clenched her fists at her side as another deep pain shot through her. Each one was worse than the last, and her stomach seemed to tighten even more with each pain. "Yes. It gets that way when I'm having . . . a contraction . . ." she panted, looking desperately around her when another pain came so soon after the last.

Doctor Templeton began giving orders: hot water; lots of clean cloths; some privacy; get Serena undressed and lying on clean sheets; everyone from the room except for those who are going to assist; and on and on . . . until Serena lay in only a cotton chemise with legs spread, ready.

She reached for Wesley's hand, feeling the cold clamminess. "Don't be frightened, Wesley," she said softly. "Just think. Soon we will have our child. And, truly, we are lucky to have the gift handed us a month early."

Wesley fell to his knees next to her, his thick lashes heavy over his eyes. "But, honey, a month early, well, that can . . . cause complications, can't it?"

Dr. Templeton answered for Serena. "We don't want to worry about that," he said, reaching up inside Serena's chemise, inserting a finger into her, while pressing down on her abdomen. He smiled warmly. "Do you think you can spare two more large pushes, Serena?" he asked, eyeing her beneath thick, black eyebrows.

She laughed a bit awkwardly. "Seems I have no control over my body and what I wish it to do or not to do at this point," she answered, readying herself for another onslaught of pains, feeling it beginning in the tightening of the skin across her stomach. She began panting, wanting so to scream when this pain hit with such a

410

sudden force, she felt her head begin to spin. She moaned, tossing her head back and forth, feeling the perspiration-soaked hair wetting her cheeks with each lashing.

"Okay," Dr. Templeton said, laughing hoarsely. "That's one. We need just one more, then I think we can tell you whether you've got a boy or girl to brag about."

Wesley moved from the bedside, cradling his head in his hands, feeling his heartbeat hastening. It was just about over . . . what he had wondered about . . . for so long . . . was just about over. He tensed, then whirled around on a heel when he heard Serena scream out with the next pain, watching, oh, watching so closely as the baby slipped from inside her into the doctor's waiting hands.

"Well, well," Dr. Templeton said smoothly. "A fine specimen of a child, if I ever did see one."

Wesley swallowed hard. He couldn't see if it was albino or not. All he could see was the mucous and blood that engulfed this small bundle of flesh that was squirming and kicking its legs and arms. He inched his way closer, warmth moving through him in quick rushes, seeing his child—his and Serena's child—and when Dr. Templeton held the baby up into the air and began to smack its behind, Wesley was able to see that he had just been handed a boy child from God. But the color. Damn it. What was the child's skin coloring? Suddenly it was important. All over again. But the blood and mucous was too thick.

As the baby began to cry, Wesley hurriedly reached for a dampened towel, and as Dr. Templeton handed the baby to Wesley, Wesley held it in one arm and began to wipe it with the other free hand, feeling his heart pound harder

411

and harder, seeing the sweet pinkish casts to the skin. It wasn't milkish-white. Not at all. And as the baby opened his eyes, a deep blue looked and blinked back at Wesley. "God, Serena. My God, our son . . . he's as you and I. . . . And he's so beautiful. . . ."

Serena reached her arms out toward Wesley, blinded with tears. "A son? Wesley, we have a son . . . ?" she murmured. "Let me have our child. Oh, Wesley, I want to see him. I want to hold him."

Wesley could see only a blur now through his rush of tears. He placed the child in Serena's waiting arms, then knelt down beside her and kissed her, over and over again. "Darling, I didn't know that we could actually do it. We've had a son. Oh, God, look at our son."

He looked around just as Dorlisa May entered the room. His face grew a bit ashen, hoping she hadn't witnessed his exuberance at having a normal child. But he knew his fears had been wrong. He could see it in the depths of her eyes. Dorlisa May was mature enough, intelligent enough, to know that anyone would want a normal child, herself having gone through so much hell having been born "different." She would have only wanted this for Serena and Wesley. She understood.

"It's a boy, Dorlisa May," Wesley said, going to her, pulling her next to him as they walked together toward the bed.

"I just knew you would have a boy," Dorlisa May sighed, bending, taking a closer look at the small bundle that was smacking its lips and still blinking its eyes.

"Serena, I must announce our son's arrival to our gathering," Wesley said anxiously, then once again let his gaze rake over the child's loveliness.

As though Serena had read his thoughts, she lifted the

baby to him. "Here, Wesley," she said softly. "Why not *show* the child to all who wait? Why not let them *see* how perfect our child is? And tell them that we have just brought a Wesley Calvert Wyndham into this world."

"Truly? Do you think we should show them?" he asked anxiously. Damn it, he had to show them. He knew what had to be on most minds . . . especially that of Lona Gale Wyndham. . . .

"Yes, go on, Wesley," Serena sighed, closing her eyes, suddenly oh, so tired. Content, yes. But exhausted from her labors.

"And we are going to name this child Wesley Calvert?" Wesley asked, reaching for a small blanket with which to wrap the baby before his first appearance in the social circles of Charleston.

"If you don't mind. . . ."

Wesley chuckled gruffly. "No. I don't mind," he said. "And your father will be just as proud as I am. He will be pleased that you have chosen to use the Calvert name for our son, since he never had a son of his own to carry the name on."

"May I go with you? Be at your side, Wesley?" Dorlisa May asked softly, peeking inside the wrapped blanket, already liking the opportunity of becoming an aunt.

"Yes, Lisa," Wesley said. "You sure can."

"Be careful of the stairs, Wesley," Serena murmured, as Dr. Templeton began to caress her brow with a dampened cloth and then moved to clean her up.

"We will," Wesley said proudly. He moved from the room and when he caught sight of eyes watching his descent on the stairs, he threw his shoulders back and smiled broadly. He glanced quickly around and could see the anxious, curious looks on most of the faces. Now that it was known that albinos were a part of the family, everyone's eyes showed the wonder of what this child might be.

Wesley searched through the faces and found Lona Gale. She hadn't even made an appearance in the upper room, where her first grandchild had been born. Wesley set his jaw firmly, knowing that she would never change. Serena had been right. Lona Gale wasn't a proud southern lady, she was a snobbish boor.

He moved into the center of the drawing room and slowly began to pull the blanket from around the baby, first one corner, then another, then when the child was shown in its full nudity, Wesley held it up above the crowd for all to see. He said proudly, "May I introduce to you all—my son, Wesley Calvert Wyndham."

He felt such a gush of warmth move through him when he saw the faces light up and when he heard the oohs and ahs. He had so long thought of how a gathering might accept an albino child. But hadn't he heard and seen when Dorlisa May had entered the room earlier in the evening? Hadn't there at first been gasps, closely followed by a strained silence, then the smiles of acceptances as Dorlisa May had broken into her usual quiet, soft smile?

A silken flutter of skirts at Wesley's side and a gentle hand on his drew his quick attention from his thoughts. His breath caught in his throat when he found his mother, misty-eyed, looking toward the baby.

"Mother?" he murmured softly.

"My grandson, Wesley. Please . . . let . . . me see my grandson," she said, pleading with her eyes.

Wesley swallowed a fast-rising lump in his throat when he lowered Wesley Calvert to be at eye level.

"He is beautiful," Lona Gale murmured.

"Mother . . ."

Her voice trembled as she reached for the baby. "May . . . I?" she said.

Wesley looked awkwardly around him, hearing the breathlessness of the crowd. Once Dorlisa May had been revealed for all society to see, feelings for Lona Gale had been suddenly changed. Wesley knew that Lona Gale was aware of this change, so suspected she was now playing on all their sympathies, by putting on a show of being the "proud grandmother" of the gathering. He wasn't sure if he would aid her in her game. He drew Wesley Calvert into the crook of his left arm and slowly folded the corners of the blanket back around him.

"Wesley?" Lona Gale murmured, paling.

"Let's go into the music room, Mother," he said in a subdued voice, already weaving his way through the crowd. He gave her a furtive glance as she moved with him, and when they were out of reach of all who might want to listen, Wesley eyed Lona Gale lingeringly.

"Why, Mother?" he said thickly. "You've shown no interest in becoming a grandmother until now. Is it because you want to be something you're not in the eyes of all who are here? You do know what their feelings must be for you now that your daughter has been presented to them. Pink eyes, milky white flesh? Now they know, don't they, Mother? They know you are a snob to hide away your daughter."

"Wesley, please," Lona Gale gasped, placing her hands to her throat.

"And, Mother, aren't you glad your grandson isn't albino? Maybe *that's* the true reason you've decided to show affection for your grandson."

415

Lona Gale lowered her eyes. "Wesley, I'm so sorry for everything," she whispered. Her eyes lifted, showing a deep inner despair as their gazes met and held. "Seeing my grandson has brought so much to my mind that I am so . . . ashamed of. . . ."

Wesley threw his head back in a quiet laughter, then he glared at her. "Mother, you've never allowed such feelings about yourself in the past," he mumbled. "And I'm sure you are lying even now. A baby, my baby, Serena's baby, couldn't effect you in such a way."

"Wesley, since having lost first your father, then Truman, and having isolated myself from family by moving to Charleston, I've had time to think and time to be lonely," she murmured, wringing her hands nervously.

Wesley laughed again. "Yes, so lonely you flaunt your new, rich gentleman friend to my social gathering."

"He is only a . . . a diversion."

"Diversion? God, Mother."

"I needed an escort to return to Wyndham Hall. To look as though I wasn't the solitary person I've truly become."

"Mother, I never know when to believe you."

"Believe me when I say I want to come home. Be a part of the family. Share in your happiness."

"I don't think it would be best, Mother," Wesley said, feeling an ache circling his heart. He so loved his mother, but he just couldn't trust that she was being totally honest. He suspected that once she returned, she would create chaos all over again. "It's best, for all, that we leave things as they are," he quickly blurted.

Lona Gale's eyes widened and her mouth went agape, realizing her son had truly, wholly rejected her.

Teetering a bit, she felt her way to a chair and crumpled down onto it. She hung her head in her hands and began to weep softly. "Wesley, I never thought things could come to this between us," she cried. "I truly thought that all I had done had been for the best interest of family. But . . . your actions . . . tell me that I'm wrong."

Wesley felt torn—with the need to return Wesley Calvert to Serena's waiting arms, and with the need to go to his mother to try and see what was causing her sudden, unusually rash behavior. It wasn't at all like her.

He turned a corner of the blanket back to check Wesley Calvert's welfare and when he saw the tiny eyes closed, he felt he could take time to go to his mother, get to the bottom of this new Lona Gale that had suddenly surfaced. In the past, hadn't she always had time for him?

He went and settled down beside her, cradling Wesley Calvert on his lap. "Mother, what things are you speaking of when you say you did so much in the best interest of family?" he said, eyeing her sharply.

Pulling a lacy handkerchief from a sleeve, she dabbed at her eyes and nose, then turned her gaze to Wesley, sniffing and clearing her throat nervously. "Wesley, please," she murmured. "Just tell me that you welcome me back to Wyndham Hall so I can be part of the family again. I truly don't want to tell things of . . . the . . . past. . . ."

"Mother, I want you here also," he said thickly, taking her hand in his, cringing a bit when he felt the tautness of the skin, realizing just how old she was. His eyes wavered a bit, then he quickly added, "But I feel we can only feel comfortable with you, if you return to us after being totally honest with us about everything. We want to pull you into our conversations with ease, we want to be able to laugh and know that you are laughing along with us . . . not at us . . ."

"Oh, Wesley," Lona Gale moaned. "Have I appeared to be such a shrew? Have I?"

"Well, in a way, you might call it that," he said, laughing nervously.

"All right," she said, squeezing his hand. "I've needed to tell someone for so long, anyway. And seeing my grandson, seeing your reaction to his eye and skin coloring, so proud, so relieved, made such a regret flow through my veins." She lowered her eyes and began to weep anew. "Wesley, I should have known what fears you had of giving birth to an albino. You see, I planted the seed of fear, unknowingly, long ago. . . ."

"What?" he gasped.

"Yes. And, oh, God, Wesley," she cried further. "When I saw you lift your child for all to see, so proud that the child was normal, it was then that I realized the torments and fears I had planted deeply inside you and how unfair it had been to you. Oh, God, Wesley, I now know how wrong I was. . . ."

Wesley removed his hand from hers, doubling it into a fist. "Mother, what on earth are you getting at?" he said thickly.

Her gaze averted upward. Her eyes were clouded with further tears. "Wesley, it is the time for truths," she murmured. "I know it is. But I'm so afraid that to reveal truths, would be to truly close the doors of Wyndham Hall in my face forever. You'll truly hate me, Wesley. You will. But I now know that I have to tell you, so your future fears will be erased. I know that you will want to father more children. It's unfair to have to burden yourself any further with the worry of fathering

418

an albino. . . ."

"Mother—"

"Please, Wesley," she said, rising, pacing. "Let me continue. Then if you request, I shall leave and never, never look back. I would deserve your hate."

Wesley's brow furrowed. His heart was racing. He shifted Wesley Calvert in his arms and moved from the chair. He paced along with his mother, then placed a hand on her arm and urged her to stop. "Mother, whatever it is, surely it isn't all this bad," he said. "You appear as though the doors of hell have opened and you're being forced to enter. . . ."

"I feel that way," she said sullenly, refusing to look his way.

"Well, then, remove this burden from inside you," he urged. "Tell me. Now."

Lona Gale sniffled into her handkerchief and quickly blurted: "Wesley, you do not have albino blood. . . ."

Something grabbed at Wesley's heart. "What are you saying?" he gasped, drawing Wesley Calvert closer to his chest. "Mother, I—"

Lona Gale dropped her handkerchief to the floor and placed her hands on Wesley's shoulders. "Wesley, the true reason I had to keep Dorlisa May hidden," she said in a near whisper. "It wasn't altogether because of her coloring."

Wesley felt a rubbery sensation enter his knees. "Good Lord, Mother, what—"

She placed a trembling forefinger to his lips, sealing his words. "Please, Wesley. No words," she said in a strain. "Let me finish. Then I shall turn my back on you and walk from this house unless you have kindness in your heart for your mother and her hidden guilts for her one

419

night of disgrace those many years ago. . . ."

Wesley was aghast at what was being said. He went to a chair and slouched down onto it, rocking Wesley Calvert back and forth in his arms, watching . . . listening. . . .

Lona Gale resumed her pacing with head bent. "It was so long ago," she murmured. "Your father had left us alone . . . you, me, Truman, on this Folly Island for weeks at a time, pleasuring himself with one of his long sea voyages. I became so lonely. Night after night. Day after day. I watched for the ship's return that would carry him back to my arms. The loneliness became unbearable."

Wesley was remembering. He hadn't been too small to understand the reasons for the sounds of weeping surfacing from behind his mother's closed bedroom door. He had been missing his father just as much. He had also stood at the window watching. He rose from the chair and went to Lona Gale. "Mother, I—"

"Shh, Wesley," she said. "Let me finish now, or I never will be brave enough again."

He grew quiet, rocking Wesley Calvert slowly back and forth.

"I met this man while shopping in Charleston. He was handsome, quite gifted with words, but a gambler. I at first ignored his advances. But after another long, lonely night, I met this man and let him lead me to his room."

Wesley paled. Was this truly his mother confessing such a truth to him? Had this woman who always appeared so cold and untouchable actually had an affair? The color returned to his face as he smiled to himself. Suddenly Wesley was seeing his mother in a different light. He wasn't as shocked as he was *glad*. She was revealing that she was human . . . with feelings. . . .

But why *was* she telling him this now? He listened more intently. . . .

Lona Gale settled onto a chair with hands clasped together on her lap, so pale, so drawn. "I was unfaithful only that one time," she murmured. "But it was time enough for me . . . to . . . get with child. . . ."

It was as though someone had poured a bucket of cold water over Wesley. He felt such a numbness. Though he had become a bit amused with the thought of his mother having an affair on the side, though it indeed was not the proper thing to do, the thought of her becoming pregnant from it hadn't crossed his mind. "Mother, what are you saying?" he said thickly. The shock registered on his face as he didn't have to be told the answer. He knew. There had been only one more child born to Lona Gale after Wesley Alston and Truman Firman.

"God," Wesley groaned. "Dorlisa?"

"Yes. Dorlisa May."

"I can't believe—"

"It is the truth, Wesley."

"How did you keep this truth hidden so well?" he stammered.

"It was a disgrace. It was something I had to keep hidden. No one speaks . . . confesses to infidelity. If only guided into such an act once. And when an albino was born to me, I felt I was being damned for having the child by a man that was not my husband, a man who had spilled his sperm inside me, a man who carried albino blood, for you see, there is no history of such in my family," she said. "There is no history of such in your father's family either. Your father knew—right away—that the child was not his."

Wesley's heart began to thump wildly. If Dorlisa May

was not his true sister, if this stranger had carried the bad blood—then Wesley had worried . . . all these years . . . for naught!

His face began slowly to flush. He went and stood over his mother, trembling. "What you're saying . . . says . . . so much more. . . ." he said thickly.

Tears glistened as Lona Gale lifted her eyes to him. "Yes, my son. I know," she murmured.

"Why, Mother?"

"Why did I let you believe you carried albino blood, when I should have known of your dread of it?"

"Yes."

"Infidelity. It's such an ugly word," she whispered. "It is such a hard thing to confess to. . . ."

"And, Father—?" Wesley said thickly. "Once he *did* know?"

"From that moment on I had no husband in the true sense of the word," she said sullenly. "So I began hating my baby, my daughter, born to me as a result of my foolish moment of loneliness. You see, it was because of her that I knew nothing but loneliness from the moment she was born. I blamed her. I hated her. It made me become cold, even cruel at times."

"The man—Dorlisa's father . . . ?"

"He disappeared. He was never seen again. He had told me that his gambling kept him moving."

"But Father and you—well—you appeared to have a normal marriage."

"It was all because of you and Truman Firman. We both loved you boys more than even life itself," she murmured. "Do you now see why I found it so hard to accept Dorlisa May? But, God, oh, how wrong I have been. I'm so very, very sorry. What have I done? She is my daughter. She should have been treated equally as well as you and Truman. I now know that. Seeing my grandson brought back the day I was first handed Dorlisa May, the brief moments of my love for her only moments after her birth, until your father walked out of the room—with disgust and hatred in his eyes. . . ."

"God, Mother, I'm . . . so . . . sorry," Wesley said. He had to forget the torturous thoughts he had carried with him all those long years. It was quite apparent that his mother had suffered even more than he. He fell to his knees before her and slowly offered her the small bundle from his arms. "Do you still wish to hold your grandson?" he said thickly.

"Oh, Wesley," Lona Gale sighed, and smiled widely as she accepted the bundle of warmth. Her eyes glistened even more as Wesley opened the blanket, so they both could share in this moment of truth and love.

Chapter Twenty-One

The winter storms had tossed up more shells than usual along Folly Island beach, but now that February had arrived, along with the herons and egrets, the beach was an inviting place to take an early afternoon stroll.

Serena placed her arm through the curve of Wesley's, inhaling deeply of the fresher air, dreaming of a summer ahead of picnics and a time for family fun. This past winter had been spent in a new townhouse that Wesley had managed to purchase on East Bay Street across from his other townhouses.

The social season had been gay, with one social gathering after another, even though too much for Serena's choosing. She loved Wyndham Hall. She loved the beach. All in all, she loved this paradise called Folly Island.

"I'm so glad to be home," she sighed, glancing upward at Wesley, seeing his thick lashes and the way they shadowed his brown eyes, making them appear even darker. His mustache was trimmed and neat, and the cleft in his chin a bit less prominent now that he had added a bit of weight.

"Contentment does that to a man," he had boasted when she had teased of his thicker waist and fatter cheeks.

She was glad that she was a part of that happiness.

Wesley's gaze met hers and held. "Do I gather from what you say, that you don't care so much for our townhouse in Charleston?" he asked, lifting his lips in a quiet smile.

"I'm not that eager to be a part of the social scene, Wesley," she replied. "I love my family. I'd much rather remain at Wyndham Hall during the social season to have the larger rooms for our children to grow up in."

"Children?" he murmured, lifting a brow.

Serena laughed softly. "Yes. Soon. I shall know soon whether or not I am with child again. Don't you think Wesley Calvert should have a baby sister?"

Wesley chuckled, peering into the distance at two clinging lovers wading barefoot in the cold water of the ocean. Serena followed his gaze and felt an inner warmth splash through her. Lisa and Adam, now almost inseparable.

"Yes. And maybe even another brother," Wesley said, chuckling again. "And Dorlisa May? I'm so glad she's found another interest in her life besides her harp."

"Isn't it romantic, Wesley?" Serena sighed. "Just look at Lisa and Adam. Have you ever seen two so in love?"

Wesley stopped and pulled Serena into his arms. "I can't believe I heard you say that," he murmured.

Serena giggled, suddenly a young girl again. "Excluding Mr. and Mrs. Wesley Alston Wyndham," she purred. "Of course, no one could ever be as in love as you and I."

"Correct," he said flatly. His lips moved gently over hers as he pulled her body to form next to his. He loved the feel of her through the cotton dresses she had chosen to wear now that they had returned to the privacy of the island. He had hated her fancy gowns, hoops, and dozens of petticoats. He had constantly fought her encumbered skirts.

But now, he could feel every line of her body and ached for her. He let a hand move between them and began to caress a breast that was almost set free from the low cut of the dress, but heard her gasp and felt her quick withdrawal from him.

"Wesley, we're not alone," she whispered, glancing around her, relieved to see that Dorlisa May and Adam were still too absorbed in their own private world to have observed such a show of affection between the "older generation." Serena was glad that the sun was hiding behind a cloud this day, enabling Dorlisa May to be able to walk parasol-free, to pull the full pleasures from the beach. Though always dressed in high-necked and full-lengthed sleeves, and with the assistance of her parasol, the sun still remained to find portions of Dorlisa May's body to torment.

"Dorlisa May and Adam wouldn't even realize it if we laid down here and caressed openly," Wesley said, stooping to pick through the sea shells, tossing the larger ones into the constant motion of waves that moved back and forth onto the beach. "They don't know there is anyone else. Only themselves."

Serena watched as a brown pelican made a dive into the surf to then carry away a beak filled with a fat, squirming fish. She then stooped down beside Wesley, gathering the skirt of her dress up and around her ankles. "And do you think June is even soon enough for the wedding for those two?" she said, giggling.

"Oh? You don't think they can be patient enough to wait that long?"

"Do you even think they have?" Serena said, lifting an eyebrow.

"Serena, shame be upon you," Wesley laughed.

"Well? What *do* you think, Wesley?"

"I think we'd best change the subject, darling," he said quietly. His face had become all shadows.

"What are you thinking about, Wesley?" Serena asked, touching his arm gently.

"I'm not able to push Adam's doubts from my mind," he said thickly.

"You mean . . . his doubts of having normal children?"

"Yes, damn it. He loves Dorlisa May. He has accepted her the way she is. But yet he is already worrying about the children they will share together."

"It's as it was for you, darling," Serena said, smoothing hair from his eyes. "I'm so sorry you had to worry about the same thing needlessly. But now that it's behind you, you can age gracefully with no burdens on your shoulders." She laughed and then added, "Not saying that you are so old, Wesley."

He looked at her, then broke into a soft laugh. "Well, I hope not," he said. "I hope I have a few more romps in the bed left in me."

"Wesley, is that all you think about . . . ?"

A rush of feet behind them drew Serena's head around. She rose quickly as she gasped and covered her mouth with a hand.

Wesley pushed himself upward, saying, "What is it, Serena?" Then he also saw the Indian standing behind them, panting. Wesley's insides grew cold. He had thought his worries about the Kiawah had also been left behind him. There hadn't been any signs of the Kiawah on Folly Island, not since Wolfram's death. But now? The firm-muscled Indian with his only attire a brief loincloth and his coal black hair pulled back into a long pigtail was standing, cross-armed, but weary-eyed.

"What the hell do you want here on Folly Island?" Wesley finally blurted, placing his arms around Serena's waist, pulling her close to him. He glanced toward her, seeing fear etched across her face, causing tiny wrinkles to deepen at her mouth and eyes.

"Halona," the Indian grumbled through widespread teeth. "She ask for you. Come."

"The hell I will," Wesley shouted.

"Halona has swamp fever. I think Halona is dying. She asks for Wesley. Come," the Indian persisted with a deep frown creasing his leathered-tan face.

Something grabbed at the pit of Wesley's stomach, realizing the Indian's words. "Halona? She is truly that ill?" he gasped. He turned his gaze toward Serena, seeing a look of puzzlement in her eyes. He had to know what she was thinking. That he and Halona had still been secretly seeing one another. She would wonder why else would the Indian come for him? But Wesley himself knew. Halona and he had had much more than a sexual relationship at one time. They had shared a childhood of romping and playing. And now? She . . . was . . . even possibly . . . dying . . . ? Suddenly she was the child

Halona—needing to be rescued from the fierceness of a swamp alligator. . . .

He turned and grasped Serena's shoulders. "I must go to her," he said in a near whisper.

"But, Wesley—" Serena stammered, feeling her insides turning icy.

"Darling, you must trust me. . . ."

Serena lowered her eyes. "I have in the past. Many times. Is now . . . so . . . truly different, Wesley?"

His grasp strengthened. He felt the moments slipping away as probably Halona's last breaths might be also doing. "Serena, this is no time for jealousy," he said firmly. "You cannot feel a need to worry about me going to Kiawah Island when it is only to see an . . . an . . . ailing Indian."

Serena's jaw set firmly and her gaze met Wesley's in a bold stare of golden browns. "Yes. An Indian maiden," she snapped.

"Yes . . . an Indian maiden . . ."

"And have you thought for even one moment that this might be a trick, Wesley?"

"Too much time has passed since Wolfram's death. No. This is no trick."

"I feel there has been *too* much silence from the Kiawah," Serena said, her gaze faltering, now fearing for Wesley's life more than her jealousies of him moving into another woman's arms.

Wesley glanced toward the Indian, who continued his silent stance with crossed arms and sealed, straight lips. Wesley truly no longer feared the Kiawah. He knew that if they had wanted him dead, they would have found a way without resorting to trickery. As quietly as they could creep from brush to brush or sand dune to sand dune, Wesley knew that he would have been a target . . . *any*time . . . if the Kiawah had chosen to make him one.

Wesley then gave Serena a gentle shake, looking into her eyes. He could see so much. He could almost read her inner soul behind the color of golden browns. "Darling, I am going. I must see if there is anything I can do for Halona," he said. He watched the familiar stubborn set to her jaw and the way she straightened her back more. He knew to expect her old self to come shining through. Then he added, "You see, long ago Halona was like a sister to me. I was even made her . . . blood brother by her father."

"I'm going with you, Wesley," she said firmly.

He smiled to himself. Hadn't he expected her to say something similar? Ah, he knew her so well. "I'd rather you didn't, Serena . . ."

"I'd rather I *did* . . ."

"The alligators . . ."

"To hell with the alligators," she argued further.

"Wesley Calvert, Serena . . ."

Her jaw slackened and her lashes fluttered nervously. "Your mother can care for him until we return," she murmured. "Wesley, I want to go. Maybe I can help."

Wesley pulled her quickly into his arms and burrowed his nose into the depths of her hair. "Darling, I knew you'd understand," he murmured. "And it is so sweet of you to want to go to see if you can help."

"I *did* work in Father's hospital quarters, Wesley . . ."

"Do you think I can ever forget . . . ?"

"Then let's go and see what can be done," Serena said,

already moving toward Dorlisa May and Adam, to tell them of the journey.

Wesley moved next to the Indian toward Kiawah River, but shouted over his shoulder at Serena, saying, "And I'm going to tell Tobias to have a carriage waiting on the other side of the river. If Halona is able, we'll get her to the hospital in Charleston. . . ."

The black water of the Kiawah River reflected the stately cypress trees and splashes of vibrant floral color as Wesley moved the oars of his johnboat back and forth, all the while watching the movements of the Indian who moved ahead of him in his own canoe. He then glanced toward Serena and the way she was clutching onto the sides of the boat, continually looking around her, fear etched across her face, though she kept assuring him that she was just as brave as anyone else who had traveled down this river.

The swamp noises increased the farther they traveled. Loud splashes of water on each side of the boat were a reminder that the alligators had just begun to return to the swamps for the long spring and summer months, and a hawk screeched high above in the hidden branches of a live oak that was draped gracefully with the lacy moss that reached from tree to tree.

Serena shivered a bit, feeling the dampness of the swamp air swirling around her in a fine mist. She moved her arms around her, hugging herself. "How much farther, Wesley?" she asked, flipping her hair to hang back away from her face. Oh, how she wished to be able to cut her hair, wear it even as a man. Then she wouldn't be bothered with the frizzy curls. One day she had even

431

stood at the mirror with scissors poised, then had decided against it. Most southern women wore their hair pulled back in long, graceful curls. She would most certainly look strange with a head of clipped hair! She had tried and tried to straighten her hair, in an effort to then use the curling iron on it, to make her hair in such long curls as all that she had seen. But she had decided that nothing would rid her of her inconvenience. Nothing!

"It's only around the bend, Serena," Wesley said, with an evident strain in his voice. His thoughts were filling more and more with Halona, being in the area that they had shared so as children, then as young adults, then even . . . later. . . .

His heart ached, thinking her to possibly be dying. She was so young. She had so many years ahead of her. How could this have happened to her? She had lived in the swamps all of her life.

"Are you sure we will be welcome, Wesley?" Serena asked, once again glancing around her for any movement in the brush. She still couldn't be as trusting of these Indians as Wesley was.

"Yes. Halona surely wouldn't have sent for me if she had thought the other members of the Kiawah wouldn't have welcomed me into their midst. You see, she surely hadn't known of her brother's vengeful ways. She had to have been innocent of all involvements in Truman's death, and then, later, when Wolfram came to her hut—" His face grew ashen. He had never mentioned being in Halona's hut to Serena. He had only told Serena that he had fought a battle with Wolfram and that Wolfram . . . had . . . lost.

Serena's heart began to pound rapidly. "What did you

432

say—about Halona's hut . . . ?" she asked cautiously.

Wesley swallowed hard. He knew that this was no time for such confessions. In only a moment's time, he had to help Halona—if indeed he wasn't too late. He couldn't get into it with Serena about the truth of Wolfram's death—where it had actually taken place.

"Nothing, Serena," he said thickly.

"No. You began to say something, Wesley," she said firmly. "Will you please just finish it? What were you about to say? What about Wolfram . . . and . . . Halona's hut . . . ?"

"It was storming, Serena," he began. "I went in out of the rain with Halona . . ."

"Wesley, I don't want to hear anymore," Serena suddenly blurted, realizing she *didn't* want to hear the details. It had all been put behind them . . . until now. She couldn't let her old jealousies and her distrust of Wesley begin all over again. Halona was ill now. Wesley was truly concerned. Yes. Her thoughts had to be pushed behind her and win Wesley's true respect by only helping him with Halona, not goading him about his past wrong deeds.

"Damn it," Wesley grumbled, then continued to think about that day, trying to remember . . .

Halona *had* lured him to the hut. . . . Wolfram *had* come to that hut, so obviously knowing that Wesley was there with Halona. At that time, had Halona hated him so much that she *did* wish him dead? Or had it been Truman that both Wolfram and Halona had expected to arrive on Kiawah Island that day?

Oh! It was all too jumbled in his head. Pinpricks of fear began to dance up and down his spine. Maybe he had been wrong to put his trust in her once again. The many months of happiness with Serena and with their child had mellowed his mind about Halona. But now that he had allowed himself to think it through all over again, he had to think that Halona might still be capable of doing anything to get her revenge on him.

Reaching inside his jacket, he secured a hand on a pistol at his waist as he let the johnboat move into some thick marsh grass next to the shore. He was glad that he had taken the time to fasten the holster around his middle. He had mainly done it for snakes. But he now knew that there were many kinds of snakes—some that crawled . . . and some that walked. . . .

Serena peered through the deep, fresh greens of the marsh grasses, then tensed when she saw the thick cluster of round, thatch-covered huts that sat back away from the water. There wasn't any sign of life anywhere. She glanced toward Wesley, seeing how his hand was now resting on his gun. Was he also fearing the worst? She looked once again toward the huts, seeing only one that had a door open. Circling upward from the top of the small dwelling, she could see gray spirals of smoke, then noticed the same at the other dwellings. She had to wonder why everyone had chosen to stay hidden. But she had to believe it was because they knew of the white man's return and possibly feared and dreaded his appearance on their private land.

"Stay close beside me, Serena," Wesley said, stepping from the johnboat, offering her a hand.

"Where is everybody?" she whispered, still glancing quickly around her, now once again seeing the one Indian who had come to request Wesley's appearance at

Halona's bedside. He was moving toward the one hut that had its door open.

"They may smell death," Wesley whispered. "Or they may smell a white man." He held onto her arm as he guided her toward Halona's hut. He knew that Halona did wish him to enter. She had left the door open. His pulsebeat increased, remembering the last time inside that dwelling. She had succeeded at sending his mind into a million different colors, but then all had come to a sudden halt when Wolfram had made his quick entrance.

"I hope it isn't *our* death they are smelling," Serena whispered, leaning closer to Wesley, tensing when the Indian turned on a heel and motioned with an arm for them to move on inside Halona's hut.

"Is that Halona's—?"

"Yes," Wesley whispered, stooping, entering, now suddenly forgetting Serena when he caught sight of Halona outstretched on a heavy pile of blankets against the far wall of the dwelling. His heart ached, seeing how different she was now. Though fully dressed in her fringed-buckskin dress, in the dim lighting of the fire, he could see that her skin was a pale color of golden and her face, as well as the rest of her body, was bloated, making her almost unrecognizable. He went to her and fell to his knees beside her, taking her hand in his, speaking her name, ever so gently. . . .

"Halona?" he said, growing numb when he felt the heat of her hand and could see the fever in her eyes when she opened them and discovered him there.

"Wesley? Halona . . . Halona . . . not well," she whispered, reaching to touch his face with her free hand.

He leaned his face into it, choking on his deep

emotions. He had hated her, their last time together, but suddenly, he felt all the love for her that he had felt as a child. He now knew, though, that this love for Halona was not the sincere love for a woman that he now felt for Serena, but that of a brother for a sister. All that they had shared in between those moments from childhood to now had been just pleasures of the body that they had discovered at a too young age and had shared openly without guilt even entering into it.

But now? His insides trembled to think that he would truly never be able to share these things with her again. She was ill. Damn ill. And he didn't know why. . . .

"I'm so sorry, Halona," he whispered, then glanced sideways when Serena fell to her knees beside him and touched Halona's brow with the back of her right hand.

"She's burning up with fever, Wesley," she said, then let her gaze settle on this smaller woman's dark, penetrating eyes. Even though glassy from fever, she could see another sort of pain when staring back at Serena. Serena now knew the depths of love this Indian maiden had for Wesley. It showed. Serena could even see now why this maiden would kill for the man she loved.

Halona's gaze moved back to Wesley. "Halona is so sorry, Wesley," she said, tears rushing from her eyes in small rivers.

"Why are you sorry, Halona?" he whispered, placing her hand back beside her on the blankets.

"Halona is the cause of much pain for you," she said, sobbing.

"Please. Don't think about the past, Halona," Wesley said, swallowing hard.

"Wesley, Halona told Wolfram that Halona hated

Wesley. This is why Wolfram tried to kill you. He also hated you. He had always hated you. He had always hated Truman Firman. He hadn't liked white man touching his sister. Even when he shared the big pipe with you, he was plotting against you. Oh, Wesley, Halona is so sorry. For . . . everything. . . ."

Serena turned her head away. Had Wesley possibly loved Halona as much, but had seen the impossibilities of such a relationship? Had Halona been truly Wesley's first choice? And had he taken Serena when nothing could have resolved this situation between a white man's love for an Indian woman? Oh, how her guts were twisting. Just twisting!

"Halona needs not be sorry for anything," Wesley said, rising. "I understand. And Halona is going to white man's hospital. Wesley is going to see to it that Halona has every chance of getting well."

Halona began shaking her head back and forth, crying even harder. "No. Halona cannot go. The gods would frown on it. . . ."

Wesley bent and scooped her up into his arms and began to walk from the hut. "I don't give a damn about your gods, Halona," he grumbled, stepping on outside, not stopping to look around him. He knew the chances he was taking. He knew that at any moment any amount of Indians could jump him and force him to return Halona to her dwelling. But he had to take that chance. He knew that she wouldn't live the night if he didn't force the issue.

Serena followed along behind Wesley, glancing quickly around her, first one way, then another. Her breathing was coming in short gasps, so afraid, she

437

couldn't remember another time that had been so threatening. Even on the long voyage from Illinois to the Carolinas, she hadn't felt as threatened. She knew the swiftness of an Indian's arrow. It wasn't like a bullet. Once it hit its mark, the person would die a quick death. She hurried to Wesley's side and tried to cling to him, but then decided to rush on ahead and get the johnboat ready for their quick departure, just hoping that an Indian wouldn't jump out and stop her.

Panting, she reached the boat and steadied it as Wesley placed Halona on its floor.

"Serena, maybe you could sit with her and place her head on your lap . . . ?" he asked, climbing into the boat, looking back at the huts, now seeing the doors slowly opening, seeing both male and female staring back at him with wonder in their eyes. He breathed easier. He now knew that he was safe. They all had wanted his return as badly as Halona. They still trusted him. Maybe it had been Wolfram whom they had dreaded and had lost trust in. Wolfram *had* been too much of a warrior. He had never been as gentle as most Kiawah that Wesley had become acquainted with. Wesley had to think that even Halona's occasional ugly tongue and ways had been formed by the guidance of her brother. But now he was gone. Only Halona remained of the late beloved elderly Chief of the Kiawah, the one whom had made Wesley the blood brother of Halona.

Serena lifted Halona's head and moved herself beneath it, trembling a bit. She had never thought of the possibilities of meeting Halona, much less of cradling her head on her lap, as she was now, tenderly caressing her brow.

"Halona thank you," Halona whispered. She closed her eyes, now laboring a bit for breath.

Serena didn't say anything, just looked away, seeing so clearly now how this Indian could steal Wesley's and even Truman's heart. There was an air of innocence about her, as though a child-woman. Serena couldn't help but like Halona.

She looked toward Wesley and could see the way his waistcoat strained at the shoulders as he flexed his muscles with each quick stroke of the oars. When he would look her way, she could see that his face was set in a locked determination, making Serena feel an emptiness at the pit of her stomach. She felt as though she was losing Wesley to this Indian once again . . . if Halona lived *or* died. Either way, Serena had to wonder if Wesley's heart could ever be completely hers again. But had . . . it . . . ever . . . been . . . ?

"I see Tobias managed to get a carriage ready," Wesley shouted, panting, staring into the distance at his faithful overseer, standing patiently beside a sleek black stallion attached to a topless carriage. He then turned a quick glance toward Halona, then Serena. The heaviness of his eyes showed his concern. "Serena, is she . . . ?" he said in a near whisper.

Serena smoothed her fingertips over Halona's brow. "She's all right, Wesley," she murmured. "She's only fallen asleep."

Wesley's gaze moved forward as he took his final two strokes with the oars. "Thank God," he murmured. "Thank God."

He maneuvered the boat next to the shore, then jumped from it and secured it onto the land. Tobias moved to his side, then bent and pulled Halona up into his massive arms. In a quick succession of movements, all were in the carriage and moving down a deeply rutted dirt road.

No words, but many glances were exchanged between Wesley and Serena. And when he reached for, and took one of her hands in his, something told Serena that things were going to be all right after all. His sweet smile, for only her, confirmed this. She relaxed her shoulders and leaned against the back of the seat, and remained there until Tobias guided the horse and carriage in front of the newly constructed Charleston hospital.

Serena climbed from the carriage and stood aside as Wesley carried Halona on inside, leaving Tobias to care for the carriage and Serena to move slowly into the hospital, feeling too much the observer once again. But she wouldn't begin that way of thinking again. She had just begun to feel that all was going to be right with the world.

Straightening her back and pushing her hair from her face, Serena went inside and moved to Wesley's side. "Where is she, Wesley?" she whispered.

Wesley nodded his head toward a closed door. "In there," he said.

Serena circled an arm through his. "Darling, things will be all right," she said. "You'll see."

"I'm not so sure. . . ."

The door swung widely open as a doctor dressed in full white moved toward them. His one cheek was puffed out like a chipmunk's as he chewed on a plug of tobacco. He offered a hand to Wesley. "Doc Shaw here," he said.

Wesley accepted the gesture of friendship. "Well?

What about Halona?" he asked impatiently.

"Don't like doctorin' Injuns. Seen enough of them where I come from," he drawled, resting his arms on his large, potbellied abdomen. "But guess she ain't truly no different than you or me."

"But, Doc Shaw, will you just tell me what you found?" Wesley said, furrowing his brow.

"Think she's got a kidney problem. A few days of rest, my whiskey treatments to lower the fever, and a diet with plenty of liquid to flush 'er system out and she'll be as good as new."

Wesley and Serena exchanged quick glances, then smiled knowingly, both remembering another time of whiskey treatments. "Whiskey treatments, did you say, Doc?" Wesley said, glancing back toward the doctor.

"Yep. Found them to be quite effective," he drawled, laughing a bit.

Wesley's voice took on a note of seriousness once again. "And you're sure Halona is going to be all right?" he asked, gazing around the doctor, toward Halona's closed door.

"Ain't swamp fever," Doc Shaw chuckled. "Every time an Injun gets a fever of *any* kind, they call it swamp fever. I've took care of cases like this one before. It's kidneys. They just ain't filterin' right."

"Can I see her?" Wesley asked, then glanced toward Serena, relieved to see understanding in her eyes.

"No. Don't think so. You go on your way. You've done your part. We should keep Halona as quiet as possible. We don't want her losin' her baby."

Wesley's breath caught in his throat. . . .

Serena's breath caught in her throat. . . .

They exchanged quick glances then Wesley spoke. "Baby?" he gasped. "Did you say . . . baby . . . ?"

"About four months along, I'd say," Doc Shaw said, moving to the front door of the hospital, spitting into the wind.

Serena turned with a start when footsteps moved up behind her. Her hands flew to her mouth when she discovered the same Indian that had just led her and Wesley to Halona. She reached a hand to Wesley and yanked on his arm, causing him to also discover the Indian standing there with sweat trickling from his brow and deep heavings of his chest. It was obvious that he had labored hard to get to this hospital where one of his own kind lay . . .

Wesley stepped in front of Serena, shielding her from the Indian. "What do you want here?" he asked hoarsely. "Why have you come?"

"Halona. Me want see Halona."

"Halona is sleeping in white man's bed," Wesley said, clearing his throat nervously. He was wondering if any other Indians had been allowed to enter the hospital. And now? To have two to deal with? He glanced toward Doc Shaw as he moved to stare openly at the Indian.

The Indian's arms crossed over his chest and his chin lifted haughtily. "Halona is my woman. Halona carry my baby. I want see Halona," he said gruffly.

Serena moved to Wesley's side and took his hand in hers. "Wesley," she said softly. "This . . . must . . . be Halona's husband. . . ."

Wesley's eyes wavered a bit, feeling a foreign stirring inside him. He at first thought it to be jealousy, but then knew it to be relief. Halona had a man. Halona no longer

442

would grieve over her loss of the man she had shared so much with as both a child and an adult. She was even with child. A smile suddenly erupted across his face as he thrust his hand outward toward the Indian, in a gesture of friendship as well as congratulations. "Wesley glad for you and Halona," he said thickly. "Halona and the baby are all right. And I'm sure Doc Shaw here will let you go sit with your woman."

The Indian's hand was firm and anxious as he gripped Wesley's. "Halona be all right? Fire Eyes be all right," he said, smiling. "Fire Eyes want to thank you."

"Fire Eyes? Is that your name?" Wesley said, smiling to himself.

"Fire Eyes given name by Halona," Fire Eyes said, shifting from one foot to the other, showing his nervousness at the situation.

"Oh, I see," Wesley chuckled, then moved to Serena's side and circled her waist with his arm.

"I guess it'd be okay if you go in to sit beside your woman's bed," Doc Shaw said, taking the Indian by the elbow, guiding him away from Serena and Wesley. "But no chanting, do you hear, Fire Eyes?"

"Quaint doctor," Serena said, laughing lightly.

"Right out of a Western novel," Wesley said, laughing also, suddenly feeling a bit lighthearted. Halona was going to be all right—she had a man, she was with child. He and Halona had resumed friendship . . . and Serena had accepted it all.

He lifted Serena's chin with a forefinger and kissed her gently. "Let's go home, darling," he said. "I believe we have some unfinished business to attend to."

"Like what?" she murmured with a pounding heart.

"I believe I've neglected this past couple of hours to tell you just how much I love you," he said further.

"Wesley, my love," she purred.

He bent to bury his nose into the depths of her hair, whispering, "I'm not only going to tell you . . . but . . . I'm going to show you. . . . Come on, darling. Let's go home."

The satin and lace of her chemise opened to a deep vee where Serena's breasts heaved in eager anticipation as Wesley stepped from his breeches. At this moment, there were only two people in the world, and they were moving toward one another, with only faint flickerings from a lone kerosene lamp to guide their way to the large bed awaiting them.

"Wesley," Serena whispered but was silenced by Wesley's forefinger sealing her lips.

"Shhh," he whispered. "Tonight is the beginning of the rest of our lives."

Serena lowered his hand. "But I need to know something—" she persisted.

Wesley guided her down onto the bed, easing her chemise from her shoulders and downward. "If you must. What is it?" he said hoarsely, smiling as she lifted her hips as he completed his task of disrobing her.

"Halona," she said. "How do you feel about her now, Wesley?"

"The way I felt the day I was first introduced into her village those many years ago."

"And how was that . . . ?"

"Like a blood brother. Nothing else."

Serena's heart warmed. "Are you absolutely sure, Wesley?"

"Yes. And Halona now realizes this also," he said, leaning his mouth over a nipple, flicking his tongue around its tautness. "The truth? She saw it today when you accompanied me to Kiawah Island. She has to know that I wouldn't have taken you there if I had been going there only for her."

"Then I don't have to worry about all tomorrows?"

"No. Not at all. . . ." he whispered. "Now will you be quiet and show *me* how much you love *me*."

"Yes, darling. . . ."

Serena reached for him and guided him down over her, letting her hands travel across his body, feeling the rippling of flesh on each spot she touched anew. When his lips moved to hers, she moaned lightly and felt the swirling in her head as his hands began to trace her body, not leaving any dip or crevice untouched. When his lips moved to the hollow of her throat, she felt a feeling similar to butterfly's wings fluttering inside her stomach and arched her body upward to meet his entrance inside her.

With her hips moving with him, Serena said, "Wesley, I remember our first time together, how sweet it was. . . ."

"And I do also," he said thickly, working in and out, feeling the pleasure rising inside him, a heat so intense, he felt as though his body would suddenly become consumed by flames.

"You were . . . my . . . enemy . . ." she whispered, clinging around his neck.

"You were . . . so . . . enchanting, my darling," he

replied, groaning a bit as the passion climbed.

Serena giggled a bit. "You were my enchanted enemy," she said. "But now . . . you are . . . just, oh, so enchanting. . . ."

Together they peaked with their passion, then lay, listening to the sounds of the night on this, their paradise of an island, an island where many battles of the heart had been fought . . . and won.

BE CAPTIVATED BY THESE HISTORICAL ROMANCES